The Emigrants of Ahadarra

William Carleton

THE EMIGRANTS OF AHADARRA.

By William Carleton

THE WORKS
OF
WILLIAM CARLETON.

VOLUME II.

JANE SINCLAIR.	THE PROCTOR'S DAUGHTER.
LHA DHU; OR, THE DARK DAY.	VATENTINE McCLUTCHY, THE IRISH AGENT
THE DEAD BOXER.	THE TITHE PROCTOR.
ELLEN DUNCAN.	THE EMIGRANTS OF AHA-DARRA.

ILLUSTRATED.

NEW YORK:
P. F. COLLIER, PUBLISHER.
1881.

CONTENTS

CHAPTER I. *A strong Farmer's Establishment and Family.*

CHAPTER II. *Gerald Cavanagh and his Family*

CHAPTER III. *Jemmy Burke Refuses to be, Made a Fool Of*

CHAPTER IV. *A Poteen Still-House at Midnight—Its Inmates.*

CHAPTER V. *Who Robbed Jemmy Burke?*

CHAPTEE VI. *Nanny Peety looks mysterious*

CHAPTER VII. *The Spinster's Kemp.*

CHAPTER VIII. *Anonymous Letter with a Name to It*

CHAPTER IX. *A Little Polities, Much Friendship, and Some Mystery*

CHAPTER X. *More of the Hycy Correspondence*

CHAPTEE XI. *Death of a Virtuous Mother.*

CHAPTER XII. *Hycy Concerts a Plot and is urged to Marry.*

CHAPTER XIII. *Mrs. M'Mahon's Funeral.*

CHAPTER XIV. *Mysterious Letter*

CHAPTER XV. *State of the Country*

CHAPTER XVI. *A Spar Between Kate and Philip Hogan*

CHAPTER XVII. *Interview between Hycy and Finigan*

CHAPTER XVIII. *A Family Dialogue*

CHAPTER XIX. Bryan Bribed—is Rejected by Kathleen.

CHAPTER XX. M'Mahon is Denounced from the Altar

CHAPTER XXI. Thomas M'Mahon is forced to determine on Emigration.

CHAPTER XII. Mystery Among the Hogans

CHAPTER XXIII. Harry Clinton's Benevolence Defeated

CHAPTER XXIV. Thoughts on Our Country and Our Countrymen

CHAPTER XXV. The Old Places—Death of a Patriarch.

CHAPTEE XXVI. Containing a Variety of Matters.

CHAPTER XXVII.   Conclusion.

List of Illustrations

Frontispiece

Peety Dhu Turned Towards the House

Country Where I'd Not See These Ould Hills

I Must Leave You—I Must Go

Hycy Received the Money, Set Spurs to his Horse

CHAPTER I.—A strong Farmer's Establishment and Family.

It was one summer morning, about nine o'clock, when a little man, in the garb and trim of a mendicant, accompanied by a slender but rather handsome looking girl about sixteen, or it may be a year more, were upon their way to the house of a man, who, from his position in life, might be considered a wealthy agriculturist, and only a step or two beneath the condition of a gentleman farmer, although much more plain and rustic in his manners. The house and place had about them that characteristic appearance of abundance and slovenly neglect which is, unfortunately, almost peculiar to our country. The house was a long slated one, and stood upon a little eminence, about three or four hundred yards from the highway. It was approached by a broad and ragged boreen or mock avenue, as it might be called, that was in very good keeping with the premises to which it led. As you entered it from the road, you had to pass through an iron gate, which it was a task to open, and which, when opened, it was another task to shut. In consequence of this difficulty, foot passengers had made themselves a way upon each side of it, through which they went to and came from the house; and in this they were sanctioned by the example of the family themselves, who, so long as these side paths were passable, manifested as much reluctance to open or close the gate as any one else.

The month was May; and nothing could be more delightful and exhilarating than the breeze which played over the green fields that were now radiant with the light which was flooded down upon them from the cloudless sun. Around them, in every field, were the tokens of that pleasant labor from which the hopes of ample and abundant harvests always spring. Here, fixed in the ground, stood the spades of a boon* of laborers, who, as was evident from that circumstance, were then at breakfast; in another place might be seen the plough and a portion of the tackle lying beside it, being expressive of the same fact. Around them, on every side, in hedges, ditches, green fields, and meadows, the birds seemed animated into joyous activity or incessant battle, by the business of nest-building or love. Whilst all around, from earth and air, streamed the ceaseless voice of universal melody and song.

A considerable number of men working together.

On reaching the gate, Peety Dhu and his pretty daughter turned up towards the house we have alluded to—which was the residence of a man named Burke. On reaching it they were observed by a couple of large dogs, who, partaking of the hospitable but neglected habits of the family, first approached and looked at them for a moment, then wagged their tails by way of welcome, and immediately scampered off into the kitchen to forage for themselves.

Burke's house and farmyard, though strongly indicative of wealth and abundance in the owner, were, notwithstanding, evidently the property of a man whose mind was far back in a knowledge of agriculture, and the industrial pursuits that depend upon it. His haggard was slovenly in the extreme, and his farmyard exceedingly offensive to most of the senses; everything lay about in a careless and neglected manner;—wheelbarrows without their trundles—sacks for days under the rain that fell from the eaves of the houses—other implements embedded in mud—car-houses tumbling down—the pump without a handle—the garden-gate open, and the pigs hard at work destroying the vegetables, and rooting up the garden in all directions. In fact, the very animals about the house were conscious of the character of the people, and acted accordingly. If one of the dogs, for instance, was hunted at the pigs, he ran in an apparent fury towards that which happened to be nearest him, which merely lifted its head and listened for a time—the dog, with loud and boisterous barking, seizing its ear, led it along for three or four yards in that position, after which, upon the pig demurring to proceed any further, he very quietly dropped it and trotted in again, leaving the destructive animal to resume its depredations.

The house inside bore the same character. Winter and summer the hall-door, which had long lost the knocker, lay hospitably open. The parlor had a very equivocal appearance; for the furniture, though originally good and of excellent materials, was stained and dinged and hacked in a manner that denoted but little sense of care or cleanliness. Many of the chairs, although not worn by age, wanted legs or backs, evidently from ill-usage alone—the grate was without fire-irons—a mahogany bookcase that stood in a recess to the right of the fireplace, with glass doors and green silk blinds, had the glass all broken and the silk stained almost out of its original color; whilst inside of it, instead of books, lay a heterogeneous collection of garden seeds in brown paper—an almanac of twenty years' standing, a dry ink-bottle, some broken delf, and a large collection of blue-moulded shoes and boots, together with an old blister of French flies, the lease of their farm, and a great number of their receipts for rent. To crown all, the clock in the other recess stood cobwebbed about the top, deprived of the minute hand, and seeming to intimate by its silence that it had given note of time's progress to this idle and negligent family to no purpose.

On the drawing-room stairs there lay what had once been a carpet, but so inseparable had been their connection that the stairs were now worn through it, and it required a sharp eye to distinguish such fragments of it as remained from the color of the dirty boards it covered and the dust that lay on both.

On entering the kitchen, Peety and his little girl found thirteen or fourteen, in family laborers and servants of both sexes, seated at a long deal table, each with a large wooden noggin of buttermilk and a spoon of suitable dimensions, digging as if for a wager into one or other of two immense wooden bowls of stirabout, so thick and firm in consistency that, as the phrase goes, a man might dance on it. This, however, was not the only picture of such enjoyment that the kitchen afforded. Over beside the dresser was turned upon one side the huge pot in which the morning meal had been made, and at the bottom of which, inside of course, a spirit of rivalry equally vigorous and animated, but by no means so harmonious, was kept up by two dogs and a couple of pigs, which were squabbling and whining and snarling among each other, whilst they tugged away at the scrapings, or residuum, that was left behind after the stirabout had been emptied out of it. The whole kitchen, in fact, had a strong and healthy smell of food—the dresser, a huge one, was covered with an immense quantity of pewter, wood, and delf; and it was only necessary to cast one's eye towards the chimney to perceive, by the weighty masses of black hung beef and the huge sides and flitches of deep yellow bacon which lined it, that plenty and abundance, even to overflowing, predominated in the family.

The "chimney-brace" projected far out over the fire-place towards the floor, and under it on each side stretched two long hobs or chimney corner seats, on which nearly a dozen persons could sit of a winter evening. Mrs. Burke, a smart, good-looking little woman, though somewhat advanced in years, kept passing in a kind of perpetual motion from one part of the house to the other, with a large bunch of bright keys jingling at one side, and a huge house-wife pocket, with a round pin-cushion dangling beside it, at the other. Jemmy Burke himself, a placid though solemn-faced man, was sitting on the hob in question complacently smoking his pipe, whilst over the glowing remnants of an immense turf fire hung a singing kettle, and beside it on three crushed coals was the teapot, "waitin'," as the servants were in the habit of expressing it, "for the masther and misthress's breakfast."

Peety, who was well known and a great favorite on his rounds, received a warm and hospitable welcome from Jemmy Burke, who made him and the girl sit upon the hob, and immediately ordered them breakfast.

"Here, Nancy Devlin, get Peety and the girsha their skinfuls of stirabout an' milk. Sit over to the fire, alanna, an' warm yourself."

"Warm, inagh!" replied Peety; "why, sure it's not a fire sich a blessed mornin' as this she'd want—an' a blessed mornin' it is, glory be to God!"

"Troth, an' you're right, sure enough, Peety," replied the good-natured farmer; "a blessed saison it is for gettin' down the crops. Go over there, now, you an' the girsha, to that other table, an'—whish!—kick them pigs an' dogs out o' the house, an' be d—d to them! One can't hear their ears for them—you an' the girsha, an' let us see what you can do. Nancy, achora, jist dash a gawliogue o' sweet milk into their noggins—they're not like us that's well fed every day—. it's but seldom they get the likes, the creatures—so dash in a brave gawliogue o' the sweet milk for them. Take your time, Peety, aisy, alanna, 'till you get what I'm sayin; it'll nourish an put strinth in you."

"Ah, Misther Burke," replied Peety, in a tone of gratitude peculiar to his class, "you're the ould* man still—ever an' always the large heart an' lavish hand—an' so sign's on it—full an' plinty upon an' about you—an' may it ever be so wid you an' yours, a chierna, I pray. An how is the misthress, sir?"

  * *That is to say, the same man still.*

"Throth, she's very well, Peety—has no raison to complain, thank God!"

"Thank God, indeed! and betther may she be, is my worst wish to her—an' Masther Hycy, sir?—but I needn't ax how he is. Isn't the whole country ringin' wid his praises;—the blessin' o' God an you, acushla"—this was to Nancy Devlin, on handing them the new milk—"draw over, darlin', nearer to the table—there now"—this to his daughter, whom he settled affectionately to her food. "Ay, indeed," he proceeded, "sure there's only the one word of it over the whole Barony we're sittin' in—that there's neither fetch nor fellow for him through the whole parish. Some people, indeed, say that Bryan M'Mahon comes near him; but only some, for it's given up to Masther Hycy all to pieces."

"Faix, an' I for one, although I'm his father—amn't I, Rosha?" he added, good-humoredly addressing his wife, who had just come into the kitchen from above stairs.

"Throth," said the wife, who never replied with good humor unless when addressed as Mrs. Burke, "you're ill off for something to speak about. How are you, Peety? an' how is your little girl?"

"In good health, ma'am, thank God an' you; an' very well employed at the present time, thanks to you still!"

To this Mrs. Burke made no reply; for it may be necessary to state here, that although she was not actually penurious or altogether without hospitality, and something that might occasionally be termed charity, still it is due to honest Jemmy to inform the reader in the outset, that, as Peety Dhu said, "the large heart and the lavish hand" were especially his own. Mrs. Burke was considered to have been handsome—indeed, a kind of rustic beauty in her day—and, like many of that class, she had not been without a due share of vanity, or perhaps we might say coquetry, if we were to speak the truth. Her teeth were good, and she had a very pretty dimple in one of her cheeks when she smiled, two circumstances which contributed strongly to sustain her good humor, and an unaccountable tendency to laughter, when the poverty of the jest was out of all proportion to the mirth that followed it. Notwithstanding this apparently light and agreeable spirit, she was both vulgar and arrogant, and labored under the weak and ridiculous ambition of being considered a woman of high pretensions, who had been most unfortunately thrown away, if not altogether lost, upon a husband whom she considered as every way unworthy of her. Her father had risen into the possession of some unexpected property when it was too late to bestow upon her a suitable education, and the consequence was that, in addition to natural vanity, on the score of beauty, she was a good deal troubled with purse-pride, which, with a foolish susceptibility of flattery, was a leading feature in her disposition. In addition to this, she was an inveterate and incurable slattern, though a gay and lively one; and we need scarcely say that whatever she did in the shape of benevolence or charity, in most instances owed its origin to the influences of the weaknesses she was known to possess.

Breakfast, at length, was over, and the laborers, with an odd hiccup here and there among them, from sheer repletion, got their hats and began to proceed towards the farm.

"Now, boys," said Jemmy, after dropping a spittle into his pipe, pressing it down with his little finger, and putting it into his waistcoat pocket, "see an' get them praties down as soon as you can, an' don't work as if you intended to keep your Christmas there; an' Paddy the Bounce, I'll thank you to keep your jokes an' your stories to yourself, an' not to be idlin' the rest till afther your work's done. Throth it was an unlucky day I had anything to do wid you, you divartin' vagabone—ha! ha! ha! When I hired him in the Micklemas fair," proceeded Jemmy, without addressing himself to any particular individual, "he killed me wid laughin' to such a degree, that I couldn't refuse the mchony whatsomever wages he axed; an' now he has the men, insteed o' mindin' their work, dancin' through the field, an' likely to split at the fun he tells them, ha! ha! ha! Be off, now, boys. Petter Murphy, you randletree, let the girl alone. That's it Peggy, lay on him; ha! devil's cure to you! take what you've got any way—you desarve it."

These latter observations were occasioned by a romping match that took place between a young laborer and a good-looking girl who was employed to drop potatoes for the men.

At length those who were engaged in the labor of the field departed in a cheerful group, and in a few minutes the noise of a horse's feet,

The Emigrants of Ahadarra

evidently proceeding at a rapid trot, was heard coming up the boreen or avenue towards the house.

"Ay," exclaimed Burke, with a sigh, "there comes Hycy at a trot, an' the wondher is it's not a gallop. That's the way he'll get through life, I fear; an' if God doesn't change him he's more likely to gallop himself to the Staff an' Bag (* Beggary.) than to anything else I know. I can't nor I won't stand his extravagance—but it's his mother's fault, an' she'll see what it'll come to in the long run."

He had scarcely concluded when his son entered the kitchen, alternately singing and whistling the Foxhunter's jig in a manner that betokened exuberant if not boisterous spirits. He was dressed in top boots, a green riding-coat, yellow waistcoat, and drab cassimere small clothes—quite in jockey trim, in fact.

Hycy rather resembled his father in the lineaments of his face, and was, consequently, considered handsome. He was about the middle size, and remarkably well proportioned. In fact, it would be exceedingly difficult to find a young fellow of manlier bearing or more striking personal attractions. His features were regular, and his complexion fresh and youthful looking, and altogether there was in his countenance and whole appearance a cheerful, easy, generous, unreflecting dash of character that not only made him a favorite on first acquaintance, but won confidence by an openness of manner that completely disarmed suspicion. It might have been observed, however, that his laugh, like his mother's, never, or at least seldom, came directly from the heart, and that there was a hard expression about his otherwise well-formed mouth, such as rarely indicated generosity of feeling, or any acquaintance with the kinder impulses of our nature. He was his mother's pet and favorite, and her principal wish was that he should be looked upon and addressed as a gentleman, and for that purpose she encouraged him to associate with those only whose rank and position in life rendered any assumption of equality on his part equally arrogant and obtrusive. In his own family his bearing towards his parents was, in point of fact, the reverse of what it ought to have been. He not only treated his father with something bordering on contempt, but joined his mother in all that ignorant pride which kept her perpetually bewailing the fate by which she was doomed to become his wife. Nor did she herself come off better at his hands. Whilst he flattered her vanity, and turned her foibles to his own advantage, under the guise of a very dutiful affection, his deportment towards her was marked by an ironical respect, which was the more indefensible and unmanly because she could not see through it. The poor woman had taken up the opinion, that difficult and unintelligible language was one test of a gentleman; and her son by the use of such language, let no opportunity pass of confirming her in this opinion, and establishing his own claims to the character.

"Where did you ride to this mornin' Misther Hycy?"

"Down to take a look at Tom Burton's mare, Crazy Jane, ma'am:—

> "'Away, my boys, to horse away,
> The Chase admits of no delay—'"

"Tom Burton!" re-echoed the father with a groan; "an so you're in Tom Burton's hands! A swindlin', horse-dalin' scoundrel that would chate St. Pether. Hycy, my man, if you go to look for wool to Tom you'll come home shorn."

> "'Our vicar still preaches that Peter and Poule
> Laid a swinging long curse on the bonny brown bowl,
> That there's wrath and despair—"

Thank you, father—much obliged; you entertain a good opinion of me."

"Do I, faith? Don't be too sure of that."

"I've bought her at any rate," said Hycy—"thirty-five's the figure; but she's a dead bargain at fifty."

"Bought her!" exclaimed the father; "an' how, in God's name, do you expect to pay for her?"

"By an order on a very excellent, worthy man and gentleman-farmer—ycleped James Burke, Esquire—who has the honor of being father to that ornament of the barony, Hycy Burke, the accomplished. My worthy sire will fork out."

"If I do, that I may—"

"Silence, poor creature!" said his wife, clapping her hand upon his mouth—"make no rash or vulgar oaths. Surely, Misther Burke—"

"How often did I bid you not to misther me? Holy scrapers, am I to be misthered and pesthered this way, an' my name plane Jemmy Burke!"

"You see, Hycy, the vulgarian will come out," said his mother. "I say, Misther Burke, are you to see your son worse mounted at the Herringstown Hunt than any other gentleman among them? Have you no pride?"

"No, thank God! barin' that I'm an honest man an' no gentleman; an', as for Hycy, Rosha—"

"Mrs. Burke, father, if you please," interposed Hycy; "remember who your wife is at all events."

"Faith, Hycy, she'll come better off if I forget that same; but I tell you that instead of bein' the laughin'-stock of the same Hunt, it's betune the stilts of a plough you ought to be, or out in the fields keepin' the men to their business."

"I paid three guineas earnest money, at all events," said the son; "but 'it matters not,' as the preacher says—

> "'When I was at home I was merry and frisky,
> My dad kept a pig and my mother sold whiskey' —

Beg pardon, mother, no allusion—my word and honor none—to you I mean—

> "'My uncle was rich, but would never be aisy
> Till I was enlisted by Corporal Casey.'

Fine times in the army, Mr. Burke, with every prospect of a speedy promotion. Mother, my stomach craves its matutinal supply—I'm in excellent condition for breakfast."

"It's ready. Jemmy, you'll—Misther Burke, I mane—you'll pay for Misther Hycy's mare."

"If I do—you'll live to see it, that's all. Give the boy his breakwhist."

"Thank you, worthy father—much obliged for your generosity—

"'Oh, love is the soul of a nate Irishman
He loves all that's lovely, loves all that he can,
With his sprig of—'

Ah, Peety Dhu, how are you, my worthy peripatetic? Why, this daughter of yours is getting quite a Hebe on our hands. Mrs. Burke, breakfast—breakfast, madam, as you love Hycy, the accomplished." So saying, Hycy the accomplished proceeded to the parlor we have described, followed by his maternal relative, as he often called his mother.

"Well, upon my word and honor, mother," said the aforesaid Hycy, who knew and played upon his mother's weak points, "it is a sad thing to see such a woman as you are, married to a man who has neither the spirit nor feelings of a gentleman—my word and honor it is."

"I feel that, Hycy, but there's no help for spilt milk; we must only make the best of a bad bargain. Are you coming to your breakfast," she shouted, calling to honest Jemmy, who still sat on the hob ruminating with a kind of placid vexation over his son's extravagance—"your tay's filled out!"

"There let it," he replied, "I'll have none of your plash to-day; I tuck my skinful of good stiff stirabout that's worth a shipload of it. Drink it yourselves—I'm no gintleman."

"Arrah, when did you find that out, Misther Burke?" she shouted back again.

"To his friends and acquaintances it is anything but a recent discovery," added Hycy; and each complimented the observation of the other with a hearty laugh, during which the object of it went out to the fields to join the men.

"I'm afraid it's no go, mother," proceeded the son, when breakfast was finished—"he won't stand it. Ah, if both my parents were of the same geometrical proportion, there would be little difficulty in this business; but upon my honor and reputation, my dear mother, I think between you and me that my father's a gross abstraction—a most substantial and ponderous apparition."

"An' didn't I know that an' say that too all along?" replied his mother, catching as much of the high English from him as she could manage: "however, lave the enumeration of the mare to me. It'll go hard or I'll get it out of him."

"It is done," he replied; "your stratagetic powers are great, my dear mother, consequently it is left in your hands."

Hycy, whilst in the kitchen, cast his eye several times upon the handsome young daughter of Peety Dhu, a circumstance to which we owe the instance of benevolent patronage now about to be recorded.

"Mother," he proceeds, "I think it would be a charity to rescue that interesting little girl of Peety Dhu's from a life of mendicancy."

"From a what?" she asked, staring at him.

"Why," he replied, now really anxious to make himself understood—"from the disgraceful line of life he's bringin' her up to. You should take her in and provide for her."

"When I do, Hycy," replied his mother, bridling, "it won't be a beggar's daughter nor a niece of Philip Hogan's—sorrow bit."

"As for her being a niece of Hogan's, you know it is by his mother's side; but wouldn't it be a feather in her cap to get under the protection of a highly respectable woman, though? The patronage of a person like you, Mrs. Burke, would be the making of her—my word and honor it would."

"Hem!—ahem!—do you think so, Hycy?"

"Tut, mother—that indeed!—can there be a doubt about it?"

"Well then, in that case, I think she may stay—that is, if the father will consent to it."

"Thank you, mother, for that example of protection and benevolence. I feel that all my virtues certainly proceed from your side of the house and are derived from yourself—there can be no doubt of that."

"Indeed I think so myself, Hycy, for where else would you get them? You have the M'Swiggin nose; an' it can't be from any one else you take your high notions. All you show of the gentleman, Hycy, it's not hard to name them you have it from, I believe."

"Spoken like a Sybil. Mother, within the whole range of my female acquaintances I don't know a woman that has in her so much of the gentleman as yourself—my word and honor, mother."

"Behave, Hycy—behave now," she replied, simpering; "however truth's truth, at any rate."

We need scarcely say that the poor mendicant was delighted at the notion of having his daughter placed in the family of so warm and independent a man as Jemmy Burke. Yet the poor little fellow did not separate from the girl without a strong manifestation of the affection he bore her. She was his only child—the humble but solitary flower that blossomed for him upon the desert of life.

"I lave her wid you," he said, addressing Mrs. Burke with tears in his eyes, "as the only treasure an' happiness I have in this world. She is the poor man's lamb, as I have hard read out of Scripture wanst; an' in lavin' her undher your care, I lave all my little hopes in this world wid her. I trust, ma'am, you'll guard her an' look afther her as if she was one of your own."

This unlucky allusion might have broken up the whole contemplated arrangement, had not Hycy stepped in to avert from Peety the offended pride of the patroness.

"I hope, Peety," he said, "that you are fully sensible of the honor Mrs. Burke does you and your daughter by taking the girl under her protection and patronage?"

"I am, God knows."

"And of the advantage it is to get her near so respectable a woman—so highly respectable a woman?"

"I am, in troth."

"And that it may be the making of your daughter's fortune?"

"It may, indeed, Masther Hycy."

"And that there's no other woman of high respectability in the parish capable of elevating her to the true principles of double and simple proportion?"

"No, in throth, sir, I don't think there is."

"Nor that can teach her the newest theories in dogmatic theology and metaphysics, together with the whole system of Algebraic Equations if the girl should require them?"

"Divil another woman in the barony can match her at them by all accounts," replied Peety, catching the earnest enthusiasm of Hycy's manner.

"That will do, Peety; you see yourself, mother," he added, taking her aside and speaking in a low voice, "that the little fellow knows right well the advantages of having her under your care and protection; and it's very much to his credit, and speaks very highly for his metempsychosis that he does so—hem!"

"He was always a daicent, sinsible, poor creature of his kind," replied his mother "besides, Hycy, between you and me, she'll be more than worth her bit."

"There now, Peety," said her son, turning towards the mendicant; "it's all settled—wait now for a minute till I write a couple of notes, which you must deliver for me."

Peety sat accordingly, and commenced to lay down for his daughter's guidance and conduct such instructions as he deemed suitable to the situation she was about to enter and the new duties that necessarily devolved upon her.

In due time Hycy appeared, and placing two letters in Peety's hands, said—"Go, Peety, to Gerald Cavanagh's, of Fenton's Farm, and if you can get an opportunity, slip that note into Kathleen's hands—this, mark, with the corner turned down—you won't forget that?"

"No, sir."

"Very well—you're then to proceed to Tom M'Mahon's, and if you find Bryan, his son, there, give him this; and if he's at the mountain farm of Ahadarra, go to him. I don't expect an answer from Kathleen Cavanagh, but I do from Bryan M'Mahon; and mark me, Peety."

"I do, sir."

"Are you sure you do?"

"Sartin, sir."

"Silent as the grave then is the word in both cases—but if I ever hear—"

"That's enough, Masther Hycy; when the grave spakes about it so will I."

Peety took the letters and disappeared with an air rendered important by the trust reposed in him; whilst Mrs. Burke looked inquiringly at her son, as if her curiosity were a good deal excited.

"One of them is to Kate or Kathleen Cavanagh, as they call her," said Hycy, in reply to her looks; "and the other for Bryan M'Mahon, who is soft and generous—*probatum est*. I want to know if he'll stand for thirty-five—and as for Kate, I'm making love to her, you must know."

"Kathleen Cavanagh," replied his mother; "I'll never lend my privileges to sich match."

"Match!" exclaimed Hycy, coolly.

"Ah," she replied warmly; "match or marriage will never—"

"Marriage!" he repeated, "why, my most amiable maternal relative, do you mean to insinuate to Hycy the accomplished, that he is obliged to propose either match or marriage to every girl he makes love to? What a prosaic world you'd have of it, my dear Mrs. Burke. This, ma'am, is only an agreeable flirtation—not but that it's possible there may be something in the shape of a noose matrimonial dangling in the background. She combines, no doubt, in her unrivalled person, the qualities of Hebe, Venus, and Diana—Hebe in youth, Venus in beauty, and Diana in wisdom; so it's said, but I trust incorrectly, as respects one of them—good-bye, mother—try your influence as touching Crazy Jane, and report favorably—

> "'Friend of my soul, this goblet sip,
> 'Twill chase the pensive tear. &c.'"

CHAPTER II.—Gerald Cavanagh and his Family

—Tom M'Mahon's return from Dublin.

The house of Gerald Cavanagh, though not so large as that of our kind-hearted friend, Jemmy Burke, was a good specimen of what an Irish farmer's residence ought to be. It was distant from Burke's somewhat better than two miles, and stood almost, immediately inside the highway, upon a sloping green that was vernal through the year. It was in the cottage style, in the form of a cross, with a roof ornamentally thatched, and was flanked at a little distance by the office-houses. The grass was always so close on this green, as to have rather the appearance of a well kept lawn. The thorn-trees stood in front of it, clipped in the shape of round tables, on one of which, exposed to all weathers, might be seen a pair of large churn-staves, bleached into a white, fresh color, that caused a person to long for the butter they made. On the other stood a large cage, in which was imprisoned a blackbird, whose extraordinary melody had become proverbial in the neighborhood. Down a little to the right of the hall-door, a pretty winding gravelled pathway led to a clear spring well that was overshadowed by a spreading white-thorn; and at each gable stood a graceful elder or mountain-ash, whose red berries during the autumn had a fine effect, and contrasted well with the mass of darker and larger trees, by which the back portion of the house and the offices was almost concealed. Both the house and green were in an elevated position, and commanded a delightful expanse of rich meadows to the extent of nearly one hundred acres, through which a placid river wound its easy way, like some contented spirit that glides calmly and happily through the gentle vicissitudes of an untroubled life.

As Peety Dhu, whilst passing from the residence of our friend Jemmy Burke to that of Gerald Cavanagh, considered himself in his vocation, the reader will not be surprised to hear that it was considerably past noon! when he arrived at Fenton's Farm; for by this name the property was known on a portion of which the Cavanaghs lived. It might be about the hours of two or three o'clock, when Peety, on arriving at the gate which led into Cavanagh's house, very fortunately saw his daughter Kathleen, in the act of feeding the blackbird aforementioned; and prudently deeming this the best opportunity of accomplishing his mission, he beckoned her to approach him. The good-natured girl did so: saying at the same time—"What is the matter, Peety?—do you want me? Won't you come into the kitchen?"

"Thank you, avourneen, but I can't; I did want you, but it was only to give you this letther. I suppose it will tell you all. Oh, thin, is it any wondher that you should get it, an' that half the parish should be dyin' in love wid you? for, in troth, it's enough to make an ould man feel young agin even to look at you. I was afraid they might see me givin' you the letther from the windy, and that's what made me sign to you to come to me here. Good-bye *a colleen dhas* (* Pretty girl.)—an' it's you that's that sure enough."

The features, neck, and bosom of the girl, on receiving this communication, were overspread with one general blush, and she stood, for a few moments, irresolute and confused. In the mean time Peety had passed on, and after a pause of a few minutes, she looked at the letter more attentively, and slowly broke it open. It was probably the first epistle she had ever received, and we need scarcely say that, as a natural consequence, she was by no means quick in deciphering written hand. Be this as it may, after having perused a few lines she started, looked at the bottom for the name, then at the letter again; and as her sister Hanna joined her, that brow on which a frown had been seldom ever seen to sit, was now crimson with indignation.

"Why, gracious goodness!" exclaims Hanna, "what is this, Kathleen? Something has vexed you!—ha! a love-letter, too! In airnest, what ails you? an' who is the letter from, if it's fair to ax?"

"The letter is not for me," replied Kathleen, putting it into her sister's hand, "but when you read it you won't wonder that I'm angry."

As Hanna began to go slowly through it, she first laughed, but on proceeding a little further her brow also reddened, and her whole features expressed deep and unequivocal resentment. Having concluded the perusal of this mysterious document, she, looked at her sister, who, in return, gazed upon her.

"Well, Kathleen, after all," said Hanna, "it's not worth while losing one's temper about it. Never think of it again; only to punish him, I'd advise you, the next time you see Peety, to send it back."

"You don't suppose, Hanna, that I intended to keep it; but indeed," she added, with a smile; "it is not worth while bein' angry about."

As the sisters stood beside each other, holding this short conversation, it would be difficult to find any two females more strikingly dissimilar both in figure, features, and complexion. Hanna was plain, but not disagreeable, especially when her face became animated with good humor. Her complexion, though not at all of a sickly hue, was of that middle tint which is neither pale nor sallow, but holds an equivocal position between both. Her hair was black, but dull, and without that peculiar gloss which accompanies either the very snowy skin of a fair beauty, or, at least, the rich brown hue of a brunette. Her figure was in no way remarkable, and she was rather under the middle size.

Her sister, however, was a girl who deserves at our hands a more accurate and lengthened description. Kathleen Cavanagh was considerably above the middle size, her figure, in fact, being of the tallest; but no earthly form could surpass it in symmetry, and that voluptuous fulness of outline, which, when associated with a modest and youthful style of beauty, is, of all others, the most fascinating and irresistible. The whiteness of her unrivalled skin, and the gloss of health which shone from it were almost dazzling. Her full bust, which literally glowed with light and warmth, was moulded with inimitable proportion, and the masses of rich brown hair that shaded her white and expansive forehead, added incredible attractions to a face that was remarkable not only for simple beauty in its finest sense, but that divine charm of ever-varying expression which draws its lights and shadows, and the thousand graces with which it is accompanied, directly from the heart. Her dark eyes were large and flashing, and reflected by the vivacity or melancholy which increased or over-shadowed their lustre, all those joys or sorrows, and various shades of feeling by which she was moved, whilst her mouth gave indication of extraordinary and entrancing sweetness, especially when she smiled.

Such was Kathleen Cavanagh, the qualities of whose mind were still superior to the advantages of her person. And yet she shone not forth at the first view, nor immediately dazzled the beholder by the brilliancy of her charms. She was unquestionably a tall, fine looking country girl, tastefully and appropriately dressed; but it was necessary to see her more than once, and to have an opportunity of examining her, time after time, to be able fully to appreciate the surprising character of her beauty, and the incredible variety of those changes which sustain its power and give it perpetual novelty to the heart and eye. It was, in fact, of that dangerous description which improves on inspection, and gradually develops itself upon the beholder, until he feels the full extent of its influence, and is sensible, perhaps, when too late, that he is its helpless and unresisting victim.

Around the two thorn-trees we have alluded to were built circular seats of the grassy turf, on which the two sisters, each engaged in knitting, now sat chatting and laughing with that unrestrained good humor and familiarity which gave unquestionable proof of the mutual confidence and affection that subsisted between them. Their natural tempers and dispositions were as dissimilar as their persons. Hanna was lively and mirthful, somewhat hasty, but placable, quick in her feelings of either joy or sorrow, and apparently not susceptible of deep or permanent impressions; whilst Kathleen, on the other hand, was serious, quiet, and placid—difficult to be provoked, of great sweetness of temper, with a tinge of melancholy that occasionally gave an irresistible charm to her voice and features, when conversing upon any subject that was calculated to touch the heart, or in which she felt deeply. Unlike her sister, she was resolute, firm, and almost immutable in her resolutions; but that was because her resolutions were seldom hasty or unadvised, but the result of a strong feeling of rectitude and great good sense. It is true she possessed high feelings of self-respect, together with an enthusiastic love for her religion, and a most earnest zeal for its advancement; indeed, so strongly did these predominate in her mind, that any act involving a personal slight towards herself, or indifference to her creed and its propagation, were looked upon by Kathleen as crimes for which there was no forgiveness. If she had any fellings, it was in these two points they lay. But at the same time, we are bound to say, that the courage and enthusiasm of Joan of Arc had been demanded of her by the state and condition of her country and her creed, she would have unquestionably sacrificed her life, if the sacrifice secured the prosperity of either.

Something of their difference of temperament might have been observed during their conversation, while sitting under the white thorn. Every now and then, for instance, Hanna would start up and commence a series of little flirtations with the blackbird, which she called her sweetheart, and again resume her chat and seat as before; or she would attempt to catch a butterfly as it fluttered about her, or sometimes give it pursuit over half the green, whilst Kathleen sat with laughing and delighted eyes, and a smile of unutterable sweetness on her lips, watching the success of this innocent frolic. In this situation we must now leave them, to follow Peety, who is on his way to deliver the other letter to Bryan M'Mahon.

Our little black Mercury was not long in arriving at the house of Tom M'Mahon, which he reached in company with that worthy man himself, whom he happened to overtake near Carriglass where he lived. M'Mahon seemed fatigued and travel-worn, and consequently was proceeding at a slow pace when Peety overtook him. The latter observed this.

"Why, thin, Tom," said he, after the first salutations had passed, "you look like a man that had jist put a tough journey over him."

"An' so I ought, Peety," he replied, "for I have put a tough journey over me."

"Musha where were you, thin, if it's fair to ax?" inquired Peety; "for as for me that hears everything almost, the never a word I heard o' this."

"I was in Dublin, thin, all the way," replied the farmer, "strivin' to get a renewal o' my laise from ould Squire Chevydale, the landlord; an' upon my snuggins, Peety, you may call a journey to Dublin an' home agin a tough one—devil a doubt of it. However, thank God, here we are at home; an' blessed be His name that we have a home to come to; for, afther all, what place is like it? Throth, Peety, my heart longed for these brave fields of ours—for the lough there below, and the wild hills above us; for it wasn't until I was away from them that I felt how strong the love of them was in my heart."

M'Mahon was an old but hale man, with a figure and aspect that were much above the common order even of the better class of peasants. There could be no mistaking the decent and composed spirit of integrity which was evident in his very manner; and there was something in his long flowing locks, now tinged with gray, as they rested upon his shoulders, that gave an air of singular respect to his whole appearance.

On uttering the last words he stood, and looking around him became so much affected that his eyes filled with tears. "Ay," said he, "thank God that we have our place to come to, an' that we will still have it to come to, and blessed be His name for all things! Come, Peety," he added, after a pause, "let us see how they all are inside; I'm longin' to see them, especially poor, dear Dora; an'—God bless me! here she is!—no, she ran back to tell them—but ay—oh, ay! here she is again, my darlin' girl, comin' to meet me."

He had scarcely uttered the words when an interesting, slender girl, about eighteen, blushing, and laughing, and crying, all at once, came flying towards him, and throwing her white arms about his neck, fell upon his bosom, kissed him, and wept with delight at his return.

"An' so, father dear, you're back to us! My gracious, we thought you'd never come home! Sure you worn't sick? We thought maybe that you took ill, or that—that—something happened you; and we wanted to send Bryan after you—but nothing happened you?—nor you worn't sick?"

"You affectionate, foolish darlin', no, I wasn't sick; nor nothing ill happened me, Dora."

"Oh, thank God! Look at them," she proceeded, directing his attention to the house, "look at them all crowdin' to the door—and here's Shibby, too, and Bryan himself—an' see my mother ready to lep out of herself wid pure joy—the Lord be praised that you're safe back!"

At this moment his second daughter ran to him, and a repetition of welcome similar to that which he received from Dora took place. His son Bryan grasped his hand, and said, whilst a tear stood even in his eye, that he was glad to see him safe home. The old man, in return, grasped his hand with an expression of deep feeling, and after having inquired if they had been all well in his absence, he proceeded with them to the house. Here the scene was still more interesting. Mrs. M'Mahon stood smiling at the door, but as he came near, she was obliged once or twice to wipe away the tears with the corner of her handkerchief. We have often observed how much fervid piety is mingled with the affections of the Irish people when in a state of excitement; and this meeting between the old man and his wife presented an additional proof of it.

"Blessed be God!" exclaimed his wife, tenderly embracing* him, "blessed be God, Tom darlin', that you're safe back to us! An' how are you, avourueen? an' wor you well ever since? an' there was nothin—musha, go out o' this, Ranger, you thief—oh, God forgive me! what am I sayin'? sure the poor dog is as glad as the best of us—arrah, thin, look at the affectionate crathur, a'most beside himself! Dora, avillish, give him the could stirabout that's in the skillet, jist for his affection, the crathur. Here, Ranger—Ranger, I say—oh no, sorra one's in the house now but yourself, Tom. Well, an' there was nothing wrong wid you?"

"Nothin', Nancy, thanks be to the Almighty—down, poor fellow—there now, Ranger—och, behave, you foolish dog—musha, see this!"

"Throth, Tom," continued his loving wife, "let what will happen, it's the last journey ever we'll let you take from us. Ever an' ever, there we wor thinkin' an' thinkin' a thousand things about you. At one time that something happened you; then that you fell sick an' had none but strangers about you. Throth we won't; let what will happen, you must stay wid vis."

"Indeed an' I never knew how I loved the place, an' you all, till I went; but, thank God, I hope it's the last journey ever I'll have to take from either you or it."

"Shibby, run down to—or do you, Dora, go, you're the souplest—to Paddy Mullen's and Jemmy Kelly's, and the rest of the neighbors, an' tell them to come up, that your father's home. Run now, acushla, an' if you fall don't wait to rise; an' Shibby, darlin', do you whang down a lot o' that bacon into rashers, 'your father must be at death's door wid hunger; but wasn't it well that I thought of having the whiskey in, for you see afther Thursday last we didn't know what minute you'd dhrop in on us, Tom, an' I said it was best to be prepared. Give Peety a chair, the crature; come forrid, Peety, an' take a sate; an' how are you? an' how is the girsha wid you, an' where is she?"

To these questions, thus rapidly put, Peety returned suitable answers; but indeed Mrs. M'Mahon did not wait to listen to them, having gone to another room to produce the whisky she had provided for the occasion.

"Here," she said, reappearing with a huge bottle in one hand and a glass in the other, "a sip o' the right sort will help you afther your long journey; you must be tired, be coorse, so take this."

"Aisy, Bridget," exclaimed her husband, "don't fill it; you'll make me hearty." (* tipsy)

"Throth an' I will fill it," she replied, "ay, an' put a heap on it. There now, finish that bumper."

The old man, with a smiling and happy face, received the glass, and taking his wife's hand in his, looked at her, and then upon them all, with an expression of deep emotion. "Bridget, your health; childre', all your healths; and here's to Carriglasa, an' may we long live happy in it, as we will, plase God! Peety, not forgettin' you!"

We need hardly say that the glass went round, nor that Peety was not omitted in the hospitality any more than in the toast.

"Here, Bryan," said Mrs. M'Mahon, "lay that bottle on the dresser, it's not worth while puttin' it past till the neighbors comes up; an' it's they that'll be the glad neighbors to see you safe back agin, Tom."

In this she spoke truth. Honest and hearty was the welcome he received from them, as with sparkling eyes and a warm grasp they greeted him on his return. Not only had Paddy Mullin and Jemmy Kelly run up in haste—the latter, who had been digging in his garden, without waiting to put on his hat or coat—but other families in the neighborhood, young and old, crowded in to welcome him home—-from Dublin—for in that lay the principal charm. The bottle was again produced, and a holiday spirit now prevailed among them. Questions upon questions were put to him with reference to the wonders they had heard of the great metropolis—of the murders and robberies committed upon travellers—the kidnapping of strangers from the country—the Lord Lieutenant's Castle, with three hundred and sixty-four windows in it, and all the extraordinary sights and prodigies which it is supposed to contain. In a few minutes after this friendly accession to their numbers had taken place, a youth entered about nineteen years of age—handsome, tall, and well-made—in fact, such a stripling as gave undeniable promise of becoming a fine, powerful young man. On being handed a glass of whiskey he shook hands with M'Mahon, welcomed him home, and then drank all their healths by name until he came to that of Dora, when he paused, and, coloring, merely nodded towards her. We cannot undertake to account for this omission, nor do more than record what actually happened. Neither do we know why Dora blushed so deeply as she did, nor why the sparkling and rapid glance which she gave him in return occasioned him to look down with an appearance of confusion and pain. That some understanding subsisted between young Cavanagh—for he was Gerald's son—and Dora might have been evident to a close observer; but in truth there was at that moment no such thing as a close observer among them, every eye being fixed with impatience and curiosity upon Tom M'Mahon, who had now most of the conversation to himself, little else being left to the share of his auditors than the interjectional phrases and exclamations of wonder at his extraordinary account of Dublin.

"But, father," said Bryan, "about the business that brought you there? Did you get the Renewal?"

"I got as good," replied the simple-hearted old man, "an' that was the, word of a gintleman—an' sure they say that that's the best security in the world."

"Well, but how was it?" they exclaimed, "an' how did it happen that you didn't get the Lease itself?"

"Why, you see," he proceeded in reply, "the poor gintleman was near his end—an' it was owin' to Pat Corrigan that I seen him at all—for Pat, you know, is his own man. When I went in to where he sat I found Mr. Fethertonge the agent wid him: he had a night-cap on, an' was sittin' in a big armchair, wid one of his feet an' a leg swaythed wid flannel. I thought he was goin' to write or sign papers. 'Well, M'Mahon,' says he—for he was always as keen as a briar, an' knew me at once—'what do you want? an' what has brought you from the country?' I then spoke to him about the new lease; an' he said to Fethertonge, 'prepare M'Mahon's lease, Fothertonge;—you shall have a new lease, M'Mahon. You are an honest man, and your family have been so for many a long year upon our property. As my health is unsartin,' he said, turning to Mr. Fethertonge, 'I take Mr. Fethertonge here to witness, that in case anything should happen me I give you my promise for a renewal—an' not only in my name alone, but in my son's; an' I now lave it upon him to fulfil my intentions an' my words, if I should not live to see it done myself. Mr. Fethertonge here has brought me papers to sign, but I am not able to hould a pen, or if I was I'd give you a written promise; but you have my solemn word, I fear my dyin' word, in Mr. Fethertonge's presence—that you shall have a lease of your farm at the ould rint. It is such tenants as you we want, M'Mahon, an' that we ought to encourage on our property. Fethertonge, do you in the mane time see that a lease is prepared for M'Mahon; an' see, at all events, that my wishes shall be carried into effect.' Sich was his last words to me, but he was a corpse on the next day but one afterwards."

"It's jist as good," they exclaimed with one voice; "for what is betther, or what can be betther than *the word of an Irish gentleman?*"

"What ought to be betther, at all events?" said Bryan. "Well, father, so far everything is right, for there is no doubt but his son will fulfil his words—Mr. Fethertonge himself isn't the thing; but I don't see why he should be our enemy. We always stood well with the ould man, an' I hope will with the son. Come, mother, move the bottle again—there's another round in it still; an' as everything looks so well and our mind is aisy, we'll see it to the bottom."

The conversation was again resumed, questions were once more asked concerning the sights and sounds of Dublin, of which one would imagine they could scarcely ever hear enough, until the evening was tolerably far advanced, when the neighbors withdrew to their respective homes, and left M'Mahon and his family altogether to themselves.

Peety, now that the joy and gratulation for the return of their father had somewhat subsided, lost no time in delivering Hycy Burke's communication into the hands of Bryan. The latter, on opening it, started with surprise not inferior to that with which Kathleen Cavanagh had perused the missive addressed to her. Nor was this all. The letter received by Bryan, as if the matter had been actually designed by the writer, produced the selfsame symptoms of deep resentment upon him that the mild and gentle Kathleen Cavanagh experienced on the perusal of her own. His face became flushed and his eye blazed with indignation as he went through its contents; after which he once more looked at the superscription, and notwithstanding the vehement passion into which it had thrown him, he was ultimately obliged to laugh.

"Peety," said he, resuming his gravity, "you carried a letter from Hycy Burke to Kathleen Cavanagh to-day?"

"Who says that?" replied Peety, who could not but remember the solemnity of his promise to that accomplished gentleman.

"I do, Peety."

"Well, I can't help you, Bryan, nor prevent you from thinking so, sure—stick to that."

"Why, I know you did, Peety."

"Well, acushla, an' if you do, your only so much the wiser."

"Oh, I understand," continued Bryan, "it's a private affair, or intended to be so—an' Mr. Hycy has made you promise not to spake of it."

"Sure you know all about it, Bryan; an' isn't that enough for you? Only what answer am I to give him?"

"None at present, Peety; but say I'll see himself in a day or two."

"That's your answer, then?"

"That's all the answer I can give till I see himself, as I said."

"Well, good-bye, Bryan, an' God be wid you!"

"Good-bye, Peety!" and thus they parted.

CHAPTER III.—Jemmy Burke Refuses to be, Made a Fool Of
—Hycy and a Confidant

Hycy Burke was one of those persons who, under the appearance of a somewhat ardent temperament, are capable of abiding the issue of an event with more than ordinary patience. Having not the slightest suspicion of the circumstance which occasioned Bryan M'Mahon's resentment, he waited for a day of two under the expectation that his friend was providing the sum necessary to accommodate him. The third and fourth days passed, however, without his having received any reply whatsoever; and Hycy, who had set his heart upon Crazy Jane, on finding that his father—who possessed as much firmness as he did of generosity—absolutely refused to pay for her, resolved to lose no more time in putting Bryan's friendship to the test. To this, indeed, he was urged by Burton, a wealthy but knavish country horse-dealer, as we said, who wrote to him that unless he paid for her within a given period, he must be under the necessity of closing with a person who had offered him a higher price. This message was very offensive to Hycy, whose great foible, as the reader knows, was to be considered a gentleman, not merely in appearance, but in means and circumstances. He consequently had come to the determination of writing again to M'Mahon upon the same subject, when chance brought them together in the market of Ballymacan.

After the usual preliminary inquiries as to health, Hycy opened the matter:—

"I asked you to lend me five-and-thirty pounds to secure Crazy Jane," said he, "and you didn't even answer my letter. I admit I'm pretty deeply in your debt, as it is, my dear Bryan, but you know I'm safe."

"I'm not at this moment thinking much of money matters, Hycy; but, as you like plain speaking, I tell you candidly that I'll lend you no money."

Hycy's manner changed all at once; he looked at M'Mahon for nearly a minute, and said in quite a different tone—

"What is the cause of this coldness, Bryan? Have I offended you?"

"Not knowingly—but you have offended me; an' that's all I'll say about it."

"I'm not aware of it," replied the other—-"my word and honor I'm not."

Bryan felt himself in a position of peculiar difficulty; he could not openly quarrel with Hycy, unless he made up his mind to disclose the grounds of the dispute, which, as matters then stood between him and Kathleen Cavanagh, to whom he had not actually declared his affection, would have been an act of great presumption on his part.

"Good-bye, Hycy," said he; "I have tould you my mind, and now I've done with it."

"With all my heart!" said the other—"that's a matter of taste on your part. You're offended, you say; yet you choose to put the offence in your pocket. It's all right, I suppose—but you know best. Good-bye to you, at all events," he added; "be a good boy and take care of yourself."

M'Mahon nodded with good-humored contempt in return, but spoke not.

"By all that deserves an oath," exclaimed Hycy, looking bitterly after him, "if I should live to the day of judgment I'll never forgive you your insulting conduct this day—and that I'll soon make you feel to your cost!"

This misunderstanding between the two friends caused Hycy to feel much mortification and disappointment. After leaving M'Mahon, he went through the market evidently with some particular purpose in view, if one could judge from his manner. He first proceeded to the turf-market, and looked with searching eye among those who stood waiting to dispose of their loads. From this locality he turned his steps successively to other parts of the town, still looking keenly about him as he went along. At length he seemed disappointed or indifferent, it was difficult to say which, and stood coiling the lash of his whip in the dust, sometimes quite unconsciously, and sometimes as if a wager depended on the success with which he did it—when, on looking down the street, he observed a little broad, squat man, with a fiery red head, a face almost scaly with freckles, wide projecting cheek-bones, and a nose so thoroughly of the saddle species, that a rule laid across the base of it, immediately between the eyes, would lie close to the whole front of his face. In addition to these personal accomplishments, he had a pair of strong bow legs, terminating in two broad, flat feet, in complete keeping with his whole figure, which, though not remarkable for symmetry, was nevertheless indicative of great and extraordinary strength. He wore neither stockings nor cravat of any kind, but had a pair of strong clouted brogues upon his feet; thus disclosing to the spectator two legs and a breast that were covered over with a fell of red close hair that might have been long and strong enough for a badger. He carried in his hand a short whip, resembling a carrot in shape, and evidently of such a description as no man that had any regard for his health would wish to come in contact with, especially from the hand of such a double-jointed but misshapen Hercules as bore it.

"Ted, how goes it, my man?"

"*Ghe dhe shin dirthu, a dinaousal?*" replied Ted, surveying him with a stare.

"D—n you!" was about to proceed from Hycy's lips when he perceived that a very active magistrate, named Jennings, stood within hearing. The latter passed on, however, and Hycy proceeded:—"I was about to abuse you, Ted, for coming out with your Irish to me," he said, "until I saw Jennings, and then I *had* you."

"Throgs, din, Meeisther Hycy, I don't like the *Bairlha* (* English tongue)—'caise I can't sphake her properly, at all, at all. Come you 'out wid the Gailick fwhor me, i' you plaise, Meeisther Hycy."

"D—n your Gaelic!" replied Hycy—"no, I won't—I don't speak it."

"The Laud forget you for that!" replied Ted, with a grin; "my ould grandmudher might larn it from you—hach, ach, ha!"

"None of your d—d impertinence, Ted. I want to speak to you."

"Fwhat would her be?" asked Ted, with a face in which there might be read such a compound of cunning, vacuity, and ferocity as could rarely be witnessed in the same countenance.

"Can you come down to me to-night?"

"No; I'll be busy."

"Where are you at work now?"

"In Glendearg, above."

"Well, then, if you can't come to me, I must only go to you. Will you be there tonight? I wish to speak to you on very particular business."

"Shiss; you *will*, dhin, wanst more?" asked the other, significantly.

"I think so."

"Shiss—ay—vary good. Fwen will she come?"

"About eleven or twelve; so don't be from about the place anywhere."

"Shiss—-dhin—vary good. Is dhat all?"

"That's all now. Are your turf *dry* or *wet** to-day?"

* *One method of selling Poteen is by bringing in kishes of turf to the neighboring markets, when those who are up to the secret purchase the turf, or pretend to do so; and while in the act of discharging the load, the Keg of Poteen is quickly passed into the house of him who purchases the turf.—Are your turf wet or dry? was, consequently, a pass- word.*

"Not vary dhry," replied Ted, with a grin so wide that, as was humorously said by a neighbor of his, "it would take a telescope to enable a man to see from the one end of it to the other."

Hycy nodded and laughed, and Ted, cracking his whip, proceeded up the town to sell his turf.

Hycy now sauntered about through the market, chatting here and there among acquaintances, with the air of a man to whom neither life nor anything connected with it could occasion any earthly trouble. Indeed, it mattered little what he felt, his easiness of manner was such that not one of his acquaintances could for a moment impute to him the possibility of ever being weighed down by trouble or care of any kind; and lest his natural elasticity of spirits might fail to sustain this perpetual buoyancy, he by no means neglected to fortify himself with artificial support. Meet him when or where you might, be it at six in the morning or twelve at night, you were certain to catch from his breath the smell of liquor, either in its naked simplicity or disguised and modified in some shape.

His ride home, though a rapid, was by no means a pleasing one. M'Mahon had not only refused to lend him the money he stood in need of, but actually quarrelled with him, as far as he could judge, for no other purpose but that he might make the quarrel a plea for refusing him. This disappointment, to a person of Hycy's disposition, was, we have seen, bitterly vexatious, and it may be presumed that he reached home in anything but an agreeable humor. Having dismounted, he was about to enter the hall-door, when his attention was directed towards that of the kitchen by a rather loud hammering, and on turning his eyes to the spot he found two or three tinkers very busily engaged in soldering, clasping, and otherwise repairing certain vessels belonging to that warm and spacious establishment. The leader of these vagrants was a man named Philip Hogan, a fellow of surprising strength and desperate character, whose feats of hardihood and daring had given him a fearful notoriety over a large district of the country. Hogan was a man whom almost every one feared, being, from confidence, we presume, in his great strength, as well as by nature, both insolent, overbearing, and ruffianly in the extreme. His inseparable and appropriate companion was a fierce and powerful bull-dog of the old Irish breed, which he had so admirably trained that it was only necessary to give him a sign, and he would seize by the throat either man or beast, merely in compliance with the will of his master. On this occasion he was accompanied by two of his brothers, who were, in fact, nearly as impudent and offensive ruffians as himself. Hycy paused for a moment, seemed thoughtful, and tapped his boot with the point of his whip as he looked at them. On entering the parlor he found dinner over, and his father, as was usual, waiting to get his tumbler of punch.

"Where's my mother?" he asked—"where's Mrs. Burke?"

On uttering the last words he raised his voice so as she might distinctly hear him.

"She's above stairs gettin' the whiskey," replied his father, "and God knows she's long enough about it."

Hycy ran up, and meeting her on the lobby, said, in a low, anxious voice—

"Well, what news? Will he stand it?"

"No," she replied, "you may give up the notion—he won't do it, an' there's no use in axin' him any more."

"He won't do it!" repeated the son; "are you certain now?"

"Sure an' sartin. I done all that could be done; but it's worse an' worse he got."

Something escaped Hycy in the shape of an ejaculation, of which we are not in possession at present; he immediately added:—

"Well, never mind. Heavens! how I pity you, ma'am—to be united to such a d—d—hem!—to such a—a—such a—gentleman!"

Mrs. Burke raised her hands as if to intimate that it was useless to indulge in any compassion of the kind.

"The thing's now past cure," she said; "I'm a marthyr, an' that's all that's about it. Come down till I get you your dinner."

Hycy took his seat in the parlor, and began to give a stave of the "Bay of Biscay:"—

> "'Loud roar'd the dreadful thunder,
> The rain a deluge pours;
> The clouds were rent asunder
> By light'ning's vivid—'

By the way, mother, what are those robbing ruffians, the Hogans, doing at the kitchen door there?"

"Troth, whatever they like," she replied. "I tould that vagabond, Philip, that I had nothing for them to do, an' says he, 'I'm the best judge of that, Rosha Burke.' An, with that he walks into the kitchen, an' takes everything that he seen a flaw in, an' there he and them sat a mendin' an' sotherin' an' hammerin' away at them, without ever sayin' 'by your lave.'"

"It's perfectly well known that they're robbers," said Hycy, "and the general opinion is that they're in connection with a Dublin gang, who are in this part of the country at present. However, I'll speak to the ruffians about such conduct."

He then left the parlor, and proceeding to the farmyard, made a signal to one of the Hogans, who went down hammer in hand to where he stood. During a period of ten minutes, he and Hycy remained in conversation, but of what character it was, whether friendly or otherwise, the distance at which they stood rendered it impossible for any one to ascertain. Hycy then returned to dinner, whilst his father in the meantime sat smoking his pipe, and sipping from time to time at his tumbler of punch. Mrs. Burke, herself, occupied an arm-chair to the left of the fire, engaged at a stocking which was one of a pair that she contrived to knit for her husband during every twelve months; and on the score of which she pleaded strong claims to a character of most exemplary and indefatigable industry.

"Any news from the market, Hycy?" said his father.

"Yes," replied Hycy, in that dry ironical tone which he always used to his parents—"rather interesting—Ballymacan is in the old place."

"Bekaise," replied his father, with more quickness than might be expected, as he whiffed away the smoke with a face of very sarcastic humor; "I hard it had gone up a bit towards the mountains—but I knew you wor the boy could tell me whether it had or not—ha!—ha!—ha!"

This rejoinder, in addition to the intelligence Hycy had just received from his mother, was not calculated to improve his temper. "You may laugh," he replied; "but if your respectable father had treated you in a spirit so stingy and beggarly as that which I experience at your hands, I don't know how you might have borne it."

"My father!" replied Burke; "take your time, Hycy—my hand to you, he had a different son to manage from what I have."

"God sees that's truth," exclaimed his wife, turning the expression to her son's account.

"I was no gentleman, Hycy," Burke proceeded.

"Ah, is it possible?" said the son, with a sneer. "Are you sure of that, now?"

"Nor no spendthrift, Hycy."

"No," said the wife, "you never had the spirit; you were ever and always a *molshy*." (* A womanly, contemptible fellow)

"An' yet *molshy* as I was," he replied, "you wor glad to catch me. But Hycy, my good boy, I didn't cost my father at the rate of from a hundre'-an'-fifty to two-hundre'-a-year, an' get myself laughed at and snubbed by my superiors, for forcin' myself into their company."

"Can't you let the boy ait his dinner in peace, at any rate?" said his mother. "Upon my credit I wouldn't be surprised if you drove him away from us altogether."

"I only want to drive him into common sense, and the respectful feeling he ought to show to both you an' me, Rosha," said Burke; "if he expects to have either luck or grace, or the blessing of God upon him, he'll change his coorses, an' not keep breakin' my heart as he's doin'."

"Will you pay for the mare I bought, father?" asked Hycy, very seriously. "I have already told you, that I paid three guineas earnest; I hope you will regard your name and family so far as to prevent me from breaking my word—besides leading the world to suppose that you are a poor man."

"Regard my name and family!" returned the father, with a look of bitterness and sorrow; "who is bringin' them into disgrace, Hycy?"

"In the meantime," replied the son, "I have asked a plain question, Mr. Burke, and I expect a plain answer; will you pay for the mare?"

"An' supposin' I don't?"

"Why, then, Mr. Burke, if you don't you won't, that's all."

"I must stop some time," replied his father, "an' that is now. I wont pay for her."

"Well then, sir, I shall feel obliged, as your respectable wife has just said, if you will allow me to eat, and if possible, live in peace."

"I'm speakin' only for your—"

"That will do now—hush—silence if you please."

"Hycy dear," said the mother; "why would you ax him another question about it? Drop the thing altogether."

"I will, mother, but I pity you; in the meantime, I thank you, ma'am, of your advice."

"Hycy," she continued, with a view of changing the conversation; "did you hear that Tom M'Bride's dead?"

"No ma'am, but I expected it; when did he die?"

Before his father could reply, a fumbling was heard at the hall-door; and, the next moment, Hogan, thrust in his huge head and shoulders began to examine the lock by attempting to turn the key in it.

"Hogan, what are you about?" asked Hycy.

"I beg your pardon," replied the ruffian; "I only wished to know if the lock wanted mendin'—that was all, Misther Hycy."

"Begone, sirra," said the other; "how dare you have the presumption to take such a liberty? you impudent scoundrel! Mother, you had better pay them," he added; "give the vagabonds anything they ask, to get rid of them."

Having dined, her worthy son mixed a tumbler of punch, and while drinking it, he amused himself, as was his custom, by singing snatches of various songs, and drumming with his fingers upon the table; whilst every now and then he could hear the tones of his mother's voice in high altercation with Hogan and his brothers. This, however, after a time, ceased, and she returned to the parlor a good deal chafed by the dispute.

"There's one thing I wonder at," she observed, "that of all men in the neighborhood, Gerald Cavanagh would allow sich vagabonds as they an Kate Hogan is, to put in his kiln. Troth, Hycy," she added, speaking to him in a warning and significant tone of voice, "if there wasn't something low an' mane in him, he wouldn't do it."

> "'Tis when the cup is smiling before us.
> And we pledge unto our hearts—'

"Your health, mother. Mr. Burke, here's to you! Why I dare say you are right, Mrs. Burke. The Cavanagh family is but an upstart one at best; it wants antiquity, ma'am—a mere affair of yesterday, so what after all could you expect from it?"

Honest Jemmy looked at him and then groaned. "An upstart family!—that'll do—oh, murdher—well, 'tis respectable at all events; however, as to havin' the Hogans about them—they wor always about them; it was the same in their father's time. I remember ould Laghlin Hogan, an' his whole clanjamfrey, men an' women, young an' old, wor near six months out o' the year about ould Gerald Cavanagh's—the present man's father; and another thing you may build upon—that whoever ud chance to speak a hard word against one o' the Cavanagh family, before Philip Hogan or any of his brothers, would stand a strong chance of a shirtful o' sore bones. Besides, we all know how Philip's father saved Mrs. Cavanagh's life about nine or ten months after her marriage. At any rate, whatever bad qualities the vagabonds have, want of gratitude isn't among them."

"'———That are true, boys, true,
The sky of this life opens o'er us,
And heaven—'

M'Bride, ma'am, will be a severe loss to his family."

"Throth he will, and a sarious loss—for among ourselves, there was none o' them like him."

"'Gives a glance of its blue—'

"I think I ought to go to the wake to-night. I know it's a bit of a descent on my part, but still it is scarcely more than is due to a decent neighbor. Yes, I shall go; it is determined on."

"'I ga'ed a waefu' gate yestreen,
A gate I fear I'll dearly rue;
I gat my death frae twa sweet een,
Twa lovely een o' bonnie blue.'

"Mine are brown, Mrs. Burke—the eyes you wot of; but alas! the family is an upstart one, and that is strongly against the Protestant interest in the case. Heigho!"

Jemmy Burke, having finished his after-dinner pipe and his daily tumbler both together, went out to his men; and Hycy, with whom he had left the drinking materials, after having taken a tumbler or two, put on a strong pair of boots, and changed the rest of his dress for a coarser 'suit, bade his mother a polite good-bye, and informed her, that as he intended to be present at M'Bride's wake he would most probably not return until near morning.

CHAPTER IV.—A Poteen Still-House at Midnight—Its Inmates.

About three miles in a south-western direction from Burke's residence, the country was bounded by a range of high hills and mountains of a very rugged and wild, but picturesque description. Although a portion of the same landscape, yet nothing could be more strikingly distinct in character than the position of the brown wild hills, as contrasted with that of the mountains from which they abutted. The latter ran in long and lofty ranges that were marked by a majestic and sublime simplicity, whilst the hills were of all shapes and sizes, and seemed as if cast about at random. As a matter of course the glens and valleys that divided them ran in every possible direction, sometimes crossing and intersecting each other at right angles, and sometimes running parallel, or twisting away in opposite directions. In one of those glens that lay nearest the mountains, or rather indeed among them, was a spot which from its peculiar position would appear to have been designed from the very beginning as a perfect paradise for the illicit distiller. It was a kind of back chamber in the mountains, that might, in fact, have escaped observation altogether, as it often did. The approach to it was by a long precipitous glen, that could be entered only at its lower end, and seemed to terminate against the abrupt side of the mountain, like a cul de sac. At the very extremity, however, of this termination, and a little on the right-hand side, there was a steep, narrow pass leading into a recess which was completely encompassed by precipices. From this there was only one means of escape independently of the gut through which it was entered. The moors on the side most approachable were level, and on a line to the eye with that portion of the mountains which bounded it on the opposite side, so that as one looked forward the space appeared to be perfectly continuous, and consequently no person could suspect that there lay so deep and precipitous a glen between them.

In the northern corner of this remarkable locality, a deep cave, having every necessary property as a place for private distillation, ran under the rocks, which met over it in a kind of gothic arch. A stream of water just sufficient for the requisite purposes, fell in through a fissure from above, forming such a little subterraneous cascade in the cavern as human design itself could scarcely have surpassed in felicity of adaptation to the objects of an illicit distiller.

To this cave, then, we must take the liberty of transporting our readers, in order to give them an opportunity of getting a peep at the inside of a Poteen Still-house, and of hearing a portion of conversation, which, although not remarkable for either elegance or edification, we are, nevertheless, obliged to detail, as being in some degree necessary to the elucidation of our narrative. Up in that end which constituted the termination of the cave, and fixed upon a large turf fire which burned within a circle of stones that supported it, was a tolerably-sized Still, made of block-tin. The mouth of this Still was closed by an air-tight cover, also of tin, called the Head, from which a tube of the same metal projected into a large keeve, or condenser, that was kept always filled with cool water by an incessant stream from the cascade we have described, which always ran into and overflowed it. The arm of this head was fitted and made air-tight, also, into a spiral tube of copper, called the Worm, which rested in the water of the cooler; and as it consisted of several convolutions, like a cork-screw, its office was to condense the hot vapor which was transmitted to it from the glowing Still into that description of spirits known as poteen. At the bottom of this cooler, the Worm terminated in a small cock or spigot, from which the spirits projected in a slender stream, about the thickness of a quill, into a vessel placed for its reception. Such was the position of the Still, Head, and Worm, when in full operation. Fixed about the cave, upon rude stone stillions, were the usual vessels requisite for the various processes through which it was necessary to put the malt, before the wort, which is its first liquid shape, was fermented, cleared off, and thrown into the Still to be singled; for our readers must know that distillation is a double process, the first product being called singlings, and the second or last, doublings—which is the perfect liquor. Sacks of malt, empty vessels, piles of turf, heaps of grains, tubs of wash, and kegs of whiskey, were lying about in all directions, together with pots, pans, wooden trenchers, and dishes, for culinary uses. The seats were round stones and black bosses which were made of a light hard moss found in the mountains and bogs, and frequently used as seats in rustic chimney corners. On entering, your nose was assailed by such a mingled stench of warm grains, sour barm, putrid potato skins, and strong whiskey, as required considerable fortitude to bear without very unequivocal tokens of *disgust.*

The persons assembled were in every way worthy of the place and its dependencies. Seated fronting the fire was our friend Teddy Phats, which was the only name he was ever known by, his wild, beetle brows lit into a red, frightful glare of savage mirth that seemed incapable, in its highest glee, to disengage itself entirely from an expression of the man's unquenchable ferocity. Opposite to him sat a tall, smut-faced, truculent-looking young fellow, with two piercing eyes and a pair of grim brows, which, when taken into conjunction with a hard, unfeeling mouth, from the corners of which two right lines ran down his chin, giving that part of his face a most dismal expression, constituted a countenance that matched exceedingly well with the visage of Teddy Phats. This worthy gentleman was a tinker, and one of Hogan's brothers, whom we have already introduced to our readers. Scattered about the fire and through the cavern were a party of countrymen who came to purchase whiskey for a wedding, and three or four publicans and shebeenmen who had come on professional business. Some were drinking, some indulging in song, and some were already lying drunk or asleep in different parts of this subterraneous pandemonium. Exalted in what was considered the position of honor sat a country hedge-schoolmaster, his mellow eye beaming with something between natural humor, a sense of his own importance, and the influence of pure whiskey, fresh it is called, from the Still-eye.

"Here, Teddy," said one of the countrymen, "will you fill the bottle again."

"No," replied Teddy, who though as cunning as the devil himself, could seldom be got to speak anything better than broken English, and that of such a character that it was often scarcely intelligible.

"No," he replied; "I gav'd you wan bottle 'idout payment fwhor her, an' by shapers I won't give none oder."

"Why, you burning beauty, aren't we takin' ten gallons, an' will you begrudge us a second bottle?"

"Shiss—devil purshue de bottle more ye'll drunk here 'idout de *airigad*, (* Money) dat's fwhat you will."

"Teddy," said the schoolmaster, "I drink propitiation to you as a profissional gintle-man! No man uses more indepindent language than you do. You are under no earthly obligation to Messrs. Syntax and Prosody. Grammar, my worthy friend, is banished as an intruder from your elocution, just as you would exclude a gauger from your Still-house."

"Fwhat about de gagur!" exclaimed Teddy, starting; "d—n him an' shun-tax an' every oder tax, rint an' all—hee! hee! hee!"

We may as well let our readers know, before we proceed farther, that in the opinion of many, Teddy Phats understood and could speak English as well as any man of his station in the country. In fairs or markets, or other public places, he spoke, it is true, nothing but Irish unless in a private way, and only to persons in whom he thought he could place every confidence. It was often observed, however, that in such conversations he occasionally arranged the matter of those who could use only English to him, in such a way as proved pretty clearly that he must have possessed a greater mastery over that language than he acknowledged. We believe the fact to be, however, that Teddy, as an illicit distiller, had found it, on some peculiar occasions connected with his profession, rather an inconvenient accomplishment to know English. He had given some evidence in his day, and proved, or attempted to prove, a few alibies on behalf of his friends; and he always found, as there is good reason to believe, that the Irish language, when properly enunciated through the medium of an interpreter, was rather the safer of the two, especially when resorted to within the precincts of the country court-house and in hearing of the judge.

"You're a fool, Teddy," said Hogan; "let them drink themselves; blind—this liquor's paid for; an' if they lose or spill it by the 'way, why, blazes to your purty mug, don't you know they'll have to pay for another cargo."

Teddy immediately took the hint.

"Barney Brogan," he shouted to a lubberly-looking, bullet-headed cub, half knave, half fool, who lived about such establishments, and acted as messenger, spy, and vidette; "listen hedher! bring Darby Keenan dere dat bottle, an' let 'em drink till de grace o' God comes on 'em—ha, ha, ha!"

"More power to you, Vaynus," exclaimed Keenan; "you're worth a thousand pounds, quarry weight."

"I am inclined to think, Mr. Keenan," said the schoolmaster, "that you are in the habit occasionally of taking slight liberties wid the haythen mythology. Little, I'll be bound, the divine goddess of beauty ever dreamt she'd find a representative in Teddy Phats."

"Bravo! masther," replied Keenan, "you're the boy can do—only that English is too tall for me. At any rate," he added, approaching the worthy preceptor, "take a spell o' this—it's a language we can all understand."

"You mane to say, Darby," returned the other, "that it's a kind of universal spelling-book amongst us, and so it is—an alphabet aisily larned. Your health, now and under all circumstances! Teddy, or Thaddeus, I drink to your symmetry and inexplicable proportions; and I say for your comfort, my worthy distillator, that if you are not so refulgent in beauty as Venus, you are a purer haythen."

"Fwhat a bloody fwhine *Bairlha* man the meeisther is," said Teddy, with a grin. "Fwhaicks, meeisthur, your de posey of Tullyticklem, spishilly wid Captain Fwhiskey at your back. You spake de Bairlha up den jist all as one as nobody could understand her—ha, ha, ha!"

The master, whose name was Finigan, or, as he wished to be called, O'Finigan, looked upon Teddy and shook his head very significantly.

"I'm afraid, my worthy distillator," he proceeded, "that the proverb which says '*latet anguis in herba*,' is not inapplicable in your case. I think I can occasionally detect in these ferret-like orbs that constitute such an attractive portion of your beauty, a passing scintillation of intelligence which you wish to keep *a secretis*, as they say."

"Mr. Finigan," said Keenan, who had now returned to his friends, "if you wouldn't be betther employed to-morrow, you'd be welcome to the weddin'."

"Many thanks, Mr. Keenan," replied Finigan; "I accept your hospitable offer wid genuine cordiality. To-morrow will be a day worthy of a white mark to all parties concerned. Horace calls it chalk, which is probably the most appropriate substance with which the records of matrimonial felicity could be registered, *crede experto*."

"At any rate, Misther Finigan, give the boys a holiday to-morrow, and be down wid us airly."

"There is not," replied Finigan, who was now pretty well advanced, "I believe widin the compass of written or spoken language—and I might on that subject appeal to Mr. Thaddeus O'Phats here, who is a good authority on that particular subject, or indeed on any one that involves the beauty of elocution—I say, then, there is not widin the compass of spoken language a single word composed of two syllables so delectable to human ears, as is that word 'dismiss,' to the pupils of a *Plantation Seminary*; (* A modest periphrasis for a Hedge-School) and I assure you that those talismanic syllables shall my youthful pupils hear correctly pronounced to-morrow about ten o'clock."

Whilst O'Finigan was thus dealing out the king's English with such complacent volubility—a volubility that was deeply indebted to the liquor he had taken—the following dialogue took place in a cautious under-tone between Batt Hogan and Teddy.

"So Hycy the sportheen is to be up here to-night?"

"Shiss."

"B—t your shiss! can't you spake like a Christian?"

"No, I won't," replied the other, angrily; "I'll spake as I likes."

"What brings him up, do you know?"

"Bekaise he's goin' to thry his misfortune upon *her* here," he replied, pointing to the still. "*You'll* have a good job of her, fwhedher or no."

"Why, will he want a new one, do you think?"

"Shiss, to be sure—would ye tink I'd begin to *run* (* A slang phrase for distilling) for him on dis ould skillet? an' be de token moreover, dat wouldn't be afther puttin' nothin' in your pockets—hee! hee! hee!"

"Well, all that's right—don't work for him widout a new one complate, Teddy—Still, Head, and Worm."

"Shiss, I tell you to be sure I won't—he thried her afore, though."

"Nonsense!—no he didn't."

"Ah, ha! ay dhin—an' she milked well too—a good cow—a brave *cheehony* she was for him."

"An' why did he give it up?"

"Fwhy—fwhy, afeard he'd be diskivered, to be sure; an' dhin shure he couldn't hunt wid de *dinnaousais*—wid de gentlemans."

"An' what if he's discovered now?"

"Fwhat?—fwhy so much the worsher for you an' me: he's ginerous now an' den, anyway; but a great rogue afther all, fwher so high a hid as he carries."

"If I don't mistake," proceeded Hogan, "either himself or his family, anyhow, will be talked of before this time to-morrow."

"Eh, Batt?" asked the other, who had changed his position and sat beside him during this dialogue—"how is dhat now?"

"I don't rightly know—I can't say," replied Hogan, with a smile murderously grim but knowing—"I'm not up; but the sportheen's a made boy, I think."

"*Dher cheerna!* you *are* up," said Teddy, giving him a furious glance as he spoke; "there must be no saycrits, I say."

"You're a blasted liar, I tell you—I am not, but I suspect—that's all."

"What brought you up dhis night?" asked Teddy, suspiciously.

"Because I hard he was to come," replied his companion; "but whether or not I'd be here."

"*Tha sha maigh*—it's right—may be so—shiss, it's all right, may be so—well?"

Teddy, although he said it was all right, did not seem however to think so. The furtive and suspicious glance which he gave Hogan from under his red beetle brows should be seen in order to be understood.

"Well?" said Hogan, re-echoing him—"it is well; an' what is more, my Kate is to be up here wid a pair o' geese to roast for us, for we must make him comfortable. She wint to thry her hand upon somebody's roost, an' it'll go hard if she fails!"

"Fwhail!" exclaimed Teddy, with a grin—"ah, the dioual a fwhail!"

"An' another thing—he's comin' about Kathleen Cavanagh—Hycy is. He wants to gain our intherest about her!"

"Well, an' what harm?"

"Maybe there is, though, it's whispered that he—hut! doesn't he say himself that there isn't a girl of his own religion in the parish he'd marry—now I'd like to see them married, Teddy, but as for anything else—"

"Hee! hee! hee!—well," exclaimed Teddy, with a horrible grimace that gave his whole countenance a facequake, "an' maybe he's right. Maybe it 'udn't be aisy to get a colleen of his religion—I tink his religion is fwhere Phiddher Fwhite's estate is—beyant the beyands, Avhere the mare foaled the fwhiddler—hee! hee! hee!"

"He had better thry none of his sckames wid any of the Cavanaghs," said Bat, "for fraid he might be brought to bed of a mistake some fine day—that's all I say; an' there's more eyes than mine upon him."

This dialogue was nearly lost in the loudness of a debate which had originated with Keenan and certain of his friends in the lower part of the still-house. Some misunderstanding relative to the families of the parties about to be united had arisen, and was rising rapidly into a comparative estimate of the prowess and strength of their respective factions, and consequently assuming a very belligerent aspect, when a tall, lank, but powerful female, made her appearance, carrying a large bundle in her hand.

"More power, Kate!" exclaimed Hogan. "I knew she would," he added, digging Teddy's ribs with his elbow.

The Emigrants of Ahadarra

"Aisy, man!" said his companion; "if you love me, say so, but don't hint it dat way."

"Show forth, Kate!" proceeded her husband; "let us see the prog—hillo!—oh, holy Moses! what a pair o' beauties!"

He then whipped up a horn measure, that contained certainly more than a naggin, and putting it under the warm spirits that came out of the still-eye, handed it to her. She took it, and coming up towards the fire, which threw out a strong light, nodded to them, and, without saying a word, literally pitched it down her throat, whilst at the same time one of her eyes presented undeniable proofs of a recent conflict. We have said that there were several persons singing and dancing, and some asleep, in the remoter part of the cave; and this was true, although we refrained from mingling up either their mirth or melody with the conversation of the principal personages. All at once, however, a series of noises, equally loud and unexpected, startled melodists, conversationalists, and sleepers all to their legs. These were no other than the piercing cackles of two alarmed geese which Hogan's wife had secured from some neighboring farmer, in order to provide a supper for our friend Hycy.

"Ted," said the female, "I lost my knife since I came out, or they'd be quiet enough before this; lend me one a minute, you blissed babe."

"Shiss, to be sure, Kate," he replied, handing her a large clasp knife with a frightful blade; "an', Kate, whisper, woman alive—you're bought up, I see."

"How is that, you red rascal?"

"Bekaise, don't I see dat de purchaser has set his mark upon ye?—hee! hee! hee!" and he pointed to her eye* as he spoke.

   * *A black eye is said to be the devil's mark.*

"No," she replied, nodding towards her husband, "that's his handy work; an' ye divil's clip!" she added, turning to Teddy, "who has a betther right?"

She then bled the geese, and, looking about her, asked—

"Have you any wet hay or straw in the place?"

"Ay, plenty of bote," replied Teddy; "an' here's de greeshavigh ready."

She then wrapped the geese, feathers and all, separately in a covering of wet hay, which she bound round them with thumb-ropes of the same material, and clearing away a space among the burning ashes, placed each of them in it, and covered them up closely.

"Now," said she, "put down a pot o' praities, and we won't go to bed fastin'."

The different groups had now melted into one party, much upon the same principle that the various little streamlets on the mountains around them all run, when swollen by a sudden storm, into some larger torrent equally precipitous and turbulent. Keenan, who was one of those pertinacious fellows that are equally quarrelsome and hospitable when in liquor, now resumed the debate with a characteristic impression of the pugilistic superiority of his family:—

"I am right, I say: I remember it well, for although I wasn't there myself, my father was, an' I often h'ard him say—God rest his sowl!"—here he reverently took off his hat and looked upwards—"I often h'ard him say that Paddy Keenan gave Mullin the first knock-down blow, an' Pether—I mane no disrespect, but far from it—give us your hand, man alive—you're going to be married upon my shisther to-morrow, plaise God!—masther, you'll come, remember? you'll be as welcome as the flowers o' May, masther—so, Pether, as I was sayin'—I mane no offince nor disrespect to you or yours, for you are, an' ever was, a daisent family, an' well able to fight your corner when it came upon you—but still, Pether—an' for all that—I say it—an' I'll stand to it—I'll stand it—that's the chat!—that, man for man, there never was one o' your seed, breed, or generation able to fight a Keenan—that's the chat!—here's luck!

> "'Oh, 'twas in the month of May,
> When the lambkins sport and play,
> As I walked out to gain raycrayation,
> I espied a comely maid.
> Sequestrin' in the shade—
> On her beauty I gazed wid admiraytion,'

No, Pether, you never could; the Mullins is good men—right good men, but they couldn't do it."

"Barney," said the brother of the bridegroom, "you may thank God that Pether is going to be married to your sisther to-morrow as you say, or we'd larn you another lesson—eh, masther? That's the chat too—ha! ha! ha! To the divil wid sich impedence!"

"Gintlemen," said Finigan, now staggering down towards the parties, "I am a man of pacific principles, acquainted wid the larned languages, wid mathematics, wid philosophy, the science of morality according to Fluxions—I grant you, I'm not college-bred; but, gintlemen, I never invied the oysther in its shell—for, gintlemen, I'm not ashamed of it, but I acquired—I absorbed my laming, I may say, upon locomotive principles."

"Bravo, masther!" said Keenan; "that's what some o' them couldn't say—"

"Upon locomotive principles. I admit Munster, gintlemen—glorious Kerry!—yes, and I say I am not ashamed of it. I do plead guilty to the peripatetic system: like a comet I travelled during my juvenile days—as I may truly assert wid a slight modicum of latitude" (here he lurched considerably to the one side)—"from star to star, until I was able to exhibit all their brilliancy united simply, I can safely assert, in my own humble person. Gintlemen, I have the honor of being able to write 'Philomath' after my name—which is O'Finigan, not Finigan, by any means—and where is the oyster in his shell could do that? Yes, and although they refused me a sizarship in Trinity College—for what will not fear and envy do?

"'Tantaene animis celesiibus irae'

Yet I have the consolation to know that my name is seldom mentioned among the literati of classical Kerry—*nudis cruribus* as they are—except as the Great O'Finigan! In the mane time—"

"Bravo, Masther!" exclaimed Keenan, interrupting him. "Here, Ted! another bottle, till the Great O'Finigan gets a glass of whiskey."

"Yes, gintlemen," proceeded O'Finigan, "the alcohol shall be accepted, *puris naturalibus*—which means, in its native—or more properly—but which comes to the same thing—in its naked state;

and, in the mane time, I propose the health of one of my best benefactors—Gerald Cavanagh, whose hospitable roof is a home—a domicilium to erudition and respectability, when they happen, as they ought, to be legitimately concatenated in the same person—as they are in your humble servant; and I also beg leave to add the pride of the barony, his fair and virtuous daughter, Kathleen, in conjunction wid the I accomplished son of another benefactor of mine—honest James Burke—in conjunction, I say, wid his son, Mr. Hyacinth. Ah, gintlemen—Billy Clinton, you thievin' villain! you don't pay attention; I say, gintlemen, if I myself could deduct a score of years from the period of my life, I should endeavor to run through the conjugations of *amo* in society wid that pearl of beauty. In the mane time—"

"Here's her health, masther," returned Keenan, "an' her father's too, an' Hycy Burke's into the bargain—is there any more o' them? Well, no matter." Then turning to his antagonist, he added, "I say agin, thin, that a Mullin's not a match for a Keenan, nor never was—no, nor never will be! That's the chat! and who's afeard to say it? eh, masther?"

"It's a lie!" shouted one of the opposite party; "I'm able to lick e'er a Keenan that ever went on nate's leather—an' that's my chat."

A blow from Keenan in reply was like a spark to gunpowder. In a moment the cavern presented a scene singularly tragic-comic; the whole party was one busy mass of battle, with the exception of Ted and Batt, and the wife of the latter, who, having first hastily put aside everything that might be injured, stood enjoying the conflict with most ferocious glee, the schoolmaster having already withdrawn himself to his chair. Even Barney Broghan, the fool, could not keep quiet, but on the contrary, thrust himself into the quarrel, and began to strike indiscriminately at all who came in his way, until an unlucky blow on the nose happening, to draw his claret very copiously, he made a bound up behind the sill, uttering a series of howlings, as from time to time he looked at his own blood, that were amusing in the extreme. As it happened, however, the influence of liquor was too strong upon both parties to enable them to inflict on each other any serious injury. Such, however, was the midnight pastime of the still-house when our friend Hycy entered.

"What in the devil's name—or the guager's—which is worse—" he asked, addressing himself to Batt and Teddy, "is the meaning of all this?"

"Faith, you know a'most as much about it," replied Hogan, laughing, "as we do; they got drunk, an' that accounts for it."

"Mr. Burke," said Finigan, who was now quite tipsy; "I am delighted to be able to—to—yes, it is he," he added, speaking to himself—"to see you well."

"I have my doubts as to that, Mr. Finigan," replied Hycy.

"Fame, Mr. Burke," continued the other, "has not been silent with regard to your exploits. Your horsemanship, sir, and the trepid pertinacity with which you fasten upon the reluctant society of men of rank, have given you a notorious celebrity, of which your worthy father, honest Jemmy, as he is called, ought to be justly proud. And you shine, Mr. Burke, in the loves as well as in the—*tam veneri quam*—I was about to add *Marti*, but it would be inappropriate, or might only remind you of poor Biddy Martin. It is well known you are a most accomplished gintleman, Mr. Burke—*homo fadus ad unguem—ad unguem*."

Hycy would have interrupted the schoolmaster, but that he felt puzzled as to whether he spoke seriously or ironically; his attention besides was divided between him and the party in conflict.

"Come," said he, addressing Hogan and Teddy, "put an end to this work, and why did you, you misbegotten vagabond," he added, turning to the latter, "suffer these fellows to remain here when you knew I was to come up?"

"I must shell my fwisky," replied Teddy, sullenly, "fwhedher you come or stay."

"If you don't clear the place of them instantly," replied Hycy, "I shall return home again."

Hogan seemed a good deal alarmed at this intimation, and said—"Ay, indeed, Terry, we had better put them out o' this."

"Fwhor fwhat?" asked Teddy, "dere my best customers shure—an' fwlay would I quarrel wid 'em all fwor wan man?"

"Good-night, then, you misshapen ruffian," said Burke, about to go.

"Aisy, Mr. Burke," said. Hogan; "well soon make short work wid them. Here, Ted, you devil's catch-penny, come an' help me! Hillo, here!" he shouted, "what are you at, you gallows crew? Do you want to go to the stone jug, I say? Be off out o' this—here's the guager, blast him, an' the sogers! Clear out, I tell you, or every mother's son of you will sleep undher the skull and cross-bones to-night." (* Meaning the County Prison)

"Here you, Barney," whispered Teddy, who certainly did not wish that Burke should return as he came; "here, you great big fwhool you, give past your yowlin' dere—and lookin' at your blood—run out dere, come in an' shout the gauger an' de sogers."

Barney, who naturally imagined that the intelligence was true, complied with the order he had received in a spirit of such alarming and dreadful earnestness, that a few minutes found the still-house completely cleared of the two parties, not excepting Hogan himself, who, having heard nothing of Teddy's directions to the fool, took it now for granted that that alarm was a real one, and ran along with the rest. The schoolmaster had fallen asleep, Kate Hogan was engaged in making preparations for supper at the lower end of the casern, and the fool had been dispatched to fetch Hogan himself back, so that Hycy now saw there was a good opportunity for stating at more length than he could in the market the purpose of his visit.

"Teddy," said he, "now that the coast's clear, let us lose no time in coming to the point. You are aware that Bryan M'Mahon has come into the mountain farm of Ahadarra by the death of his uncle."

"Shiss; dese three years."

"You will stick to your cursed brogue," said the other; "however, that's your own affair. You are aware of this?"

"I am."

"Well, I have made my mind up to take another turn at this," and he tapped the side of the still with his stick; "and I'll try it there. I don't know a better place, and it is much more convenient than this."

Teddy looked at him from under his brows, but seemed rather at a loss to comprehend his meaning.

"Fwor fhy 'ud you go to Ahadarra?"

"It's more convenient, and quite as well adapted for it as this place, or nearly."

"Well! Shiss, well?"

"Well; why that's all I have to say about it, except that I'm not to be seen or known in the business at all—mark that."

"Shiss—well? De Hogans must know it?"

"I am aware of that; we couldn't go on without them. This running of your's will soon be over; very well. You can go to Ahadarra to-morrow and pitch upon a proper situation for a house. These implements will do."

"No, dey won't; I wouldn't tink to begin at all wid dat ould skillet. You must get de Hogans to make a new Still, Head and Worm, an' dat will be money down."

"Very well; I'll provide the needful; let Philip call to me in a day or two."

"Dat Ahadarra isn't so safe," said Teddy. "Fwhy wouldn't you carry it on here?" and he accompanied the query with a piercing-glance as he spoke.

"Because," replied Hycy, "I have been seen here too often already, and my name must not in any way be connected with your proceedings. This place, besides, is now too much known. It's best and safest to change our bob, Ted."

"Dere's trewt in dhat, anyhow," said the other, now evidently more satisfied as to Hycy's motive in changing. "But," he added, "as you is now to schange, it 'ud be gooder to shange to some better place nor Ahadarra."

"I know of none better or safer," said Burke.

"Ay, fifty," returned his companion, resuming his suspicious looks; "but no matter, any way you must only plaise yerself—'tis all the shame to me."

"Ahadarra it must be then," said the other, "and that ends it."

"Vary well, den, Ahadarra let her be," said Ted, and the conversation on this subject dropped.

The smuggler's supper now made it's appearance. The geese were beautifully done, and as Hycy's appetite had got a keen stimulus by his mountain walk, he rendered them ample justice.

"Trot," said Teddy, "sich a walk as you had droo de mountains was enough to sharpen anybody's appetite."

Hogan also plied him with punch, having provided himself with sugar for that express purpose. Hycy, however, was particularly cautious, and for a long time declined to do more than take a little spirits and water. It was not, in fact, until he had introduced the name of Kathleen Cavanagh that he consented to taste punch. Between the two, however, Burke's vanity was admirably played on; and Hogan wound up the dialogue by hinting that Hycy, no matter how appearances might go, was by no means indifferent to the interesting daughter of the house of Cavanagh.

At length, when the night was far advanced, Burke rose, and taking his leave like a man who had forgotten some appointment, but with a very pompous degree of condescension, sought his way in the direction of home, across the mountains.

He had scarcely gone, when Hogan, as if struck by a sudden recollection, observed as he thought it would be ungenerous to allow him, at that hour of the night, to cross the mountains by himself. He accordingly whispered a few words to his wife, and left them with an intention, as he said, to see Mr. Hycy safe home.

CHAPTER V.—Who Robbed Jemmy Burke?

On the second morning after the night described in the last chapter, Bryan M'Mahon had just returned to his father's house from his farm in Ahadarra, for the purpose of accompanying him to an Emigration auction in the neighborhood. The two farms of Carriglass and Ahadarra had been in the family of the M'Mahon's for generations, and were the property of the same landlord. About three years previous to the period of our narrative, Toal M'Mahon, Bryan's uncle, died of an inflammatory attack, leaving to his eldest nephew and favorite the stock farm of Ahadarra. Toal had been a bachelor who lived wildly and extravagantly, and when he died Bryan suceeeded to the farm, then as wild, by the way, and as much neglected as its owner had been, with an arrear of two years' rent upon it. In fact the house and offices had gone nearly to wreck, and when Bryan entered into occupation he found that a large sum of money should be expended in necessary improvements ere the place could assume anything like a decent appearance. As a holding, however, it was reasonable; and we may safely assert that if Toal M'Mahon had been either industrious or careful he might have lived and died a wealthy man upon it. As Ahadarra lay in the mountain district, it necessarily covered a large space; in fact it constituted a townland in itself. The greater portion of it, no doubt, was barren mountain, but then there were about three hundred acres of strong rough land that was either reclaimed or capable of being so. Bryan, who had not only energy and activity, but capital to support both, felt, on becoming master of a separate farm, that peculiar degree of pride which was only natural to a young and enterprising man. He had now a fair opportunity, he thought, of letting his friends see what skill and persevering exertion could do. Accordingly he commenced his improvements in a spirit which at least deserved success. He proceeded upon the best system then known to intelligent agriculturalists, and nothing was left undone that he deemed necessary to work out his purposes. He drained, reclaimed, made fences, roads, and enclosures. Nor did he stop here. We said that the house and offices were in a ruinous state when they came into his possession, and the consequence was that he found it necessary to build a new dwelling house and suitable offices, which he did on a more commodious and eligible site. Altogether his expenditure on the farm could not have been less than eight hundred pounds at the period of the landlord's death, which, as the reader knows is that at which we have commenced our narrative.

Thomas M'Mahon's family consisted of—first, his father, a grey-haired patriarch, who, though a very old man, was healthy and in the full possession of all his faculties; next, himself; then his wife; Bryan, the proprietor of Ahadarra; two other sons, both younger, and two daughters, the eldest twenty, and the youngest about eighteen. The name of the latter was Dora, a sweet and gentle girl, with beautiful auburn hair, dark, brilliant eyes, full of intellect and feeling, an exquisite mouth, and a figure which was remarkable for natural grace and great symmetry.

"Well, Bryan," said the father, "what news from Ahadarra?"

"Nothing particular from Ahadarra," replied the son, "but our good-natured friend, Jemmy Burke, had his house broken open and robbed the night before last."

"Wurrah deheelish" exclaimed his mother, "no, he hadn't!"

"Well, mother," replied Bryan, laughing, "maybe not. I'm afeard it's too true though."

"An' how much did he lose?" asked his father.

"Between seventy and eighty pounds," said Bryan.

"It's too much," observed the other; "still I'm glad it's no more; an' since the villains did take it, it's well they tuck it from a man that can afford to lose it."

"By all accounts," said Arthur, or, as he was called, Art, "Hycy, the sportheen, has pulled him down a bit. He's not so rich now, they say, as he was three or four years ago."

"He's rich enough still," observed his father; "but at any rate, upon my sowl I'm sorry for him; he's the crame of an honest, kind-hearted neighbor; an' I believe in my conscience if there's a man alive that hasn't an ill-wisher, he is."

"Is it known who robbed him?" asked the grandfather, "or does he suspect anybody?"

"It's not known, of course, grandfather," replied Bryan, "or I suppose they would be in limbo before now; but there's quare talk about it. The Hogans is suspected, it seems. Philip was caught examinin' the hall-door the night before; an' that does look suspicious."

"Ay," said the old man, "an' very likely they're the men. I remember them this many a long day; it's forty years since Andy Hogan—he was lame—Andy Boccah they called him—was hanged for the murdher of your great-granduncle, Billy Shevlin, of Frughmore, so that they don't like a bone in our bodies. That was the only murdher I remember of them, but many a robbery was laid to their charge; an' every now and then there was always sure to be an odd one transported for thievin', an' house-breakin', and sich villainy."

"I wouldn't be surprised," said Mrs. M'Mahon, "but it was some o' them tuck our two brave geese the night before last."

"Very likely, in throth, Bridget," said her husband; "however, as the ould proverb has it, 'honesty's the best policy.' Let them see which of us I'll be the best off at the end of the year."

"There's an odd whisper here an' there about another robber," continued Bryan; "but I don't believe a word about it. No, no;—he's wild, and not scrupulous in many things, but I always thought him generous, an' indeed rather careless about money."

"You mane the sportheen?" said his brother Art.

"The Hogans," said the old man, recurring to the subject, as associated with them, "would rob anybody barrin' the Cavanaghs; but I won't listen to it, Bryan, that Hycy Burke, or the son of any honest man that ever had an opportunity of hearin' the Word o' God, or livin' in a Christian counthry, could ever think of robbin' his own father—his own father! I won't listen to that."

"No, nor I, grandfather," said Bryan, "putting everything else out of the question, its too unnatural an act. What makes you shake your head, Art?"

"I never liked a bone in his body, somehow," replied Art.

"Ay, but my goodness, Art," said Dora, "sure nobody would think of robbin' their own father?"

"He has been doin' little else these three years, Dora, by all accounts," replied Art.

"Ay, but his father," continued the innocent girl; "to break into the house at night an' rob him like a robber!"

"Well, I say, it's reported that he has been robbin' him these three years in one shape or other," continued Art; "but here's Shibby, let's hear what she'll say. What do you think, shibby?"

"About what, Art?"

"That Hycy Burke would rob his father!"

"Hut, tut! Art, what puts that into your head? Oh, no, Art—not at all—to rob his father, an' him has been so indulgent to him!"

"Indeed, I agree with you, Shibby," said Bryan; "for although my opinion of Hycy is changed very much for the worse of late, still I can't and won't give in to that."

"An what has changed it for the worse?" asked his mother. "You an' he wor very thick together always—eh? What has changed it, Bryan?"

Bryan began to rub his hand down the sleeve of his coat, as if freeing it from dust, or perhaps admiring its fabric, but made no reply.

"Eh, Bryan," she continued, "what has changed your opinion of him?"

"Oh, nothing of much consequence, mother," replied her son; "but sometimes a feather will toll one how the wind blows."

As he spoke, it might have been observed that he looked around upon the family with an appearance of awakened consciousness that was very nearly allied to shame. He recovered his composure, however, on perceiving that none among them gave, either by look or manner, any indication of understanding what he felt. This relieved him: but he soon found that the sense of relief experienced from it was not permitted to last long. Dora, his favorite sister, glided over to his side and gently taking his hand in hers began to play with his fingers, whilst a roguish laugh, that spoke a full consciousness of his secret, broke her pale but beautiful features into that mingled expression of smiles and blushes which, in one of her years, gives a look of almost angelic purity and grace. After about a minute or two, during which she paused, and laughed, and blushed, and commenced to whisper, and again stopped, she at last put her lips to his ear and whispered:—"Bryan, I know the reason you don't like Hycy."

"You do?" he said, laughing, but yet evidently confused in his turn;—"well—an'—ha!—ha!—no, you fool, you don't."

"May I never stir if I don't!"

"Well, an' what is it?"

"Why, bekaise he's coortin' Kathleen Cavanagh—now!"

"An' what do I care about that?" said her brother.

"Oh, you thief!" she replied; "don't think you can play upon me. I know your saycret."

"An' maybe, Dora," he replied, "I have my saycrets. Do you know who was inquirin' for you to-day?"

"No," she returned, "nor I don't care either—sorra bit."

"I met James Cavanagh there below"—he proceeded, still in a whisper, and he fixed his eyes upon her countenance as he spoke. The words, however, produced a most extraordinary effect. A deep blush crimsoned her whole neck and face, until the rush of blood seemed absolutely to become expressive of pain. Her eye, however, did not droop, but turned upon him with a firm and peculiar sparkle. She had been stooping with her mouth near his ear, as the reader knows, but she now stood up quickly, shook back her hair, that had been hanging in natural and silken curls about her blushing cheeks, and exclaimed: "No—no. Let me alone Bryan;" and on uttering these words she hurried into another room."

"Bryan, you've vexed Dora some way," observed her sister. "What did you say to her?"

"Nothing that vexed her, I'll go bail," he replied, laughing; "however, as to what I said to her, Shibby, ax me no questions an' I'll tell you no lies."

"Becaise I thought she looked as if she was angry," continued Shibby, "an', you know, it must be a strong provocation that would anger her."

"Ah, you're fishin' now, Shibby," he replied, "and many thanks for your good intentions. It's a saycret, an' that's all you're going to know about it. But it's as much as 'll keep you on the look out this month to come; and now you're punished for your curiosity—ha!—ha!—ha! Come, father, if we're to go to Sam Wallace's auction it's time we should think of movin'. Art, go an' help Tom Droogan to bring out the horses. Rise your foot here, father, an' I'll put on your spur for you. We may as well spake to Mr. Fethertonge, the agent, about the leases. I promised we'd call on Gerald Cavanagh, to—an' he'll be waitin' for us—hem!"

His eye here glanced about, but Dora was not visible, and he accordingly seemed to be more at his ease. "I think, father," he added, "I must trate you to a pair of spurs some of these days. This one, it's clear, has been a long time in the family."

"Throth, an' on that account," replied M'Mahon, "I'm not goin' to part wid it for the best pair that ever were made. No, no, Bryan; I like everything that I've known long. When my heart gets accustomed to anything or to anybody"—here he glanced affectionately at his wife—"I can't bear to part wid them, or to think of partin' wid them."

The horses were now ready, and in a brief space he and his son were decently mounted, the latter smartly but not inappropriately dressed; and M'Mahon himself, with his right spur, in a sober but comfortable suit, over which was a huge Jock, his inseparable companion in every fair, market, and other public place, during the whole year. Indeed, it would not be easy to find two better representatives of that respectable and independent class of Irish yeomanry of which our unfortunate country stands so much in need, as was this man of high integrity and his excellent son.

On arriving at Gerald Cavanagh's, which was on their way to the auction, it appeared that in order to have his company it was necessary they should wait for a little, as he was not yet ready. That worthy man they found in the act of shaving himself, seated very upright upon a chair in the kitchen, his eyes fixed with great steadiness upon the opposite wall, whilst lying between his legs upon the ground was a wooden dish half filled with water, and on a chair beside him a small looking-glass, with its backup, which, after feeling his face from time to time in an experimental manner, he occasionally peeped into, and again laid down to resume the operation.

In the mean time, Mrs. Cavanagh set forward a chair for Tom M'Mahon, and desired her daughter Hannah to place one for Bryan, which she did. The two girls were spinning, and it might have been observed that Kathleen appeared to apply herself to that becoming and feminine employment with double industry after the appearance of the M'Mahons. Kate Hogan was sitting in the chimney corner, smoking a pipe, and as she took it out of her mouth to whiff away the smoke from time to time, she turned her black piercing eyes alternately from Bryan M'Mahon to Kathleen with a peculiar keenness of scrutiny.

"An' how are you all up at Carriglass?" asked Mrs. Cavanagh.

"Indeed we can't complain, thank God, as the times goes," replied M'Mahon.

"An' the ould grandfather?—musha, but I was glad to see him look so well on Sunday last!"

"Troth he's as stout as e'er a one of us."

"The Lord continue it to him! I suppose you hard o' this robbery that was done at honest Jemmy Burke's?"

"I did, indeed, an' I was sorry to hear it."

"A hundre' an' fifty pounds is a terrible loss to anybody in such times."

"A hundre' an' fifty!" exclaimed M'Mahon—"hut, tut!—no; I thought it was only seventy or eighty. He did not lose so much, did he?"

"So I'm tould."

"It was two—um—it was two—urn—urn—it was—um—um—it was two hundre' itself," observed Cavanagh, after he had finished a portion of the operation, and given himself an opportunity of speaking—"it war two hundre' itself, I'm tould, an' that's too much, by a hundre' and ninety-nine pounds nineteen shillings an' eleven pence three fardens, to be robbed of."

"Troth it is, Gerald," replied M'Mahon; "but any way there's nothin' but thievin' and robbin' goin'. You didn't hear that we came in for a visit?"

"You!" exclaimed Mrs. Cavanagh—"is it robbed? My goodness, no!"

"Why," he proceeded, "we'll be able to get over it afore we die, I hope. On ere last night we had two of our fattest geese stolen."

"Two!" exclaimed Mrs. Cavanagh—"an' at this saison of the! year, too. Well, that same's a loss."

"Honest woman," said M'Mahon, addressing Kate Hogan, "maybe you'd give me a draw o' the pipe?"

"Maybe so," she replied; "an' why wouldn't I? Shough! that is here!"

"Long life to you, Katy. Well," proceeded the worthy man, "if it was a poor person that wanted them an' that took them from hardship, why God forgive them as heartily as I do: but if they wor stole by a thief, for thievin's sake, I hope I'll always be able to afford the loss of a pair betther than the thief will to do without them; although God mend his or her heart, whichever it was, in the mane time."

During this chat Bryan and Hanna Cavanagh were engaged in that good-humored badinage that is common to persons of their age and position.

"I didn't see you at Mass last Sunday, Bryan?" said she, laughing; "an' that's the way you attend to your devotions. Upon my word you promise well!"

"I seen you, then," replied Bryan, "so it seems if I haven't betther eyes I have betther eyesight."

"Indeed I suppose," she replied, "you see everything but what you go to see."

"Don't be too sure of that," he replied, with an involuntary glance at Kathleen, who seemed to enjoy her sister's liveliness, as was evident from the sweet and complacent smile which beamed upon her features.

"Indeed I suppose you're right," she replied; "I suppose you go to say everything but your prayers."

"An' is it in conversation with Jemmy Kelly," asked Bryan, jocularly, alluding to her supposed admirer, "that you perform your own devotions, Miss Hanna?"

"Hanna, achora," said the father, "I think you're playin' the second fiddle there—ha! ha! ha!"

The laugh was now general against Hanna, who laughed as loudly, however, as any of them.

"Throth, Kathleen," she exclaimed, "you're not worth knot's o' straws or you'd help me against this fellow here; have you nothing," she proceeded, addressing Bryan, and nodding towards her sister, "to say to her? Is everything to fall on my poor shoulders? Come, now," with another nod in the same direction, "she desarves it for not assistin' me. Who does she say her devotions with?"

"Hem—a—is it Kathleen you mane?" he inquired, with rather an embarrassed look.

"Not at all," she replied ironically, "but my mother there—ha! ha! ha! Come, now, we're waitin' for you."

"Come, now?" he repeated, purposely misunderstanding her—"oh, begad, that's a fair challenge;" and he accordingly rose to approach her with the felonious intent of getting a kiss; but Hanna started from her wheel and ran out of the house to avoid him.

"Throth, you're a madcap, Hanna," exclaimed her mother, placidly—"an antick crather, dear knows—her heart's in her mouth every minute of the day; an' if she gets through the world wid it always as light, poor girl, it'll be well for her."

"Kathleen, will you get me a towel or praskeen of some sort to wipe my face wid," said her father, looking about for the article he wanted.

"I left one," she replied, "on the back of your chair—an' there it is, sure."

"Ay, achora, it's you that laves nothing undone that ought to be done; an' so it is here, sure enough."

"Why, then, Gerald," asked Tom M'Mahon, "in the name o' wonder what makes you stick to the meal instead o' the soap when you're washin' yourself?"

"Throth, an' I ever will, Tom, an' for a good raison—becaise it's best for the complexion."

The unconscious simplicity with which Cavanagh uttered this occasioned loud laughter, from which Kathleen herself was unable to refrain.

"By the piper, Gerald," said M'Mahon, "that's the best thing I h'ard this month o' Sundays. Why, it would be enough for one o' your daughters to talk about complexion. Maybe you paint too—ha! ha! ha!"

Hanna now put in her head, and asked "what is the fun?" but immediately added, "Kathleen, here's a message for you."

"For me!" said Kathleen; "what is it?"

"Here's Peety Dhu's daughter, an' she says she has something to say to you."

"An' so Rosha Burke," said Mrs. Cavanagh, "has taken her to live wid them; I hope it'll turn out well for the poor thing."

"Will you come out, Kathleen," said Hanna, again peeping in; "she mustn't tell it to anyone but yourself."

"If she doesn't she may keep it, then," replied Kathleen. "Tell her I have no secrets," she added, "nor I won't have any of her keeping."

"You must go in," said Hanna, turning aside and addressing the girl—"you must go in an' spake to her in the house."

"She can tell us all about the robbery, anyway," observed Mr. Cavanagh. "Come in, a-colleen—what are you afeard of?"

"I have a word to say to her," said the girl—"a message to deliver; but it must be to nobody but herself. Whisper," she proceeded, approaching Kathleen, and about to address her.

Kathleen immediately rose, and, looking on the messenger, said, "Who is it from, Nanny?"

"I mustn't let *them* know," replied the girl, looking at the rest.

"Whatever it is, Or whoever it's from, you must spake it out then, Nanny," continued Kathleen.

"It's from Hycy Burke, then," replied the girl; "he wants to know if you have any answer for him?"

"Tell Hycy Burke," replied Kathleen, "that I have no answer for him; an' that I'll thank him to send me no more messages."

"Hut tut! you foolish girl," exclaimed her mother, rising up and approaching her daughter; "are you mad, Kathleen?"

"What's come over you," said the father, equally alarmed; "are you beside yourself, sure enough, to send Hycy Burke sich a message as that? Sit down, ma colleen, sit down, an' never mind her—don't think of bringin' him back sich a message. Why, then," he added, "in the name o' mercy, Kathleen, what has come over you, to trate a respectable young man like. Hycy Burke in that style?"

"Simply, father, because I don't wish to receive any messages at all from him."

"But your mother an' I is of a different opinion, Kathleen. We wish you to resave messages from him; an' you know you're bound both by the laws of God an' man to obey us an' be guided by us."

"I know I am, father," she replied; "an' I hope I haven't been an undutiful child to either of you for so far."

"That's true, Kathleen—God sees it's truth itself."

"What message do you expect to bring back, Nanny?" said the mother, addressing the girl.

"An answer," replied the girl, seeing that everything must be and was above board—"an answer to the letther he sent her."

"Did he send you a letther?" asked her father, seriously; "an' you never let us know a word about it?—did he send you a letther?"

Kathleen paused a moment and seemed to consult Hanna's looks, who had now joined them. At length she replied, slowly, and as if in doubt whether she ought to speak in the affirmative or not—"no, he sent me no letter."

"Well now, take care, Kathleen," said her mother; "I seen a letther in your hands this very mornin'."

Kathleen blushed deeply; but as if anxious to give the conversation another turn, and so to relieve herself, she replied, "I can't prevent you, mother, or my father either, from sending back whatever answer you wish; but this I say that, except the one I gave already, Hycy Burke will never receive any message or any answer to a message from me; an' now for the present let us drop it."

"Very well," said her mother; "in the mane time, my good girsha, sit down. Is it thrue that Jemmy Burke's house was robbed a couple o' nights ago?"

"True enough," said the girl.

"And how much did he lose?" asked M'Mahon; "for there's disputes about it—some say more and some say less."

"Between seventy and eighty pounds," replied Nanny; "the masther isn't sure to a pound or so; but he knows it was near eighty, any way."

"That's just like him," said Cavanagh; "his careless way of managin'. Many a time I wondher at him; he clobbers everything about that you'd think he'd beggar himself, an' yet the luck and prosperity flows to him. I declare to my goodness I think the very dirt under his feet turns to money. Well, girsha, an' have they any suspicion of the robbers?"

"Why," said the girl, "they talk about"—she paused, and it was quite evident from her manner that she felt not only embarrassed, but distressed by the question. Indeed this was no matter of surprise; for ever since the subject was alluded to, Kate Hogan's black piercing eyes had not once been removed from hers, nor did the girl utter a single word in reply to the questions asked of her without first, as it were, consulting Kate's looks.

A moment's reflection made Cavanagh feel that the question must be a painful one to the girl, not only on her own account, but on that of Kate herself; for even then it was pretty well known that Burke's family entertained the strongest suspicion that the burglary had been committed by these notorious vagabonds.

"Well, ahagur," said Cavanagh, "no matter now—it's all over unless they catch the robbers. Come now," he added, addressing M'Mahon and his son, "if you're for the road I'm ready."

"Is it true, Mrs. Burke," asked Bryan, "that you're goin' to have a Kemp in your barn some o' these days?"

"True enough, indeed," replied the good woman, "an' that's true, too, tell the girls, Bryan, and that they must come."

"Not I," said the other, laughing; "if the girls here—wishes them to come, let them go up and ask them."

"So we will, then," replied Hanna, "an' little thanks to you for your civility."

"I wish I knew the evenin'," said Bryan, "that I might be at Carriglass."

"When will we go, Kathleen," asked her sister, turning slyly to her.

"Why, you're sich a light-brained cracked creature," replied Kathleen, "that I can't tell whether you're joking or not."

"The sorra joke I'm jokin'," she replied, striving suddenly to form her features into a serious expression. "Well, then, I have it," she proceeded. "Some Thursday, Bryan, in the middle o' next week—now you know I'm not jokin', Kathleen."

"Will you come, Kathleen?" inquired Bryan.

"Why, if Hanna goes, I suppose I must," she replied, but without looking up.

"Well then I'll have a sharp look-out on Thursday."

"Come now," said Gerald, "let us move. Give the girsha something to ate among you, for the credit of the house, before she goes back," he added. "Paddy Toole, girth that horse tighter, I tell you; I never can get you to girth him as he ought to be girthed."

On bidding the women good-bye, Bryan looked towards Kathleen for a moment, and her eye in return glanced on him as he was about to go. But that simple glance, how significant was its import, and how clearly did it convey the whole history of as pure a heart as ever beat within a female bosom!

CHAPTEE VI.—Nanny Peety looks mysterious

—Hycy proves himself a good Judge of Horse-Flesh.

The day was all light, and life, and animation. The crops were going down fast in every direction, and the fields were alive and cheerful with the voice of mirth and labor. As they got into the vicinity of Wallace's house they overtook or were over-taken by several of their neighbors, among whom was seen our old friend, Jemmy, or as I his acquaintances generally called him, honest Jemmy Burke, mounted upon a brood mare with a foal at her heels, all his other horses having been engaged in the labor of the season.

After having sympathized with him upon the loss he had sustained, they soon allowed the subject to drop; for it was quite clear from the expression of care, if not of sorrow, that was legible in his face, that the very mention of it only caused him to feel additional anxiety.

At length they reached Wallace's house, where they found a tolerably large crowd of people waiting for the auction, which was not to commence until the hour of one o'clock.

Sam Wallace was a respectable Protestant farmer, who finding, as he said, that there was no proper encouragement given to men who were anxious and disposed to improve their property, had deemed it a wiser step to dispose of his stock and furniture than to remain as he was—not merely with no certain prospect of being able to maintain even his present position, but with the chances against him of becoming every day a poorer and more embarrassed man. His brother, who like himself, after having been on the decline for a considerable period, had emigrated to America, where he was prospering, now urged him to follow his example and leave a country in which he said, in language that has become a proverb, "everything was going to the bad." Feeling that his brother's words were unfortunately too true, Wallace, at all events, came to the determination of following his example.

The scene at which our friends arrived was indeed a striking and impressive one. The majority of the crowd consisted of those who belonged either to the Protestant or Presbyterian forms of worship;

and it might be with truth asserted, that nothing could surpass the clear unquestionable character of independent intelligence which prevailed among them. Along with this, however, there was an obvious spirit of dissatisfaction, partial, it is true, as to numbers, but yet sufficiently marked as to satisfy an observer that such a people, if united upon any particular subject or occasion, were not for a moment to be trifled with or cajoled. Their feelings upon the day in question were stirred into more than usual warmth. A friend, a neighbor, a man of an old and respectable family, frugal, industrious, and loyal, as they said, both to king and country, was now forced from want of due encouragement from his landlord, to disturb all his old associations of friendship and kindred, and at rather an advanced state of life to encounter the perils of a long voyage, and subject himself and his family to the changes and chances which he must encounter in a new world, and in a different state of society. Indeed, the feeling which prompted the expression of these sentiments might be easily gathered from the character that pervaded the crowd. Not to such an extent, however, with respect to Wallace himself or any portion of his family, There might be observed upon him and them a quiet but resolute spirit, firm, collected, and cheerful; but still, while there were visible no traces of dejection or grief, it was easy to perceive that under this decent composure there existed a calm consciousness of strong stern feeling, whose dignity, if not so touching, was quite as impressive as the exhibition of louder and more clamorous grief.

"Bryan," said M'Mahon to his son, as the auction was proceeding, "I'll slip up to the agent's, and do you see if them sheep goes for a fair value—if they do, give a bid or two any how. I'm speakin' of that lot we wor lookin' at, next the wall there."

"I'll pay attention to it," said Bryan; "I know you'll find the agent at home now, for I seen him goin' in a while ago; so hurry up, an' ax him if he can say how soon we may expect the leases."

"Never fear, I will."

On entering Fethertonge's Hall, M'Mahon was treated with very marked respect by the servant, who told him to walk into the parlor, and he would let his master know.

"He entertains a high opinion of you, Mister M'Mahon," said he; "and I heard him speak strongly about you the other day to some gentlemen that dined with us—friends of the landlord's. Walk into the parlor."

In a few minutes M'Mahon was shown into Fethertonge's office, the walls of which were, to a considerable height, lined with tin boxes, labelled with the names of those whose title-deeds and other valuable papers they contained.

Fethertonge was a tall, pale, placid looking man, with rather a benevolent cast of countenance, and eyes that were mild, but very small in proportion to the other features of his face. His voice was exceedingly low, and still more musical and sweet than low; in fact it was such a voice as, one would imagine, ought to have seldom been otherwise employed than in breathing hope and, consolation to despairing sinners on their bed of death. Yet he had nothing of either the parson or the preacher in his appearance. So far from that he was seldom known to wear a black coat, unless when dressed for dinner, and not very frequently even then, for he mostly wore blue.

"M'Mahon," said he, "take a seat. I am glad to see you. How are your family?"

"Both I an' they is well, I'm thankful to you, sir," replied the farmer.

"I hope you got safe home from the metropolis. How did you travel?"

"Troth, I walked it, sir, every inch of the way, an' a long stretch it is. I got safe, sir, an' many thanks to you."

"That was a sudden call poor Mr. Chevydale got, but not more so than might, at his time of life, have been expected; at all events I hope he was prepared for it, and indeed I have reason to think he was."

"I trust in God he was, sir," replied M'Mahon; "so far as I and mine is consarned, we have raison to wish it; he didn't forget us, Mr. Fethertonge."

"No," said the other, after some pause, "he did not indeed forget you, M'Mahon."

"I tuck the liberty of callin' down, sir," proceeded M'Mahon, "about the leases he spoke of, an' to know how soon we may expect to have them filled."

"That is for your son Bryan and yourself. How is Bryan proceeding with Ahadarra, by the way? I spoke to him some time ago about his system of cropping that farm, and some other matters of the kind; I must ride up one of these days to see how he is doing. As to the leases, there is no difficulty in the way, M'Mahon, except to get our young landlord to sign them. That we will easily do, of course; in the meantime, do you go on, improve your land, and strive to do something for your children, M'Mahon; for, in this world, he that won't assist himself will find very few that will. The leases are in Dublin; if you wish, I'll send for them, and have them ready for the landlord's signature whenever he comes down here; or I'll leave them in town, where I shall be more likely to see him."

"Very well, sir," replied M'Mahon, "I lave it all in your own hands, for I know that if you won't be my friend, you won't be my enemy."

"Well—certainly—I hope not. Will you take anything? Here, James, bring in some brandy."

M'Mahon's protest against the brandy was anything but invincible. Fethertonge's manner was so kind, so familiar, and his interest in the success of himself and his family so unaffectedly warm and sincere, that, after drinking his health, he took his leave with a light and happy heart.

Their journey home was a little more lively than the depression of Jemmy Burke's mind had allowed it to be on their way to the auction. Yet each had his own peculiar feelings, independently of those which were elicited by the conversation. Jemmy Burke, who had tasted some of Wallace's liquor, as indeed, with the exception of Bryan, they all did, was consequently in a better and more loquacious humor than he had been during the day. On this occasion his usual good fortune attended him for it was the opinion of every one there, that he had got the best bargain disposed of during the day—a lot of twenty-five wethers in prime condition. Gerald Cavanagh, who had also tasted the poteen, stuck as closely as possible to his skirts, moved thereto by a principle of adhesion, with which our readers are already acquainted; and Bryan, who saw and understood his motives, felt by no means comfortable at witnessing such strong symptoms of excessive attachment. Old M'Mahon did not speak much, for, in truth, he could not overcome the depressing effects of the scene he had witnessed, nor of the words uttered by Wallace, as they bade each other farewell.

Burke, however, and his companion, Cavanagh, looked like men between whom a warm friendship was about to grow up. Whenever they came to a public-house or a shebeen, they either dismounted and had a cordial drop together, or took it in the saddle after touching each other's glasses in token of love and amity. It is true some slight interruption occurred, that disturbed the growing confidence and familiarity of their dialogue, which interruption consisted in the endless whinnying of the mare whenever her foal delayed a moment behind her, or in the sudden and abrupt manner in which she wheeled about with a strong disposition to return and look for it.

On the discovery of Burke's robbery an investigation was set on foot, but with no prospect of success, and without in any way involving the Hogans, who were strongly suspected. It was clearly proved that Philip and one of his brothers slept in their usual residence — Cavanagh's corn-kiln — on that night, but it was admitted that Batt Hogan and his wife Kate were both abroad the greater portion of it. On them suspicion might, indeed, very naturally have rested, were it not for the evidence of Hycy himself, who at once admitted that he could exonerate them from any suspicion, as he knew both how and where they had passed the night in question. So far, therefore, the Hogans, dishonest as they were unquestionably reputed to be, now stood perfectly exonerated from all suspicion.

The lapse of a very few days generally cools down the ferment occasioned by matters of this kind, especially when public curiosity is found to be at fault in developing the whole train of circumstances connected with them. All the in-door servants, it is true, were rigorously examined, yet it somehow happened that Hycy could not divest himself of a suspicion that Nanny Peety was in some way privy to the disappearance of the money. In about three or four days he happened to see her thrust something into her father's bag, which he carried as a mendicant, and he could not avoid remarking that there was in her whole manner, which was furtive and hurried, an obvious consciousness of something that was not right. He resolved, however, to follow up the impression which he felt, and accordingly in a few minutes after her father had taken his departure, he brought her aside, and without giving her a moment to concoct a reply, he asked what it was that he saw her thrusting in such a hurried manner into his bag. She reddened like scarlet, and, after pausing a moment, replied, "Nothing, sir, but an ould pair of shoes."

"Was that all?" he asked.

"That was all, sir," she replied.

The blush and hesitation, however, with which she answered him were far from satisfactory; and without more ado he walked briskly down the avenue, and overtook her father near the gate at its entrance.

"Peety," said he, "what was that your daughter Nanny put into your bag a while ago? I wish to know?"

"Deed an its scarcely worth your while, Master Hycy," replied the mendicant; "but since you'd like to know, it was a pair of ould brogues, and here they are," he added, "if you wish to see them."

He laid down the bag as he spoke, and was proceeding to pull them out, when Hycy, who felt angry with himself as well as ashamed at being detected in such a beggarly and unbecoming act of espionage, turned instantly back, after having vented several hearty curses upon the unfortunate mendicant and his bags.

As he approached the hall-door, however, he met Nanny crossing into the kitchen-yard, and from the timid and hesitating glance she cast at him, some vague suspicion again occurred, and he resolved to enter into further conversation with her. It struck him that she had been watching his interview with her father, and could not avoid yielding to the impression which had returned so strongly upon him.

"I saw your father, Nanny," he said, in as significant and dry a tone as possible.

"Did you, sir?" said she; and he remarked that while uttering the words, she again colored deeply and did not raise her eyes to his face.

"Yes," he replied; "but he did not bear out what you said—he had no pair of shoes in his bag."

"Did you see what he had in it, Master Hycy?"

"Why," said he, "a—hem—a—a—I didn't look—but I'll tell you what, Nanny, I think you look as if you were in possession of some secret. I say so, and don't imagine you can for a moment impose upon me. I know what your father had in his bag."

"Well then, if you do, sir," she replied, "you know the saycrit."

"So there is a secret, then?"

"So you say, Masther Hycy."

"Nanny," he proceeded, "it occurs to me now that you never underwent a formal examination about this robbery that took place in our house."

"That wasn't my fault," she replied; "I mostly happened to be out."

"Well, but do you know anything about it?"

"Not a thing—no more than yourself, Mr. Hycy."

Her interrogator turned upon her a hard scrutinizing glance, in which it was easy to see that she read a spirit of strong and dissatisfied suspicion. She was evidently conscious of this; for as Hycy stood gazing upon her, she reddened, and betrayed unequivocal symptons of confusion.

"Because, Nanny," he proceeded, "if you knew anything about it, and didn't mention it at once to the family, you would be considered as one of the robbers."

"An' wouldn't I be nearly as bad if I didn't?" she replied; "surely the first thing I'd do would be to tell."

"It's very strange," observed Hycy, "that such a robbery could be committed in a house where there are so many servants, without any clue whatsoever to a discovery."

"Well, I don't agree with you there, Mr. Hycy—if what your father and mother an' all o' them say is true—that it wasn't often the hall-door was bolted at night; and that they can't say whether it was fastened on that night or not. Sure if it wasn't, there was nothing to prevent any one from comin' in."

"Very true, Nanny," he replied, "very true; and we have paid severely for our negligence."

This closed the conversation, but Hycy felt that, proceed from whatever source it might, it was impossible to dismiss certain vague suspicions as connected with the mendicant's daughter. He determined, however, to watch her narrowly; and somehow he could not divest himself of the impression that she saw through his design. This incident occurred a few days after the robbery.

Jemmy Burke, though in many respects a man of easy and indolent character, was nevertheless a person who, as is familiarly! said, "always keep an eye to the main chance." He was by no means over-tidy either in his dress or farming; but it mattered little in what light you contemplated him, you were always certain to find him a man not affected by trifles, nor rigidly systematic in anything; but at the same time you could not help observing that he was a man of strong points, whose life was marked by a course of high prosperity, that seemed to flow in upon him, as it were, by some peculiar run of good fortune. This luck, however, was little less than the natural result of shrewd mother-wit, happily applied to the: ordinary transactions of life, and assuming the appearance of good fortune rather than of sound judgment, in consequence of the simplicity of character under which it acted. Ever since the night of the robbery, he had devoted himself more to the pipe than he had ever been known to do before; he spoke little, too; but what he did say was: ironical, though not by any means without a tinge of quiet but caustic humor.

Hycy, on entering the parlor, found him! seated in an arm-chair, smoking as usual, whilst his mother, who soon came down stairs, appeared dressed in more than her usual finery.

"What keeps Patsy Dolan wid the car?" she inquired. "Hycy, do you see any appearance of him?"

"No, ma'am," replied the son; "I didn't know you wanted him."

Jemmy looked at her with a good deal of surprise, and, after whiffing away the smoke, asked—"And well, Rosha—begs pardon—Mrs. Burke—is it a fair question to ax where you are bound for?"

"Fair enough, Mr. Burke," she replied; "but I'm not goin' to answer it."

"You're bound for a journey, ma'am, I think?"

"I'm bound for a journey, sir."

"Is it a long journey, Mrs. Burke?"

"No, indeed; it's a short journey, Mister Burke."

"Ah!" replied her husband, uttering a very significant groan; "I'm afraid it is."

"Why do you groan, Mr. Burke?"

"Oh it doesn't signify," he replied, dryly; "it's no novelty, I believe, to hear a man—a married man—groan in this world; only if you wor for a long journey, I'd be glad to give you every assistance in my power."

"You hear that, Hycy; there's affection?" she exclaimed—"wishin' me to go my long journey!"

"Would you marry again, Mr. Burke?" asked the worthy son.

"I think not," replied Jemmy. "There's gintlemen enough o' the name—I'm afraid one too many."

"Well," exclaimed his wife, assuming something as near to her conception of the look of a martyr as possible, "I'm sufferin' at all events; but I know my crown's before me."

"Sich as it is," replied her husband, "I dare say it is."

"I'll not be back for a few hours, Hycy; an'—but here's the car. Come fardher up, Patsy."

Hycy politely handed his mother out, and assisted her on the car. "Of course, he'll discover it all," said he, laughing.

"I know he will," she replied; "but when it's over, it's over, and that's all."

Jemmy now met his son at the hall-door, and asked him if he knew where his mother had gone.

"I really cannot undertake to say," replied the other. "Mrs. Burke, father, is a competent judge of her own notions; but I presume to think that she may take a drive upon her own car, without being so severely, if not ungenerously catechised about it. I presume to think so, sir; but I daresay I am wrong, and that even that is a crime on my part."

His father made no reply, but proceeded at an easy and thoughtful pace to join his men in the field where they were at labor.

Hycy, after his mother's return that evening, seemed rather in low spirits, if one could form any correct estimate of his character by appearances. He was very silent, and somewhat less given to those broken snatches of melody than was his wont; and yet a close observer might have read in his deportment, and especially in the peculiar expression of his eye, that which seemed to indicate anything rather than depression or gloom. His silence, to such an observer, might have appeared rather the silence of satisfaction and triumph, than of disappointment or vexation.

His father, indeed, saw little of him that night, in consequence of the honest man having preferred the hob of his wealthy and spacious kitchen to the society of his wife and son in the parlor. The next morning, however, they met at breakfast, as usual, when Hycy, after some ironical compliments to his father's good taste, asked him, "if he would do him the favor to step towards the stable and see his purchase."

"You don't mane Crazy Jane?" said the other, coolly.

"I do," replied Hycy; "and as I set a high value on your opinion, perhaps you would be kind enough to say what you think of her."

Now, Hycy never for a moment dreamt that his father would have taken him at his word, and we need hardly say that he was a good deal disconcerted at the cool manner in which the other expressed his readiness to do so.

"Well, Mr. Burke," he proceeded, when they had reached the stable, "there she is. Pray what do you think of her?"

The old man looked at her from various points, passed his hand down her limbs, clapped her on the back, felt her in different places, then looked at her again. "She's a beauty," said he, "a born beauty like Billy Neelin's foal; what's this you say you paid for her?"

"Thirty-five pounds."

"Tare-an-ounty, Hycy, she's dog chape—thirty-five!—why she's value for double the sum."

"Nearly," replied Hycy, quite elevated and; getting into good humor; "is she not really now, father, a precious bit of flesh?"

"Ah! you may swear that, Hycy; I tell you you won't act the honest man, if you don't give him fifteen or twenty pounds over an' above what you paid him. Tom Burton I see's too simple for you. Go and do what I bid you; don't defraud the poor man; you have got a treasure, I tell you—a beauty bright—an extraordinary baste—a wonderful animal—oh, dear me! what a great purchase! Good-bye, Hycy. Bless my sowl! what a judge of horseflesh you are!"

Having uttered these words in a tone of grave and caustic irony, he left his worthy son in a state of chagrin almost bordering on resentment, at the strong contempt for Crazy-Jane, implied by the excessive eulogium he had passed upon her. This feeling, however, was on reflection considerably checked by his satisfaction on finding that the matter was taken by his father so coolly. He had calculated on receiving a very stormy lecture from him the moment he should become aware of his having the animal in his possession; and he now felt rather relieved that he should have escaped so easily. Be this as it may, Hycy was now in excellent spirits. Not only had Crazy Jane been secured, but there were strong symptoms of his being in cash. In a few days after the incident of the stable, he contrived to see Philip Hogan, with whom he appointed a final meeting in Cavanagh's kiln on the night of the Kemp; at which meeting, Teddy Phats and the other two Hogans were also to be present, in order to determine upon the steps which he ultimately proposed to take, with a view to work out his purposes, whatever those purposes may have been.

CHAPTER VII.—The Spinster's Kemp.

A kemp, or camp, is a contest of industrial skill, or a competition for priority in a display of rustic labor. Among men it is principally resorted to in planting potatoes or reaping of corn, and generally only on the day which closes the labor at each for the season; but in the sense in which it is most usually practised and contested, it means a trial of female skill at the spinning of linen yarn. It is, indeed, a very cheerful assemblage of the fair sex; and, although strong and desperate rivalry is the order of the day, yet it is conducted in a spirit so light-hearted and amicable that we scarcely know a more laudable or delightful recreation in country life. Its object is always good, and its associations praiseworthy, inasmuch as they promote industry, a spirit of becoming emulation, and principles of good will and kindness to our neighbor.

When a kemp is about to be held, the matter soon becomes generally known in the neighborhood. Sometimes the young women are asked, but in most instances, so eager are they to attend it that invitations are unnecessary. In the whiter months, and in mountain districts, it is often as picturesque as it is pleasant. The young women usually begin to assemble about four o'clock in the morning; and, as they always go in groups, accompanied besides by their sweethearts or some male relatives, each of the latter bearing a large torch of well-dried bogfir, their voices, and songs, and loud laughter break upon the stillness of night with a holiday feeling, made ten times more delightful by the surrounding darkness and the hour. When they have not the torches the spinning-wheels are carried by the males, amidst an agreeable din of fun, banter, repartee, and jest, such as scarcely any other rustic amusement with which we are acquainted ever occasions. On arriving at the house where the kemp is to be held, they are placed in the barn or some clean outhouse; but indeed the numbers are usually such as to crowd every available place that can be procured for their accommodation. From the moment they arrive the lively din is incessant. Nothing is heard but laughter, conversation, songs, and anecdotes, all rising in a loud key, among the louder humming of the spinning-wheels and the stridulous noise of the reeds, as they incessantly crack the cuts in the hands of the reelers, who are perpetually turning them from morning to night, in order to ascertain the quantity which every competitor has spun; and she, of course, who has spun most wins the kemp, and is the queen for the night.

A kemp invariably closes with a dance—and a dance too upon an unusually extensive scale. Indeed, during the whole day the fair competitors are regaled from time to time with the enlivening strains of the fiddle or bagpipes, and very often with the united melody of both together.

On that morning the dwelling-house and mostly all the out-offices of Gerald Cavanagh bore, in stir and bustle, a stronger resemblance to the activity of so many bee-hives about to swarm than to anything else to which we can think of comparing them. Mirth in all its shapes, of laughter, glee, and song, rang out in every direction. The booming of wheels and the creaking of reels, the loud banter, the peals of laughter, the sweet Irish songs that filled up the pauses of the louder mirth, and the strains of the fiddle that ever and anon added to the enlivening spirit of the scene, all constituted such a full and general chorus of hilarity as could seldom be witnessed.

There were many girls present who took no part in the competition, but who, as friends and acquaintances of Kathleen and Hanna, came to enjoy the festive spirit of the day. Hanna herself, however, who had earned some celebrity as a spinster, started for the honor of winning, as did Dora M'Mahon, whose small and beautiful fingers seemed admirably adapted for this graceful and peculiarly feminine process of Minerva. Towards evening the neighbors assembled in considerable numbers, each interested in the success of some peculiar favorite, whose former feats had induced her friends to entertain on her behalf strong, if not certain, hopes of victory. Kathleen, from a principle of generosity, patronized her young friend, Dora M'Mahon; and Shibby M'Mahon, on the other hand, took Hanna Cavanagh under her protection. As the evening advanced, and the spectators and friends of the parties began to call, in order to be present at the moment of victory, it would be difficult to witness any assemblage of young women placed under circumstances of such striking interest. The mirth and song and general murmur diminished by degrees, until they altogether ceased, and. nothing was to be heard but the perpetual cracking of the reels, the hum of the rapid wheels, and the voices of the reelers, as they proclaimed the state of this enlivening pool of industry. As for the fair competitors themselves, it might have been observed that even those among them who had no, or at least but slight pretensions to beauty, became actually interesting from the excitement which prevailed. Their eyes lit by the active spirit of rivalry within them, sparkled with peculiar brilliancy, their cheeks became flushed or got pale as they felt themselves elevated or depressed by the prospect or loss of victory. Nor were there wanting on this occasion some vivid glances that were burthened, as they passed aslant, their fair faces, with pithier feelings than those that originated from a simple desire of victory. If truth must be told, baleful flashes, unmeasured both in number and expression, were exchanged in a spirit of true defiance between the interested and contending parties, as the close of the contest approached. At length, by the proclamation of the reelers, the great body of the competitors were thrown out, and they consequently gave up the contest. It was now six o'clock, and the first sound of seven o'clock by Captain Millar's bell was to close the proceedings, and enable the reelers to proclaim the victor. Only four names now remained to battle it out to the last; to wit, a country farmer's daughter, named Betty Aikins, Dora M'Mahon, Hanna Cavanagh, and a servant-girl belonging to another neighbor, named Peggy Bailly. This ruck, as they say on the turf, was pretty well up together, but all the rest nowhere. And now, to continue the metaphor, as is the case at Goodwood or the Curragh, the whole interest was centered upon these four. At the commencement of the last hour the state of the case was proclaimed as follows: Betty Aikins, three dozen and eight cuts; Dora M'Mahon, three dozen and seven cuts; Hanna Cavanagh, three dozen and five cuts; and Peggy Bailly, three dozen and four cuts. Every individual had now her own party anxious for her success, and amidst this hour of interest how many hearts beat with all hopes and fears that are incident even to the most circumscribed contest of human life. Opposite Dora stood the youth whom we have already noticed, James Cavanagh, whose salvation seemed but a very trifling thing when compared or put into opposition with her success. Be this as it may, the moment was a most exciting one even to those who felt no other interest than that which naturally arises from human competition. And it was unquestionably a beautiful thing to witness this particular contest between, four youthful and industrious young women. Dora's otherwise pale and placid features were now mantling, and her beautiful dark eyes flashing, under the proud and ardent spirit of ambition, for such in fact was the principle which now urged and animated the contest. When nearly half an hour had passed, Kathleen came behind her, and stooping down, whispered, "Dora, don't turn your wheel so quickly: you move the, foot-board too fast—don't twist the thread too much, and you'll let down more."

Dora smiled and looked up to her with a grateful and flashing eye. "Thank you, Kathleen," she replied, nodding, "I'll take your advice." The state of the contest was then proclaimed:—Betty Aikins—three dozen and ten cuts; Dora M'Mahon—three dozen and ten cuts; Hanna Cavanagh —three dozen, six cuts and a half; Peggy Bailly— three dozen, five and a half.

On hearing this, Betty Aikin's cheek became scarlet, and as it is useless to disguise the fact, several flashing glances that partook more of a Penthesilean fire than the fearful spirit which usually characterizes the industrious pursuits of Minerva, were shot at generous Dora, who sustained her portion of the contest with singular spirit and temper.

"You may as well give it up, Dora M'Mahon," exclaimed Betty; "there never was one of your blood could open against an Aikins— the stuff is not in you to beat me."

"A very little time will soon tell that," replied Dora; "but indeed, Betty, if I am doin' my best to win the kemp, I hope it's not in a bad or unfriendly spirit, but in one of fair play and good humor."

The contest now went on for about fifteen minutes, with surpassing interest and animation, at the expiration of which period, the seven o'clock bell already alluded to, rang the hour for closing their labors and determining the victory. Thus stood their relative position— Dora M'Mahon, four hanks and three cuts; Betty Aikins, four hanks; Hanna Cavanagh, three hanks and nine cuts; Peggy Bailly, three hanks and eight cuts.

The Emigrants of Ahadarra

When this result was made known, Betty Aikins burst into a loud fit of grief, in which she sobbed as if her very heart would break, and Kathleen stooping down, congratulated the beautiful girl upon her victory, kissing her at the same time as she spoke—an act of love and kindness in which she would have joyfully been followed by several of her male friends, if they had dared to take that delicious liberty.

The moment of victory, we believe, is that which may be relied upon as the test of true greatness. Dora M'Mahon felt the pride of that moment in its fullest extent, but she felt it only to influence her better and nobler principles. After casting her eyes around to gather in, as it were, that honest approbation which is so natural, and exchanging some rapid glances with the youth we have alluded to, she went over to her defeated competitor, and taking her hand said, "Don't cry, Betty, you have no right to be ashamed; sure, as you say, it's the first time you wor ever beaten; we couldn't all win; an' indeed if I feel proud now, everyone knows an' says I have a right to be so; for where was there—ay, or where is there—such a spinner as you are?

"Shake hands now an' there's a kiss for you. If I won this kemp, it was won more by chance than by anything else."

These generous expressions were not lost on Betty; on the contrary, they soothed her so much that she gave her hand cordially to her young and interesting conqueress, after which they all repaired to a supper of new milk and flummery, than which there is nothing more delicious within the wide range of luxury. This agreeable meal being over, they repaired to the large barn where Mickey M'Grory the fiddler, was installed in his own peculiar orchestra, consisting of an arm-chair of old Irish oak, brought out from Gerald Cavanagh's parlor.

It would indeed be difficult to find together such a group of happy faces. Gerald Cavanagh and his wife, Tom M'Mahon and his better half, and several of the neighbors, of every age and creed, were all assembled; and, in this instance, neither gray hairs nor length of years were looked upon as privileged from a participation in the festivities of the evening. Among the rest, gaunt and grim, were the three Hogans, looking through the light-hearted assemblage with the dark and sinister visages of thorough ruffians, who were altogether incapable of joining in the cheerful and inoffensive amusements that went forward around them. Kate Hogan sat in an obscure corner behind the fiddler, where she was scarcely visible, but from which she enjoyed a full view of everything that occurred in the house.

A shebeen-man, named Parra Bradagh, father to Barney, whom the reader has already met in the still-house, brought a cask of poteen to the stable, where he disposed of it *sub silentio*, by which we mean without the knowledge of Gerald Cavanagh, who would not have suffered any such person about his place, had the circumstance been made known to him. Among the rest, in the course of the evening, our friend O'Finigan the Philomath made his appearance, and as was his wont very considerably advanced in liquor. The worthy pedagogue, on inquiring for the queen of the kemp, as he styled her, was told that he might know her by the flowers in her hair. "There she is, masther," said one of them, "wid the roses on her head."

"Well," said O'Finigan, looking about him with surprise, "I have, before now, indulged in the Cerelian juice until my eyes have become possessed of that equivocal quality called the double vision, but I must confess that this is the first occasion on which the quality aforesaid has been quadrupled. Instead of one queen, wid Flora's fragrant favors in her lock, I think I see four."

Finigan indeed was right. Dora, on being presented with a simple chaplet of flowers, as the heroine of the night, in a spirit of true magnanimity generously divided the chaplet among her three rivals, thus, like every brave heart, resting satisfied with the consciousness of victory, and anxious that those who had approached her so nearly should also share in its honors.

It is not our intention to enter into a detailed account of the dancing, nor of the good humor which prevailed among them. It is enough to say that the old people performed minuets and cotillions, and the young folks, jigs, reels, and country dances; hornpipes were performed upon doors, by rural dancers, and all the usual variations of mirth and amusement were indulged in on the occasion.

We have said that Tom M'Mahon and his family were there, but we should have added, with one exception. Bryan did not arrive until the evening was far advanced, having been prevented by pressing business connected with his farm. On making his appearance, he was greeted by a murmur of welcomes, and many an honest hand was extended to him. Up until then there were two individuals who observed Kathleen Cavanagh closely, and we must ourselves admit that both came to the same conclusion. Its was clear that during the whole evening she had been unusually pensive, if not actually depressed, although a general observer would have seen nothing in her beyond the natural sedateness of her manner. The two in question were Kate Hogan and Dora M'Mahon. On Bryan's arrival, however, the color of her cheek deeped into a richer beauty, the eye became more sparkling, and a much slighter jest than before moved her into mirth. Such, however, we are, and such is the mystery of our nature. It might have been remarked that the Hogans eyed Bryan, soon after making his appearance, with glances expressive of anything but good feeling. It was not, however, when he first arrived, or danced with Hanna Cavanagh, that these boding glances were turned upon him, but on the occasion of his performing a reel with Kathleen. It might have been noticed that they looked at him, and afterwards at each other, in a manner that could admit of but little misapprehension.

"Philip," observed Finigan, addressing the elder Hogan,—"Philip, the Macedonian—monarch of Macedon, I say, is not that performance a beautiful specimen of the saltatory art? There is manly beauty, O Philip! and modest carriage.

> "'With aquil beauty formed, and aquil grace,
> Hers the soft blushes of the opening morn,
> And his the radiance of the risen day.'"

"It's night now, misther, if you plaise," returned Hogan, gruffly; "but we don't want your opinion here—stick to your pothooks and hangers—keep to your trade."

"The *pot-hooks* and *hangers* are more *tui generis*, you misbegotten satyr," replied the schoolmaster; "that is, more appropriately concatenated with your own trade than wid mine. I have no trade, sirra, but a profession, and neither have you. You stand in the same degraded ratio to a tradesman that a rascally quack does to a regular surgeon."

"You had better keep a civil tongue in jour head," replied Hogan, nettled at the laughter which the schoolmaster raised at his expense.

"What! a civil tongue for you! Polite language for a rascally sotherer of ould skillets and other anonymous utensils. Why, what are you?—firstly, a general violation of the ten commandments; and, secondly, a misshapen but faithful impersonation of the seven deadly sins. Take my word for it, my worthy Macedonian, you will die any death but a horizontal one—it's veracity I'm telling you. Yet there is some comfort for you too—some comfort, I say again; for you who never lived one upright hour will die an upright death. A certain official will erect a perpendicular with you; but for that touck of Mathematics you must go to the hangman, at whose hands you will have to receive the rites of your church, you monstrous bog-trotting Gorgon. Mine a trade! Shades of Academus, am I to bear this!"

Finigan was, like most of his class, a privileged man; but on this occasion the loudness of the mirth prevented Hogan's reply from being heard. As to violence, nobody that knew the poor pedagogue could ever dream of using it towards him, and there is little doubt that the consciousness of this caused him to give his tongue a license when provoked, which he otherwise would not have dared to venture upon. When he first made his appearance he was so far advanced in liquor as scarcely to be able to stand, and it was quite evident that the heat of the crowded house by no means improved him.

In about a quarter of an hour after Bryan and Kathleen had danced, the good people of the kemp were honored by the appearance of Hycy Burke among them—not in his jockey dress, but in a tight-fitting suit, that set off his exceedingly well-made person to great advantage. In fact, Hycy was a young fellow of a remarkably handsome face, full of liveliness and apparent good humor, and a figure that was nearly perfect. He addressed the persons present with an air of easy condescension, and went over immediately and shook hands, in a very cordial manner, with Gerald Cavanagh and his wife, after which he turned round and bowed to the daughters. He then addressed Bryan, beside whom Kathleen was sitting.

"Bryan," said he, "there will be mistakes in the best of families. I hate enmity. How, do you do?"

Bryan nodded, and replied, "Pretty well, Hycy—how are you?"

Cavanagh and his wife were evidently quite delighted to see him; the good man rose and made him take his own seat, and Mrs. Cavanagh paid him every conceivable mark of attention.

"Mrs. Cavanagh," said he, after some chat, "may I be permitted to indulge in the felicity of a dance with Miss Cavanagh?"

"Which of them?" asked the mother, and then added, without waiting for a reply—"to be sure you may."

"The felicity of a dance! that was well expressed, Mr. Hycy; but it was not for nothing that you broke grammatical ground under Patricius Finigan—ah, no; the early indoctrinations will tell;—that is clear."

"I mean Miss Kathleen," replied Hycy, without paying any attention to Finigan's observations.

"Why not?" exclaimed both; "of course you will—go over and bring her out."

Hycy, approaching her, said, in his blandest and most persuasive manner, "Miss Cavanagh, will you allow me the gratification of dancing a reel with you?"

"I'm obliged to you, Mr. Burke," she replied gravely; "I have just danced a reel with Bryan M'Mahon here, and I don't intend to dance any more to-night."

"A simple reel?" said Hycy; "perhaps you will so far favor me? I shall consider it as a favor, I assure you."

"Excuse me, Mr. Burke, but I won't dance any more to-night."

"That's hard," he replied, "especially as I came all the way to have that pleasure. Perhaps you will change your mind, Miss Cavanagh?"

"I'm not in the habit of changing my mind, Mr. Burke," she replied, "and I don't see any reason why I should do so now. I say once for all that I won't dance any more to-night."

"What is it," asked the mother, on perceiving her hesitation; "won't she dance wid you? Hut, tut, Kathleen, what nonsense is this? To be sure you must dance wid Mr. Burke; don't take any refusal, Mr.

Burke—is that all you know about girls.—sure nineteen refusals is aquil to one consent. Go over, Gerald, and make her dance wid him," she added, turning to her husband.

"Wha3t's the matter, Kathleen, that you won't dance wid Mr. Hycy?" asked the good man.

"Because I have danced all I will dance to-night, father."

"Tut, nonsense, you foolish girl—it's proud you ought to be that he'd ax you. Get up and dance a reel wid him."

Hanna, who knew her sister's resolution when once formed, immediately came to her rescue. "Don't ask her, father," she said; "the truth is, that I believe she has a headache—however, I'll take her place—have you any objection to me, Mr. Burke?"

None in the world—he would be very happy—only he regretted that he could not have that pleasure also with his sister.

"Ah, Mr. Hycy—which is properly Hyacinthus," said Finigan; "I am able to perceive that Cupid declines to be propitious in that quarter, or perhaps it's the *irae amantium*,—-which is, on being rendered into vernacularity, a falling out of lovers; and if so, do not despair; for as certain as it is, it will be followed by that most delectable of processes, the *redintegratio amoris*, or the renewing of love. In fact, he is a little better than a tyro—an ignoramus, who doesn't quarrel at least once a week, wid the fair object of his amorous inclinations, an' that for the sake of the reconciliaitons."

Hycy and Hanna were now about to dance, when Philip Hogan came forward, and, with an oath, declared that Kathleen must dance—"He wouldn't see Mr. Burke insulted that way by any such airs—and by—she must dance. Come," said he, "what stuff is this—we'll see whether you or I is strongest;" and as he spoke he seized her rudely by the arm, and was about to pull her out on the floor.

Bryan M'Mahon sprung to his feet. "Let her go, you ruffian," he exclaimed; "let her go this instant."

"No, I won't," replied the savage; "an' not for you, at any rate. Come, Miss Kathleen, out you'll go:—for you indeed," he added, in a ferocious parenthesis, looking at Bryan; "it's you that's the cause of all this. Come, miss, dance you must."

The words were scarcely uttered when M'Mahon, by a single blow on the neck, felled him like an ox, and in an instant the whole place was a scene of wild commotion. The Hogans, however, at all times unpopular, had no chance in an open affray on such an occasion as this. The feeling that predominated was, that the ruffianly interference of Philip had been justly punished; and ere many minutes the usual harmony, with the exception of some threatening looks and ferocious under growls from the Hogans, was restored. Hycy and Hanna then went on with their dance, and when it was over, the schoolmaster rose to depart.

"Mr. Burke," said he, "you are and have the reputation of being a perfect gentleman *homo factus ad unguem*—as has been said by the learned little Roman, who, between you and me, was not overburthened with an excess of morality. I take the liberty, jinteels, of wishing you a good-night—*precor vobia prosperam noctem!* Ah, I can do it yet; but it wasn't for nothing that I practised the peripatetics in larned Kerry, where the great O'Finigan is not yet forgotten. I shall now seek a contiguous place of repose, until the consequences of some slight bacchanalin libations on my part shall have dispersed themselves into thin air."

He accordingly departed, but from the unsteadiness of his step it was clear that, as he said, the place of his repose must be contiguous indeed. Had he been conscious of his own motions it is not likely he would have sought for repose in Cavanagh's kiln, then the habitation of the Hogans. It was probably the fact of the door having been left open, which was generally the case in summer, that induced him to enter—for enter he did—ignorant, it is to be presumed, that the dwelling he was about to enter was then inhabited by the Hogans, whom he very much disrelished.

The place was nearly waste, and had a very desolate look. Scattered around, and littered upon shake-down beds of straw, some half dozen young besmutted savages, male and female, lay stretched in all positions, some north, others south, without order or decency, but all seeming in that barbarous luxury which denotes strong animal health and an utter disregard of cleanliness and bodily comfort. Over

The Emigrants of Ahadarra

in one of the corners lay three or four budgets, old iron skillets, hammers, lumps of melted lead, broken pots, a quantity of cows' horns for spoons, wooden dishes that required clasping, old kettles that wanted repair, a couple of cast off Poteen Stills, and a new one half made—all of which were visible by the light of a large log of bog-fir which lay burning in the fire-place. On looking around him, he descended a flight of stone steps that led to the fireplace or the kiln or opening in which the fuel used to dry the grain was always burned. This corner, which was eight or ten feet below the other portion of the floor, being, in general, during the summer months filled with straw, received the drowsy pedagogue, who, in a few minutes, was as sound asleep as any of them about him.

Hycy, who was conscious of his good figure, danced two or three times afterwards.

Dora M'Mahon had the honor of being his partner, as had one or two of the best looking girls present. At the close of the last dance he looked significantly at the Hogans, and nodded towards the door; after which it might have been observed, that they slunk out one at a time, followed in a few minutes by Kate Hycy, after some further chat with Gerald Cavanagh and his wife, threw half a crown to Mickey M'Grory, and in his usual courteous phraseology, through which there always ran, by the way, a vein of strong irony, he politely wished them all a good night.

CHAPTER VIII.—Anonymous Letter with a Name to It

—Finigan's Dialogue with Hycy

The severest tax upon Hycy's powers of invention was, in consequence of his habits of idleness, to find means of occupying his time. Sometimes, it is true, he condescended to oversee the men while at work, but there it was generally found that so far from keeping them to their employment, he was a considerable drawback upon their industry. The ordinary business of his life, however, was riding about the country, and especially into the town of Ballymacan and home again. He was also a regular attendant in all the neighboring fairs; and we may safely assert that no race in the province ever came off without him.

On the second day after his interview with Teddy Phats and the Hogans, he was riding past the post-office, when he heard the window tapped, and, on approaching, a letter was handed out to him, which on opening he found to contain the following communication:—

"Worthy Mr. Hyacinthus—

"A friend unknown to you, but not altogether so to fame, and one. whom no display of the subtlest ingenuity on behalf of your acute and sagacious intellect could ever decypher through the medium of this epistle, begs to convey to you a valuable portion of anonymous information. When he says that he is not unknown to fame, the assertion, as far as it goes, is pregnant wid veracity. Mark that I say, as far as it goes, by which is meant the assertion as well as the fame of your friend, the inditer of this significant epistle. Forty-eight square miles of good sound fame your not inerudite correspondent can conscientiously lay claim to; and although there is, with regret I admit it, a considerable portion of the square superficies alluded to, waste and uncultivated moor, yet I can say, wid that racy touch of genial and expressive pride which distinguishes men of letters in general, that the other portions of this fine district are inhabited by a multitudinity of population in the highest degree creditable to the prolific powers of the climate. 'Tisn't all as one, then, as that thistle-browsing quadruped. Barney Heffeman, who presumes, in imitation of his betters, to write Philomath after his name, and whose whole extent of literary reputation is not more than two or three beggarly townlands, whom, by the way, he is inoculating successfully wid his own ripe and flourishing ignorance. No, sir; nor like Gusty Gibberish, or (as he has been most facetiously christened by his Reverence, Father O'Flaherty) Demosthenes M'Gosther, inasmuch as he is distinguished for an aisy and prodigal superfluity of mere words, unsustained by intelligibility or meaning, but who cannot claim in his own person a mile and a half of dacent reputation. However, *quid multis* Mr. Hyacinthus; 'tis no indoctrinated or obscure scribe who now addresses you, and who does so from causes that may be salutary to your own health and very gentlemanly fame, according as you resave the same, not pretermitting interests involving, probably, on your part, an abundant portion of pecuniarity.

"In short, then, it has reached these ears, Mr. Hyacinthus, and between you and me, they are not such a pair as, in consequence of their longitudinity, can be copiously shaken, or which rise and fall according to the will of the wearer; like those of the thistle-browser already alluded to; it has reached them that you are about to substantiate a a disreputable—excuse the phrase—co-partnership wid four of the most ornamental villains on Hibernian earth, by which you must understand me to mane that the villains aforesaid are not merely accomplished in all the plain principles and practices of villainy, but finished off even to its natest and most inganious decorations. Their whole life has been most assiduously and successfully devoted to a general violation of the ten commandments, as well as to the perpetual commission of the seven deadly sins. Nay, the 'reserved cases' themselves can't escape them, and it is well known that they wont rest satisfied wid the wide catalogue of ordinary and general iniquity, but they must, by way of luxury, have a lick at blasphemy, and some of the rarer vices, as often as they can, for the villains are so fastidious that they won't put up wid common wickedness like other people. I cannot, however, wid anything approximating to a safe conscience, rest here. What I have said has reference to the laws of God, but what I am about to enumerate relates to the laws of man—to the laws of the land Wid respect, then, to them, I do assure you, that although I myself look upon the violation of a great number of the latter wid a very vanial squint, still, I say, I do assure you that they have not left a single law made by Parliament unfractured. They have gone over the whole statute-book several times, and I believe are absolutely of opinion that the Parliament is doing nothing. The most lynx-eyed investigator of old enactments could not find one which has escaped them, for the villains are perfectly black letter in that respect; and what is in proper keeping wid this, whenever they hear of a new Act of Parliament they cannot rest either night or day until they break it. And now for the inference: be on your guard against this pandemonial squad. Whatever your object may be in cultivating and keeping society wid them, theirs is to ruin you—fleece was the word used—an I then to cut and run, leaving Mr. Hycy—the acute, the penetrating, the accomplished—completely in the lurch. Be influenced, then, by the amicitial admonitions of the inditer of this correspondence. Become not a smuggler—forswear poteen. The Lord forgive me, Mr. Hycy—no, I only wished to say forswear—not the poteen—but any connection wid the illegal alembic from which it is distillated, otherwise they will walk off wid the 'doublings,' or strong liquor, leaving you nothing but the residuum or feints. Take a friend's advice, therefore, and retrograde out of all society and connection wid the villains I have described; or if you superciliously overlook this warning, book it down as a fact that admits of no negation, that you will be denuded of reputation, of honesty, and of any pecuniary contingencies that you may happen to possess. This is a sincere advice from

"Your Anonymous Friend,

"Patricius O'Finigan, Philomath."

After perusing this characteristic production, Hycy paused for a little, and felt it very probable that there might be some reasonable grounds for its production, although he could scarcely understand upon what motive these fellows should proceed to practice treachery towards him. That they were without principle or honesty he was perfectly satisfied; but he knew it was their interest to keep within bounds in all matters connected with their employment, He laughed very heartily at Finigan's blunder—for such it evidently was—in signing his name to a document that he intended to be anonymous.

"At all events," thought he, "I will ride over to his 'seminary,' as he calls it, and see what he can mean, or what his object is in sending me such a warning."

He accordingly did so, and in some twenty minutes reached a small cabin that stood about a couple of hundred yards from the highroad. A little bridle way led to it, as did several minor pathways, each radiating from a different direction. It was surrounded by four or five acres of common, where the children played from twelve to one, at which hour Mr. O'Finigan went to the house of some wealthy benefactor to dine. The little village of Ballydruthy, at a short distance from which it stood, was composed of a couple dozen dwelling-houses, a chapel, a small grocer's and publican's, together with a Pound at the entrance, through which ran a little stream necessary to enable the imprisoned cattle to drink.

On riding up to the school, Hycy, as he approached the door, heard his own name repeated by at least two dozen voices.

"Here's a gintleman, masther"—"It's Misther Hycy Burke, sir "—"It is, bedad, sir, Hycy the sportheen—"

"Him that rides the race, masther"—"Ay, an' he has on top-boots and buckskins, an's as gran' as a gintleman—"

"Silence!" said Finigan, "silence! I say; is this proper scholastic decorum in the presence of a stranger? Industry and taciturnity, you reptiles, or castigation shall result. Here, Paddy Sparable," he added, rising up—"here, you nailroad, assume my office, and rule the establishment till I return; and, mark me, as the son of a nailer, sirra, I expect that you will rule them with a rod of iron—ha! ha! ha!"

"Ay, but Paddy Pancake's here to-day, sir, an' he's able to welt me; so that's it's only leathered I'd get, sir, i' you plase."

"But have you no officers? Call in aid, I ordher you. Can't you make Sam Scaddhan and Phiddher Mackleswig there two policeman get Pancake down—flatten him—if he prove contumacious during my absence. Pancake, mark me, obedience is your cue, or, if not, the castigator here is your alternative; there it is, freshly cut—ripe and ready—and you are not to be told, at this time o' day, what portion of your corpus will catch it. Whish-h-h!—silence! I say. How do you do, Mr. Burke? I am proud of a visit from you, sir; perhaps you would light down and examine a class. My Greeks are all absent to-day; but I have a beautiful class o' Romans in the Fourth Book of Virgil—immortal Maro. Do try them, Mr. Hycy; if they don't do Dido's death in a truly congenial spirit I am no classic. Of one thing I can assure you, that they ought; for I pledge my reputation it is not the first time I've made them practice the Irish cry over it. This, however, was but natural; for it is now well known to the learned that, if Dido herself was not a fair Hibernian, she at least spoke excellent Irish. Ah, Mr. Hycy," he added, with a grin, "the birch is the only pathetic switch growing! Will you come in, sir?"

"No, thank you, Mr. Finigan; but perhaps you would have the goodness to come out for a little;" and, as he spoke, he nodded towards the public-house. "I know the boys will be quiet until you return."

"If they don't," replied Finigan, "the alternative is in no shape enigmatical. Mark what I've already said, gintlemen. Sparable, do you keep a faithful journal of the delinquents; and observe that there are offices of importance in this world besides flagellating erudition into reptiles like you."

He then looked about him with an air of vast importance, and joined Hycy on his way to the public-house. Having ordered in the worthy pedagogue's favorite beverage, not forgetting something of the same kind for himself, he addressed Finigan as follows:—

"Finigan, I received a devilish queer letter from you to-day—take your liquor in the mean time—what did you mean by it?"

"From me, Mr. Hycy—*nego*, I say—*pugnis et calce bu nego*."

"Come, come, you know you wrote me an anonymous letter, referring to some ridiculous copartnership or other that I can neither make head nor tail of. Tell me candidly what you meant."

"Very good, Mr. Burke; but sure I know of old that jocularity was always your forte—even when laying in under my own instruction that sound classical substratum on which the superstructure of your subsequent knowledge was erected, you were always addicted to the facetious and the fabulous—both of which you contrived to blend together with an ease and volubility of language that could not be surpassed."

"That is all very well; but you need not deny that you wrote me the letter. Let me ask you seriously, what was it you warned me against?"

"*Propino tibi salulem*—here's to you. No, but let me ask you what you are at, Mr. Hycy? You may have resaved an anonymous letter, but I am ignorant why you should paternize it upon me."

"Why, because it has all the marks and tokens of you."

"Eh?—to what does that amount? Surely you know my handwriting?"

"Perfectly; but this is disguised evidently."

"Faith," said the other, laughing, "maybe the inditer of it was disguised when he wrote it."

"It might be," replied Hycy; "however, take your liquor, and in the mean time I shall feel exceedingly obliged to you, Mr. Finigan, if you will tell me the truth at once—whether you wrote it or whether you did not?"

"My response again is in the negative," replied Finigan—"I disclaim it altogether. I am not the scribe, you may rest assured of it, nor can I say who is."

"Well, then," said Hycy, "I find I must convict you yourself of the fabulous at least; read that," said he, placing the letter in his own hands. "Like a true Irishman you signed your name unconsciously; and now what have you to say for yourself?"

"Simply," replied the other, "that some knave, of most fictitious imagination, has forged my name to it. No man can say that that is my manuscript, Mr. Hycy." These words he uttered with great coolness; and Hycy, who was in many things a shrewd young fellow, deemed it better to wait until the liquor, which was fast disappearing, should begin to operate. At length, when about three-quarters of an hour had passed, he resolved to attack his vanity.

"Well, well, Finigan, as regards this letter, I must say I feel a good deal disappointed."

"Why so, Mr. Hycy?"

"Why, because I did not think there was any other man in the country who could have written it."

"Eh? how is that now?"

"Faith, it's very simple; the letter is written with surprising ability—the language is beautiful—and the style, like the land of Canaan, flowing with milk and honey. It is certainly a most uncommon production."

"Now, seriously, do you think so? At all events, Mr. Hycy, it was written by a friend of yours—that's a clear case."

"I think so; but what strikes me is its surprising ability; no wonder the writer should say that he is not unknown to fame—he could not possibly remain in obscurity."

"Mr. Hycy, your health—I remember when you were wid me you certainly were *facile princeps* for a ripe judgment, even in your rudiments; so then, you are of opinion that the epistle in question has janius? I think myself it is no everyday production; not I believe such as the thistle-browser Heffernan, or Misther Demosthenes M'Gosther could achieve—the one wid his mile and a half, and the other wid his three townlands of reputation. No, sir, to the divil I pitch them both; they could never indite such a document. Your health, Mr. Hycy—*propino tibi*, I say; and you are right, *ille ego*—it's a a fact; I am the man, sir—I acknowledge the charge."

This admission having been made, we need scarcely add that an explanation was at at once given by Finigan of the motive which had induced him to write the letter.

"On laving the kemp," said he, "and getting into the open air—*sub diu*, Mr. Hycy—I felt a general liquidation of my whole bodily strength, with a strong disposition to make short excursions to the right or to the left rather than hold my way straight a-head, with, I must confess, an equal tendency to deposit my body on my mother earth and enact the soporiferous. On passing Gerald Cavanagh's kiln, where the Hogans kennel, I entered, and was greeted wid such a chorus of sternutation as you might expect from a pigsty in midsummer, and made me envy the unlicked young savages who indulged in it. At the period spoken of neither you nor they had come in from the kemp. Even this is but a dim recollection, and I remember nothing more until I overheard your voice and theirs in dialogue as you were about to depart. After you went, I heard the dialogue which I hinted at in the letter, between Teddy Phats and them; and knowing my position and the misbegotten satyrs by whom I was surrounded, I patiently waited until they were asleep, when I quietly took my departure."

Burke could not help inferring from Finigan's manner, that he had overheard a greater portion of their conversation on the occasion alluded to than he seemed disposed to acknowledge.

"Now, Finigan," he said, "I feel disposed to place every confidence in you. Will you answer candidly the question I am about to propose to you? Did you hear Bryan M'Mahon's name mentioned?"

"You say, Mr. Hycy," replied Finigan, emptying his glass, "that you would entherthain no apprehension in placing confidence in me?"

"Not the slightest," replied Hycy; "I believe you to be the very soul of honor; and, besides, are you not my old master? As you say yourself, did I not break grammatical ground, under you?"

"The soul of honor," replied the pedagogue, complacently—"that is excellently said. Well, then, Mr. Burke, I shall not deal out my confidence by beggarly instalments—I did hear Bryan M'Mahon's name mentioned; and I heard a plan alluded to between you and them for reducing him to—"

"That was all humbug, Finigan, so far as I am concerned; but for the present I am obliged to let them suppose what you allude to, in order to keep them honest to myself if I can. You know they have a kind of hereditary hatred against the M'Mahons; and if I did not allow them to take their own way in this, I don't think I could depend on them."

"Well, there is raison in that too," replied Finigan.

"I am sure, Finigan," proceeded Hycy, "that you are too honorable a man to breathe either to Bryan M'Mahon or any one else, a single syllable of the conversation which you overheard merely by accident. I say I am certain you will never let it transpire, either by word of mouth or writing. In me you may always calculate on finding a sincere friend; and of this let me assure you, that your drink, if everything goes right with us, won't cost you much—much! not a penny; if you had two throats instead of one—as many necks as Hydra, we should supply them all."

"Give me your hand, Mr. Hycy—you are a gintleman, and I always said would be one—I did, sir—I prognosticated as much years ago; and sincerely felicitous am I that my prognostications have been verified for so far. I said you would rise—that exaltation was before you—and that your friends might not feel at all surprised at the elevated position in which you will die. *Propino tibi*, again—and do not fear that ever revelation of mine shall facilitate any catastrophe that may await you."

Hycy looked keenly into the schoolmaster's face as he uttered the last observation; but in the maudlin and collapsed features then before him he could read nothing that intimated the sagacity of a double meaning. This satisfied him; and after once more exacting from Finigan a pledge of what he termed honorable confidence, he took his departure.

CHAPTER IX.—A Little Polities, Much Friendship, and Some Mystery

This communication determined Hycy to forego his intention for the present, and he consequently allowed the summer and autumn to pass without keeping up much intercourse with either Teddy Phats or the Hogans. The truth is, that Burke, although apparently frank and candid, was constitutionally cautious, and inclined a good deal to suspicion. He feared that no project, the knowledge of which was held in common with Finigan, could be long kept a secret; and for that reason he make up his mind to postpone the matter, and allow it to die away out of the schoolmaster's mind ere he bestowed any further attention upon it. In the meantime, the state of the country was gradually assuming a worse and more depressing character. The season was unfavorable; and although we do not assert that many died of immediate famine, yet we know that hundreds—nay, thousands—died from the consequences of scarcity and destitution—or, in plainer words, from fever and other diseases induced by bad and insufficient food, and an absence of the necessary comforts of life. Indeed, at the period of our narrative, the position of Ireland was very gloomy; but when, we may ask, has it been otherwise, within the memory of man, or the records of history? Placed as the country was, emigration went forward on an extensive scale,—emigration, too, of that peculiar description which every day enfeebles and impoverishes the country, by depriving her of all that approaches to anything like a comfortable and independent yeomanry. This, indeed, is a kind of depletion which no country can bear long; and, as it is, at the moment we are writing this, progressing at a rate beyond all precedent, it will not, we trust, be altogether uninteresting to inquire into some of the causes that have occasioned it. Let not our readers apprehend, however, that we are about to turn our fictitious narrative into a dissertation on political economy. Of course the principle cause of emigration is the poverty and depressed state of the country; and it follows naturally, that whatever occasions our poverty will necessarily occasion emigration. The first cause of our poverty then, is Absenteeism, which, by drawing six or seven millions out of the country, deprives our people of employment and means of life to that amount. The next is the general inattention of Irish landlords to the state and condition of their own property, and an inexcusable want of sympathy with their tenantry, which, indeed, is only a corollary from the former; for it can hardly be expected that those who wilfully neglect themselves will feel a warm interest in others. The next is the evil of subletting, by which property becomes overloaded with human beings, who, for the most part, are bound by no ties whatsoever to the owner of the soil. He is not their landlord, nor are they his tenants; and so far from their interests being in any way reciprocal, they are actually adversative. It is his interest to have them removed, and, as circumstances unfortunately stand, it is theirs to remain, inasmuch as their alternative is ruin since they have no place of shelter to receive them.

Political corruption, in the shape of the forty-shilling franchise, was another cause, and one of the very worst, which led to the prostration of the country by poverty and moral degradation, and for this the proprietors of the soil are solely responsible. Nor can the use of the potato, as the staple food of the laboring classes, in connection with the truck system, and the consequent absence of money payments, in addition to the necessary ignorance of domestic and social comforts that resulted from them, be left out of this wretched catalogue of our grievances. Another cause of emigration is to be found in the high and exorbitant rents at which land is held by all classes of farmers—with some exceptions we admit, as in the case of old leases—but especially by those who hold under middlemen, or on the principle of subletting generally. By this system a vast deal of distress and petty but most harrassing oppression is every day in active operation upon the property of the head landlord, which he can never know, and for which he is in no other way responsible unless by having ever permitted the existence of it for any purpose whatsoever.

In a country distracted like Ireland, it would be impossible to omit the existence of political and religious animosity as a strong and prominent cause of our wretched poverty, and consequently of emigration. The priest, instead of leaving temporal affairs to temporal men, most improperly mingles himself in the angry turmoils of politics, to which, by his interference, he communicates a peculiar and characteristic bitterness. The landlord, on the other hand, having his own interests to consult, does not wish to arm a political opponent with such powers as he knows will most assuredly be turned against himself, and consequently often refuses to grant a lease unless to those who will pledge themselves to support him. This state of things, involving, as it does, much that is wrong on both sides, is, has been, and will be, a present and permanent curse to the country—a curse, too, which, until there is more of humanity and justice on the one side, and of education and liberal feeling on the other, is not likely to disappear from the country.

Though last, not least, comes the unaccountable and guilty neglect of our legislature (if we can call it ours) in everything that pertained to Irish interests. This, together with its almost necessary consequence of dishonest agitation on the one hand, and well founded dissatisfaction on the other, nearly completes the series of the causes which have produced the poverty of the country, and, as a direct result, the emigration of all that is most comfortable, independent, and moral among us.

This poverty, arising, as it does, from so many causes, has propagated itself with a rapidity which is startling; for every one knows that poverty is proverbially prolific. And yet it is a grievous anomaly to reflect that a country so far steeped in misery and destitution as to have nearly one-half of its population in a state of most pitiable pauperism, possesses a soil capable of employing and maintaining three times the number of its inhabitants. When the causes, however, which we have just enumerated are seriously looked at and considered, we think its extraordinary result is, after all, so very natural, that the wonder would indeed be were the state of Ireland otherwise than it is. As matters stand at present, and as they are likely to continue, unless parliament shall interfere by a comprehensive measure of legislation, we must only rest contented with seeing the industrious, moral, and respectable portion of our countrymen abandoning the land of their birth and affections, and nothing but the very dregs—degraded alike by idleness and immorality—remaining behind to multiply and perpetuate their own wretchedness and degradation.

It has been often said, and with great truth, that no man is more devotedly attached to his native soil than an Irishman; yet it may reasonably be asked, how this principle of attachment can be reconciled with the strong tendency to emigration which characterizes our people. We reply, that the tendency in question is a proof of the love of honest industry, enterprise, and independence, by which our countrymen, when not degraded by neglect and poverty, are actuated. It is not of this class, however so degraded, that we now speak. On the contrary we take the decent and respectable farmer as the subject of our illustration—the man who, loving his native fields as if they were of his blood, would almost as soon part with the one as the other. This man it is, who, with the most child-like tenderness of affection towards the land on which he and his have lived for centuries, will, nevertheless, the moment he finds himself on the decline, and with no cheering hope of prosperity or encouragement before him or his family, resolutely determine to forget everything but the noble duties which he owes to himself and them. He sees clearly, from the unhappy state of the country, and the utter want of sympathy and attention which he experiences at the hands of those who ought to have his interests at heart, that if he attempt to hold his position under circumstances so depressing and unfavorable, he must gradually sink, until he and his become mingled with the great mass of pauperism which lies lik a an incubus upon the energies of the country. What, therefore, can possibly prove more strongly than this that the Irishman who is not dragged into the swamp of degradation, in which hope and energy are paralyzed, is strongly and heroically characterized by I those virtues of industry and enterprise that throw their lustre over social life?

There are other and still more indefensible causes, however, which too frequently drive the independent farmer out of the country. In too many cases it happens that the rapacity and dishonesty of the agent, countenanced or stimulated by the necessities and reckless extravagance of the landlord, fall, like some unwholesome blight, upon that enterprise and industry which would ultimately, if properly encouraged, make the country prosperous and her landed proprietors independent men. We allude to the nefarious and monstrous custom of ejecting tenants who have made improvements, or, when permitted to remain, making them pay for the improvements which they have made. A vast proportion of this crying and oppressive evil must be laid directly to the charge of those who fill the responsible situation of agents to property in Ireland, than whom in general there does not exist, a more unscrupulous, oppressive, arrogant, and dishonest class of men. Exceptions of course there are, and many, but speaking of them as a body, we unhappily assert nothing but what the condition of property, and of those who live upon it, do at this moment and have for many a year testified.

Several months had now elapsed, and although the M'Mahons had waited upon the agent once or twice since the interview which we have already described between him and Tom, yet there seemed no corresponding anxiety on the part of Fethertonge to have the leases prepared or executed. This neglect or reluctance did not occasion much uneasiness to the old man, who was full of that generous and unsuspecting confidence that his countrymen always repose in the promise of a landlord respecting a lease, which they look upon, or did at least, as something absolutely inviolable and sacred, as indeed it ought to be. Bryan, however, who, although a young man, was not destitute of either observation or the experience which it bestows, and who, moreover, had no disposition to place unlimited confidence in Fethertonge, began to entertain some vague suspicions with reference to the delay. Fethertonge, however, had not the reputation of being a harsh man, or particularly unjust in his dealings with the world; on the contrary, he was rather liked than otherwise; for so soft was the melody of his voice, and so irresistible the friendship and urbanity of his manner, that many persons felt as much gratified by the refusal of a favor from him as they did at its being granted by another. At length, towards the close of October, Bryan himself told his father that he would, call upon the agent and urge him to expedite the matter of the leases. "I don't know how it is," said he, "but some way or other I don't feel comfortable about this business: Fethertonge is very civil and very dacent, and is well spoken of in general; but for all that there's always a man here an' there that says he's not to be depended on."

"Troth an' he is to be depended on," said his generous father; "his words isn't like the words of a desaver, and it isn't till he shows the cloven foot that I'll ever give in that he's, dishonest."

"Well," said Bryan, "I'm sure I for one hope you may be right; but, at any rate, as he's at home now I'll start and see him."

"Do then," said his father, "bekaise I know you're a favorite of his; for he tould me so wid his own lips."

"Well," replied the other, laughing, "I hope you're right there too; I'm sure I have no objection;" and he accordingly set out to see Fethertonge, but with something of an impression that the object of his visit was not likely to be accomplished without difficulty, if accomplished at all.

On reaching the agent's house he met a thin, tall man, named Clinton, with a hooked nose and sinister aspect, riding down the avenue, after having paid Fethertonge a visit. This person was the gauger of the district, a bachelor and a man of considerable wealth, got together, it is suspected, by practices that were not well capable of bearing the light. His family consisted of a niece and a nephew, the latter of whom had recently become a bosom friend of the accomplished Hycy Burke, who, it was whispered, began to look upon Miss Clinton with a partial eye. Hycy had got acquainted with him at the Herringstown races, where he, Hycy, rode and won a considerable sweepstakes; and as both young gentlemen were pretty much of the same habits of life, a very warm intimacy had, for some time past, subsisted between them. Clinton, to whom M'Mahon was known, addressed him in a friendly manner, and, after some chat, he laid the point of his whip gently upon Bryan's shoulder, so as to engage his attention.

"M'Mahon," said he, "I am glad I have met you, and I trust our meeting will be for your good. You have had a dispute with Hycy Burke?"

"Why, sir," replied Bryan, smiling, "if I had it wasn't such as it was worth his while to talk about."

"Well, M'Mahon, that's generously said on your part—now, listen to me; don't allow yourself to be drawn into any illegal or illicit proceedings by any one, friend or foe—if so, you will only put yourself into the power of your enemies; for enemies you have, I can assure you."

"They say, sir, there is no one without them," replied Bryan, smiling; "but so far as I am consarned, I don't exactly understand what you mane. I have no connection with anything, either illegal or—or—wrong in any way, Mr. Clinton, and if any one tould you so, they spoke an untruth."

"Ay, ay," said Clinton, "that may be so, and I hope it is so; but you know that it could not be expected you would admit it even if it be true. Will you in the mean time, be guided by a friend? I respect your father and his family; I respect yourself, M'Mahon; and, consequently, my advice to you is—keep out of the meshes of the law—avoid violating it—and remember you have enemies. Now think of these words, and so good-bye, M'Mahon! Indeed, I am glad for your own sake I met you—good-bye!"

As he uttered the last words he dashed on and left Bryan in a state of perfect amazement at the strange and incomprehensible nature of the communication he had just received. Indeed, so full was his mind of the circumstance, that forgetting all his suspicions of Fethertonge, and urged by the ingenuous impulse of an honest heart, he could not prevent himself in the surprise and agitation of the moment from detailing the conversation which he had just had with the gauger.

"That is singular enough," said Fethertonge—"he named Hycy Burke, then?"

"He did, sir."

"It is singular," proceeded the other, as if speaking to himself; "in truth, my dear M'Mahon, we were talking about you, discussing, in fact, the same subject not many minutes ago; and what you tell me now is only an additional proof that Clinton, who is sometimes harshly spoken of by the way, is a straightforward, honest man."

"What could he mane, sir?" asked Bryan, "I never had anything to do contrary to the law—I haven't now, nor do I ever intend to have—"

"Well, I'm sure I do not know," replied the agent: "he made no illusion of that kind to me, from a generous apprehension, I dare say, lest he might injure you in my opinion. He only desired me not rashly to listen to anything prejudicial to your character; for that you had enemies who were laboring to injure you in some way—but how—he either would not tell, or perhaps did not know. I am glad, however, he mentioned it; for I shall be guarded should I hear anything to your prejudice."

"I tell you beforehand, sir," said Bryan, with the conscious warmth of rectitude, "and I think I ought to know best, that if you ever hear anything against my honesty or want of principle, or if any one should say that I will be consarned in what's contrary to either law or justice, you'll hear a falsehood—I don't care who it comes from—and the man who tells you so is a liar."

"I should be sorry to believe otherwise, my dear Bryan; it would grieve me to be forced to believe otherwise. If you suffer yourself to be drawn into anything wrong or improper, you will be the first individual of your family that ever brought a stain upon it. It would grieve me—deeply would it grieve me, to witness such a blot upon so honest—but no, I will not, for I cannot suppose it."

Bryan, whose disposition was full of good-nature and cheerfulness, could not help bursting into a hearty laugh, on reverting to the conversation which he had with Clinton, and comparing it with that in which they were now engaged; both of which were founded upon some soap-bubble charge of which he knew nothing.

"You take it lightly," said Fethertonge, with something of a serious expression; "but remember, my dear Bryan, that I now speak as one interested in, and, in fact, representing the other members of your family. Remember, at all events, you are forewarned, and, in the meantime, I thank Clinton—although I certainly would not have mentioned names. Bryan, you can have no objection that I should speak to your father on this subject?"

The Emigrants of Ahadarra

"Not the slightest, sir," replied Bryan; "spake to any one you like about it; but, putting that aside, sir, for the present—about these leases?"

"Why, what apprehension have you about them, Byran?"

"No apprehension, sir, sartinly; but you know yourself, Mr. Fethertonge, that to a man like me, that's layin' out and expendin' money every day upon Adaharra farm, and my father the same way upon Carriglass—I say, to a man like me, to be layin' out his money, when you know yourself that if the present landlord should refuse to carry his father's dying words into effect—or, as you said this minute yourself, sir, if some enemy should turn you against me, amn't I and my father and the whole family liable to be put out, notwithstanding all the improvements we've made, and the money we've spent in makin' them?"

"Bryan," said Fethertonge, after a pause, "every word you say is unfortunately too true—too true—and such things, are a disgrace to the country; indeed, I believe, they seldom occur in any country but this. Will it in the mean time satisfy you when I state that, if old Mr. Chevydale's intentions are not carried into effect by his son, I shall forthwith resign my agency?"

Bryan's conscience, generous as he was, notwithstanding his suspicions, smote him deeply on hearing this determination so unequivocally expressed. Indeed the whole tenor of their dialogue, taken in at one view—especially Fethertonge's intention of speaking to Tom M'Mahon upon the mysterious subject of Bryan's suspected delinquencies against the law—so thoroughly satisfied him of the injustice he had rendered Fethertonge, that he was for a time silent.

At length he replied—"That, sir, is more than we could expect; but at any rate there's one thing I'm now sartin of—that, if we're disappointed, you won't be the cause of it."

"Yes; but of course you must put disappointment out of the question. The landlord, will, without any doubt, grant the leases—I am satisfied of that; indeed, there can be no doubt about it. By the way, I am anxious to see Ahadarra and to ascertain the extent to which you have carried your improvements. Clinton and I will probably take a ride up there some day soon; and in the meantime do you keep improving, M'Mahon, for that's the secret of all success—leave the rest to me. How is your father?"

"Never was better, sir, I'm thankful to you."

"And your grandfather? how does he bear up?"

"Faith, sir, wonderfully, considering his age."

"He must be very old now?"

"He's ninety-four, sir, and that's a long age sure enough; but I'm sorry to say that my mother's health isn't so well."

"Why, what is the matter with her? I'm sorry to hear this."

"Indeed we can't say; she's very poorly—her appetite is gone—she has a cough, an' she doesn't get her rest at night."

"Why don't you get medical advice?"

"So we did, sir. Dr. Sexton's attendin' her; but I don't think somehow that he has a good opinion of her."

"Sexton's a skilful man, and I don't think she could be in better hands; however, Bryan, I shall feel obliged if you will send down occasionally to let me know how she gets on—once a week or so."

"Indeed we will, sir, an' I needn't say how much we feel obliged to you for your kindness and good wishes."

"It must be more than good wishes, Bryan; but I trust that she will get better. In the meantime leave the other matters to me, and you may expect Clinton and I up at your farm to look some of these days."

"God forgive me," thought Bryan, as he left the hall-door, "for the injustice I did him, by supposin' for one minute that he wasn't disposed to act fairly towards us. My father was right; an' it was foolish of me to put my wit against his age an' experience. Oh, no, that man's honest—there can;t be any mistake about it."

From this topic he could not help reverting, as he pursued his way home, to the hints he had received with respect to Hycy Burke's enemity towards him, the cause of which he could not clearly understand. Hycy Burke had, in general, the character of being a generous, dashing young fellow, with no fault unless a disposition to gallantry and a thoughtless inclination for extravagance; for such were the gentle terms in which habits of seduction and an unscrupulous profligacy in the expenditure of money were clothed by those who at once fleeced and despised him, but who were numerous enough to impress those opinions upon a great number of the people. In turning over matters as they stood between them, he could trace Burke's enmity to no adequate cause; nor indeed could he believe it possible that he entertained any such inveterate feeling of hostility against him. They had of late frequently met, on which occasion Hycy spoke to him with nearly as much cordiality as ever. Still, however, he could not altogether free himself from the conviction, that both Clinton and Fethertonge must have had unquestionable grounds for the hints which they had in such a friendly way thrown out to him.

In this mood he was proceeding when he heard the noise of horses' feet behind, and in a few minutes Hycy himself and young Clinton overtook him at a rapid pace. Their conversation was friendly, as usual, when Bryan, on seeing Hycy about to dash off at the same rapid rate, said, "If you are not in a particular hurry, Hycy, I'd wish to have a word with you."

The latter immediately pulled up, exclaiming, "a word, Bryan! ay, a hundred—certainly. Clinton, ride on a bit, will you? till I have some conversation with M'Mahon. Well, Bryan?"

"Hycy," proceeded Bryan, "I always like to be aboveboard. Will you allow me to ask if you have any bad feelings against me?"

"Will you answer me another question?" replied Hycy.

"If I can I will," said Bryan.

"Well, then," replied Hycy, "I will answer you most candidly, Bryan—not the slightest; but I do assure you that I thought you had such a feeling against me."

"And you wor right, too," returned Bryan "for I really had."

"I remember," proceeded Hycy, "that when I asked you to lend me thirty-five pounds—and by the way that reminds me that I am still pretty deep in your debt—you would neither lend it nor give any satisfactory reason why you refused me; now, what occasioned that feeling, Bryan?"

"It's by the merest chance that I happen to have the cause of it in my pocket," replied M'Mahon, who, as he spoke, handed him the letter which Peety Dhu had delivered to him from Hycy himself. "Read that," said he, "and I think you'll have no great trouble in understanding why I felt as I did;—an' indeed, Hycy, to tell you the truth, I never had the same opinion of you since." Hycy, to his utter amazement, read as follows:

"My Dear Miss Cavanagh:—

"Will you permit little Cupid, the god of Love, to enrol the name of Hycy Burke on the long list of your adorers? And if you could corrupt the little stone-blind divinity to blot out every name on it but my own, I should think that a very handsome anticipation of the joys of Paradise could be realized by that delightful fact. I say anticipation—for my creed is, that the actual joys of Paradise exist no where, but within the celestial circle of your ambrosial arms. That is the Paradise which I propose to win; and you may rest assured that I shall bring the most flaming zeal, the most fervent devotion, and all the genuine piety of a true worshipper, to the task of attaining it. I shall carry, for instance, a little Bible of Love in my pocket—for I am already a divinity student or a young collegian under little Cupid aforesaid—and I will have it all dogeared with refreshing texts for my edification. I should state, however, that I am, as every good Christian is, awfully exclusive in my creed; and will suffer no one, if I can prevent it, to approach the Paradise I speak of but myself. In fact I am as jealous as the very Deuce—whoever that personage may be—quite an Othello in my way—a perfect raw-head-and-bloody-bones—with a sharp appetite and teeth like a Walrus, ready to bolt my rivals in dozens. It is said, my divine creature, or rather it is hinted, that a certain clodhopping boor, from the congenial wilds of Ahadarra, is favored by some benignant glances from those lights of yours that do mislead the moon. I hope this is not so—bow wow!—ho! ho!—I smell the blood of a rival; and be he great or small, red or black, or of any color in the rainbow, I shall have him for my breakfast—ho! ho! You see now, my most divine Kathleen, what a terrible animal to all rivals and competitors for your affections I shall be; and that if it were only for their own sakes, and to prevent carnage and cannibalism, it will be well for you to banish them once and forever, and be content only with myself.

"Seriously, my dear Kathleen, I believe I am half-crazed; and, if so, you are the sole cause of it. I can think of no other object than your beautiful self; and I need scarcely say, that I shall have neither peace nor happiness unless I shall be fortunate enough to gain a place in your tender bosom. As for the Ahadarra man, I am surprised you should think of such an ignorant clodhopper—a fellow whose place Providence especially allotted to between the stilts of a plough, and at the tail of a pair of horses. Perhaps you would be kind enough to take a walk on Thursday evening, somewhere near the river—where I hope I shall have an opportunity of declaring my affection for you in person. At all events I shall be there with the ardent expectation of meeting you.

"Ever your devoted worshipper,

"Hycy Burke.

"P.S.—Beware the clodhopper—bow wow!—ho! ho!"

On looking at the back of this singular production he was thunderstruck to perceive that it was addressed to "Mr. Bryan M'Mahon, Ahadarra"—the fact being that, in the hurry of the moment, he had misdirected the letters—Bryan M'Mahon having received that which had been intended for Kathleen, who, on the contrary, was pressingly solicited to lend him thirty-fine pounds in order to secure "Crazy Jane."

Having perused this precious production, Hycy, in spite of his chagrin, was not able to control a most irresistible fit of laughter, in which he indulged for some minutes. The mistake being now discovered in Bryan's case was necessarily discovered in that of both, a circumstance which to Hycy, who now fully understood the mature and consequences of his blunder, was, as we have stated, the subject of extraordinary mirth, in which, to tell the truth, Bryan could not prevent himself from joining him.

"Well, but after all, Bryan," said he, "what is there in this letter to make you angry with me? Don't you see it's a piece of humbug from beginning to end."

"I do, and I did," replied Bryan; "but at that time I had never spoken upon the subject of love or marriage to Kathleen Cavanagh, and I had no authority nor right to take any one to task on her account, but, at the same time, I couldn't even then either like or respect, much less lend money to, any man that could humbug her, or treat such a girl with disrespect—and in that letther you can't deny that you did both."

"I grant," said Hycy, "that it was a piece of humbug certainly, but not intended to offend her."

"I'm afraid there was more in it, Hycy," observed Bryan; "an' that if she had been foolish or inexperienced enough to meet you or listen to your discourse, it might a' been worse for herself. You were mistaken there though."

"She is not a girl to be humbugged, I grant, Bryan—very far from it, indeed; and now that you and she understand each other I will go farther for both your sakes, and say, that I regret having written such a letter to such an admirable young woman as she is. To tell you the truth, Bryan, I shall half envy you the possession of such a wife."

"As to that," replied the other, smiling, "we'll keep never minding—but you have spoken fairly and honestly on the subject of the letther, an' I'm thankful to you; still, Hycy, you haven't answered my first question—have you any ill feeling against me, or any intention to injure me?"

"Neither one nor the other. I pledge you my honor and word I have no ill feeling against you, nor any design to injure you."

"That's enough, Hycy," replied his companion; "I think I'm bound to believe your words."

"You are, Bryan; but will you allow me to ask if any one ever told you that I had—and if so, who was the person?"

"It's enough for you to know," said Bryan, "that whoever told it to me I don't believe it."

"I certainly have a right to know," returned Hycy; "but as the matter is false, and every way unfounded, I'll not press you upon it—all I can say to satisfy you is, what I have said already—that I entertain no ill will or unfriendly feeling towards you, and, consequently, can have no earthly intention of doing you an injury even if I could, although at the present moment I don't see how, even if I was willing."

"You have nothing particular that you'd wish to say to me?"

"No: devil a syllable."

"Nor a proposal of any kind to make me?"

Hycy pulled up his horse.

"Bryan, my good friend, let me look at you," he exclaimed. "Is it right to have you at large? My word and honor I'm beginning to fear that there's something wrong with your upper works."

"Never mind," replied Bryan, laughing, "I'm satisfied—the thing's a mistake—so there's my hand to you, Hycy. I've no suspicion of the kind against you and it's all right."

"What proposal, in heaven's name, could I have to make to you?" exclaimed Hycy..

"There now," continued Bryan, "that'll do; didn't I say I was satisfied? Move on, now and overtake your friend—by the way he's a fine horseman, they say?"

"Very few better," said Hycy; "but some there are—and one I know—ha! ha! ha! Good-bye, Bryan, and don't be made a fool of for nothing."

Bryan nodded and laughed, and Hycy dashed on to overtake his friend Clinton.

M'Mahon's way home lay by Gerald Cavanagh's house, near which as he approached he saw Nanny Peety in close conversation with Kate Hogan. The circumstance, knowing their relationship as he did, made no impression whatsoever upon him, nor would he have bestowed a thought upon it, had he been left to his own will in the matter. The women separated ere he had come within three hundred yards of them; Kate, who had evidently been convoying her niece a part of the way, having returned in the direction of Cavanagh's, leaving Nanny to pursue her journey home, by which she necessarily met M'Mahon.

"Well, Nanny," said the latter, "how are you?"

"Faix, very well, I thank you, Bryan; how are all the family in Carriglass?"

"Barring my mother, they're all well, Nanny. I was glad to hear you got so good a place, an' I'm still betther plaised to see you look so well—for it's a proof that you feel comfortable in it."

"Why I can't complain," she replied; "but you know there's no one widout their throubles."

"Troubles, Nanny," said Bryan, with surprise; "why surely, Nanny, barrin' it's love, I don't see what trouble you can have."

"Well, and may be it is," said the girl, smiling.

"Oh, in that case," replied Bryan, "I grant you're to be pitied; poor thing, you look so ill and pale upon it, too. An' what is it like, Nanny—this same love that's on you?"

"Faix," she replied, archly, "it's well for you that Miss Kathleen's not to the fore or you daren't ax any one sich a question as that."

"Well done, Nanny," he returned; "do you think she knows what it's like?"

"It's not me," she replied again, "you ought to be axin' sich a question from; if you don't know it I dunna who ought."

"Begad, you're sharp an' ready, Nanny," replied Bryan, laughing; "well, and how are you all in honest Jemmy Burke's?"

"Some of us good, some of us bad, and some of us indifferent, but, thank goodness, all in the best o' health."

"Good, bad, and indifferent," replied Bryan, pausing a little. "Well, now, Nanny, if one was to ask you who is the good in your family, what would you say?"

"Of coorse myself," she returned; "an' stay—let me see—ay, the masther, honest Jemmy, he and I have the goodness between us."

"And who's the indifferent, Nanny?"

"Wait," she replied; "yes—no doubt of it—if not worse—why the mistress must come in for that, I think."

"And now for the bad, Nanny?"

She shook her head before she spoke. "Ah," she proceeded, "there would be more in that house on the bad list than there is, if he, had his way."

"If who had his way?"

"Masther Hycy."

"Why is he the bad among you?"

"Thank God I know him now," she replied, "an' he knows I do; but he doesn't know how well I know him."

"Why, Nanny, are you in airnest?" asked Bryan, a good deal surprised, and not a little interested at what he heard, "surely I thought Mr. Hycy a good-hearted, generous young fellow that one could depend upon, at all events?"

"Ah, it's little you know him," she replied; "and I could"—she looked at him and paused.

"You could what?" he asked.

"I could tell you something, but I daren't."

"Daren't; why what ought you be afraid of?"

"It's no matther, I daren't an' thats enough; only aren't you an' Kathleen Cavanagh goin' to be married?"

"We will be married, I hope."

"Well, then, keep a sharp look-out, an take care her father an' mother doesn't turn against you some o' these days. There a many a slip between the cup and the lip; that's all I can say, an' more than I ought; an' if you ever mention my name, its murdhered I'll be."

"An' how is Hycy consarned in this? or is he consarned in it?"

"He is, an' he is not; I dursn't tell you more; but I'm not afraid of him, so far from that, I could soon—but what am I sayin'? Good-bye, an' as I said, keep a sharp lookout;" and having uttered these words, she tripped on hastily and left him exceedingly surprised at what she had said.

CHAPTER X.—More of the Hycy Correspondence

A Family Debate—Honest Speculations.

Kathleen's refusal to dance, at the kemp, with Hycy Burke, drew down upon her the loud and vehement indignation of her parents, both of whom looked upon a matrimonial alliance with the Burkes as an object exceedingly desirable, and such as would reflect considerable credit on themselves. Gerald Cavanagh and his wife were certainly persons of the strictest integrity and virtue. Kind, charitable, overflowing with hospitality, and remarkable for the domestic virtues and affections in an extraordinary degree, they were, notwithstanding, extremely weak-minded, and almost silly, in consequence of an over-weening anxiety to procure "great matches" for their children. Indeed it may be observed, that natural affection frequently assumes this shape in the paternal heart, nor is the vain ambition confined to the Irish peasant alone. On the contrary, it may be seen as frequently, if not more so, in the middle and higher classes, where it has ampler scope to work, than in humbler and more virtuous life. It is this proud and ridiculous principle which consigns youth, and beauty, and innocence, to the arms of some dissipated profligate of rank, merely because he happens to inherit a title which he disgraces. There is, we would wager, scarcely an individual who knows the world, but is acquainted with some family laboring under this insane anxiety for connection. Sometimes it is to be found on the paternal side, but, like most of those senseless inconsistencies which entail little else than ridicule or ruin, and sometimes both, upon those who are the object of them, it is, for the most part, a female attribute.

Such as it is, however, our friend, Gerald Cavanagh, and his wife—who, by the way, bore the domestic sceptre in all matters of importance—both possessed it in all its amplitude and vigor. When the kemp had been broken up that night, and the family assembled, Mrs. Cavanagh opened the debate in an oration of great heat and bitterness, but sadly deficient in moderation and logic.

"What on earth could you mane, Kathleen," she proceeded, "to refuse dancin' wid such a young man—a gintleman I ought to say—

as Hycy Burke, the son of the wealthiest man in the whole parish, barring the gentry? Where is the girl that wouldn't bounce at him?—that wouldn't lave a single card unturned to secure him? Won't he have all his father's wealth?—won't he have all his land when the ould man dies? and indeed it's he that will live in jinteel style when he gets everything into his own hands, as he ought to do, an' not go dhramin' an' dhromin' about like his ould father, without bein' sartin whether he's alive or not. He would be something for you, girl, something to turn out wid, an' that one could feel proud out of; but indeed, Kathleen, as for pride and decency, you never had as much o' them as you ought, nor do you hold your head as high as many another girl in your place would do. Deed and throth I'm vexed at you, and ashamed of you, to go for to hurt his feelins as you did, widout either rhyme or raison."

"Troth," said her father, taking up the argument where she left it, "I dunno how I'll look the respectable young man in the face afther the way you insulted him. Why on airth wouldn't you dance wid him?"

"Because, father, I don't like him."

"An' why don't you like him?" asked her mother. "Where is there his aquil for either face or figure in the parish, or the barony itself? But I know the cause of it; you could dance with Bryan M'Mahon. But take this with you—sorra ring ever Bryan M'Mahon will put on you wid my consent or your father's, while there's any hope of Hycy Burke at any rate."

Kathleen, during this long harangue, sat smiling and sedate, turning her beautiful and brilliant eyes sometimes upon one parent, sometimes upon another, and occasionally glancing with imperturbable sweetness and good nature at her sister Hanna. At length, on getting an opportunity of speaking, she replied,—

"Don't ask me, mother, to give anything in the way of encouragement to Hycy Burke; don't ask me, I entrate you, for God's sake—the thing's impossible, and I couldn't do it. I have no wish for his father's money, nor any wish for the poor grandeur that you, mother dear, and my father, seem to set your heart upon. I don't like Hycy Burke—I could never like him; and rather than marry him, I declare solemnly to God, I would prefer going into my grave."

As she uttered the last words, which she did with an earnestness that startled them, her fine features became illuminated, as it were, with a serene and brilliant solemnity of expression that was strikingly impressive and beautiful.

"Why couldn't you like him, now?" asked her father; "sure, as your mother says, there's not his aquil for face or figure within many a mile of him?"

"But it's neither face nor figure that I look to most, father."

"Well, but think of his wealth, and the style he'll live in, I'll go bail, when he gets married."

"That style maybe won't make his wife happy. No, father, it's neither face, nor figure, nor style that I look to, but truth, pure affection, and upright principle; now, I know that Hycy Burke has neither truth, nor affection, nor principle; an' I wondher, besides, that you could think of my ever marrying a man that has already destroyed the happiness of two innocent girls, an' brought desolation, an' sorrow, an' shame upon two happy families. Do you think that I will ever become the wife of a profligate? An' is it you, father, an' still more you, mother, that's a woman, that can urge me to think of joining my fate to that of a man that has neither shame nor principle? I thought that if you didn't respect decency an' truth, and a regard for what is right and proper, that, at all events, you would respect the feelings of your child that was taught their value."

Both parents felt somewhat abashed by the force of the truth and the evident superiority of her character; but in a minute or two her worthy father, from whose dogged obstinacy she inherited the firmness and resolution for which she had ever been remarkable, again returned to the subject.

"If Hycy Burke was wild, Kathleen, so was many a good man before him; an' that's no raison but he may turn out well yet, an' a credit to his name, as I have no doubt he will. All that he did was only folly an' indiscretion—we can't be too hard or uncharitable upon our fellow-craytures."

"No," chimed in her mother, "we can't. Doesn't all the world know that a reformed rake makes a good husband?—an' besides, didn't them two huzzies bring it on themselves?—why didn't they keep from him as they ought? The fault, in such cases, is never all on one side."

Kathleen's brow and face and whole neck became crimson, as her mother, in the worst spirit of a low and degrading ambition, uttered the sentiments we have just written. Hanna had been all this time sitting beside her, with one arm on her shoulder; but Kathleen, now turning round, laid her face on her sister's bosom, and, with a pressure that indicated shame and bitterness of heart, she wept. Hanna returned this melancholy and distressing caress in the same mournful spirit, and both wept together in silence.

Gerald Cavanagh was the first who felt something like shame at the rebuke conveyed by this tearful embrace of his pure-hearted and ingenuous daughters, and he said, addressing his wife:—

"We're wrong to defend him, or any one, for the evil he has done, bekaise it can't be defended; but, in the mane time, every day will bring him more sense an' experience, an' he won't repute this work; besides, a wife would settle him down."

"But, father," said Hanna, now speaking for the first time, "there's one thing that strikes me in the business you're talkin' about, an' it's this—how do you know whether Hycy Burke has any notion, good, bad, or indifferent, of marrying Kathleen?"

"Why," replied her mother, "didn't he write to her upon the subject?"

"Why, indeed, mother, it's not an easy thing to answer that question," replied Hanna. "She sartinly resaved a letther from him, an' indeed, I think," she added, her animated face brightening into a smile, "that as the boys is gone to bed, we had as good read it."

"No, Hanna, darling, don't," said Kathleen—"I beg you won't read it."

"Well, but I beg I will," she replied; "it'll show them, at any rate, what kind of a reformation is likely to come over him. I have it here in my pocket—ay, this is it. Now, father," she proceeded, looking at the letter, "here is a letter, sent to my sister—'To Miss Cavanagh,' that's what's on the back of it—and what do you think Hycy, the sportheen, asks her to do for him?"

"Why, I suppose," replied her mother, "to run away wid him?"

"Na"

"Then to give her consent to marry him?" said her father.

"Both out," replied Hanna; "no, indeed, but to lend him five-and-thirty pounds to buy a mare, called Crazy Jane, belonging to Tom Burton, of the Race Road!"

"'My Dear Bryan—For heaven's sake, in addition to your other generosities—for-which I acknowledge myself still in your debt—will you lend me thirty-five pounds, to secure a beautiful mare belonging to Tom Burton, of the Race Road? She is a perfect creature, and will, if I am not quick, certainly slip through my fingers. Jemmy, the gentleman'—

"This is what he calls his father, you must know.

"'Jemmy, the gentleman, has promised to stand to me some of these days, and pay off all my transgressions, like a good, kind-hearted, soft-headed old Trojan as he is; and, for this reason, I don't wish to press him now. The mare is sold under peculiar circumstances; otherwise I could have no chance of her at such a price. By the way, when did you see Katsey'—

"Ay, Katsey!—think of that, now—doesn't he respect your daughter very much, father?

"'By the way, when did you see Katsey Cavanagh?—'"

"What is this you're readin' to me?" asked her father. "You don't mean to say that this letter is to Kathleen?"

"Why, no; but so much the better—one has an opportunity now of seein' what he is made of. The letter was intended for Bryan M'Mahon; but he sent it, by mistake, to Kathleen. Listen—-

"'When did you see Katsey Cavanagh? She certainly is not ill-looking, and will originate you famous mountaineers. Do, like a good fellow, stand by me at this pinch, and I will drink your health and Kat-sey's, and that you may—' (what's this?) 'col—colonize

Ahadarra with a race of young Colossusses that the world will wonder at.

"'Ever thine,

"'H. Burke.'

"Here's more, though: listen, mother, to your favorite, that you want to marry Kathleen to:—

"'P.S. I will clear scores with you for all in the course of a few months, and remember that, at your marriage, I must, with my own hand, give you away to Katsey, the fair Oolossa.'"

The perusal of this document, at least so far as they could understand it, astonished them not a little. Until they heard it read, both had been of the opinion that Hycy had actually proposed for Kathleen, or at least felt exceedingly anxious for the match.

"An' does he talk about givin' her away to Bryan M'Mahon?" asked her mother. Sorrow on his impidence!—Bryan M'Mahon indeed! Throth, it's not upon his country side of wild mountain that Kathleen will go to live. An' maybe, too, she has little loss in the same Hycy, for, afther all, he's but a skite of a fellow, an' a profligate into the bargain."

"Paix an' his father," said Gerald—"honest Jemmy—tould me that he'd have it a match whether or not."

"His father did!" exclaimed Mrs. Cavanagh; "now, did he say so, Gerald?"

"Well, in troth he did—said that he had I set his heart upon it, an' that if she hadn't a gown to her back he'd make him marry her."

"The Lord direct us for the best!" exclaimed his wife, whose opinion of the matter at this last piece of information had again changed in favor of Hycy. "Sure, afther all, one oughtn't to be too sevare on so young a man. However, as the sayin' is, 'time will tell,' an' Kathleen's own good sense will show her what a match he'd be."

The sisters then retired to bed; but before they went, Kathleen approached her mother, and putting an open palm affectionately upon each of the good woman's cheeks, said, in a voice in which there was deep feeling and affection:—

"Good-night, mother dear! I'm sure you love me, an' I know it is because you do that you spake in this way; but I know, too, that you wouldn't make me unhappy and miserable for the wealth of the world, much less for Hycy Burke's share of it. There's a kiss for you, and good-night!—there's another for you, father; God bless you! and good-night, too. Come, Hanna darling, come!"

In this state matters rested for some time. Bryan M'Mahon, however, soon got an opportunity of disclosing his intentions to Kathleen, if that can be called disclosing, which was tolerably well known for a considerable time previous to the disclosure. Between them it was arranged that he and his father should make a formal proposal of marriage to her parents, as the best means of bringing the matter to a speedy issue. Before this was done, however, Gerald, at the instigation of his wife, contrived once more to introduce the subject as if by accident, in a conversation with Jemmy Burke, who repeated his anxiety for the match as the best way of settling down his son, and added, that he would lay the matter before Hycy himself, with a wish that a union should take place between them. This interview with old Burke proved a stumbling-block in the way of M'Mahon. At length, after a formal proposal on the behalf of Bryan, and many interviews with reference to it, something like a compromise was effected. Kathleen consented to accept the latter in marriage, but firmly and resolutely refused to hear Burke's name as a lover or suitor mentioned. Her parents, however, hoping that their influence over her might ultimately prevail, requested that she would not engage herself to any one for two years, at the expiration of which period, if no change in her sentiments should take place, she was to be at liberty to marry M'Mahon. For the remainder of the summer and autumn, and up until November, the period at which our narrative has now arrived, or, in other words, when Bryan M'Mahon met Nanny Peety, matters had rested precisely in the same position. This unexpected interview with the mendicant's daughter, joined to the hints he had already received, once more caused M'Mahon to feel considerably perplexed with regard to Hycy Burke. The coincidence was very remarkable, and the identity of the information, however limited, appeared to him to deserve all the consideration which he could bestow upon it, but above all things he resolved, if possible, to extract the secret out of Nanny Peety.

One cause of Hycy Burke's extravagance was a hospitable habit of dining and giving dinners in the head inn of Ballymacan. To ask any of his associates to his father's house was only to expose the ignorance of his parents, and this his pride would not suffer him to do. As a matter of course he gave all his dinners, unless upon rare occasions, in Jack Shepherd's excellent inn; but as young Clinton and he were on terms of the most confidential intimacy, he had asked him to dine on the day in question at his father's.

"You know, my dear Harry," he said to his friend, "there is no use in striving to conceal the honest vulgarity of Jemmy the gentleman from you who know it already. I may say ditto to madam, who is unquestionably the most vulgar of the two—for, and I am sorry to say it, in addition to a superabundant stock of vulgarity, she has still a larger assortment of the prides; for instance, pride of wealth, of the purse, pride of—I was going to add, birth—ha! ha! ha!—of person, ay, of beauty, if you please—of her large possessions—but that comes under the purse again—and lastly—but that is the only well-founded principle among them—of her accomplished son, Hycy. This, now, being all within your cognizance already, my dear Hal, you take a pig's cheek and a fowl with me to-day. There will be nobody but ourselves, for when I see company at home I neither admit the gentleman nor the lady to table. Damn it, you know the thing would be impossible. If you wish it, however, we shall probably call in the gentleman after dinner to have a quiz with him; it may relieve us. I can promise you a glass of wine, too, and that's another reason why we should keep him aloof until the punch comes. The wine's always a *sub silencio* affair, and, may heaven pity me, I get growling enough from old Bruin on other subjects."

"Anything you wish, Hycy, I am your man; but somehow I don't relish the idea of the quiz you speak of. 'Children, obey your parents,' says Holy Scripture; and I'd as soon not help a young fellow to laugh at his father."

"A devilish good subject he is, though—but you must know that I can draw just distinctions, Hal. For instance, I respect his honesty—"

"And copy it, eh?"

"Certainly—I respect his integrity, too—in fact, I appreciate all his good qualities, and only laugh at his vulgarity and foibles."

"You intend to marry, Hycy?"

"Or, in other words, to call you brother some of these days."

"And to have sons and daughters?"

"Please the fates."

"That will do," replied Clinton, dryly.

"Ho! ho!" said Hycy, "I see. Here's a mentor with a vengeance—a fellow with a budget of morals cut and dry for immediate use—but hang all morality, say I; like some of my friends that talk on the subject, I have an idiosyncrasy of constitution against it, but an abundant temperament for pleasure."

"That's a good definition," said Clinton; "a master-touch, a very correct likeness, indeed. I would at once know you from it, and so would most of your friends."

"This day is Friday," said Hycy, "more growling."

"Why so?"

"Why, when I eat meat on a Friday, the pepper and sauce cost me nothing. The 'gentlemen' lays on hard, but the lady extenuates, 'in regard to it's bein' jinteel.'"

"Well, but you have certainly no scruple yourself on the subject?"

"Yes, I have, sir, a very strong one—in favor of the meat—ha! ha! ha!"

"D—n me, whoever christened you Hycy the accomplished, hit you off."

"I did myself; because you must know, my worthy Hal, that, along with all my other accomplishments, I am my own priest.'

"And that is the reason why you hate the clergy? eh—ha! ha! ha!"

"A hit, a hit, I do confess."

"Harke, Mr. Priest, will you give absolution—to Tom Corbet?"

"Ah! Hal, no more an' thou lovest me—that sore is yet open. Curse the villain. My word and honor, Hal, the gentleman' was right there. He told me at the first glance what she was. Here comes a shower, let us move on, and reach Ballymacan, if possible, before it falls. We shall be home in fair time for dinner afterwards, and then for my proposal, which, by the word and honor—"

"And morality?"

"Nonsense, Harry; is a man to speak nothing but truth or Scripture in this world?—No—which I say by the honor of a gentleman, it will be your interest to consider and accept."

"Very well, most accomplished. We shall see, and we shall hear, and then we shall determine."

A ham and turkey were substituted for the pig's cheek and fowl, and we need not say that Hycy and his friend accepted of the substitution with great complacency. Dinner having been discussed, and a bottle of wine finished, the punch came in, and each, after making himself a stiff tumbler, acknowledged that he felt comfortable. Hycy, however, anxious that he should make an impression, or in other words gain his point, allowed Clinton to grow a little warm with liquor before he opened the subject to which he had alluded. At length, when he had reached the proper elevation, he began:—

"There's no man, my dear Harry, speaks apparently more nonsense than I do in ordinary chat and conversation. For instance, to-day I was very successful in it; but no matter, I hate seriousness, certainly, when there is no necessity for it. However, as a set-off to that, I pledge you my honor that no man can be more serious when it is necessary than myself. For instance, you let out a matter to me the other night that you probably forget now. You needn't stare—I am serious enough and honorable enough to keep as an inviolable secret everything of the kind that a man may happen to disclose in an unguarded moment."

"Go on, Hycy, I don't forget it—I don't, upon my soul."

"I allude to M'Mahon's farm in Ahadarra."

"I don't forget it; but you know, Hycy, my boy, I didn't mention either M'Mahon or Ahadarra."

"You certainly did not mention them exactly; but, do you think I did not know at once both the place and the party you allude to? My word and honor, I saw them at a glance."

"Very well, go on with your word and honor;—you are right, I did mean M'Mahon and Ahadarra—proceed, most accomplished, and most moral—"

"Be quiet, Harry. Well, you have your eye upon that farm, and you say you have a promise of it."

"Something like it; but the d—d landlord, Chevydale, is impracticable—so my uncle says—and doesn't wish to disturb the M'Mahons, although he has been shown that it is his interest to do so—but d—n the fellow, neither he nor one of his family ever look to their interests—d—n the fellow, I say."

"Don't curse or swear, most moral. Well, the lease of Ahadarra has dropped, and of Carriglass too;—with Carriglass, however, we—that is you—have nothing at all to do."

"Proceed?'

"Now, I have already told you my affection for your sister, and I have not been able to get either yes or no out of you."

"No."

"What do you mean?"

"That you have not been able to get yes or no out of me—proceed, most accomplished. Where do you get your brandy? This is glorious. Well!"

"Now, as you have a scruple against taking the farm in any but a decent way, if I undertake to manage matters so as that Bryan M'Mahon shall be obliged to give up his farm, will you support my suit with Miss Clinton?"

"How will you do it?"

"That is what you shall not know; but the means are amply within my power. You know my circumstances, and that I shall inherit all my father's property."

"Come; I shall hold myself neuter—will that satisfy you? You shall have a clear stage and no favor, which, if you be a man of spirit, is enough."

"Yes; but it is likely I may require your advocacy with Uncle; and, besides, I know the advantage of having an absent friend well and favorably spoken of, and all his good points brought out."

"Crazy Jane and Tom Burton, to wit; proceed, most ingenuous!"

"Curse them both! Will you promise this—to support me so far?"

"Egad, Hycy, that's a devilish pretty girl that attends us with the hot water, and that waited on us at dinner—eh?"

"Come, come, Master Harry, 'ware spring-guns there; keep quiet. You don't answer?"

"But, worthy Hycy, what if Maria should reject you—discard you—give you to the winds?—eh?"

"Even in that case, provided you support me honestly, I shall hold myself bound to keep my engagement with you, and put M'Mahon out as a beggar."

"What! as a beggar?"

"Ay, as a beggar; and then no blame could possibly attach to you for succeeding him, and certainly no suspicion."

"Hum! as a beggar. But the poor fellow never offended me. Confound it, he never offended me, nor any one else as far as I know. I don't much relish that, Hycy."

"It cannot be done though in any other way."

"I say—how do you call that girl?—Jenny, or Peggy, or Molly, or what?"

"I wish to heaven you could be serious, Harry. If not, I shall drop the subject altogether."

"There now—proceed, O Hyacinthus."

"How can I proceed, when you won't pay attention to me; or, what is more, to your own interests?"

"Oh! my own interests!—well I am alive to them."

"Is it a bargain, then?"

"It is a bargain, most ingenuous, most subtle, and most conscientious Hycy! Enable me to enter upon the farm of Ahadarra—to get possession of it—and calculate upon my most—let me see—what's the best word—most strenuous advocacy. That's it: there's my hand upon it. I shall support you, Hycy; but, at the same time, you must not hold me accountable for my sister's conduct. Beyond fair and reasonable persuasion, she must be left perfectly free and uncontrolled in whatever decision she may come to."

"There's my hand, then, Harry; I can ask no more."

After Clinton had gone, Hycy felt considerably puzzled as to the manner in which he had conducted himself during the whole evening. Sometimes he imagined he was under the influence of liquor, for he had drunk pretty freely; and again it struck him that he manifested an indifference to the proposal made to him, which he only attempted to conceal lest Hycy might perceive it. He thought, however, that he observed a seriousness in Clinton, towards the close of their conversation, which could not have been assumed; and as he gave himself a good deal of credit for penetration, he felt satisfied that circumstances were in a proper train, and likely, by a little management, to work out his purposes.

Hycy, having bade him good night at the hall-door, returned again to the parlor, and called Nanny Peety—"Nanny," said he, "which of the Hogans did you see to-day?"

"None o' them, sir, barrin' Kate: they wor all out."

"Did you give her the message?"

"Why, sir, if it can be called a message, I did."

"What did you say, now?"

"Why, I tould her to tell whichever o' them she happened to see first, that St. Pether was dead."

"And what did she say to that?"

"Why, sir, she said it would be a good story for you if he was."

"And what did she mean by that, do you think?"

"Faix, then, I dunna—barrin' that you're in the black books wid him, and that you'd have a better chance of gettin' in undher a stranger that didn't know you."

"Nanny," he replied, laughing, "you are certainly a very smart girl, and indeed a very pretty girl—a very interesting young woman, indeed, Nanny; but you won't listen to reason."

"To raison, sir, I'll always listen; but not to wickedness or evil."

"Will you have a glass of punch? I hope there is neither wickedness nor evil in that."

"I'm afraid, sir, that girls like me have often found to their cost too much of both in it. Thank you, Masther Hycy, but I won't have it; you know I won't."

"So you will stand in your own light, Nanny?"

"I hope not, sir; and, wanst for all, Mr. Hycy, there's no use in spakin' to me as you do. I'm a poor humble girl, an' has nothing but my character to look to."

"And is that all you're afraid of, Nanny?"

"I'm afear'd of Almighty God, sir: an' if you had a little fear of Him, too, Mr. Hycy, you wouldn't spake to me as you do."

"Why, Nanny, you're almost a saint on our hands."

"I'm glad to hear it, sir, for the sinners is plenty enough."

"Very good, Nanny; well said. Here's half a crown to reward your wit."

"No, no, Mr. Hycy: I'm thankful to you; but you know I won't take it."

"Nanny, are you aware that it was I who caused you to be taken into this family?"

"No," sir; "but I think it's very likely you'll be the cause of my going out of it."

"It certainly is not improbable, Nanny. I will have no self-willed, impracticable girls here."

"You won't have me here long, then, unless you mend your manners, Mr. Hycy."

"Well, well, Nanny; let us not quarrel at all events. I will be late out to-night, so that you must sit up and let me in. No, no, Nanny, we must not quarrel; and if I have got fond of you, how can I help it? It's very natural thing, you know, to love a pretty girl."

"But not so natural to lave her, Mr. Hycy, as you have left others before now—I needn't name them—widout name, or fame, or hope, or happiness in this world."

"I won't be in until late, Nanny," he replied, coolly. "Sit up for me. You're a sharp one, but I can't spare you yet a while;" and, having nodded to her with a remarkably benign aspect he went out.

"Ay," said she, after he had gone; "little you know, you hardened and heartless profligate, how well I'm up to your schemes. Little you know that I heard your bargain this evenin' wid Clinton, and that you're now gone to meet the Hogans and Teddy Phats upon some dark business, that can't be good or they wouldn't be in it; an' little you know what I know besides. Anybody the misthress plaises may sit up for you, but I won't."

CHAPTEE XI.—Death of a Virtuous Mother.

It could not be expected that Bryan M'Mahon, on his way home from Fethertonge's, would pass Gerald Cavanagh's without calling. He had, in his interview with that gentleman, stated the nature of his mother's illness, but at the same time without feeling any serious apprehensions that her life was in immediate danger. On reaching Cavanagh's, he found that family over-+shadowed with a gloom for which he could not account. Kathleen received him gravely, and even Hanna had not her accustomed jest. After looking around him for a little, he exclaimed—"What is the matter? Is anything wrong? You all look as if you were in sorrow."

Hanna approached him and said, whilst her eyes filled with tears—"We are in sorrow, Bryan; for we are goin', we doubt, to lose a friend that we all love—as every one did that knew her."

"Hanna, darling," said Kathleen, "this won't do. Poor girl! you are likely to make bad worse; and besides there may, after all, be no real danger. Your mother, Bryan," she proceeded, "is much worse than she has been. The priest and doctor have been sent for; but you know it doesn't follow that there is danger, or at any rate that the case is hopeless."

"Oh, my God!" exclaimed Bryan, "is it so? My mother—and such a mother! Kathleen, my heart this minute tells me it is hopeless. I must leave you—I must go."

"We will go up with you," said Kathleen. "Hanna, we will go up; for, if she is in danger, I would like to get the blessing of such a woman before she dies; but let us trust in G-od she won't die, and that it's only a sudden attack that will pass away."

"Do so, Kathleen," said her mother; "and you can fetch us word how she is. May the Lord bring her safe over it at any rate; for surely the family will break their hearts afther her, an' no wondher, for where was her fellow?"

Bryan was not capable of hearing these praises, which he knew to be so well and so justly her due, with firmness; nor could he prevent his tears, unless by a great effort, from bearing testimony to the depth of his grief. Kathleen's gaze, however, was turned on him with an expression which gave him strength; for indeed there was something noble and. sustaining in the earnest and consoling sympathy which he read in her dark and glorious eye. On their way to Carriglass there was little spoken. Bryan's eye every now and then sought that of Kathleen; and he learned, for the first time, that it is only in affliction that the exquisite tenderness of true and disinterested love can be properly appreciated and felt. Indeed he wondered at his own sensations; for in proportion as his heart became alarmed at the contemplation of his mother's loss, he felt, whenever he looked upon Kathleen, that it also burned towards her with greater tenderness and power—so true is it that sorrow and suffering purify and exalt all our nobler and better emotions.

Bryan and his companions, ere they had time to reach the house, were seen and. recognized by the family, who, from the restlessness and uncertainty which illness usually occasions, kept moving about and running out from time to time to watch the arrival of the priest or doctor. On this occasion Dora came to meet them; but, alas! with what a different spirit from that which animated her on the return of her father from the metropolis. Her gait was now slow, her step languid; and they could perceive that, as she approached them, she wiped away the tears. Indeed her whole appearance was indicative of the state of her mother; when they met her, her bitter sobbing and the sorrowful earnestness of manner with which she embraced the sisters, wore melancholy assurances that the condition of the sufferer was not improved. Hanna joined her tears with hers; but Kathleen, whose sweet voice in attempting to give the affectionate girl consolation, was more than once almost shaken out of its firmness, did all she could to soothe and relieve her.

On entering the house, they found a number of the neighboring females assembled, and indeed the whole family, in consequence of the alarm and agitation visible them, might not inaptly be compared to a brood of domestic fowl when a hawk, bent on destruction, is seen hovering over their heads.

As is usual with Catholic families in their state of life, there were several of those assembled, and also some of themselves, at joint prayer in different parts of the house; and seated by her bedside was her youngest son, Art, engaged, with sobbing voice and eyes every now and then blinded with tears, in the perusal, for her comfort, of Prayers for the Sick. Tom M'Mahon himself went about every now and then clasping his hands, and turning up his eyes to heaven in a distracted manner, exclaiming—"Oh! Bridget, Bridget, is it come to this at last! And you're lavin' me—you're lavin' me! Oh, my God! what will I do—how will I live, an' what will become of me!"

On seeing Bryan, he ran to him and said,—"Oh! Bryan, to what point will I turn?—where will I get consolation?—how will I bear it? Sure, she was like a blessin' from heaven among us; ever full of peace, and charity, and goodness—the kind word an' the sweet smile to all; but to me—to me—oh! Bridget, Bridget, I'd rather die than live afther you!"

"Father, dear, your takin' it too much to heart," replied Bryan; "who knows but God may spare her to us still? But you know that even if it's His will to remove her from amongst us"—his voice here failed him for a moment—"hem—to remove her from amongst us, it's our duty to submit to it; but I hope in God she may recover still. Don't give way to sich grief till we hear what the docthor will say, at all events. How did she complain or get ill; for I think she wasn't worse when I left home?"

"It's all in her stomach," replied his father. "She was seized wid cramps in her stomach, an' she complains very much of her head; but her whole strength is gone, she can hardly spake, and she has death in her face."

At this moment his brother Michael came to them, and said— "Bryan—Bryan"—but he could proceed no farther.

"Whisht, Michael," said the other; "this is a shame; instead of supportin' and cheer-in' my father, you're only doing him harm. I tell you all that you'll find there's no raison for this great grief. Be a man, Michael—"

"She has heard your voice," proceeded his brother, "and wishes to see you."

This proof of her affection for him, at the very moment when he was attempting to console others, was almost more than he could bear.

Bryan knew that he himself had been her favorite son, so far as a heart overflowing with kindness and all the tender emotions that consecrate domestic life and make up its happiness, could be said to have a favorite. There was, however, that almost imperceptible partiality, which rarely made its appearance unless in some slight and inconsiderable circumstances, but which, for that very reason, was valuable in proportion to its delicacy and the caution with which it was guarded. Always indeed in some quiet and inoffensive shape was the partiality she bore him observable; and sometimes it consisted in a postponement of his wishes or comforts to those of her other children, because she felt that she might do with him that which she could not with the others—thus calculating as it were upon his greater affection. But it is wonderful to reflect in how many ways, and through what ingenious devices the human heart can exhibit its tenderness.

Arthur, as Bryan entered, had concluded the devotions he had been reading for her, and relinquished to him the chair he had occupied. On approaching, he was at once struck by the awful change for the worse, which so very brief a period had impressed upon her features. On leaving home that morning she appeared to be comparatively strong, and not further diminished in flesh than a short uneasy ailment might naturally occasion. But now her face, pallid and absolutely emaciated, had shrunk into half its size, and was, beyond all possibility of hope or doubt, stamped with the unequivocal impress of death.

Bryan, in a state which it is impossible to describe and very difficult to conceive, took her hand, and after a short glance at her features, now so full of ghastliness and the debility which had struck her down, he stooped, and, kissing her lips, burst out into wild and irrepressible sorrow.

"Bryan, dear," she said, after a pause, and when his grief had somewhat subsided, "why will you give way to this? Sure it was on you I placed my dependence—I hoped that, instead of settin' the rest an example for weakness, you'd set them one that they might and ought to follow—I sent for you, Bryan, to make it my request that, if it's the will of God to take me from among you, you might support an' console the others, an' especially your poor father; for I needn't tell you that along wid the pain I'm bearin', my heart is sore and full o sorrow for what I know he'll suffer when I'm gone. May the Lord pity and give him strength! —for I can say on my dyin' bed that, from the first day I ever seen his face until now, he never gave me a harsh word or an unkind look, an' that you all know."

"Oh how could he, mother dear? how could any one give you that? Who was it that ever knew you could trate you with anything but respect and affection?"

"I hope I always struv to do my duty, Bryan, towards God an' my childre', and my fellow-creatures; an' for that raison I'm not frightened at death. An', Bryan, listen to the words of your dyin' mother—"

"Oh, don't say that yet, mother," replied her son, sobbing; "don't say so yet; who knows but God will spare your life, an' that you may be many years with us still; they're all alarmed too much, I hope; but it's no wondher we should, mother dear, when there's any appearance at all of danger about you."

"Well, whether or not, Bryan, the advice I'm goin' to give you is never out o' saison. Live always with the fear of God in your heart; do nothing that you think will displease Him; love your fellow-creatures—serve them and relieve their wants an' distresses as far as you're able; be like your own father—kind and good to all about you, not neglectin' your religious duties. Do this, Bryan, an' then when the hour o' death comes, you'll feel a comfort an' happiness in your heart that neither the world nor anything in it can give you. You'll feel the peace of God there, an' you will die happy—happy."

Her spirit, animated by the purity and religious truth of this simple but beautiful morality, kindled into pious fervor as she proceeded, so much so indeed, that on turning her eyes towards heaven, whilst she uttered the last words, they sparkled with the mild and serene light of that simple but unconscious enthusiasm on behalf of all goodness which had characterized her whole life, and which indeed is a living principle among thousands of her humble countrywomen.

"This, dear Bryan, is the advice I gave to them all; it an' my love is the only legacy I have to lave them. An' my darlin' Dora, Bryan—oh, if you be kind and tendher to any one o' them beyant another, be so to her. My darlin' Dora! Oh! her heart's all affection, an' kindness, an' generosity. But indeed, as I said, Bryan, the task must fall to you to strengthen and console every one o' them. Ay!—an' you must begin now. You wor ever, ever, a good son; an' may God keep you in the right faith, an' may my blessin' an' His be wid you for ever! Amin."

There was a solemn and sustaining spirit in her words which strengthened Bryan, who, besides, felt anxious to accomplish to the utmost extent the affectionate purpose which had caused her to send for him.

"It's a hard task, mother darlin," he replied; "but I'll endeavor, with God's help, to let them see that I haven't been your son for nothing; but you don't know, mother, that Kathleen's here, an' Hanna. They wish to see you, an' to get your blessin'."

"Bring them in," she replied, "an' let Dora come wid them, an' stay yourself, Bryan, becaise I'm but weak, an' I don't wish that they should stay too long. God sees its not for want of love for the other girls that I don't bid you bring them in, but that I don't wish to see them sufferin' too much sorrow; but my darlin' Dora will expect to be where Kathleen is, an' my own eyes likes to look upon her, an' upon Kathleen, too, Bryan, for I feel my heart bound to her as if she was one of ourselves, as I hope she will be."

"Oh, bless her! bless her! mother," he said, with difficulty, "an' tell her them words—say them to herself. I'll go now and bring them in."

He paused, however, for a minute or two, in order to compose his voice and features, that he might not seem to set them an example of weakness, after which he left the apartment with an appearance of greater composure than he really felt.

In a few minutes the four returned: Bryan, with Kathleen's hand locked in his, and Hanna, with her arm affectionately wreathed about Dora's neck, as if the good-hearted girl felt anxious to cherish and comfort her under the heavy calamity to which she was about to be exposed, for Dora wept bitterly. Mrs. M'Mahon signed to Hanna to approach, who, with her characteristic ardor of feeling, now burst into tears herself, and stooping down kissed her and wept aloud, whilst Dora's grief also burst out afresh.

The sick woman looked at Bryan, as if to solicit his interference, and the look was immediately understood by Kathleen as well as by himself.

"This is very wrong of you, Hanna," said her sister; "out of affection and pity to them, you ought to endeavor to act otherwise. They have enough, an' to much, to feel, without your setting them example; and, Dora dear, I thought you had more courage than you have. All this is only grieving and disturbing your mother; an' I hope that, for her sake, you'll both avoid it. I know it's hard to do so, but it's the difficulty and the trial that calls upon us to have strength, otherwise what are we better than them that we'd condemn or think little of for their own weakness."

The truth and moral force of the words, and the firmness of manner that marked Kathleen as she spoke, were immediately successful. The grief of the two girls was at once hushed; and, after a slight pause, Mrs. M'Mahon called Kathleen to her.

"Dear Kathleen," she said, "I did hope to see the day when you'd be one of my own family, but it's not the will of God, it appears, that I should; however, may His will be done! I hope still that day will come, an' that your friends won't have any longer an objection to your marriage wid Bryan. I am his mother, an' no one has a better right to know his heart an' his temper, an' I can say, upon my dyin' bed, that a better heart an' a better temper never was in man. I believe, Kathleen, it was never known that a good son ever made a bad husband. However, if it's God's will to bring you together, He will, and if it isn't, you must only bear it patiently."

Bryan was silent, but his eye, from time to time, turned with a long glance of love and sorrow upon Kathleen, whose complexion became pale and red by turns. At length Dora, after her mother had concluded, went over to Kathleen, and putting her arms around her neck, exclaimed, "Oh! mother dear, something tells me that Kathleen will be my sisther yet, an' if you'd ask her to promise—"

Kathleen looked down upon the beautiful and expressive features of the affectionate girl, and gently raising her hand she placed it upon Dora's lips, in order to prevent the completion of the sentence. On doing so she received a sorrowful glance of deep and imploring entreaty from Bryan, which she returned with another that seemed to reprove him for doubting her affection, or supposing that such a promise was even necessary. "No, Dora dear," she said, "I could make no promise without the knowledge of my father and mother, or contrary to their wishes; but did you think, darling, that such a thing was necessary?" She kissed the sweet girl as she spoke, and Dora felt a tear on her cheek that was not her own.

Mrs. M'Mahon had been looking with a kind of mournful admiration upon Kathleen during this little incident, and then proceeded. "She says what is right and true; and it would be wrong, my poor child, to ask her to give such a promise. Bryan, thry an' be worthy of that girl—oh, do! an' if you ever get her, you'll have raison to thank God for one of the best gifts He ever gave to man. Hanna, come here—come to me—let me put my hand upon your head. May my blessin' and God's blessin' rest upon you for ever more. There now, be stout, acushla machree." Hanna kissed her again, but her grief was silent; and Dora, fearing she might not be able to restrain it, took her away.

"Now," proceeded the dying woman, "come to me, you Kathleen, my daughter—sure you're the daughter of my heart, as it is. Kneel down and stay with me awhile. Why does my heart warm to you as it never did to any one out o' my own family? Why do I love you as if you were my own child? Because I hope you will be so. Kiss me, asthore machree."

Kathleen kissed her, and for a few moments Mrs. M'Mahon felt a shower of warm tears upon her face, accompanied by a gentle and caressing pressure, that seemed to corroborate and return the hope she had just expressed. Kathleen hastily wiped away her tears, however, and once more resuming her firmness, awaited the expected blessing.

"Now, Kathleen dear, for fear any one might say that at my dyin' hour, I endeavored to take any unfair advantage of your feelings for my son, listen to me—love him as you may, and as I know you do."

"Why should I deny it?" said Kathleen, "I do love him."

"I know, darlin', you do, but for all that, go not agin the will and wishes of your parents and friends; that's my last advice to you."

She then placed her hand upon her head, and in words breathing of piety and affection, she invoked many a blessing upon her, and upon any that was clear to her in life, after which both Bryan and Kathleen left her to the rest which she now required so much.

The last hour had been an interval from pain with Mrs. M'Mahon. In the course of the day both the priest and the doctor arrived, and she appeared somewhat better. The doctor, however, prepared them for the worst, and in confirmation of his opinion, the spasms returned with dreadful violence, and in the lapse of two hours after his visit, this pious and virtuous woman, after suffering unexampled agony with a patience and fortitude that could not be surpassed, expired in the midst of her afflicted family.

It often happens in domestic life, that in cases where long and undisturbed affection is for the first time deprived of its object by death, there supervenes upon the sorrow of many, a feeling of awful sympathy with that individual whose love for the object has been, the greatest, and whose loss is of course the most irreparable. So was it with the M'Mahons. Thomas M'Mahon himself could not bear to witness the sufferings of his wife, nor to hear her moans. He accordingly left the house, and walked about the garden and farm-yard, in a state little short of actual distraction. When the last scene was over, and her actual sufferings closed for ever, the outrage of grief among his children became almost hushed from a dread of witnessing the sufferings of their father; and for the time a great portion of their own sorrow was merged in what they felt for him. Nor was this feeling confined to themselves. His neighbors and acquaintances, on hearing of Mrs. M'Mahon's death, almost all exclaimed:—

"Oh, what will become of him? they are nothing an will forget her soon, as is natural, well as they loved her; but poor Tom, oh! what on earth will become of him?" Every eye, however, now turned toward Bryan, who was the only one of the family possessed of courage enough to undertake the task of breaking the heart-rending intelligence to their bereaved father.

"It must be done," he said, "and the sooner it's done the better; what would I give to have my darlin' Kathleen here. Her eye and her advice would give me the strength that I stand so much in need of.

My God, how will I meet him, or break the sorrowful tidings to him at all! The Lord support me!"

"Ah, but Bryan," said they, "you know he looks up to whatever you say, and how much he is advised by you, if there happens to be a doubt about anything. Except her that's gone, there was no one—"

Bryan raised his hand with an expression of resolution and something like despair, in order as well as he could to intimate to them, that he wished to hear no allusion made to her whom they had lost, or that he must become incapacitated to perform the task he had to encounter, and taking his hat he proceeded to find his father, whom he met behind the garden.

It may be observed of deep grief, that whenever it is excited by the loss of what is good and virtuous, it is never a solitary passion, we mean within the circle of domestic life. So far from that, there is not a kindred affection under the influence of a virtuous heart, that is not stimulated, and strengthened by its emotions. How often, for instance, have two members of the same family rushed into each other's arms, when struck by a common sense of the loss of some individual that was dear to both, because it was felt that the very fact of loving the same object had now made them dear to each other.

The father, on seeing Bryan approach, stood for a few moments and looked at him eagerly; he then approached him with a hasty and unsettled step, and said, "Bryan, Bryan, I see it in your face, she has left us, she has left us, she has left us all, an' she has left me; an' how am I to live without her? answer me that; an then give me consolation if you can."

He threw himself on his son's neck, and by a melancholy ingenuity attempted to seduce him as it were from the firmness which he appeared to preserve in the discharge of this sorrowful task, with a hope that he might countenance him in the excess of his grief—"Oh," he added, "I've have lost her, Bryan—you and I, the two that she— that—she—Your word was everything to her, a law to her; and she was so proud out of you—I an' her eye would rest upon you smilin', as much as to say—there's my son, haven't I a right to feel proud of him, for he has never once vexed his mother's heart? nayther did you, Bryan, nayther did you, but now who will praise you as she

The Emigrants of Ahadarra

did? who will boast of you behind your back, for she seldom did it to your face; and now that smile of love and kindness will never be on her blessed lips more. Sure you won't blame me, Bryan—oh, sure above all men livin', you won't blame me for feelin' her loss as I do."

The associations excited by the language of his father were such as Bryan was by no means prepared to meet. Still he concentrated all his moral power and resolution in order to accomplish the task he had undertaken, which, indeed, was not so much to announce his mother's death, as to support his father under it. After a, violent effort, he at length said:—

"Are you sorry, father, because God has taken my mother to Himself? Would you wish to have her here, in pain and suffering? Do you grudge her heaven? Father, you were always a brave and strong, fearless man, but what are you now? Is this the example you are settin' to us, who ought to look up to you for support? Don't you know my mother's in heaven? Why, one would think you're sorry for it? Come, come, father, set your childre' an example now when they want it, that they can look up to—be a man, and don't forget that she's in God's Glory, Come in now, and comfort the rest."

"Ay, but when I think of what she was, Bryan; of what she was to me, Bryan, from the first day I ever called her my wife, ay, and before it, when she could get better matches, when she struggled, and waited, and fought for me, against all opposition, till her father an' mother saw her heart was fixed upon me; hould your tongue, Bryan, I'll have no one' to stop my grief for her, where is she? where's my wife, I tell you? where's Bridget M'Mahon?—Bridget, where are you? have you left me, gone from me, an' must I live here widout you? must I rise in the mornin,' and neither see you nor hear you? or must I live here by myself an' never have your opinion nor advice to ask upon anything as I used to do—Bridget M'Mahon, why did you leave me? where are you from me?"

"Here's Dora," said a sweet but broken voice; "here's Dora M'Mahon—your own Dora, too—and that you love bekaise I was like her. Oh, come with me, father, darlin'. For her sake, compose yourself and come with me. Oh, what are we to feel! wasn't she our mother? Wasn't she?—wasn't she? What am I sayin'? Ay, but, now—we have no mother, now!"

The Emigrants of Ahadarra

M'Mahon still leaned upon his son's neck, but on hearing his favorite daughter's voice, he put his arm round to where she stood, and clasping her in, brought her close to him and Bryan, so that the three individuals formed one sorrowing group together.

"Father," repeated Dora, "come with me for my mother's sake."

He started. "What's that you say, Dora? For your mother's sake? I will, darlin'—for her sake, I will. Ay, that's the way to manage me—for her sake. Oh, what wouldn't I do for her sake? Come, then, God bless you, darlin', for puttin' that into my head. You may make me do anything now, Dora, jewel—if you just ax it for her sake. Oh, my God! an is it come to this? An' am I talkin' this way?—but—well, for her sake, darlin'—for her sake. Come, I'll go in—but—but—oh, Bryan, how can I?"

"You know father," replied Bryan, who now held his arm, "we must all die, and it will be well for us if we can die as she died. Didn't father Peter say that if ever the light of heaven was in a human heart, it was in hers?"

"Ay, but when I go in an' look upon her, an' call Bridget, she won't answer me."

"Father dear, you are takin' it too much to heart."

"Well, it'll be the first time she ever refused to answer me—the first time that ever her lips will be silent when I spake to her."

"But, father," said the sweet girl at his side, "think of me. Sure I'll be your Dora more than ever, now. You know what you promised me this minute. Oh, for her sake, and for God's sake, then, don't take it so much to heart. It was my grandfather sent me to you, an' he says he want's to see you, an' to spake to you."

"Oh!" he exclaimed, "My poor father, an' he won't be long afther her. But this is the way wid all, Bryan—the way o' the world itself. We must go. I didn't care, now, how soon I followed her. Oh, no, no."

"Don't say so, father; think of the family you have; think of how you love them, and how they love you, father dear. Don't give way so much to this sorrow. I know it's hard to bid you not to do it; but you know we must strive to overcome ourselves. I hope there's happy days and years before us still. We'll have our leases soon, you know, an' then we'll feel firm and comfortable: an' you know you'll be—we'll all be near where she sleeps."

"Where she sleeps. Well, there's comfort in that, Bryan—there's comfort in that."

The old man, though very feeble, on seeing him approach, rose up and met him. "Tom," said he, "be a man, and don't shame my white hairs nor your own. I lost your mother, an' I was as fond of her, an' had as good a right, too, as ever you were of her that's now an angel in heaven; but if I lost her, I bore it as a man ought. I never yet bid you do a thing that you didn't do, but I now bid you stop cryin', an don't fly in the face o' God as you're doin'. You respect my white hairs, an' God will help you as he has done!"

The venerable appearance of the old man, the melancholy but tremulous earnestness with which he spoke, and the placid spirit of submission which touched his whole bearing with the light of an inward piety that no age could dim or overshadow, all combined to work a salutary influence upon M'Mahon. He evidently made a great effort at composure, nor without success. His grief became calm; he paid attention to other matters, and by the aid of Bryan, and from an anxiety lest he should disturb or offend his father by any further excess of sorrow, he was enabled to preserve a greater degree of composure than might have been expected.

CHAPTER XII.—Hycy Concerts a Plot and is urged to Marry.

The Hogans, who seldom missed a Wake, Dance, Cockfight or any other place of amusement or tumult, were not present, we need scarcely assure our readers, at the wake-house of Mrs. M'Mahon. On that night they and Teddy Phats were all sitting in their usual domicile, the kiln, already mentioned, expecting Hycy, when the following brief dialogue took place, previous to his appearance:

"What keeps this lad, Hycy?" said Bat; "an' a complate lad is in his coat, when he has it on him. Troth I have my doubts whether this same gentleman is to be depended on."

"Gentleman, indeed," exclaimed Philip, "nothing short of that will sarve him, shure. To be depinded on, Bat! Why, thin, its more than I'd like to say. Howanever, he's as far in, an' farther than we are."

"There's no use in our quarrelin' wid him," said Phats, in his natural manner. "If he's in our power, we're in his; an' you know he could soon make the counthry too hot to hold us. Along wid all, too, he's as revengeful as the dioule himself, if not a thrifle more so."

"If he an' Kathleen gets bothered together," said Philip, "'twould be a good look up for us, at any rate."

Kate Hogan was the only female present, the truth being that Philip and Ned were both widowers, owing, it was generally believed, to the brutal treatment which their unfortunate wives received at their hands.

"Don't quarrel wid him," said she, "if you can, at any rate, till we get him more in our power, an' that he'll be soon, maybe. If we fall out wid him, we'd have to lave the place, an' maybe to go farther than we intend, too. Wherever we went over the province, this you know was our headquarters. Here's where all belongin' to us—I mane that ever died a natural death, or drew their last breath in the counthry—rests, an' I'd not like to go far from it."

"Let what will happen," said Philip, with an oath, "I'd lose my right arm before Bryan M'Mahon puts a ring on Kathleen."

"I can tell you that Hycy has no notion of marryin' her, thin," said Kate.

"How do you know that?" asked her husband.

"I've a little bird that tells me," she replied.

"Gerald Cavanagh an' his wife doesn't think so," said Philip. "They and Jemmy Burke has the match nearly made."

"They may make the match," said Kate, "but it's more than they'll be able to do to make the marriage. Hycy's at greater game, I tell you; but whether he is or not, I tell you again that Bryan M'Mahon will have her in spite of all opposition."

"May be not," said Phats; "Hycy will take care o' that; he has him set; he'll work him a charm; he'll take care that Bryan won't be long in a fit way to offer himself as a match for her."

"More power to him in that," said Philip; "if he makes a beggarman of him he may depend on us to the back-bone."

"Have no hand in injurin' Bryan M'Mahon," said Kate. "Keep him from marryin' Kathleen if you like, or if you can; but, if you're wise, don't injure the boy."

"Why so?" asked Philip.

"That's nothing to you," she replied; "for a raison I have; and mark me, I warn you not to do so or it'll be worse for you."

"Why, who are we afraid of, barrin Hycy himself?"

"It's no matther; there's them livin' could make you afeard, an' maybe will, too, if you injure that boy."

"I'd just knock him on the head," replied the ferocious ruffian, "as soon as I would a mad dog."

"Whisht," said Phats, "here's Hycy; don't you hear his foot?"

Hycy entered in a few moments afterwards, and, after the usual greetings, sat down by the fire.

"De night's could," said Phats, resuming his brogue; "but here," he added, pulling out a bottle of whiskey, "is something to warm de blood in us. Will you thry it, Meeisther Hycy?"

"By-and-by—not now; but help yourselves."

"When did you see Miss Kathleen, Masther Hycy," asked Kate.

"You mean Miss Kathleen the Proud?" he replied—"my Lady Dignity—I have a crow to pluck with her."

"What crow have you to pluck wid her?" asked Kate, fiercely. "You'll pluck no crow wid her, or, if you do, I'll find a bag to hould the fedhers—mind that."

"No, no," said Philip; "whatever's to be done, she must come to no harm."

"Why, the crow I have to pluck with her, Mrs. Hogan, is—let me see—why—to—to marry her—to bind her in the bands of holy wedlock; and you know, when I do, I'm to give you all a house and place free gratis for nothing during your lives—that's what I pledge myself to do, and not a rope to hang yourselves, worthy gentlemen, as Finigan would say. I pass over the fact," he proceeded, laughing, "of the peculiar intimacy which, on a certain occasion, was established between Jemmy, the gentleman's old oak drawers, and your wrenching-irons; however, that is not the matter at present, and I am somewhat in a hurry."

"You heard," said Bat, "that Bryan M'Mahon has lost his mother?"

"I did," said the other; "poor orphan lad, I pity him."

"We know you do," said Bat, with a vindictive but approving sneer.

"I assure you," continued Hycy, "I wish the young man well."

"Durin' der lives," repeated Phats, who had evidently been pondering over Hycy's promised gift to the Hogans;—"throth," he observed with a grin, "dere may be something under dat too. Ay! an' she wishes Bryan M'Mahon well," he exclaimed, raising his red eyebrows.

"Shiss," replied Hycy, mimicking him, "her does."

"But you must have de still-house nowhere but in Ahadarra for alls dat."

"For alls dats" replied the other. "Dat will do den," said Phats, composedly. "Enough of this," said Hycy. "Now, Phats, have you examined and pitched upon the place?"

"Well, then," replied Phats, speaking in his natural manner, "I have; an' a betther spot isn't in Europe than there is undher the hip of Cullamore. But do you know how Roger Cooke sarved Adam Blakely of Glencuil?"

"Perfectly well," replied Hycy, "he ruined him."

"But we don't know it," said Ned; "how was it, Teddy?"

"Why, he set up a still on his property—an' you know Adam owns the whole townland, jist as Bryan M'Mahon does Ahadarra—an' afther three or four runnin she gets a bloody scoundrel to inform upon Adam, as if it was him an' not himself that had the still. Clinton the gauger—may the devil break his neck at any rate!—an' the redcoats—came and found all right, Still, Head, and Worm."

"Well," said Bat, "an' how did that ruin him?"

"Why, by the present law," returned Phats, "it's the townland that must pay the fine. Poor Adam wasn't to say very rich; he had to pay the fine, however, and now he's a beggar—root an' branch, chick an' child out of it. Do you undherstand that, Misther Hycy?"

"No," replied Hycy, "you're mistaken; I have recourse to the still, because I want cash. Honest Jemmy the gentleman has taken the *sthad* an' won't fork out any longer, so that I must either run a cast or two every now an' then, or turn clodhopper like himself. So much I say for your information, Mr. Phats. In the meantime let us see what's to be done. Here, Ned, is a five pound note to buy barley; keep a strict account of this; for I do assure you that I am not a person to be played on. There's another thirty-shilling note—or stay, I'll make it two pounds—to enable you to box up the still-house and remove the vessels and things from Glendearg. Have you all ready, Philip?" he said, addressing himself to Hogan.

"All," replied Philip; "sich a Still, Head, and Worm, you'd not find in Europe—ready to be set to work at a minute's notice."

"When," said Hycy, rising, "will it be necessary that I should see you again?"

"We'll let you know," replied Phats, "when we want you. Kate here can drop in, as if by accident, an' give the hand word."

"Well, then, good-night—stay, give me a glass of whiskey before I go; and, before I do go, listen. You know the confidence I place in every one of you on this occasion?"

"We do," replied Philip; "no doubt of it."

"Listen, I say. I swear by all that a man can swear by, that if a soul of you ever breathes—I hope, by the way, that these young savages are all asleep—"

"As sound as a top," said Bat, "everyone o' them."

"Well, if a single one of you ever breathes my name or mentions me to a human being as in any way connected, directly or indirectly, with the business in which we are engaged, I'll make the country too hot to hold you—and you need no ghost to tell you how easily I could dispose of you if it went to that."

Kate, when he had repeated these words, gave him a peculiar glance, which was accompanied by a short abrupt laugh that seemed to have something derisive in it.

"Is there anything to be laughed at in what I am saying, most amiable Mrs. Hogan?" he asked.

Kate gave either a feigned or a real start as he spoke.

"Laughed at!" she exclaimed, as if surprised; "throth I wasn't thinkin of you at all, Mr. Hycy. What wor you sayin'?"

"That if my name ever happens to be mentioned in connection with this business, I'll send the whole kit of you—hammers, budgets, and sothering-irons—to hell or Connaught; so think of this now, and goodnight."

"There goes as d——d vagabond," said Ned, "as ever stretched hemp; and only that it's our own business to make the most use we can out of him, I didn't care the devil had him, for I don't like a bone in his skin."

"Why," said Philip, "I see what he's at now. Sure enough he'll put the copin'-stone on Bryan. M'Mahon at any rate—that, an' if we can get the house and place out of him—an' what need we care?"

"Send us to hell or Connaught," said Kate; "well, that's not bad—ha! ha! ha!"

"What are you neigherin' at?" said her husband; "and what set you a-caoklin' to his face a while ago?"

She shook her head carelessly. "No matther," she replied, "for a raison I had."

"Would you let me know your raison, if you plaise?"

"If I plaise—ay, you did well to put that in, for I don't plaise to let you know any more about it. I laughed bekaise I liked to laugh; an' I hope one may do that 'ithout being brought over the coals about it. Go to bed, an' give me another glass o' whiskey, Ted—it always makes me sleep."

Ted had been for some minutes evidently ruminating.

"He is a good boy," said he; "but at any rate our hands is in the lion's mouth, an' its not our policy to vex him."

Hycy, on his way home, felt himself in better spirits than he had been in for some time. The arrangement with young Clinton gave him considerable satisfaction, and he now resolved to lose as little time as possible in executing his own part of the contract. Clinton himself, who was a thoughtless young fellow, fond of pleasure, and with no great relish for business, was guided almost in everything by his knowing old uncle the gauger, on whom he and his sister depended, and who looked upon him as unfit for any kind of employment unless the management of a cheap farm, such as would necessarily draw his attention from habits of idleness and expense to those of application and industry. Being aware, from common report, that M'Mahon's extensive and improvable holding in Ahadarra was out of lease, he immediately set his heart upon it, but knew not exactly in what manner to accomplish his designs, in securing it if he could, without exposing himself to suspicion and a good deal of obloquy besides. Old Clinton was one of those sheer and hardened sinners who, without either scruple or remorse, yet think it worth while to keep as good terms with the world as they can, whilst at the same time they laugh and despise in their hearts all that is worthy of honor and respect in it. His nephew, however, had some positive good, and not a little of that light and reckless profligacy which is often mistaken for heart and spirit. Hycy and he, though not very long acquainted, were, at the present period of our narrative, on very intimate terms. They had, it is true, a good many propensities in common, and these were what constituted the bond between them. They were companions but not friends; and Clinton saw many things in Hycy which disgusted him exceedingly, and scarcely anything more than the contemptuous manner in which he spoke of and treated his parents. He liked his society, because he was lively and without any of that high and honorable moral feeling which is often troublesome to a companion who, like Clinton, was not possessed of much scruple while engaged in the pursuit of pleasures. On this account, therefore, we say that he relished his society, but could neither respect nor esteem him.

On the following morning at breakfast, his uncle asked him where he had dined the day before.

"With Hycy Burke, sir," replied the nephew.

"Yes; that is honest Jemmy's son—a very great man in his own conceit, Harry. You seem to like him very much."

Harry felt a good deal puzzled as to the nature of his reply. He knew very well that his uncle did not relish Hycy, and he felt that he could not exactly state his opinion of him without bringing in question his own penetration and good taste in keeping his society. Then, with respect to his sister, although he had no earthly intention of seeing her the wife of such a person, still he resolved to be able to say to Hycy that he had not broken his word, a consideration which would not have bound Hycy one moment under the same circumstances.

"He's a very pleasant young fellow, sir," replied the other, "and has been exceedingly civil and attentive to me."

"Ay!—do you like him—do you esteem him, I mean?"

"I dare say I will, sir, when I come to know him better."

"Which is as much as to say that at present you do not. So I thought. You have a portion of good sense about you, but in a thousand things you're a jackass, Harry."

"Thank you, sir," replied his nephew, laughing heartily; "thank you for the compliment. I am your nephew, you know."

"You have a parcel of d——d scruples, I say, that are ridiculous. What the devil need a man care about in this world but appearances? Mind your own interests, keep up appearances, and you have done your duty."

"But I should like to do a little more than keep up appearances," replied his nephew.

"I know you would," said his uncle, "and it is for that especial reason that I say you're carrying the ears. I'm now a long time in the world, Masther Harry—sixty-two years—although I don't look it, nor anything like it, and in the course of that time—or, at all events, ever since I was able to form my own opinions, I never met a man that wasn't a rogue in something, with the exception of—let me see—one—two—three—four—five—I'm not able to make out the half-dozen."

"And who were the five honorable exceptions?" asked his niece, smiling.

"They were the five fools of the parish, Maria—and yet I am wrong, still—for Bob M'Cann was as thievish as the very devil whenever he had an opportunity. And now, do you know the conclusion I come to from all this?"

"I suppose," said his niece, "that no man's honest but a fool."

"Thank you, Maria, Well done—you've hit it. By the way, it's seems M'Mahon's wife, of Carriglass, is dead."

"Is she?" said Harry; "that is a respectable family, father, by all accounts."

"Why, they neither rob nor steal, I believe," replied his uncle. "They are like most people, I suppose, honest in the eye of the law—honest because the laws keep them so."

"I did not think your opinion of the world was so bad, uncle," said Maria; "I hope it is not so bad as you say it is."

"All I can say, then," replied the old Cynic, "that if you wait till you find an honest man for your husband, you'll die an old maid."

"Well, but excuse me, uncle, is that safe doctrine to lay down before your nephew, or myself?"

"Pooh, as to you, you silly girl, what have you to do with it? We're taikin' about men, now—about the world, I say, and life in general."

"And don't you wish Harry to be honest?"

"Yes, where it is his interest; and ditto to roguery, where it can be done safely."

"I know you don't feel what you say, uncle," she observed, "nor believe it either."

"Not he, Maria," said her brother, awakening out of a reverie; "but, uncle, as to Hycy Burke—I don't—hem."

"You don't what?" asked the other, rising and staring at him.

His nephew looked at his sister, and was silent.

"You don't mean what, man?—always speak out. Here, help me on with this coat. Fethertonge and I are taking a ride up tomorrow as far as Ahadarra."

"That's a man I don't like," said the nephew. "He's too soft and too sweet, and speaks too low to be honest."

"Honest, you blockhead! Who says he's honest?" replied his uncle. "He's as good a thing, however, an excellent man of the world that looks to the main point, and—keeps up appearances. Take care of yourselves;" and with these words, accompanied with a shrewd, knavish nod that was peculiar to him, in giving which with expression he was a perfect adept, he left them.

When he was gone, the brother and his sister looked at each, other, and the latter said, "Can it be possible, Harry, that my uncle is serious in all he says on this subject?"

Her brother, who paid more regard to the principles of his sister than her uncle did, felt great reluctance in answering her in the affirmative, so much so, indeed, that he resolved to stretch a little for the sake of common decency.

"Not at all, Maria; no man relishes honesty more than he does. He only speaks in this fashion because he thinks that honest men are scarce, and so they are. But, by-the-way, talking about Hycy Burke, Maria, how do you like him?"

"I can't say I admire him," she replied, "but you know I have had very slight opportunities of forming any opinion."

"From what you have seen of him, what do you think?"

"Let me see," she replied, pausing; "why, that he'll meet very few who will think so highly of him as he does of himself."

"He thinks very highly of you, then."

"How do you know that?" she asked somewhat quickly.

"Faith, Maria, from the best authority—because he himself told me so."

"So, then, I have had the honor of furnishing you with a topic of conversation?"

"Unquestionably, and you may prepare yourself for a surprise. He's attached to you."

"I think not," she replied calmly.

"Why so?" he asked.

"Because, if you wish to know the truth, I do not think him capable of attachment to any one but himself."

"Faith, a very good reason, Maria; but, seriously, if he should introduce the subject, I trust, at all events, that you will treat him with respect."

"I shall certainly respect myself, Harry. He need not fear that I shall read him one of my uncle's lectures upon life and honesty."

"I have promised not to be his enemy in the matter, and I shall keep my word."

"So you may, Harry, with perfect safety. I am much obliged to him for his good opinion; but" — she paused.

"What do you stop at, Maria?"

"I was only about to add," she replied, "that I wish it was mutual."

"You wish it," he exclaimed. "What do you mean by that, Maria?"

She laughed. "Don't you know it is only a form of speech? a polite way of saying that he does not rank high in my esteem?"

"Well, well," he replied, "settle that matter between you; perhaps the devil is not so black as he's painted."

"A very unhappy illustration," said his sister, "whatever has put it into your head.'

"Faith, and I don't know what put it there. However, all I can say in the matter I have already said. I am not, nor shall I be, his enemy. I'll trouble you, as you're near it, to touch the bell till George gets the horse. I am going up to his father's, now. Shall I tell him that John Wallace is discarded; that he will be received with smiles, and that—"

"How can you be so foolish, Harry?"

"Well, good-bye, at any rate. You are perfectly capable of deciding for yourself, Maria."

"I trust so," she replied. "There's George with your horse now."

"It's a blue look-up, Master Hycy," said Clinton to himself as he took his way to Burke's. "I think you have but little chance in that quarter, oh, most accomplished Hycy, and indeed I am not a whit sorry; but should be very much so were it otherwise."

It is singular enough that whilst Clinton was introducing the subject of Hycy's attachment to his sister, that worthy young gentleman was sustaining a much more serious and vehement onset upon a similar subject at home. Gerald Cavanagh and his wife having once got the notion of a marriage between Kathleen and Hycy into their heads, were determined not to rest until that desirable consummation should be brought about. In accordance with this resolution, we must assure our readers that Gerald never omitted any opportunity

The Emigrants of Ahadarra

of introducing the matter to Jemmy Burke, who, as he liked the Cavanaghs, and especially Kathleen herself, who, indeed, was a general favorite, began to think that, although in point of circumstances she was by no means a match for him, Hycy might do still worse. It is true, his wife was outrageous at the bare mention of it; but Jemmy, along with a good deal of blunt sarcasm, had a resolution of his own, and not unfrequently took a kind of good-natured and shrewd delight in opposing her wishes whenever he found them to be unreasonable. For several months past he could not put his foot out of the door that he was not haunted by honest Gerald Cavanagh, who had only one idea constantly before him, that of raising his daughter to the rank and state in which he knew, or at least calculated that Hycy Burke would keep her. Go where he might, honest Jemmy was attended by honest Gerald, like his fetch. At mass, at market, in every fair throughout the country was Cavanagh sure to bring up the subject of the marriage; and what was the best of it, he and his neighbor drank each other's healths so repeatedly on the head of it, that they often separated in a state that might be termed anything but sober. Nay, what is more, it was a fact that they had more than once or twice absolutely arranged the whole matter, and even appointed the day for the wedding, without either of them being able to recollect the circumstances on the following morning.

Whilst at breakfast on the morning in question, Burke, after finishing his first cup of tea, addressed his worthy son as follows:—

"Hycy, do you intend to live always this way?"

"Certainly not, Mr. Burke. I expect to dine on something more substantial than tea."

"You're very stupid, Hycy, not to understand me; but, indeed, you never were overstocked wid brains, unfortunately, as I know to my cost—but what I mane is, have you any intention of changing your condition in life? Do you intend to marry, or to go on spendin' money upon me at this rate!"

"The old lecture, Mrs. Burke," said Hycy, addressing his mother. "Father, you are sadly deficient in originality. Of late you are perpetually repeating yourself. Why, I suppose to-morrow or next day, you will become geometrical on our hands, or treat us to a grammatical praxis. Don't you think it very likely, Mrs. Burke!"

"And if he does," replied his mother, "it's not the first time he has been guilty of both; but of late, all the little shame he had, he has lost it."

"Faith, and if I hadn't got a large stock, I'd a been run out of it this many a day, in regard of what I had to lose in that way for you, Hycy. However I'll thank you to listen to me. Have you any intention of marryin' a wife?"

"Unquestionably, Mr. Burke. Not a doubt of it."

"Well, I am glad to hear it. The sooner you're married, the sooner you'll settle down. You'll know, then, my lad, what life is."

Honest Jemmy's sarcasm was likely to carry him too far from his purpose, which was certainly not to give a malicious account of matrimony, but, on the contrary, to recommend it to his worthy son.

"Well, Mr. Burke," said Hycy, winking at his mother, "proceed."

"The truth is, Hycy," he added, "I have a wife in my eye for you."

"I thought as much," replied the other. "I did imagine it was there you had her; name—Mr. Burke—name?"

"Troth, I'm ashamed, Hycy, to name her and yourself on the same day."

"Well, can't you name her to-day, and postpone me until to-morrow?"

"It would be almost a pity to have her thrown away upon you. A good and virtuous wife, however, may do a great deal to reclaim a bad husband, and, indeed, you wouldn't be the first profligate that was reformed in the same way."

"Many thanks, Mr. Burke; you are quite geological this morning; isn't he, ma'am?"

"When was he ever anything else? God pardon him! However, I know what he's exterminatin' for; he wants you to marry Kathleen Cavanagh."

"Ay do I, Rosha; and she might make him a respectable man yet,—that is, if any woman could."

"Geological again, mother; well, really now, Katsey Cavanagh is a splendid girl, a fine animal, no doubt of it; all her points are good, but, at the same time, Mr. Burke, a trifle too plebeian for Hycy the accomplished."

"I tell you she's a devilish sight too good for you; and if you don't marry her, you'll never get such a wife."

"Troth," answered Mrs. Burke, "I think myself there's something over you, or you wouldn't spake as you do—a wife for Hycy—one of Gerald Cavanagh's daughters make a wife for him!—not while I'm alive at any rate, plaise God."

"While you're alive; well, may be not:—but sure if it plases God to bring it about, on your own plan, I must endaivor to be contented, Rosha; ay, an' how do you know but I'd dance at their weddin' too! ha! ha! ha!"

"Oh, then, it's you that's the bitther pill, Jemmy Burke! but, thank God, I disregard you at all events. It's little respect you pay to my feelings, or ever did."

"I trust, my most amiable mother, that you won't suffer the equability of your temper to be disturbed by anything proceeding from such an antiphlogistic source. Allow me to say, Mr. Burke, that I have higher game in view, and that for the present I must beg respectfully to decline the proposal which you so kindly made, fully sensible as I am of the honor you intended for me. If you will only exercise a little patience, however, perhaps I shall have the pleasure ere long of presenting to you a lady of high accomplishments, amiable manners, and very considerable beauty."

"Not a 'Crazy Jane' bargain, I hope?"

"Really, Mr. Burke, you are pleased to be sarcastic; but as for honest Katsey, have the goodness to take her out of your eye as soon as possible, for she only blinds you to your own interest and to mine."

"You wouldn't marry Kathleen, then?"

"For the present I say most assuredly not," replied the son, in the same ironical and polite tone.

"Because," continued his father, with a very grave smile, in which there was, to say truth, a good deal of the grin visible, "as poor Gerald was a good deal anxious about the matther, I said I'd try and make you marry her—*to oblige him.*"

Hycy almost, if not altogether, lost his equanimity by the contemptuous sarcasm implied in these words. "Father," said he, to save trouble, and to prevent you and me both from thrashing the wind in this manner, I think it right to tell you that I have no notion of marrying such a girl as Cavanagh's daughter."

"No," continued his mother, "nor if you had, I wouldn't suffer it."

"Very well," said the father; "is that your mind?"

"That's my mind, sir."

"Well, now, listen to mine, and maybe, Hycy, I'll taiche you better manners and more respect for your father; suppose I bring your brother home from school,—suppose I breed him up an honest farmer,—and suppose I give him all my property, and lave Mr. Gentleman Hycy to lead a gentleman's life on his own means, the best way he can. There now is something for you to suppose, and so I must go to my men."

He took up his hat as he spoke and went out to the fields, leaving both mother and son in no slight degree startled by an intimation so utterly unexpected, but which they knew enough of him to believe was one not at all unlikely to be acted on by a man who so frequently followed up his own determinations with a spirit amounting almost to obstinacy.

"I think, mother," observed the latter, "we must take in sail a little; 'the gentleman' won't bear the ironical to such an extent, although he is master of it in his own way; in other words, Mr. Burke won't bear to be laughed at."

"Not he," said his mother, in the tone of one who was half angry at him on that very account, "he'll bear nothing."

"D—n it, to tell that vulgar bumpkin, Cavanagh, I suppose in a state of maudlin drunkenness, that he would make me marry his daughter—to oblige, him!—contempt could go no further; it was making a complete cipher of me."

"Ay, but I'm disturbed about what he said going out, Hycy. I don't half like the face he had on him when he said it; and when he comes to discover other things, too, money matthers—there will be no keepin the house wid him."

"I fear as much," said Hycy; "however, we must only play our cards as well as we can; he is an impracticable man, no doubt of it, and it is a sad thing that a young fellow of spirit should be depending on such a—

> "'Ye banks and braes o' bonnie Doon,
> How can you bloom so fresh and fair,
> How can ye chant, ye little birds,
> And I sae weary fu' o' care, &c., &c.

"Well, well—I do not relish that last hint certainly, and if other projects should fail, why, as touching the fair Katsey, it might not be impossible that—however, time will develop. She is a fine girl, a magnificent creature, no doubt of it, still, most maternal relative, as I said, time will develop—by the way, Mrs. M'Mahon, the clodhopper's mother, is to be interred to-morrow, and I suppose you and 'the gentleman' will attend the funeral."

"Sartinly, we must."

"So shall 'the accomplished.' Clinton and I shall honor that lugubrious ceremony with our presence; but as respecting the clodhopper himself, meaning thereby Bryan of Ahadarra, he is provided for. What an unlucky thought to enter into the old fellow's noddle! However, *non constat*, as Finigan would say, time will develop."

"You're not gainin' ground with him at all events," said his mother; "ever since that Crazy Jane affair he's changed for the worse towards both of us, or ever since the robbery I ought to say, for he's dark and has something on his mind ever since."

"I'm in the dark there myself, most amiable of mothers; however, as I said just now, I say time will develop."

He then began to prepare himself for the business of the day, which consisted principally in riding about seeking out new adventures, or, as they term it, hunting in couples, with Harry Clinton.

CHAPTER XIII.—Mrs. M'Mahon's Funeral.

On the morning of Mrs. M'Mahon's funeral, the house as is usual in such cases, was filled with relatives and neighbors, each and all anxious to soothe and give comfort to the afflicted family. Protestants and Presbyterians were there, who entered as deeply and affectionately into the sorrow which was felt as if they were connected to them by blood. Moving about with something like authority, was Dennis O'Grady, the Roman Catholic Parish Clerk, who, with a semi-clerical bearing, undertook to direct the religious devotions which are usual on such occasions. In consequence of the dearth of schools and teachers that then existed in our unfortunate country, it frequently happened, that persons were, from necessity, engaged in aiding the performance of religious duties, who were possessed of very little education, if not, as was too often the case, absolutely and wholly illiterate. Dennis was not absolutely illiterate, but, in good truth, he was by no means far removed from that uncomfortable category. Finigan, the schoolmaster, was also present; and as he claimed acquaintance with the classics, and could understand and read with something like correctness the Latin offices, which were frequently repeated on these occasions it would be utterly impossible to describe the lofty scorn and haughty supercilious contempt with which he contemplated poor Dennis, who kept muttering away at the *Confiteor* and *De Profundis* with a barbarity of pronunciation that rendered it impossible for human ears to understand a single word he said. Finigan, swollen with an indignation which he could no longer suppress, and stimulated by a glass or two of whiskey, took three or four of the neighbors over to a corner, where, whilst his eyes rested on Dennis with a most withering expression of scorn, he exclaimed—"Here, hand me that manual, and get out o' my way, you illiterate nonentity and most unsufferable appendage to religion."

He then took the book, and going over to the coffin, read in a loud and sonorous voice the *De Profundis* and other prayers for the dead, casting his eyes from time to time upon the unfortunate clerk with a contemptuous bitterness and scorn that, for force of expression, could not be surpassed. When he had concluded, he looked around him with a sense of lofty triumph that was irresistible in its way. "There," said he, "is something like accent and quantity for you—there is something that may, without derogation to religion, be called respectable perusal—an' yet to say that a man like me, wid classical accomplishments and propensities from my very cradle, should be set aside for that illiterate vulgarian, merely because, like every other janius, I sometimes indulge in the delectable enjoyment of a copious libation, is too bad."

This in fact was the gist of his resentment against O'Grady. He had been in the habit for some time of acting as clerk to the priest, who bore with his "copious libations," as he called them, until common decency rendered it impossible to allow him any longer the privilege of taking a part as clerk in the ceremonies of religion.

When this was over, a rustic choir, whom the parish clerk had organized, and in a great measure taught himself, approached the body and sang a hymn over it, after which the preparations for its removal began to be made.

Ever since the death of his wife, Thomas M'Mahon could not be prevailed upon to taste a morsel of food. He went about from place to place, marked by such evidences of utter prostration and despair that it was painful to look upon him, especially when one considered the truth, purity, and fervor of the affection that had subsisted between him and the inestimable woman he had lost. The only two individuals capable of exercising any influence upon him now were Bryan and his daughter Dora; yet even they could not prevail upon him to take any sustenance. His face was haggard and pale as death, his eyes red and bloodshot, and his very body, which had always been erect and manly, was now stooped and bent from the very intensity of his affliction.

He had been about the garden during the scene just described, and from the garden he passed round through all the office-houses, into every one of which he entered, looking at them in the stupid bereavement of grief, as if he had only noticed them for the first time. On going into the cow-house where the animals were at their food, he approached one of them—that which had been his wife's favorite, and which would suffer no hand to milk her but her own— "Oh, Bracky," he said, "little you know who's gone from you—even you miss her already, for you refused for the last three days to let any one of them milk you, when she was not here to do it. Ah, Bracky, the kind hand and the kind word that you liked so well will never be wid you more—that low sweet song that you loved to listen to, and that made you turn round while she was milkin' you, an' lick her wid your tongue from pure affection—for what was there that had life that didn't love her? That low, sweet song, Bracky, you will never hear again. Well, Bracky, for her sake I'm come to tell you, this sorrowful mornin', that while I have life an' the means of keepin' you, from me an' them she loved you will never part."

While he spoke the poor animal, feeling from the habit of instinct that the hour of! milking had arrived, turned round and uttered once or twice that affectionate lowing with which she usually called upon the departed to come and relieve her of her fragrant burthen. This was more than the heart-broken man could bear, he walked back, and entering the wake-house, in a burst of vehement sorrow—"Oh, Bridget, my wife, my wife—is it any wondher we should feel your loss, when your favorite, Bracky, is callin' for you; but you won't come to her—that voice that so often charmed her will never charm the poor affectionate creature again."

"Father dear," said Bryan, "if ever you were called upon to be a man it is now."

"But, Byran, as God is to judge me," replied his father, "the cow—her own cow—is callin' for her in the cow-house widin—its truth—doesn't everything miss her—even poor Bracky feels as if she was dasarted. Oh, my God, an' what will we do—what will we do!"

This anecdote told by the sorrowing husband was indeed inexpressingly affecting. Bryan, who had collected all his firmness with a hope of being able to sustain his father, was so much overpowered by this circumstance that, after two or three ineffectual attempts to soothe him, he was himself fairly overcome, and yielded for the moment to bitter tears, whilst the whole family broke out into one general outburst, of sorrow, accompanied in many cases by the spectators, who were not proof against the influence of so natural and touching an incident.

Their neighbors and friends, in the meantime, were pouring in fast from all directions. Jemmy Burke and his wife—the latter ridiculously over-dressed—drove there upon their jaunting-car, which was considered a great compliment, followed soon afterwards by Hycy and Harry Clinton on horse-back. Gerald Cavanagh and his family also came, with the exception of Kathleen and Hanna, who were, however, every moment expected. The schoolmaster having finished the *De Profundis*, was, as is usual, treated to glass of whiskey—a circumstance which just advanced him to such a degree of fluency and easy assurance as was necessary properly to develop the peculiarities of his character. Having witnessed Bryan's failure at consolation, attended as it was by the clamorous grief of the family, he deemed it his duty, especially as he had just taken some part in the devotions, to undertake the task in which Bryan had been so unsuccessful.

"Thomas M'Mahon," said he, "I'm disposed to blush—do you hear me, I say? I am disposed to blush, I repate, for your want of—he doesn't hear me:—will you pay attention? I am really disposed to blush"—and as he uttered the words he stirred M'Mahon by shaking his shoulders two or three times, in order to gain his attention.

"Are you?" replied the other, replying in an absent manner to his words. "God help you then, and assist you, for it's few can do it."

"Can do what?"

"Och, I don't know; whatever you wor sayin'."

"Patience, my good friend, Thomas M'Mahon. I would call you Tom familiarly, but that you are in affliction, and it is well known that every one in affliction is, or at least ought to be, treated with respect and much sympathetical consolation. You are now in deep sorrow; but don't you knows that death is the end of all things? and believe me there are many objects in this world which a wise and experienced man would lose wid much greater regret than he would a mere wife. Think, for instance, how many men there are—dreary and subdued creatures—who dare not call their souls, if they have any, or anything else they do possess, their own; think, I repate, of those who would give nine-tenths of all they are worth simply to be in your present condition! Wretches who from the moment they passed under the yoke matrimonial, to which all other yokes are jokes, have often heard of liberty but never enjoyed it for one single hour—the Lord help them!"

"Amen!" exclaimed M'Mahon, unconsciously.

"Yes," proceeded Finigan, "unfortunate devils whose obstinacy has been streaked by a black mark, or which ought rather to be termed a black and blue mark, for that is an abler and more significant illustration, Poor quadrupeds who have lived their whole miserable lives as married men under an iron dynasty; and who know that the thunderings of Jupiter himself, if he were now in vogue, would be mere music compared to the fury of a conjugal tongue when agitated by any one of the thousand causes that set it a-going so easily. Now, Thomas, I am far from insinuating that ever you stood in that most pitiable category, but I know many who have—heigho!—and I know many who do, and some besides who will; for what was before may be agin, and it will be nothing but ascendancy armed with her iron rod on the one hand, against patience, submission, and tribulation, wid their groans and penances on the other. Courage then, my worthy friend; do not be overwhelmed wid grief, for I can assure you that as matters in general go on the surface of this terraqueous globe, the death of a wife ought to be set down as a proof that heaven does not altogether overlook us. 'Tis true there are tears shed upon such occasions, and for very secret reason's too, if the truth were known. Joy has its tears as well as grief, I believe, and it is often rather difficult, under a blessing so completely disguised as the death of a wi—of one's matrimonial partner, to restrain them. Come then, be a man. There is Mr. Hycy Burke, a tender-hearted young gentleman, and if you go on this way you will have him weeping' for sheer sympathy, not pretermitting Mr. Clinton, his companion, who is equally inclined to be pathetic, if one can judge from apparent symptoms."

"I'm obliged to you, Masther," replied M'Mahon, who had not heard, or rather paid attention to, a single syllable he had uttered. "Of course it's thruth you're savin'—-it is—it is, *fureer gair* it is; and she that's gone from me is a proof of it. What wondher then that I should shed tears, and feel as I do?"

The Emigrants of Ahadarra

The unconscious simplicity of this reply to such a singular argument for consolation as the schoolmaster had advanced, caused many to smile, some to laugh outright, and others to sympathize still more deeply with M'Mahon's sorrow. Finigan's allusion to Hycy and his companion was justified by the contrast which the appearance of each presented. Hycy, who enjoyed his lecture on the tribulations of matrimonial life very much, laughed as he advanced in it, whilst Clinton, who was really absorbed in a contemplation of the profound and solemn spirit which marked the character of the grief he witnessed, and who felt impressed besides by the touching emblems of death and bereavement which surrounded him, gradually gave way to the impressions that gained on him, until he almost felt the tears in his eyes.

At this moment Kathleen and her sister Hanna entered the house, and a general stir took place among those who were present, which was caused by her strikingly noble figure and extraordinary beauty—a beauty which, on the occasion in question, assumed a peculiarly dignified and majestic character from the deep and earnest sympathy with the surrounding sorrow that was impressed on it.

Hycy and his companion surveyed her for many minutes; and the former began to think that after all, if Miss Clinton should fail him, Kathleen would make an admirable and most lovely wife. Her father soon after she entered came over, and taking her hand said, "Come with me, Kathleen, till you shake hands wid a great friend of yours— wid Misther Burke. This is herself, Misther Burke," he added, significantly, on putting her hand into that of honest Jemmy, "an' I think no father need be ashamed of her."

"Nor no father-in-law," replied Jemmy, shaking her cordially by the hand, "and whisper, darlin'," said he, putting his mouth close to her ear, and speaking so as that he might not be heard by others, "I hope to see you my daughter-in-law yet, if I could only get that boy beyant to make himself worthy of you."

On speaking he turned his eyes on Hycy, who raised himself up, and assuming his best looks intimated his consciousness of being the object of his father's allusion to him. He then stepped over to where she stood, and extending his hand with an air of gallantry and good humor said, "I hope Miss Cavanagh, who has so far honored our worthy father, won't refuse to honor the son."

Kathleen, who had blushed at his father's words, now blushed more deeply still; because in this instance, there was added to the blush of modesty that of offended pride at his unseasonable presumption.

"This, Mr. Hycy," she replied, "is neither a time nor a place for empty compliments. When the son becomes as worthy as the father, I'll shake hands with him; but not till that time comes."

On returning to the place she had left, her eyes met those of Bryan, and for a period that estimable and true-hearted young fellow forgot both grief and sorrow in the rush of rapturous love which poured its unalloyed sense of happiness into his heart. Hycy, however, felt mortified, and bit his lip with vexation. To a young man possessed of excessive vanity, the repulse was the more humiliating in proportion to its publicity. Gerald Cavanagh was as deeply offended as Hycy, and his wife could not help exclaiming aloud, "Kathleen! what do you mane? I declare I'm ashamed of you!"

Kathleen, however, sat down beside her sister, and the matter was soon forgotten in the stir and bustle which preceded the setting out of the funeral.

This was indeed a trying and heart-rending scene. The faithful wife, the virtuous mother, the kind friend, and the pious Christian, was now about to be removed for ever from that domestic scene which her fidelity, her virtue, her charity, and her piety, had filled with peace, and love, and happiness. As the coffin, which had been resting upon two chairs, was about to be removed, the grief of her family became loud and vehement.

"Oh, Bridget!" exclaimed her husband, "and is it to come to this at last! And you are lavin' us for evermore! Don't raise the coffin," he proceeded, "don't raise it. Oh! let us not part wid her till to-morrow; let us know that she's undher the same roof wid us until then. An', merciful Father, when I think where you're goin' to bring her to! Oh! there lies the heart now widout one motion—dead and cowld—the heart that loved us all as no other heart ever did! Bridget, my wife, don't you hear me? But the day was that you'd hear me, an' that your kind an' lovin' eye would turn on me wid that smile that was never broken. Where is the wife that was true? Where is the lovin' mother, the charitable heart to the poor and desolate, and the hand that was ever ready to aid them that was in distress? Where are they all now? There, dead and cowld forever, in that coffin. What has become of my wife, I say? What is death at all, to take all we love from us this way? But sure God forgive me for saying so, for isn't it the will of God? but oh! it is the heaviest of all thrials to lose such a woman as she was!"

Old grandfather, as he was called, had latterly become very feeble, and was barely able to be out of bed on that occasion. When the tumult reached the room where he sat with some of the aged neighbors, he inquired what had occasioned it, and being told that the coffin was about to be removed to the hearse, he rose up.

"That is Tom's voice I hear," said he, "and I must put an end to this." He accordingly made his appearance rather unexpectedly among them, and approaching his son, said, putting his hand commandingly upon his shoulder, and looking in his face with a solemn consciousness of authority that was irresistible, "I command you, Tom, to stop. It's not many commands that I'll ever give you—maybe this will be the last—and it's not many ever I had occasion to give you, but now I command you to stop and let the funeral go on." He paused for a short time and looked upon the features of his son with a full sense of what was due to his authority. His great age, his white hairs, his venerable looks and bearing, and the reverence which the tremulous but earnest tones of his voice were calculated to inspire, filled his son with awe, and he was silent.

"Father," said he, "I will; I'll try and obey you—I will."

"God bless you and comfort you, my dear son," said the old man. "Keep silence, now," he proceeded, addressing the others, "and bring the coffin to the hearse at wanst. And may God strengthen and support you all, for it's I that knows your loss; but like a good mother as she was, she has left none but good and dutiful childre' behind her."

Poor Dora, during the whole morning, had imposed a task upon herself that was greater than her affectionate and sorrowing heart could bear. She was very pale and exhausted by the force of what she had felt, and her excessive weeping; but it was observed that she now appeared to manifest a greater degree of fortitude than any of the rest. Still, during this assumed calmness, the dear girl, every now and then, could not help uttering a short convulsive sob, that indicated at once her physical debility and extraordinary grief. She was evidently incapable of entering into conversation, or at least, averse to it, and was consequently very silent during the whole morning. As they stooped, however, to remove the coffin, she threw herself upon it, exclaiming, "Mother, its your own Dora—mother—mother—don't, mother—don't lave me don't—I won't let her go—I won't let her go! I—I—" Even before she could utter the words she intended to say, her head sank down, and her pale but beautiful cheek lay exactly beside the name, Bridget M'Mahon, that was upon it.

"The poor child has fainted," they exclaimed, "bring her to the fresh air."

Ere any one had time, however, to raise her, James Cavanagh rushed over to the coffin, and seizing her in his arms, bore her to the street, where he placed her upon one of the chairs that had been left there to support the coffin until keened over by the relatives and friends, previous to its being-placed in the hearse; for such is the custom. There is something exceedingly alarming in a swoon to a person who witnesses it for the first time; which was the case with James Cavanagh. Having placed her on the chair, he looked wildly upon her; then as wildly upon those who were crowding round him. "What ails her?" he exclaimed—"what ails her?—she is dead!—she is dead! Dora—Dora dear—Dora dear, can't you spake or hear me?"

Whilst he pronounced the words, a shower of tears gushed rapidly from his eyes and fell upon her beautiful features, and in the impressive tenderness of the moment, he caught her to his heart, and with rapturous distraction and despair kissed her lips and exclaimed, "She is dead!—she is dead!—an' all that's in the world is nothing to the love I had for her!"

"Stand aside, James," said his sister Kathleen; "leave this instantly. Forgive him, Bryan," she said, looking at her lover with a burning brow, "he doesn't know what he is doing."

"No, Kathleen," replied, her brother, with a choking voice, "neither for you nor for him, nor for a human crature, will I leave her."

"James, I'm ashamed of you," said Hanna, rapidly and energetically disengaging his arms from about the insensible girl; "have! you no respect for Dora? If you love her as you say, you could hardly act as you did."

"Why," said he, staring at her, "what did I do?"

Bryan took him firmly by the arm, and said, "Come away, you foolish boy; I don't think you know what you did. Leave her to the girls. There, she is recoverin'."

She did soon recover; but weak and broken down as she was, no persuasion nor even authority could prevail upon her to remain at home. Jemmy Burke, who had intended to offer Kathleen a seat upon his car, which, of course, she would not have accepted, was now outmanoeuvred by his wife, 'who got Dora beside herself, after having placed a sister of Tom M'Mahon's beside him.

At length, the coffin was brought out, and the keene raised over it, on the conclusion of which it was placed in the hearse, and the procession began to move on.

There is nothing in the rural districts of this country that so clearly indicates the respect entertained for any family as the number of persons which, when a death takes place in it, attend the funeral. In such a case, the length of the procession is the test of esteem in which the party has been held. Mrs. M'Mahon's funeral was little less than a mile long. All the respectable farmers and bodaghs, as they call them, or half-sirs in the parish, were in attendance, as a mark of, respect for the virtues of the deceased, and of esteem for the integrity and upright spirit of the family that had been deprived of her so unexpectedly.

Hycy and his friend, Harry Clinton, of course rode together, Finigan, the schoolmaster, keeping as near them as he could; but not so near as to render his presence irksome to them, when he saw that they had no wish for it.

"Well, Harry," said his companion, "what do you think of the last scene?"

"You allude to Cavanagh's handsome young son, and the very pretty girl that fainted, poor thing!"

"Of course I do," replied Hycy.

"Why," said the other, "I think the whole thing was very simple, and consequently very natural. The young fellow, who is desperately in love—there is no doubt of that—thought she had died; and upon my soul, Hycy, there is a freshness and a purity in the strongest raptures of such a passion, that neither you nor I can dream of. I think, however, I can understand, or guess at rather, the fulness of heart and the tenderness by which he was actuated."

"What do you think of Miss Cavanagh?" asked Hycy, with more of interest than he had probably ever felt in her before.

"What do I think?" said the other, looking at him with a good deal of surprise. "What can I think? What could any man, that has either taste or common-sense think? Faith, Hycy, to be plain with you, I think her one of the finest girls, if not the very finest, I ever saw. Heavens! what would not that girl be if she had received the advantages of a polished and comprehensive education?"

"She is very much of a lady as it is," added Hycy, "and has great natural dignity and unstudied grace, although I must say that she has left me under no reason to feel any particular obligations to her."

"And yet there is a delicate and graceful purity in the beauty of little Dora, which is quite captivating," observed Clinton.

"Very well," replied the other, "I make jou a present of the two fair rustics; give me the interesting Maria. Ah, Harry, see what education and manner do. Maria is a delightful girl."

"She is an amiable and a good girl," said her brother; "but, in point of personal attractions, quite inferior to either of the two we have been speaking of."

"Finigan," said Hycy—"I beg your pardon, O'Finigan—the great O'Finigan, Philomath—are you a good judge of beauty?"

"Why, then, Mr. Hycy," replied the pedagogue, "I think, above all subjects, that a thorough understanding of that same comes most natural to an Irishman. It is a pleasant topic to discuss at all times."

"Much pleasanter than marriage, I think," said Clinton, smiling.

"Ah, Mr. Clinton," replied the other, with a shrug, "*de mortuis nil nisi bonum*; but as touching beauty, in what sense do you ask my opinion?"

"Whether now, for instance, would your learned taste prefer Miss Cavanagh or Miss Dora M'Mahon? and give your reasons."

"Taste, Mr. Hycy, is never, or at least seldom, guided by reason; the question, however, is a fair one."

"One at least on a fair subject," observed Clinton.

"Very well said, Mr. Clinton," replied the schoolmaster, with a grin—"there goes wit for us, no less—and originality besides. See what it is to have a great janius!—ha! ha! ha!"

"Well, Mr. O'Finigan," pursued Hycy, "but about the ladies? You have not given us your opinion."

"Why, then, they are both highly gifted wid beauty, and strongly calculated to excite the amorous sentiments of refined and elevated affection."

"Well done, Mr. Plantation," said Hycy; "you are improving—proceed."

"Miss Cavanagh, then," continued Finigan, "I'd say was a goddess, and Miss M'Mahon her attendant nymph."

"Good again, O'Finigan," said Clinton; "you are evidently at home in the mythology."

"Among the goddesses, at any rate," replied the master, with another grin.

"Provided there is no matrimony in the question," said Clinton.

"Ah, Mr. Clinton, don't, if you please. That's a subject you may respect yet as much as I do; but regarding my opinion of the two beauties in question, why was it solicited, Mr. Hycy?" he added, turning to that worthy gentlemen.

"Faith, I'm not able to say, most learned Philomath; only, is it true that Bryan, the clodhopper, has matrimonial designs upon the fair daughter of the regal Cavanagh?"

"*Sic vult fama*, Mr. Hycy, upon condition that a certain accomplished young gentleman, whose surname commences with the second letter of the alphabet, won't offer—for in that case, it is affirmed, that the clodhopper should travel. By the way, Mr. Clinton, I met your uncle and Mr. Fethertonge riding up towards Ahadarra this morning."

"Indeed!" exclaimed both; and as they spoke, each cast a look of inquiry at the other.

"What could bring them to Ahadarra, gentlemen?" asked Finigan, in a tone of voice which rendered it a nice point to determine whether it was a simple love of knowledge that induced him to put the question, or some other motive that might have lain within a kind of ironical gravity that accompanied it.

"Why, I suppose a pair of good horses," replied Hycy, "and their own inclination."

"It was not the last, at all events," said Finigan, "that ever brought a thief to the gallows—ha! ha! ha! we must be facetious sometimes, Mr. Hycy."

"You appear to enjoy that joke, Mr. Finigan," said Hycy, rather tartly.

"Faith," replied Finigan, "it's a joke that very few do enjoy, I think."

"What is?"

"Why, the gallows, sir—ha! ha! ha! but don't forget the O if you plaise—ever and always the big O before Finigan—ha! ha! ha!"

"Come, Clinton," said Hycy, "move on a little. D—n that fellow!" he cried—"he's a sneering scoundrel; and I'm half inclined to think he has more in him than one would be apt to give him credit for."

"By the way, what could the visit to Ahadarra mean?" asked Clinton. "Do you know anything about it, Hycy?"

"Not about this; but it is very likely that I shall cause them, or one of them at least, to visit it on some other occasion ere long; and that's all I can say now. Curse that keening, what a barbarous practice it is!'

"I think not," said the other; "on the contrary, I am of opinion that there's something strikingly wild and poetical in it something that argues us Irish to be a people of deep feeling and strong imagination: two of the highest gifts of intellect."

"All stuff," replied the accomplished Hycy, who, among his other excellent qualities, could never afford to speak a good word to his country Or her people. "All stuff and barbarous howling that we learned from the wolves when we had them in Ireland. Here we are at the graveyard."

"Hycy," said his friend, "it never occurred to me to thing of asking what religion you believe in."

"It is said," replied Hycy, "that a fool may propose a question which a wise man can't answer. As to religion, I have not yet made any determination among the variety that is abroad. A man, however, can be at no loss; for as every one of them is the best, it matters little which of them he chooses. I think it likely I shall go to church with your sister, should we ever do matrimony together. To a man like me who's indifferent, respectability alone ought to determine."

Clinton made no reply to this; and in a few minutes afterward they entered the churchyard, the coffin having been taken out of the hearse and borne on the shoulders of her four nearest relatives,— Tom M'Mahon, in deep silence and affliction, preceding it as chief mourner.

There is a prostrating stupor, or rather a kind of agonizing delirium that comes over the mind when we are forced to mingle with crowds, and have our ears filled with the voices of lamentation, the sounds of the death-bell, or the murmur of many people in conversation. 'Twas thus M'Mahon felt during the whole procession. Sometimes he thought it was relief, and again he felt as if it was only the mere alternation of suffering into a sharper and more dreadful sorrow; for, change as it might, there lay tugging at his heart the terrible consciousness that she, I the bride of his youthful love and the companion of his larger and more manly affection—the blameless wife and the stainless woman—was about to be consigned to the grave, and that his eyes in this life must; never rest upon her again.

When the coffin was about to be lowered down, all the family, one after another, clasped their arms about it, and kissed it with a passionate fervor of grief that it was impossible to witness with firmness. At length her husband, who had been looking on, approached it, and clasping it in his arms like the rest, he said—"for ever and for ever, and for ever, Bridget—but, no, gracious God, no; the day will come, Bridget, when I will be with you here—I don't care now how soon. My happiness is gone, asthore machree—life is nothing to me now—all's empty; and there's neither joy, nor ease of mind, nor comfort for me any more. An' this is our last parting—this is our last farewell, Bridget dear; but from this out my hope is to be with you here; and if nothing else on my bed of death was to console me, it would be, and it will be, that you and I will then sleep together, never to be parted more. That will be my consolation."

"Now, father dear," said Bryan, "we didn't attempt to stop or prevent you, and I hope you'll be something calm and come away for a little."

"Best of sons! but aren't you all good, for how could you be otherwise with her blood in your veins?—bring me away; come you, Dora darlin'—ay, that's it—support the: blessed child between you and Hanna, Kathleen darlin'. Oh, wait, wait till we get out of hearin, or the noise of the clay fallin' on the coffin will kill me."

They then walked to some distance, where they remained until the "narrow house" was nearly filled, after which they once more surrounded it until the last sod was beaten in. This being over, the sorrowing group sought their way home with breaking hearts, leaving behind them her whom they had loved so well reposing in the cold and unbroken solitude of the grave.

CHAPTER XIV.—Mysterious Letter

—Hycy Disclaims Sobriety—Ahadarra's in for it.

One day about a month after Mrs. M'Mahon's funeral, Harry Clinton was on his way to Jemmy Burke's, when he met Nanny Peety going towards Ballymacan.

"Well, Nanny," he inquired, "where are you bound for, now?"

"To the post-office with a letter from Masther Hycy, sir. I wanted him to tell me who it was for, but he would not. Will you, Mr. Clinton?" and she held out the letter to him as she spoke.

Clinton felt a good deal surprised to see that it was addressed to his uncle, and also written in a hand which he did not recognize to be that of Hycy Burke.

"Are you sure, Nanny," he asked, "that this letter was written by Mr. Hycy?"

"Didn't I see him, sir?" she replied; "he wrote it before my eyes a minute before he handed it to me. Who is it for, Mr. Clinton?"

"Why are you so very anxious to know, Nanny?" he inquired.

"Sorra thing," she replied, "but curiosity—a woman's curiosity, you know."

"Well, Nanny, you know, or ought to know, that it would not be right in me to tell you who the letter is for, when Mr. Hycy did not think proper to do so."

"True enough, sir," she replied; "an I beg your pardon, Mr. Clinton, for asking you; indeed it was wrong in me to tell you who it came from even, bekaise Mr. Hycy told me not to let any one see it, only jist to slip it into the post-office unknownst, as I passed it; an' that was what made me wish to know who it was goin' to, since the thruth must be tould."

Clinton in turn now felt his curiosity stimulated as to the contents of this mysterious epistle, and he resolved to watch, if possible, what effect the perusal of it might have on his uncle, otherwise he was never likely to hear a syllable that was contained in it, that worthy relative being, from official necessity, a most uncommunicative person in all his proceedings.

"I wonder," observed Clinton, "that Mr. Hycy would send to any one a letter so slurred and blotted with ink as that is."

"Ay, but he blotted it purposely himself," replied Nanny, "and that too surprised me, and made me wish to know what he could mane by it."

"Perhaps it's a love-letter, Nanny," said Clinton, laughing.

"I would like to know who it is to, at any rate," said the girl; "but since you won't, tell me, sir, I must try and not lose my rest about it. Good-bye, Mr. Clinton."

"Good-bye, Nanny;" and so they started.

Young Clinton, who, though thoughtless and fond of pleasure, was not without many excellent points of character, began now to perceive, by every day's successive intimacy, the full extent of Hycy Burke's profligacy of morals, and utter want of all honorable principle. Notwithstanding this knowledge, however, he felt it extremely difficult, nay, almost impossible, to separate himself from Hycy, who was an extremely pleasant young fellow, and a very agreeable companion when he pleased. He had in fact gained that personal ascendancy over him, or that licentious influence which too many of his stamp are notorious for exercising over better men than themselves; and he found that he could not readily throw Hyoy off, without being considerably a loser by the act.

"I shall have nothing to do with his profligacy," said he, "or his want of principle, and I shall let him know, at all events, that I will not abide by the agreement or compromise entered into between us some time since at his father's. He shall not injure an honest man for me, nor shall I promise him even neutrality with respect to his proposal for my sister, whom I would rather see dead a hundred times than the wife of such a fellow."

The next morning, about half an hour before breakfast, he told his uncle that he was stepping into town and would bring him any letters that might be for him in the post-office. He accordingly did so, and received two letters, one Hycy's and the other with the crest and frank of the sitting member for the county, who was no other than young Chevydale. His uncle was at breakfast when he handed them to him, and we need hardly say that the M.P. was honored by instant attention. The Still-hound read it over very complacently. "Very well," he exclaimed; "very well, indeed, so far. Harry, we must be on the alert, now the elections are approaching, and Chevydale will be stoutly opposed, it seems. We must work for him, and secure as many votes as we can. It is our interest to do so, Harry,—and he will make it our interest besides."

"Has principle nothing to do with it, sir?"

"Principle! begad, sir," retorted the uncle, "there's no such thing as principle—lay that down as a fact—there's no such thing in this world as principle."

"Well, but consistency, uncle. For instance, you know you always vote on the Tory side, and Chevydale is a Liberal and an Emancipator."

"Consistency is all d—d stuff, Harry, as principle. What does it mean? why that if a man's once wrong he's always to be wrong— that is just the amount of it. There's Chevydale, for instance, he has a brother who is a rank Tory and a Commissioner of Excise, mark that; Chevydale and he play into each other's hands, and Chevydale some of these days will sell the Liberals, that is, if he can get good value for them. If I now vote on the Tory side against Chevydale, his brother, the Tory Commissioner, will be my enemy in spite of all his Toryism; but if I vote and exert myself for Chevydale, the Liberal, I make his Tory of a brother my friend for life. And now, talk to me about principle, or consistency either."

His nephew could not but admit, that the instances adduced by his uncle were admirably calculated to illustrate his argument, and he accordingly pursued the subject no further.

"Ay!" exclaimed the Still-hound, "what d—d scrawl have we got here? Ay, ay, why this is better than I expected."

"What is better, uncle?" said the nephew, venturing an experiment.

"Why," replied the sagacious old rascal, "for you to mind your business, if you have any, and to let me mind mine, without making impertinent inquiries, Master Harry." With these words he went and. locked up both letters in his desk. As we, however, possess the power of unlocking his desk, and reading the letter to boot, we now take the liberty of laying it in all its graphic beauty and elegance before our readers—

"To MISTHER KLINTON, SIR:

"Af you go this nite bout seven clocks or thereaway, you'd find a Still-Hed an' Worm At full work, in they tipper End iv The brown Glen in Ahadarra. Sir, thrum wan iv Die amstrung's Orringemen an' a fren to the axshize."

The gauger after breakfast again resumed the conversation as follows:—

"Have you changed your mind, Harry, regarding the Excise? because if you have I think I may soon have an opportunity of getting you a berth."

"No, sir, I feel an insurmountable repugnance to the life of a Still—hem."

"Go on, man, to the life of a Still-hunter. Very well. Your father's death last year left you and your sister there dependent upon me, for the present at least; for what could a medical man only rising into practice, with a, family to support and educate, leave behind him?"

"Unfortunately, sir, it is too true."

"In the mean time you may leave 'unfortunate' out, and thank God that you had the shelter of my roof to come to; and be on your knees, too, that I was a bachelor. Well, I am glad myself that I had and have a home for you; but still, Harry, you ought to think of doing something for yourself; for I may not live always, you know, and beside I am not rich. You don't relish surgery, you say?"

"I can't endure it, uncle."

"But you like farming?"

"Above every other mode of life."

"Very well, I think it's likely I shall have a good farm to put you into before long."

"Thank you, uncle. You may rest assured that both Maria and myself are fully sensible of the kindness we have experienced at your hands."

"Small thanks to me for that. Who the devil would I assist, if not my brother's orphans? It is true, I despise the world, but still we must make our use of it. I know it consists of only knaves and fools. Now, I respect the knaves; for if it were'nt for their roguery, the world would never work; it would stand still and be useless. The fools I despise, not so much because they are fools, as because they would be knaves if they could; so that, you see I return again to my favorite principle of honesty. I am going to Ballymacan on business, so good-bye to you both."

"Uncle," said his nephew, "one word with you before you go."

"What is it?"

"Would you suffer me to offer you a word of advice, and will you excuse me for taking such a liberty with a man of your experience?"

"Certainly, Harry, and shall always feel thankful to any one that gives me good advice."

"If this is not good advice, it is at least well intended."

"Let us hear it first, and then we shall judge better."

"You say you will procure me a farm. Now, uncle, there is one thing I should wish in connection with that transaction, which is, that you would have no underhand—hem!—no private understanding of any kind with Mr. Hycy Burke."

"Me a private understanding with Hycy Burke! What in the devil's name has put such a crotchet as that into your head?"

"I only speak as I do, because I believe you have received a private communication from him."

"Have I, faith! If so I am obliged to you—but I am simply ignorant of the fact you mention; for, with my own knowledge', I never received a line from him in my life."

"Then I must be wrong," replied Harry; "that is all."

"Wrong! Certainly you are wrong. Hycy Burke, I am told, is a compound of great knave and gross fool, the knavery rather prevailing. But how is this? Are not you and he inseparable?"

"He is a companion, uncle, but not a friend in the true sense—nor, indeed, in any sense of that word. I spoke now, however, with reference to a particular transaction, and not to his general character."

"Well, then, I have no underhand dealings with him, as you are pleased to call them, nor ever had. I never to my knowledge received a line from him in my life; but I tell you that if he comes in my way, and that I can make use of him, I will. Perhaps he may serve us in the Elections. Have you anything else to ask?"

"No sir," replied Harry, laughing. "Only I hope you will excuse me for the liberty I took."

"Certainly, with all my heart, and you shall be always welcome to take the same liberty. Good-bye, again."

Clinton now felt satisfied that Hycy's letter to his uncle was an anonymous one, and although he could not divine its contents, he still felt assured that it was in some way connected with the farm transaction, or at all events detrimental to Bryan M'Mahon. He consequently resolved to see Hycy, against whom, or rather against whose principles he was beginning to entertain a strong repugnance, and without any hesitation to repudiate the engagement he had entered into with him.

He found Hycy at home, or rather he found him in conversation with Bat Hogan behind his father's garden.

"What was that ruffian wanting with you, Hycy, if it's a fair question?"

"Perfectly," said Hycy, "from you; but not in sooth from your worthy uncle."

"How is that?"

"Simply, he wants to know if I'd buy a keg of Poteen which, it seems, he has to sell. I declined because I have a sufficiently ample stock of it on hands."

"My uncle," said Clinton, prefers it to any other spirits; indeed, at home he never drinks any other, and whenever he dines, thanks those who give it the preference."

"Come in, and let us have a glass of poteen grog, in the mean time," said Hycy, "for it's better still in grog than in punch. It's a famous relish for a slice of ham; but, as the Scotch say, baith's best."

Having discussed the grog and ham, the conversation went on.

"Hycy," proceeded his companion, "with respect to that foolish arrangement or bargain we made the other night, I won't have anything to say or do in it. You shall impoverish or ruin no honest man on my account. I was half drunk or whole drunk, otherwise I wouldn't have listened to such a proposal."

"What do you mean?" said Hycy, with a look of very natural surprise, and a pause of some time, "I don't understand you."

"Don't you remember the foolish kind of stipulation we entered into with reference to M'Mahon's farm, of Ahadarra, on the one hand, and my most amiable (d—n me but I ought to be horsewhipped for it) sister on the other?"

"No," replied Hycy, "devil a syllable. My word and honor, Harry."

"Well, if you don't, then, it's all right. You didn't appear to be tipsy, though."

"I never do, Harry. In that respect I'm the d—dest, hypocritical rascal in Europe. I'm a perfect phenomenon; for, in proportion as I get drunk in intellect, I get sober both in my carriage and appearance. However, in Heaven's name let me know the bargain if there was one?"

"No, no," replied his friend, "it was a disgraceful affair on both sides, and the less that's said of it the better."

By some good deal of persuasion, however, and an additional glass of grog, he prevailed on Clinton to repeat the substance of the stipulation; on hearing which, as if for the first time, he laughed very heartily.

"This liquor," he proceeded, "is a strange compound, and puts queer notions into our head. Why if there's an honest decent fellow in Europe, whom I would feel anxious to serve beyond another, next to yourself, Harry, it is Bryan M'Mahon. But why I should have spoken so, I can't understand at all. In the first place, what means have of injuring the man? And what is stronger still, what inclination have I, or could have—and what is still better—should have?"

"I do assure you it did not raise you in my opinion."

"Faith, no wonder, Harry, and I am only surprised you didn't speak to me sooner about it. Still," he proceeded, smiling, 'there is one portion of it I should not wish to see cancelled—I mean your advocacy with Miss Clinton."

"To be plain with you, Hycy, I wash my hands out of that affair too; I won't promise advocacy."

"Well neutrality?"

"The truth is, neither neutrality nor advocacy would avail a rush. I have reason to think that my sister's objections against you are insuperable."

"On what do they rest?" asked the other.

"They are founded upon your want of morals," replied Clinton.

"Well, suppose I reform my morals?"

"That is, substitute hypocrisy for profligacy; I fear, Hycy, the elements of reformation are rather slight within you."

"Seriously, you do me injustice; and, besides, a man ought not to be judged of his morals before marriage, but after."

"Faith, both before and after, in my opinion, Hycy. No well-educated, right-minded girl would marry a man of depraved morals, knowing him to be such."

"But I really am not worse than others, nor so bad as many. Neither have I the reputation of being an immoral man. A little wild and over-impulsive from animal spirits I may be, but all that will pass off with the new state. No, no, d—n it, don't allow Miss Clinton to imbibe such prejudices. I do not say that I am a saint; but I shall settle down and bring her to church very regularly, and hear the sermon with most edifying attention. Another glass of grog?"

"No, no."

"But I hope and trust, my dear Harry, that you have not been making impressions against me."

"Unquestionably not. I only say you have no chance whatever in that quarter."

"Will you allow me to try?" asked Hycy.

"I have not the slightest objection," replied the other, "because I know how it will result."

"Very well,—thank you even for that same, my dear Harry; but, seriously speaking, I fear that neither you nor I are leading the kind of lives we ought, and so far I cannot quarrel with your sister's principles. On the contrary, they enable me to appreciate her if possible still more highly; for a clear and pure standard of morals in a wife is not only the best fortune but the best security for happiness besides. You might stop and dine?"

"No, thank you, it is impossible. By the way, I have already spoiled my dinner with that splendid ham of yours. Give me a call when in town."

Hycy, after Clinton's departure, began to review his own position. Of ultimately succeeding with Miss Clinton he entertained little doubt. So high and confident was his vanity, that he believed himself capable of performing mighty feats, and achieving great successes, with the fair sex,—all upon the strength of having destroyed the reputation of two innocent country girls. Somehow, notwithstanding his avowed attachment for Miss Clinton, he could not help now and then reverting to the rich beauty and magnificent form of Kathleen Cavanagh; nor was this contemplation of his lessened by considering that, with all his gentlemanly manners, and accomplishments, and wealth to boot, she preferred the clod-hopper, as he called Bryan M'Mahon, to himself.

He felt considerably mortified at this reflection, and the more especially, as he had been frequently taunted with it and laughed at for it by the country girls, whenever he entered into any bantering conversation. A thought now struck him by which he could, as he imagined, execute a very signal revenge upon M'Mahon through Kathleen, and perhaps, ultimately upon Kathleen herself, if he should succeed with Miss Clinton; for he did not at all forgive Kathleen the two public instances of contempt with which she had treated him. There was still, however, another consideration. His father had threatened to bring home his brother Edward, then destined for the church, and altogether to change his intentions in that respect. Indeed, from the dry and caustic manner of the old man towards him of late, he began to entertain apprehensions upon the subject. Taking therefore all these circumstances into consideration, he resolved in any event to temporize a little, and allow the father to suppose that he might be prevailed upon to marry Kathleen Cavanagh.

In the course of that evening, after dinner, while his father and he were together and his mother not present, he introduced the subject himself.

"I think, Mr. Burke, if I remember correctly, you proposed something like a matrimonial union between the unrivalled Katsey Cavanagh and the accomplished Hycy."

"I did, God forgive me."

"I have been thinking over that subject since."

"Have you, indeed," said his father; "an' am I to make Ned a priest or a farmer?" he asked, dryly.

"The church, I think, Mr. Burke, is, or ought to be, his destination."

"So, after all, you prefer to have my money and my property, along wid a good wife, to your brother Ned—Neddy I ought to call him, out of compliment to you—ha! ha! ha!"

"Proceed, Mr. Burke, you are pleased to be facetious."

"To your brother Ned—Neddy—having them, and maybe along wid them the same, wife too?"

"No, not exactly; but out of respect to your wishes.

"What's that?" said the old man, staring at him with a kind of comic gravity—"out of respect to my wishes!"

"That's what I've said," replied the son. "Proceed."

His father looked at' him again, and replied, "Proceed yourself—-it was you introduced the subject. I'm now jack-indifferent about it."

"All I have to say," continued Hycy, "is that I withdraw my ultimate refusal, Mr. Burke. I shall entertain the question, as they say; and it is not improbable but that I may dignify the fair Katsey with the honorable title of Mrs. Burke."

"I wish you had spoken a little sooner, then," replied his father, "bekaise it so happens that Gerald Cavanagh an' I have the match between her and your brother Ned as good as made."

"My brother Ned! Why, in the name of; all that's incredible, how could that be encompassed?"

"Very aisily," said his father, "by the girl's waitin' for him. Ned is rather young! yet, I grant you; he's nineteen, however, and two years more, you know, will make him one-and-twenty—take him out o' chancery, as they say."

"Very good, Mr. Burke, very good; in that case I have no more to say."

"Well," pursued the father, in the same dry, half-comic, half-sarcastic voice, "but what do you intend to do with yourself?"

"As to that," replied Hycy, who felt that the drift of the conversation was setting in against him, "I shall take due time to consider."

"What height are you?" asked the father, rather abruptly.

"I can't see, Mr. Burke, I really can't see what my height has to do with the question."

"Bekaise," proceeded the other, "I have some notion of putting you into the army. You spoke of it wanst yourself, remimber; but then there's an objection even to that."

"Pray, what is the objection, Mr. Burke?"

"Why, it's most likely you'd have to fight—if you took to the milintary trade."

"Why, upon my word, Mr. Burke, you shine in the sarcastic this evening."

"But, at any rate, you must take your chance for that. You're a fine, active young fellow, and I suppose if they take to runnin' you won't be the last of them."

"Good, Mr. Burke—proceed, though."

"An accordingly I have strong notions of buying you a corplar's or a sargent's commission. A good deal of that, however, depends upon yourself; but, as you say, I'll think of it."

Hycy, who could never bear ridicule, especially from the very man whom he attempted to ridicule most, bounced up, and after muttering something in the shape of an oath that was unintelligible, said, assuming all his polite irony:—

"Do so, Mr. Burke; in the mean time I have the pleasure of wishing you a very good evening, sir."

"Oh, a good-evening, sir," replied the old fellow, "and when you come home from the wars a full non-commissioned officer, you'll be scowerin' up your halbert every Christmas an' Aisther, I hope; an' telling us long stories—of all you killed an' ate while you were away from us."

Harry Clinton, now aware that the anonymous letter which his uncle had received that morning was the production of Hycy, resolved to watch the gauger's motions very closely. After a great deal of reflection upon Hycy's want of memory concerning their bargain, and upon a close comparison between his conduct and whole manner on the night in question, and his own account of the matter in the course of their last interview, he could not help feeling that his friend had stated a gross falsehood, and that the pretended want of recollection was an ingenious after-thought, adopted for the purpose of screening himself from the consequences of whatever injury he might inflict upon Bryan M'Mahon.

"Harry," said his uncle, as nine o'clock approached, "I am going upon duty tonight."

"In what direction, sir? may I ask."

"Yes, you may, but I'm not bound to tell you. In this instance, however, there is no necessity for secrecy; it is now too late to give our gentleman the hard word, so I don't care much if I do tell you. I am bound for Ahadarra."

"For Ahadarra—you say for Ahadarra, uncle?"

"I do, nephew."

"By heavens, he is the deepest and most consummate scoundrel alive," exclaimed Harry; "I now see it all. Uncle, I wish to God you would—would—-I don't know what to say."

"That's quite evident, nor what to think either. In the mean time the soldiers are waiting for me in Ballymacan, and so I must attend to my duty, Harry."

"Is it upon the strength of the blotted letter you got this morning, sir, that you are now acting"?"

"No, sir; but upon the strength of a sure spy dispatched this day to the premises. I am a little too shrewd now, Master Harry, to act solely upon anonymous information. I have been led too many devil's dances by it in my time, to be gulled in my old age on the strength of it."

He immediately prepared himself for the excursion, mounted his horse, that was caparisoned in a military saddle, the holsters furnished with a case of pistols, which, with a double case that he had on his person and two daggers, constituted his weapons of offence and defence.

Their path lay directly to the south for about two miles. Having traversed this distance they reached cross-roads, one of which branched towards the left and was soon lost in a rough brown upland, into which it branched by several little pathways that terminated in little villages or solitary farmer's houses. For about two miles more they were obliged to cross a dark reach of waste moor, where the soil was strong and well capable of cultivation. Having avoided the villages and more public thoroughfares, they pushed upward until they came into the black heath itself, where it was impossible that horses could travel in such darkness as then prevailed; for it was past ten o'clock, near the close of December. Clinton consequently left his horse in the care of two soldiers on a bit of green meadow by the side of Ahadarra Lough—a small tarn or mountain lake about two hundred yards in diameter. They then pushed up a long round swelling hill, on the other side of which was a considerable stretch of cultivated land with Bryan M'Mahon's new and improved houses at the head of it. This they kept to their right until they came in sight of the wild but beautiful and picturesque Glen of Althadhawan, which however was somewhat beyond the distance they had to go. At length, after breasting another hill which was lost in the base of Cullimore, they dropped down rapidly into a deep glen through which ran a little streamlet that took its rise not a quarter of a mile above them, and which supplied the apparatus for distillation with soft clear water. This they followed until near the head of the glen, where, in a position which might almost escape even a gauger's eye, they found the object of their search.

Tumbled around them in all directions were a quantity of gigantic rocks thrown as it were at random during some Titanic war-fare or diversion—between two of which the still-house was built in such a way, that, were it not for the smoke in daylight, it would be impossible to discover it, or at all events, to suppose that it could be the receptacle of a human being.

On entering, Clinton and his men were by no means surprised to find the place deserted, for this in fact was frequently the case on such occasions. On looking through the premises, which they did by the light of a large fire, they found precisely that which had been mentioned in Hycy's letter—to wit, the Still, the Head, and the Worm; but with the exception of an old broken rundlet or two, and a crazy vessel of wash that was not worth removing, there was nothing whatsoever besides.

The Still was on the fire half filled with water, the Head was on the Still, and the Worm was attached to the Head precisely as if they were in the process of distillation.

"Ay," said Clinton, on seeing how matters stood, "I think I understand this affair. It's a disappointment in one sense—but a sure enough card in another. The fine is certain, and Ahadarra is most undoubtedly in for it."

CHAPTER XV.—State of the Country

—Hycy's Friendship for Bryan M'Mahon—Bryan's Interview with his Landlord.

M'Mahon's last interview with Fethertonge was of so cheering a nature, and indicated on the part of that gentleman so much true and sterling kindness towards the young man and his family, that he felt perfectly satisfied on leaving him, and after having turned their conversation over in his mind, that he might place every confidence in the assurance he had given him. His father, too, who had never for a moment doubted Feathertonge, felt equally gratified at Bryan's report of their interview, as indeed did the whole family; they consequently spared neither labor nor expense in the improvements which they were making on their farms.

The situation of the country and neighborhood at this period was indeed peculiar, and such as we in this unhappy country have experienced both before and since. I have already stated, that there was a partial failure of the potato crop that season, a circumstance which uniformly is the forerunner of famine and sickness. The failure, however, on that occasion was not caused by a blight in the haulm, or to use plainer words, by a sudden withering of the stalks, but by large portions of the seed failing to grow. The partial scarcity, however, occasioned by this, although it did not constitute what can with propriety be termed famine, cause the great mass of pauperism which such a season always extends and increases, to press so heavily upon the struggling farmers, that their patience and benevolence became alike tired out and exhausted. This perpetually recurring calamity acts with a most depressing effect upon those persons in the country who have any claim to be considered independent. It deprives them of hope, and consequently of energy, and by relaxing the spirit of industry which has animated them, tends in the course of time to unite them to the great body of pauperism which oppresses and eats up the country. But let us not be misunderstood. This evil alone is sufficiently disastrous to the industrial energies of the class we mention; but when, in addition to this, the hitherto independent farmer has to contend with high rents, want of sympathy in his landlord, who probably is ignorant of his very existence, and has never seen him perhaps in his life; and when it is considered that he is left to the sharp practice and pettifogging, but plausible rapacity of a dishonest agent, who feels that he is irresponsible, and may act the petty tryant and vindictive oppressor if he wishes, having no restraint over his principles but his interest, which, so far from restraining, only guides and stimulates them;— when we reflect upon all this, and feel, besides, that the political principles upon which the country is governed are those that are calculated to promote British at the expense of Irish interests—we say, when we reflect upon and ponder over all this, we need not feel surprised that the prudent, the industrious, and the respectable, who see nothing but gradual decline and ultimate pauperism before them—who feel themselves neglected and overlooked, and know that every sixth or seventh year they are liable to those oppressive onsets of distress, sickness, and famine—we need not, we repeat, feel at all surprised that those who constitute this industrious and respectable class should fly from the evils which surround them, and abandon, whilst they possess the power of doing so, the country in which such evils are permitted to exist.

It is upon this principle, or rather upon these principles, and for these reasons, that the industry, the moral feeling, the independence, and the strength of the country have been passing out of it for years—leaving it, season after season, weaker, more impoverished, and less capable of meeting those periodical disasters which, we may almost say, are generated by the social disorder and political misrule of the country.

The fact is, and no reasonable or honest man capable of disencumbering himself of political prejudices can deny it, that up until a recent period the great body of the Irish people—the whole people—were mainly looked upon and used as political instruments in the hands of the higher classes, but not at all entitled to the possession of separate or independent interests in their own right. It is true they were allowed the possession of the forty-shilling franchise; but will any man say that the existence of that civil right was a benefit to the country? So far from that, it was a mere engine of corruption, and became, in the hands of the Irish landlords, one of the most oppressive and demoralizing curses that ever degraded a people. Perjury, fraud, falsehood, and dishonesty, were its fruits, and the only legacy it left to the country was an enormous mass of pauperism, and a national morality comparatively vitiated and depraved, in spite of all religious influence and of domestic affections that are both strong and tender. Indeed it is exceedingly difficult to determine whether it has been more injurious to the country in a political than in a moral sense. Be that as it may, it had a powerful effect in producing the evils that we now suffer, and our strong tendencies to social disorganization. By it the landlords were induced, for the sake of multiplying, votes, to encourage the subdivision of small holdings into those that were actually only nominal or fictitious, and the consequences were, that in multiplying votes they were multiplying families that had no fixed means of subsistence—multiplying in fact a pauper population—multiplying not only perjury, fraud, falsehood, and dishonesty, but destitution, misery, disease and death. By the forty-shilling franchise, the landlords encumbered the soil with a loose and unsettled population that possessed within itself, as poverty always does, a fearful facility of reproduction—a population which pressed heavily upon the independent class of farmers and yeomen, but which had no legal claim upon the territory of the country. The moment, however, when the system which produced and ended this wretched class, ceased to exist, they became not only valueless in a political sense, but a dead weight upon the energies of the country, and an almost insuperable impediment to its prosperity. This great evil the landlords could conjure up, but they have not been able to lay it since. Like Frankenstein in the novel, it pursues them to the present moment, and must be satisfied or appeased in some way, or it will unquestionably destroy them. From the abolition of the franchise until now, an incessant struggle of opposing interests has been going on in the country. The "forties" and their attendants must be fed; but the soul on which they live in its present state is not capable of at the same time supporting them and affording his claims to the landlord; for the food must go to England to pay the rents and the poor "forties" must starve. They are now in the way of the landlord—they are now in the way of the farmer—they are in fact in way of each other, and unless some wholesome and human principle, either of domestic employment or colonial emigration, or perhaps both, shall be adopted, they will continue to embarrass the country, and to drive out of it, always in connection with other causes, the very class of persons that constitute its remaining strength.

At the present period of our narrative the neighborhood of Ballymacan was in an unsettled and distressful state. The small farmers, and such as held from six to sixteen acres, at a rent which they could at any period with difficulty pay, were barely able to support themselves and their families upon the produce of their holdings, so that the claims of the landlord were out of the question. Such a position as this to the unhappy class we speak of, is only another name for ruin. The bailiff, who always lives upon the property, seeing their condition, and knowing that they are not able to meet the coming gale, reports accordingly to the agent, who, now cognizant that there is only one look-up for the rent, seizes the poor man's corn and cattle, leaving himself and his family within cold walls, and at an extinguished hearth. In this condition were a vast number in the neighborhood of the locality laid in our narrative. The extraordinary, but natural anxiety for holding land, and the equally ardent spirit of competition which prevails in the country, are always ready arguments in the mouth of the landlord and agent, when they wish to raise the rent or eject the tenant. "If you won't pay me such a rent, there are plenty that will. I have been offered more than you pay, and more than I ask, and you know I must look to my own interests!" In this case it is very likely that the landlord speaks nothing but the truth; and as he is pressed on by his necessities on the one hand, and the tenant on the other, the state of a country so circumstanced with respect to landed property and its condition may be easily conceived.

In addition, however, to all we have already detailed, as affecting the neighborhood of Ahadarra, we have to inform our readers that the tenantry upon the surrounding property were soon about to enjoy the luxury of a contested election. Chevydale had been the sitting member during two sessions of Parliament. He was, as we have already stated, an Emancipator and Liberal; but we need scarcely say that he did not get his seat upon these principles. He had been a convert to Liberalism since his election, and at the approaching crisis stood, it was thought, but an indifferent chance of being re-elected.

The gentleman who had sat before was a sturdy Conservative, a good deal bigoted in politics, but possessing that rare and inestimable quality, or rather combination of qualities which constitute an honest man. He was a Major Vanston, a man of good property, and although somewhat deficient in the *suaviter in modo*, yet in consequence of his worth and sincerity, he was rather a favorite with the people, who in general relish sincerity and honesty wherever they find them in public men.

Having thus far digressed, we now beg leave to resume our narrative and once more return, from the contemplation of a state of things so painful to the progress of those circumstances which involve the fate of our humble individuals who constitute our *dramatis personae*.

The seizure of the distillery apparatus on M'Mahon's farm of Ahadarra, was in a few days followed by knowledge of the ruin in which it must necessarily involve that excellent and industrious young man. At this time there was an act of parliament in existence against illicit distillation, but of so recent a date that it was only when a seizure similar to the foregoing had been made, that the people in any particular district became acquainted with it. By this enactment the offending individual was looked upon as having no farther violated the laws in that case made and provided, than those who had never been engaged in such pursuits at all. In other words, the innocent, were equally punished with the guilty. A heavy fine was imposed—not on the offender, but on the whole townland in which he lived; so that the guilt of one individual was not visited as it ought to have been on the culprit himself, but equally distributed in all its penalties upon the other inhabitants of the district in question, who may have had neither act nor part in any violation of the laws whatsoever.

Bryan M'Mahon, on discovering the fearful position in which it placed him, scarcely knew on what hand to turn. His family were equally alarmed, and with just reason. Illicit distillation had been carried to incredible lengths for the last two or three years, and the statute in question was enacted with, a hope that it might unite the people in a kind of legal confederacy against a system so destructive of industry and morals. The act, however ill-judged, and impolitic at best, was not merely imperative,—but fraught with ruin and bloodshed. It immediately became the engine of malice and revenge between individual enemies—often between rival factions, and not unfrequently between parties instigated against each other by political rancor and hatred. Indeed, so destructive of the lives and morals of the people was it found, that in the course of a very few years it was repealed, but not until it had led to repeated murders and brought ruin and destruction upon many an unoffending and industrious family.

Bryan now bethought him of the warnings he had received from the gauger and Fethertonge, and resolved to see both, that he; might be enabled, if possible, to trace to its source the plot that had been laid, for his destruction. He accordingly went down to his father's at Carriglass, where he had not been long when Hycy Burke made his appearance, "Having come that far on his way," he said, "to see him, and to ascertain the truth of the report that had gone abroad respecting the heavy responsibility under which the illicit distillation had placed him." Bryan was naturally generous and without suspicion; but notwithstanding this, it was impossible that he should not entertain some slight surmises touching the sincerity of Burke.

"What is this, Bryan?" said the latter. "Can it be possible that you're in for the Fine, as report goes?"

"It's quite possible," replied Bryan; "on yesterday I got a notice of proceedings from the Board of Excise."

"But," pursued his friend, "what devil could have tempted you to have anything to do with illicit distillation? Didn't you know the danger of it?"

"I had no more to do with it," replied Bryan, "than you had—nor I don't even rightly know yet who had; though, indeed, I believe I may say it was these vagabonds, the Hogans, that has their hands in everything that's wicked and disgraceful. They would ruin me if they could," said Bryan, "and I suppose it was with the hope of doing so that they set up the still where they did."

"Well, now," replied Hycy, with an air of easy and natural generosity, "I should be sorry to think so: they are d—d scoundrels, or rather common ruffians, I grant you; but still, Bryan, I don't like to suspect even such vagabonds without good grounds. Bad as we know them to be, I have my doubts whether they are capable of setting about such an act for the diabolical purpose of bringing you to ruin. Perhaps they merely deemed the place on your farm a convenient one to build a still-house in, and that they never thought further about it."

"Or what," replied Bryan, "if there was some one behind their backs who is worse than themselves? Mightn't sich a thing as that be possible?"

"True," replied Hycy, "true, indeed—that's not improbable. Stay—no—well it may be—but—no—I can't think it."

"What is it you can't think?"

"Why, such a thing might be," proceeded Hycy, "if you have an enemy; but I think, Bryan, you are too well liked—and justly so too—if you will excuse me for saying so to your face—to have any enemy capable of going such nefarious lengths as that."

Bryan paused and seemed a good deal struck with the truth of Hycy's observation—"There's raison, sure enough in what you say, Hycy," he observed. "I don't know that I have a single enemy—unless the Hogans themselves—that would feel any satisfaction in drivin' me to destruction."

"And besides," continued Hycy, "between you and me now, Bryan, who the devil with an ounce of sense in his head would trust such scoundrels, or put himself in their power?"

Bryan considered this argument a still more forcible one than the other.

"That's stronger still," Re replied, "and indeed I am inclined to think that after all, Hycy, it happened as you say. Teddy Phats I think nothing at all about, for the poor, misshapen vagabone will distil poteen for any one that employs him."

"True," replied the other, "I agree with you; but what's to be done, Bryan? for that's the main point now."

"I scarcely know," replied Bryan, who now began to feel nothing but kindness towards Hycy, in consequence of the interest which that young fellow evidently took in his misfortune, for such, in serious truth, it must be called. "I am the only proprietor of Ahadarra," he proceeded, "and, as a matter of course, the whole fine falls on my shoulders."

"Ay, that's the devil of it; but at all events, Bryan, there is nothing got in this world without exertion and energy. Mr. Chevydale, the Member, is now at home: he has come down to canvass for the coming-election. I would recommend you to see him at once. You know—but perhaps you don't though—that his brother is one of the Commissioners of Excise; so that I don't know any man who can serve you more effectually than Chevydale, if he wishes."

"But what could he do?" asked Bryan.

"Why, by backing a memorial from you, stating the particulars, and making out a strong case, he might get the fine reduced. I shall draw up such a memorial if you wish."

"Thank you, Hycy—I'm obliged to you—these, I dare say, will be the proper steps to take—thank you."

"Nonsense! but perhaps I may serve you a little in another way. I'm very intimate with Harry Clinton, and who knows but I may be able to influence the uncle a little through the nephew."

"It's whispered that you might do more through the niece," replied Bryan, laughing; "is that true?"

"Nonsense, I tell you," replied Hycy, affecting confusion; "for Heaven's sake, Bryan, say nothing about that; how did it come to your ears?"

"Faith, and that's more than I can tell you," replied the other; "but I know I heard it somewhere of late."

"It's not a subject, of course," continued Hycy, "that I should wish to become the topic of vulgar comment or conversation, and I'd much rather you would endeavor to discountenance it whenever you hear it spoken of. At all events, whether with niece or nephew," proceeded Hycy, "you may rest assured, that whatever service I can render you, I shall not fail to do it. You and I have had a slight misunderstanding, but on an occasion like this, Bryan, it should be a bitter one indeed that a man—a generous man at least,—would or ought to remember."

This conversation took place whilst Bryan was proceeding to Fethertonge's, Hycy being also on his way home. On arriving at the turn of the road which led to Jemmy Burke's, Hycy caught the hand of his companion, which he squeezed with an affectionate warmth, so cordial and sincere in its character that Bryan cast every shadow of suspicion to the winds,

"Cheer up, Bryan, all will end better than you think, I hope. I shall draw up a memorial for you this evening, as strongly and forcibly as possible, and any other assistance that I can render you in this unhappy difficulty I will do it. I know I am about ninety pounds in your debt, and instead of talking to you in this way, or giving you fair words, I ought rather to pay you your money. The 'gentleman,' however, is impracticable for the present, but I trust—"

"Not a word about it," said Bryan, "you'll oblige me if you'll drop that part of the subject; but listen, Hycy,—I think you're generous and a little extravagant, and both is a good man's case—but that's not what I'm going to spake about, truth's best at all times; I heard that you were my enemy, and I was desired to be on my guard against you."

Hycy looked at him with that kind of surprise which is natural to an innocent man, and simply said, "May I ask by whom, Bryan?"

"I may tell you some other time," replied Bryan, "but I won't now; all I can say is, that I don't believe it, and I'm sure that ought to satisfy you."

"I shall expect you to tell me, Bryan," said the other, and then after returning a few steps, he caught M'Mahon's hand again, and shaking it warmly, once more added, "God bless you, Bryan; you are a generous high-minded young fellow, and I only wish I was like you."

Bryan, after they had separated, felt that Hycy's advice was the very best possible under the circumstances, and as he had heard for the first time that Chevydale was in the country, he resolved to go at once and state to him the peculiar grievance under which he labored.

Chevydale's house was somewhat nearer Ahadarra than Fethertonge's, but on the same line of road, and he accordingly proceeded to the residence of his landlord. The mansion indeed was a fine one. It stood on the brow of a gentle eminence, which commanded a glorious prospect of rich and highly cultivated country. Behind, the landscape rose gradually until it terminated in a range of mountains that protected the house from the north. The present structure was modern, having been built by old Chevydale, previous to his marriage. It was large and simple, but so majestic in appearance, that nothing could surpass the harmony that subsisted between its proportions and the magnificent old trees which studded the glorious lawn that surrounded, it, and rose in thick extensive masses that stretched far away behind the house. It stood in a park, which for the beauties of wood and. water was indeed worthy of its fine simplicity and grandeur—a park in which it was difficult to say whether the beautiful, the picturesque, or the wild, predominated most. And yet in this princely residence Mr. Chevydale did not reside more than a month, or at most two, during the whole year.

On reaching the hall-door, M'Mahon inquired from the servant who appeared, if he could see Mr. Chevydale.

"I'm afraid not," said the servant, "but I will see; what's your name?"

"Bryan M'Mahon, of Ahadarra, one of his tenants."

The servant returned to him in a few moments, and said, "Yes, he will see you; follow me."

Bryan entered a library, where he found his landlord and Fethertonge apparently engaged in business, and as he was in the act of doing so, he overheard Chevydale saying—"No, no, I shall always see my tenants."

Bryan made his obeisance in his own plain way, and Chevydale said—"Are you M'Mahon of Ahadarra?"

"I am, sir," replied Bryan.

"I thought you were a much older man," said Chevydale, "there certainly must be, some mistake here," he added, looking at Fethertonge.

"M'Mahon of Ahadarra was a middle-aged man several years ago, but this person is young enough to be his man."

"You speak of his uncle," replied Fethertonge, "who is dead. This young man, who now owns his uncle's farm, is son to Thomas M'Mahon of Carriglass. How is your father, M'Mahon? I hope he bears up well under his recent loss."

"Indeed but poorly, sir," replied Bryan, "I fear he'll never be the same man."

Chevydale here took to reading a newspaper, and in a minute or two appeared to be altogether unconscious of Bryan's presence.

"I'm afeard, sir," said Bryan, addressing himself to the agent, who was the only person likely to hear him, "I'm afeard, sir, that I've got into trouble."

"Into trouble? how is that?"

"Why, sir, there was a Still, Head, and Worm found upon Ahadarra, and I'm going to be fined for it."

"M'Mahon," replied the agent, "I am sorry to hear this, both on your own account and that of your family. If I don't mistake, you were cautioned and warned against this; but it was useless; yes, I am sorry for it; and for you, too."

"I don't properly understand you, sir," said Bryan.

"Did I not myself forewarn you against having anything to do in matters contrary to the law? You must remember I did, and on the very last occasion, too, when you were in my office."

"I remember it right well, sir," replied Bryan, "and I say now as I did then, that I am not the man to break the law, or have act or part in anything that's contrary to it. I know nothing about this business, except that three ruffianly looking fellows named Hogan, common tinkers, and common vagabonds to boot—men that are my enemies—are the persons by all accounts who set up the still on my property. As for myself, I had no more to do in it or with it than yourself or Mr. Chevydale here."

"Well," replied Fethertonge, "I hope not. I should feel much disappointed if you had, but you know, Bryan," he added, good-humoredly, "we could scarcely expect that you should admit such a piece of folly, not to call it by a harsher name."

"If I had embarked in it," replied M'Mahon, "I sartinly would not deny it to you or Mr. Chevydale, at least; but, as I said before, I know nothing more about it, than simply it was these ruffians and a fellow named Phats, a Distiller, that set it a-working,—however, the question is, what am I to do? If I must pay the fine for the whole townland, it will beggar me—ruin me. It was that brought me to my landlord here," he added; "I believe, sir, you have a brother a Commissioner of Excise?"

"Eh? what is that?" asked Chevydaie, looking up suddenly as Bryan asked the question.

M'Mahon was obliged to repeat all the circumstances once more, as did Feathertonge the warning he had given him against having any connection with illegal proceedings.

"I am to get a memorial drawn up tomorrow, sir," proceeded Bryan, "and I was thinking that by giving the Board of Excise a true statement of the case, they might reduce the fine; if they don't, I am ruined—that's all."

"Certainly," said his landlord, "that is a very good course to take; indeed, your only course."

"I hope, sir," proceeded Bryan, "that as you now know the true circumstances of the case, you'll be kind, enough to support my petition; I believe your brother, sir, is one of the Commissioners; you would sartinly be able to do something with him."

"No," replied Chevydaie, "I would not ask anything from him; but I shall support your Petition, and try what I can do with the other Commissioners. On principle, however, I make it a point never to ask anything from my brother."

"Will I bring you the Petition, sir?" asked Bryan.

"Fetch me the Petition."

"And Bryan," said Fethertonge, raising his finger at him as if by way of warning—and laughing—"hark ye, let this be the last."

"Fethertonge," said the landlord, "I see 'Pratt has been found guilty, and the sentence confirmed by the Commander-in-Chief."

"You will insist on it," said Bryan, in reply to the agent, "but—"

"There now, M'Mahon," said the latter, "that will do; good day to you."

"I think it is a very harsh sentence, Fethertonge; will you touch the bell?"

"I don't know, sir," replied the other, ringing as he spoke; "Neville's testimony was very strong against him, and the breaking of the glass did not certainly look like sobriety."

"I had one other word to say, gentlemen," added M'Mahon, "if you'll allow me, now that I'm here."

Fethertonge looked at him with a face in which might be read a painful but friendly rebuke for persisting to speak, after the other had changed the subject. "I rather think Mr. Chevydale would prefer hearing it some other time, Bryan."

"But you know the proverb, sir," said Bryan, smiling, "that there's no time like the present; besides it's only a word."

"What is it?" asked the landlord.

"About the leases, sir," replied M'Mahon, "to know when it would be convenient for you to sign them."

Chevydale looked, from Bryan to the agent, and again from the agent to Bryan, as if anxious to understand what the allusion to leases meant. At this moment a servant entered, saying, "The horses are at the door, gentlemen."

"Come some other day, M'Mahon," said Fethertonge; "do you not see that we are going out to ride now—going on our canvass? Come to my office some other day; Mr. Chevydale will remain for a considerable time in the country now, and you need not feel so eager in the matter."

"Yes, come some other day, Mr.—Mr.—ay—M'Mahon; if there are leases to sign, of course I shall sign them; I am always anxious to do my duty as a landlord. Come, or rather Fethertonge here will manage it. You know I transact no business here; everything is done at his office, unless when he brings me papers to sign. Of course I shall sign any necessary paper."

Bryan then withdrew, after having received another friendly nod of remonstrance, which seemed to say, "Why will you thus persist, when you see that he is not disposed to enter into these matters now? Am I not your friend?" Still, however, he did not feel perfectly at ease with the result of his visit. A slight sense of uncertainty and doubt crept over him, and in spite of every effort at confidence, he found that that which he had placed in Fethertonge, if it did not diminish, was most assuredly not becoming stronger.

CHAPTER XVI.—A Spar Between Kate and Philip Hogan

—Bryan M'Mahon is Cautioned against Political Temptation—He Seeks Major Vanston's Interest with the Board of Excise.

The consequences of the calamity which was hanging over Bryan M'Mahon's head, had become now pretty well understood, and occasioned a very general and profound sympathy for the ruin in which it was likely to involve him. Indeed, almost every one appeared to feel it more than he himself did, and many, who on meeting him, were at first disposed to offer him consolation, changed their purpose on witnessing his cheerful and manly bearing under it. Throughout the whole country there was but one family, with another exception, that felt gratified at the blow which had fallen on him. The exception we speak of was no other than Mr, Hycy Burke, and the family was that of the Hogans. As for Teddy Phats, he was not the man to trouble himself by the loss of a moment's indifference upon any earthly or other subject, saving and excepting always that it involved the death, mutilation, or destruction in some shape, of his great and relentless foe, the Gauger, whom he looked upon as the impersonation of all that is hateful and villainous in life, and only sent into this world to war with human happiness at large. That great professional instinct, as the French say, and a strong unaccountable disrelish of Hycy Burke, were the only two feelings that disturbed the hardened indifference of his nature.

One night, shortly after Bryan's visit to his landlord, the Hogans and Phats were assembled in the kiln between the hours of twelve and one o'clock, after having drunk nearly three quarts of whiskey among them. The young savages, as usual, after the vagabond depredations or mischievous exercises of the day, were snoring as we have described them before; when Teddy, whom no quantity of liquor could affect beyond a mere inveterate hardness of brogue and an indescribable effort at mirth and melody, exclaimed—"Fwhy, dhen, dat's the stuff; and here's bad luck to him that paid fwor it."

"I'll not drink it, you ugly *keout*," exclaimed Philip, in his deep and ruffianly voice; "but come—all o' yez fill up and drink my toast.

Come, Kate, you crame of hell's delights, fill till I give it. No," he added abruptly, "I won't drink that, you leprechaun; the man that ped for it is Hycy Burke, and I like Hycy Burke for one thing, an' I'll not dhrink bad luck to him. Come, are yez ready?"

"Give it out, you hulk," said Kate, "an' don't keep us here all night over it."

"Here, then," exclaimed the savage, with a grin of ferocious mirth, distorting his grim colossal features into a smile that was frightful and inhuman—"Here's may Bryan M'Mahon be soon a beggar, an' all his breed the same! Drink it now, all o' yez, or, by the mortal counthryman, I'll brain the first that'll refuse it."

The threat, in this case, was a drunken one, and on that very account the more dangerous.

"Well," said Teddy, "I don't like to drink it; but if—"

"*Honomondiaul!* you d——d disciple," thundered the giant, "down wid it, or I'll split your skull!"

Teddy had it down ere the words were concluded.

"What!" exclaimed Hogan, or rather roared again, as he fastened his blazing eyes on Kate—"what, you yalla mullotty, do you dar to refuse?"

"Ay, do dar to refuse!—an' I'd see you fizzin' on the devil's fryin'-pan, where you'll fiz yet, afore I'd dhrink it. Come, come," she replied, her eye blazing now as fiercely as his own, "keep quiet, I bid you—keep calm; you ought to know me now, I think."

"Drink it," he shouted, "or I'll brain you."

"Howl him," said Teddy—"howl him; there's murdher in his eye. My soul to happiness but he'll kill her."

"Will he, indeed?" said Bat, with a loud laugh, in which he was joined by Ned—"will he, indeed?" they shouted. "Go on, Kate, you'll get fair play if you want it—his eye, Teddy! ay, but look at her's, man alive—look at her altogether! Go on, Kate—more power!"

Teddy, on looking at her again, literally retreated a few paces from sheer terror of the tremendous and intrepid fury who now stood before him. It was then for the first time that he observed the huge bones and immense muscular development that stood out into terrible strength by the force of her rising passion. It was the eye, however, and the features of the face which filled him with such an accountable dread. The eyes were literally blazing, and the muscles of the face, now cast into an expression which seemed at the same time to be laughter and fury, were wrought up and blended together in such a way as made the very countenance terrible by the emanation of murder which seemed to break from every feature of it. "Drink it, I say again," shouted Philip. Kate made no reply, but, walking over to where he stood, she looked closely into his eyes, and said, with grinding teeth—"Not if it was to save you from the gallows, where you'll swing yet; but listen." As she spoke her words were hoarse and low, there was a volume of powerful strength in her voice which stunned one like the roar of a lioness. "Here," she exclaimed, her voice now all at once rising or rather shooting up to a most terrific scream—"here's a disgraceful death to Hycy Burke! and may all that's good and prosperous in this world, ay, and in the next, attend Bryan M'Mahon, the honest man! Now, Philip, my man, see how I drink them both." And, having concluded, she swallowed the glass of whiskey, and again drawing her face within an inch of his she glared right into his eyes.

"Howl me," he shouted, "or I'll sthrike, an' we'll have a death in the house."

She raised one hand and waved it behind her, as an intimation that they should not interfere.

The laughter of the brothers now passed all bounds. "No, Kate, go on—we won't interfere. You had better seize him."

"No," she replied, "let him begin first, if he dar."

"Howl me," shouted Philip, "she'll only be killed."

Another peal of laughter was the sole reply given to this by the brothers. "He's goin'," they exclaimed, "he's gone—the white fedher's in him—it's all over wid him he's afeerd of her, an' not for nothing either—ha! ha! ha! more power, Kate!"

Stung by the contemptuous derision contained in this language, Philip was stepping back in order to give himself proper room for a blow, when, on the very instant that he moved, Kate, uttering something between a howl and a yell, dashed her huge hands into his throat—which was, as is usual with tinkers, without a cravat—and in a moment a desperate and awful struggle took place between them. Strong as Philip was, he found himself placed perfectly on the defensive by the terrific grip which this furious opponent held of his throat. So powerful was it, indeed, that not a single instant was allowed him for the exercise of any aggressive violence against her by a blow, all his strength being directed to unclasp her hands from his throat that he might be permitted to breathe. As they pulled and tugged, however, it was evident that the struggle was going against him—a hoarse, alarming howl once or twice broke from him, that intimated terror and distress on his part.

"That's right, Kate," they shouted, "you have him—press tight—the windpipe's goin'—bravo! he'll soon stagger an' come down, an' then you may do as you like."

They tugged on, and dragged, and panted, with the furious vehemence of the exertion; when at length Philip shouted, in a voice half-stifled by strangulation, "Let g—o—o—o, I—I sa—y—y; ah! ah! ah!"

Bat now ran over in a spirit of glee and triumph that cannot well be described, and clapping his wife on the back, shouted—"Well done, Kate; stick to him for half a minute and he's yours. Bravo! you clip o' perdition, bravo!"

He had scarcely uttered the words when the giant carcass of Philip tottered and fell, dragging Kate along with it, who never for a moment lost or loosened her hold. Her opponent now began to sprawl and kick out his feet from a sense of suffocation, and in attempting to call for assistance, nothing but low, deep gurgling noises could issue from his lips, now livid with the pressure on his throat and covered with foam. His face, too, at all times dark and savage, became literally black, and he uttered such sternutations as, on seeing that they were accompanied by the diminished struggles which betoken exhaustion, induced Teddy to rush over for the purpose of rescuing him from her clutches.

"Aisy," said the others; "let them alone—a little thing will do it now—it's almost over—she has given him his gruel—an' divil's cure to him—he knew well enough what she could do—but he would have it."

Faint convulsive movements were all now that could be noticed in the huge limbs of their brother, and still the savage tigress was at his throat, when her husband at length said:—

"It's time, Ned—it's time—she may carry it too far—he's quiet enough now. Come away, Kate, it's all right—let him alone—let go your hoult of him."

Kate, however, as if she had tasted his blood, would listen to no such language; all the force, and energies, and bloody instincts of the incarnate fury were aroused within her, and she still stuck to her victim.

"Be japers she'll kill him," shouted Bat, rushing to her; "come, Ned, till we unclasp her—take care—pull quickly—bloody wars, he's dead!—Kate, you divil!—you fury of hell! let go—let go, I say."

Kate, however, heard him not, but still tugged and stuck to the throat of Philip's quivering carcass, until by a united effort they at length disentangled her iron clutches from it, upon which she struggled and howled like a beast of prey, and attempted with a strength that seemed more akin to the emotion of a devil than that of a woman to get at him again and again, in order to complete her work.

"Come, Kate," said her husband, "you're a Trojan—by japers you're a Trojan; you've settled him any way—is there life in him?" he asked, "if there is, dash wather or something in his face, an' drag him up out o' that—ha! ha! Well done, Kate; only for you we'd lead a fine life wid him—ay! an' a fine life that is—a hard life we led until you did come—there now, more power to you—by the livin' Counthryman, there's not your aquil in Europe—come now, settle down, an' don't keep all movin' that way as if you wor at him again—sit down now, an' here's another glass of whiskey for you."

In the mean time, Ned and Teddy Phats succeeded in recovering Philip, whom they dragged over and placed upon a kind of bench, where in a few minutes he recovered sufficiently to be able to speak—but ever and anon he shook his head, and stretched his neck, and drew his breath deeply, putting his hands up from time to time as if he strove to set his windpipe more at ease.

"Here Phil, my hairo," said his triumphant brother Bat, "take another glass, an' may be for all so strong and murdherin' as you are wid others you now know—an' you knew before what our woman' can do at home wid you."

"I've—hoch—hoch—I've done wid her—she's no woman; there's a devil in her, an' if you take my advice, it's to Priest M'Scaddhan you'd bring her, an' have the same devil prayed out of her—I that could murdher ere a man in the parist a'most!"

"Lave Bryan M'Mahon out," said Kate.

"No I won't," replied Phil, sullenly, and with a voice still hoarse, "no, I won't—I that could make smash of ere a man in the parish, to be throttled into perdition by a blasted woman. She's a devil, I say; for the last ten minutes I seen nothin' but fire, fire, fire, as red as blazes, an' I hard somethin' yellin', yellin', in my ears."

"Ay!" replied Kate, "I know you did—that was the fire of hell you seen, ready to resave you; an' the noise you hard was the voices of the devils that wor comin' for your sowl—ay, an' the voices of the two wives you murdhered—take care then, or I'll send you sooner to hell than you dhrame of."

The scowl which she had in return for this threat was beyond all description.

"Oh, I have done wid you," he replied; "you're not right, I say—but never mind, I'll put a pin in M'Mahon's collar for this—ay will I."

"Don't!" she exclaimed, in one fearful monosyllable, and then she added in a low condensed whisper, "or if you do, mark the consequence."

"Trot, Phil," said Teddy, "I think you needn't throuble your head about M'Mahon—he's done fwhor."

"An' mark me," said Kate, "I'll take care of the man that done for him. I know him well, betther than he suspects, an' can make him sup sorrow whenever I like—an' would, too, only for one thing."

"An' fwhat's dhat wan thing?" asked Phats.

"You'll know it when you're ouldher, may be," replied Kate; "but you must be ouldher first—I can keep my own secrets, thank God, an' will, too—only mark me all o' yez; you know well what I am—let no injury come to Bryan M'Mahon. For the sake of one person he must be safe."

"Well," observed Teddy, "let us hear no more about them; it's all settled that we are to set up in Glen Dearg above again—for this Hycy,—who's sthrivin' to turn the penny where he can."

"It is," said Bat; "an', to-morrow night, let us bring the things up—this election will sarve us at any rate—but who will come in?" (* That is, be returned.)

"The villain of hell!" suddenly exclaimed Kate, as if to herself; "to go to ruin the young man! That girl's breakin' her heart for what has happened."

"What are you talkin' about?" asked her husband.

"Nothing," she replied; "only if you all intend to have any rest to-night, throw yourselves in the shake-down there, an' go sleep. I'm not to sit up the whole night here, I hope?"

Philip, and Ned, and Teddy tumbled themselves into the straw, and in a few minutes were in a state of perfect oblivion.

"Hycy Burke is a bad boy, Bat," she said, as the husband was about to follow their example; "but he is marked—I've set my mark upon him."

"You appear to know something particular about him," observed her husband.

"Maybe I do, an' maybe I don't," she replied; "but I tell you, he's marked—that's all—go to bed now."

He tumbled after the rest, Kate stretched herself in an, opposite corner, and in a few minutes this savage orchestra was in full chorus.

What an insoluble enigma is woman! From the specimen of feminine delicacy and modest diffidence which we have just presented to the reader, who would imagine that Kate Hogan was capable of entering into the deep and rooted sorrow which Kathleen Cavanagh experienced when made acquainted with the calamity which was about to crush her lover. Yet so it was. In truth this fierce and furious woman who was at once a thief, a liar, a drunkard, and an impostor, hardened in wickedness and deceit, had in spite of all this a heart capable of virtuous aspirations, and of loving what was excellent and good. It is true she was a hypocrite herself, yet she detested Hycy Burke for his treachery. She was a thief and a liar, yet she liked and respected Bryan M'Mahon for his truth and honesty. Her heart, however, was not all depraved; and, indeed, it is difficult to meet a woman in whose disposition, however corrupted by evil society, and degraded by vice, there is not to be found a portion of the angelic essence still remaining. In the case before us, however, this may be easily accounted for. Kate Hogan, though a hell-cat and devil, when provoked, was, amidst all her hardened violence and general disregard of truth and honesty, a virtuous woman and a faithful wife. Hence her natural regard for much that was good and pure, and her strong sympathy with the sorrow which now fell upon Kathleen Cavanagh.

Kathleen and her sister had been sitting sewing at the parlor window, on the day Bryan had the interview we have detailed with Chevydale and the agent, when they heard their father's voice inquiring for Hanna.

"He has been at Jemmy Burke's, Kathleen," said her sister, "and I'll wager a nosegay, if one could get one, that he has news of this new sweetheart of yours; he's bent, Kathleen," she added, "to have you in Jemmy Burke's family, cost what it may."

"So it seems, Hanna."

"They say Edward Burke is still a finer-looking young fellow than Hycy. Now, Kathleen," she added, laughing, "if you should spoil a priest afther all! Well! un-likelier things have happened."

"That may be," replied Kathleen, "but this won't happen for all that, Hanna. Go, there he's calling for you again."

"Yes—yes," she shouted; "throth, among you all, Kathleen, you're making a regular go-between of me. My father thinks I can turn you round my finger, and Bryan M'Mahon thinks—yes, I'm goin'," she answered again. "Well, keep up your spirits; I'll soon have news for you about this spoiled priest."

"Poor Hanna," thought Kathleen; "where was there ever such a sister? She does all she can to keep my spirits up; but it can't be. How can I see him ruined and beggared, that had the high spirit and the true heart?"

Hanna, her father, and mother, held a tolerably long discussion together, in which Kathleen could only hear the tones of their voices occasionally. It was evident, however, by the emphatic intonations of the old couple, that they were urging some certain point, which her faithful sister was deprecating, sometimes, as Kathleen could learn, by seriousness, and at other times by mirth. At length she returned with a countenance combating between seriousness and jest; the seriousness, however, predominating.

"Kathleen," said she, "you never had a difficulty before you until now. They haven't left me a leg to stand upon. Honest Jemmy never had any wish to make Edward a priest, and he tells my father that it was all a trick of the wife to get everything for her favorite; and he's now determined to disappoint them. What will you do?"

"What would you recommend me?" asked Kathleen, looking at her with something of her own mood, for although her brow was serious, yet there was a slight smile upon her lips.

"Why," said the frank and candid girl, "certainly to run away with Bryan M'Mahon; that, you know, would settle everything."

"Would it settle my father's heart," said Kathleen, "and my mother's?—would it settle my own character?—would it be the step that all the world would expect from Kathleen Cavanagh?—and putting all the world aside, would it be a step that I could take in the sight of God, my dear Hanna?"

"Kathleen, forgive me, darlin'," said her sister, throwing her arms about her neck, and laying her head upon her shoulder; "I'm a foolish, flighty creature; indeed, I don't know what's to be done, nor I can't advise you. Come out and walk about; the day's dry an' fine."

"If your head makes fifty mistakes," said her sister, "your heart's an excuse for them all; but you don't make any mistakes, Hanna, when you're in earnest; instead of that your head's worth all our heads put together. Come, now."

They took the Carriglass road, but had not gone far when they met Dora M'Mahon who, as she said, "came down to ask them up a while, as the house was now so lonesome;" and she added, with artless naivete, "I don't know how it is, Kathleen, but I love you better now than I ever did before. Ever since my darlin' mother left us, I can't look upon you as a stranger, and now that poor Bryan's in distress, my heart clings to you more and more."

Hanna, the generous Hanna's eyes partook of the affection and admiration which beamed in Dora's, as they rested on Kathleen; but notwithstanding this, she was about to give Dora an ironical chiding for omitting to say anything gratifying to herself, when happening to look back, she saw Bryan at the turn of the road approaching them.

"Here's a friend of ours," she exclaimed; "no less than Bryan M'Mahon himself. Come, Dora, we can't go' up to Carriglass, but we'll walk back with you a piece o' the way."

Bryan, who was then on his return from Chevydale's, soon joined them, and they proceeded in the direction of his father's, Dora and Hanna having, with good-humored consideration, gone forward as an advanced guard, leaving Bryan and Kathleen to enjoy their tete-a-tete behind them.

"Dear Kathleen," said Bryan, "I was very anxious to see you. You've h'ard of this unfortunate business that has come upon me?"

"I have," she replied, "and I need not say that I'm sorry for it. Is it, or will it be as bad as they report?"

"Worse, Kathleen. I will have the fine for all Ahadarra to pay myself."

"But can nothing be done. Wouldn't they let you off when they come to hear that, although the Still was found upon your land, yet it wasn't yours, nor it wasn't you that was usin' it?"

"I don't know how that may be. Hycy Burke tells me that they'll be apt to reduce the fine, if I send them a petition or memorial, or whatever they call it, an' he's to have one Written for me tomorrow."

"I'm afraid Hycy's a bad authority for anybody, Bryan."

"I don't think you do poor Hycy justice, Kathleen; he's not, in my opinion, so bad as you think him. I don't know a man, nor I haven't met a man that's sorrier for what has happened me; he came to see me yesterday, and to know in what way he could serve me, an' wasn't called upon to do so."

"I hope you're right, Bryan; for why should I wish Hycy Burke to be a bad man, or why should I wish him ill? I may be mistaken in him, and I hope I am."

"Indeed, I think you are, Kathleen; he's wild a good deal, I grant, and has a spice of mischief in him, and many a worthy young fellow has both."

"That's very true," she replied; "however, we have h'ard bad enough of him. There's none of us what we ought to be, Bryan. If you're called upon to pay this fine, what will, be the consequence?"

"Why, that I'll have to give up my farm—that I won't be left worth sixpence."

"Who put the still up in Ahadarra?" she inquired. "Is it true that it was the Hogan's?"

"Indeed I believe there's no doubt about it," he replied; "since I left the landlord's, I have heard what satisfies me that it was them and Teddy Phats."

Kathleen paused and sighed. "They are a vile crew," she added, after a little; "but, be they what they may, they're faithful and honest, and affectionate to our family; an' that, I believe, is the only good about them. Bryan, I am very sorry for this misfortune that has come upon you. I am sorry for your own sake."

"And I," replied Bryan, "am sorry for—I was goin' to say—yours; but it would be, afther all, for my own. I haven't the same thoughts of you now, dear Kathleen."

She gazed quickly, and with some surprise at him, and asked, "Why so, Bryan?"

"I'm changed—I'm a ruined man," he replied; "I had bright hopes of comfort and happiness—hopes that I doubt will never come to pass. However," he added, recovering himself, and assuming a look of cheerfulness, "who knows if everything will turnout so badly as we fear?"

"That's the spirit you ought to show," returned Kathleen; "You have before you the example of a good father; don't be cast down, nor look at the dark side; but you said you had not the same thoughts of me just now; I don't understand you."

"Do you think," he replied, with a smile, "that I meant to say my affection for you was changed? Oh, no, Kathleen; but that my situation is changed, or soon will be so; and that on that account we can't be the same thing to one another that we have been."

"Bryan," she replied, "you may always depend upon this, that so long as you are true to your God and to yourself, I will be true to you. Depend upon this once and forever."

"Kathleen, that's like yourself, but I could not think of bringing you to shame." He paused, and turning his eyes full upon her, added—"I'm allowin' myself to sink again. Everything will turn out better than we think, plaise God."

"I hope so," she added, "but whatever happens, Bryan do you always act an open, honest, manly part, as I know you will do; act always so as that your conscience can't accuse you, or make you feel that you have done anything that is wrong, or unworthy, or disgraceful; and then, dear Bryan, welcome poverty may you say, as I will welcome Bryan M'Mahon with it."

Both had paused for a little on their way, and stood for about a minute moved by the interest which each felt in what the other uttered. As Bryan's eye rested on the noble features and commanding figure of Kathleen, he was somewhat started by the glow of enthusiasm which lit both her eye and her cheek, although he was too unskilled in the manifestations of character to know that it was enthusiasm she felt.

They then proceeded, and after a short silence Bryan observed— "Dear Kathleen, I know the value of the advice you are giving me, but will you let me ask if you ever seen anything in my conduct, or heard anything in my conversation, that makes you think it so necessary to give it to me?"

"If I ever had, Bryan, it's not likely I'd be here at your side this day to give it to you; but you're now likely to be brought into trials and difficulties—into temptation—and it is then that you may think maybe of what I'm sayin' now."

"Well, Kathleen," he replied, smiling, "you're determined at all events that the advice will come before the temptation; but, indeed, my own dearest girl, my heart this moment is proud when I think that you are so full of truth, an' feelin', and regard for me, as to give me such advice, and to be able to give it. But still I hope I won't stand in need of it, and that if the temptations you spoke of come in my way, I will have your advice—ay, an' I trust in God the adviser, too—to direct me."

"Are you sure, Bryan," and she surveyed him closely as she spoke— "are you sure that no part of the temptation has come across you already?"

He looked surprised as she asked him this singular question. "I am," said he; "but, dear Kathleen, I can't rightly understand you. What temptations do you mane?"

"Have you not promised to vote for Mr. Vanston, the Tory candidate, who never in his life voted for your religion or your liberty?"

"Do you mane me, dearest Kathleen?"

"You, certainly; who else could I mean when I ask you the question?"

"Why, I never promised to vote for Vanston," he replied; "an' what is more—but who said I did?"

"On the day before yesterday," she proceeded, "two gentlemen came to our house to canvass votes, and they stated plainly that you had promised to vote for them—that is for Vanston."

"Well, Kathleen, all I can say is, that the statement is not true. I didn't promise for Vanston, and they did not even ask me. Are you satisfied now? or whether will you believe them or me?"

"I am satisfied, dear Bryan; I am more than satisfied; for my heart is easy. Misfortune! what signifies mere misfortune, or the loss of a beggarly farm?"

"But, my darling Kathleen, it is anything but a beggarly farm."

Kathleen, however, heard him not, but proceeded. "What signifies poverty, Bryan, or struggle, so long as the heart is right, and the conscience clear and without a spot? Nothing—oh, nothing! As God is to judge me, I would rather beg my bread with you as an honest man, true, as I said awhile ago, to your God and your religion, than have an estate by your side, if you could prove false to either."

The vehemence with which she uttered these sentiments, and the fire which animated her whole mind and manner, caused them to pause again, and Bryan, to whom this high enthusiasm was perfectly new, now saw with something like wonder, that the tears were flowing down her cheeks.

He caught her hand and said "My own darling Kathleen, the longer I know you the more I see your value; but make your mind easy; when I become a traitor to either God or my religion, you may renounce me!"

"Don't be surprised at these tears, Bryan; don't, my dear Bryan; for you may look upon them as a proof of how much I love you, and what I would feel if the man I love should do anything unworthy, or treacherous, to his religion or his suffering country."

"How could I," he replied, "with my own dear Kathleen, that will be a guardian angel to me, to advise and guide me? Well, now that your mind is aisy, Kathleen, mine I think is brighter, too. I have no doubt but we'll be happy yet—at least I trust in God we will. Who knows but everything may prove betther than our expectations; and as you say, they may make a poor man of me, and ruin me, but so long as I can keep my good name, and am true to my country, and my God, I can never complain."

CHAPTER XVII.—Interview between Hycy and Finigan

—The Former Propones for Miss Clinton—A love Scene

Hycy, after his conversation with Bryan M'Mahon, felt satisfied that he had removed all possible suspicion from himself, but at the same time he ransacked his mind in order to try who it was that had betrayed him to Bryan. The Hogans he had no reason to suspect, because from experience he knew them to be possessed of a desperate and unscrupulous fidelity, in excellent keeping with their savage character; and to suspect Teddy Phats, was to suppose that an inveterate and incurable smuggler would inform upon him. After a good deal of cogitation, he at length came to the conclusion that the school-master, Finigan, must have been the traitor, and with this impression he resolved to give that worthy personage a call upon his way home. He found him as usual at full work, and as usual, also, in that state which is commonly termed half drunk, a state, by the way, in which the learned pedagogue generally contrived to keep himself night and day. Hycy did not enter his establishment, but after having called him once or twice to no purpose—for such was the din of the school that his voice could not penetrate it—he at length knocked against the half open door, which caused him to be both seen and heard more distinctly. On seeing him, the school-master got to his limbs, and was about to address him, when Hycy said—

"Finigan, I wish to speak a few words to you."

"O'Finigan, sir—O'Finigan, Mr. Burke. It is enough, sir, to be deprived of our hereditary territories, without being clipped of our names; they should lave us those at all events unmutilated. O'Finigan, therefore, Mr. Burke, whenever you address me, if you plaise."

"Well, Mr. O'Finigan," continued Hycy, "if not inconvenient, I should wish to speak a few words with you."

"No inconvenience in the world, Mr. Burke; I am always disposed to oblige my friends whenever I can do so wid propriety. My advice, sir, my friendship, and my purse, are always at their service. My advice to guide them—my friendship to sustain—and my purse—

hem!—ha, ha, ha—I think. I may clap a payriod or full stop there," he added, laughing, "inasmuch as the last approaches very near to what philosophers term a vacuum or nonentity. Gintlemen," he proceeded, addressing the scholars, "I am going over to Lanty Hanratty's for a while to enjoy a social cup wid Mr. Burke here, and as that fact will cause the existence of a short interegnum, I now publicly appoint Gusty Carney as my *locum tenens* until I resume the reins of government on my return. Gusty, put the names of all offenders down on a slate, and when I return 'condign' is the word; an' see, Gusty—mairk me well—no bribery—no bread nor buttons, nor any other materials of corruption from the culprits—otherwise you shall become their substitute in the castigation, and I shall teach you to look one way and feel another, my worthy con-disciple."

"Now, Finigan—I beg your pardon—O'Finigan," said Hycy, when they were seated in the little back tap-room of the public-house with refreshments before them, "I think I have reason to be seriously displeased with you."

"Displeased with me!" exclaimed his companion; "and may I take the liberty to interrogate wherefore, Mr. Hycy?"

"You misrepresented me to Bryan M'Mahon," said Hycy.

"Upon what grounds and authority do you spake, sir?" asked Finigan, whose dignity was beginning to take offence.

"I have good grounds and excellent authority for what I say," replied Hycy. "You have acted a very dishonorable part, Mr. Finigan, and the consequence is that I have ceased to be your friend."

"I act a dishonorable part. Why, sir, I scorn the imputation; but how have I acted a dishonorable part? that's the point."

"You put Bryan M'Mahon upon his guard against me, and consequently left an impression on his mind that I was his enemy."

"Well," said the other, with a good deal of irony, "that is good! Have I, indeed? And pray, Mr. Burke, who says so?"

"I have already stated that my authority for it is good."

"But you must name you authority, sir, no lurking assassin shall be permitted wid impunity to stab my fair reputation wid the foul dagger of calumny and scandal. Name your authority, sir?"

"I could do so."

"Well, sir, why don't you? Let me hear the name of the illiterate miscreant, whoever he is, that has dared to tamper with my unblemished fame."

"All I ask you," continued Hycy, "is to candidly admit the fact, and state why you acted as you did."

"Name your authority, sir, and then I shall speak. Perhaps I did, and perhaps I did not; but when you name your authority I shall then give you a more satisfactory reply. That's the language—the elevated language—of a gentleman, Mr. Burke."

"My authority then is no other than Bryan M'Mahon himself," replied Hycy, "who told me that he was cautioned against me; so that I hope you're now satisfied."

"Mr. Burke," replied Finigan, assuming a lofty and impressive manner, "I have known the M'Mahons for better than forty years; so, in fact, has the country around them; and until the present moment I never heard that a deliberate falsehood, or any breach of truth whatsoever, was imputed to any one of them. Tom M'Mahon's simple word was never doubted, and would pass aquil to many a man's oath; and it is the same thing wid the whole family, man and women. They are proverbial, sir, for truth and integrity, and a most spontaneous effusion of candor under all circumstances. You will pardon me then, Mr. Hycy, if I avow a trifle of heresy in this matter. You are yourself, wid great respect be it spoken, sometimes said to sport your imagination occasionally, and to try your hand wid considerable success at a *lapsus veritatis*. Pardon me, then, if I think it somewhat more probable that you have just now stated what an ould instructor of mine used to call a moral thumper; excuse me, I say; and at all events I have the pleasure of drinking your health; and if my conjecture be appropriate, here's also a somewhat closer adhesion to the *veritas* aforesaid to you!"

"Do you mean to insinuate that I'm stating what is not true?" said Burke, assuming an offended look, which, however, he did not feel.

"No, sir," replied Finigan, retorting his look with one of indignant scorn, "far be it from me to insinuate any such thing. I broadly, and in all the latitudinarianism of honest indignation, assert that it is a d—d lie, begging your pardon, and drinking to your moral improvement a second time; and ere you respond to what I've said, it would be as well, in order to have the matter copiously discussed, if you ordhered in a fresh supply of liquor, and help yourself, for, if the proverb be true—*in vino veritas*—there it is again, but truth will be out, you see—who knows but we may come to a thrifle of it from you yet? Ha! ha! ha! Excuse the jest, Mr. Hycy. You remember little Horace,—

"'*Quid vetat ridentem dicere verum?*'"

"Do you mean to say, sirra," said Hycy, "that I have stated a lie?"

"I mean to say that whoever asserts that I misrepresented you in any way to Bryan M'Mahon, or ever cautioned him against you, states a lie of the first magnitude—a moral thumper, of gigantic dimensions."

"Well, will you tell me what you did say to him?"

"What I did say," echoed Finigan. "Well," he added, after a pause, during which he I surveyed Hycy pretty closely—having now discovered that he was, in fact, only proceeding upon mere suspicion—"I believe I must acknowledge a portion of the misrepresentation. I must, on secondary consideration, plead guilty to that fact."

"I thought as much," said Hycy.

"Here then—," proceeded Finigan, with a broad and provoking grin upon his coarse but humorous features, "here, Mr. Hycy, is what I did say—says I, 'Bryan, I have a word to say to you, touching an accomplished young gentleman, a friend of yours.'

"'What is that?' asked the worthy Beit-nardus.

"'It is regarding the all-accomplished Mr. Hyacinthus Burke,' I replied, 'who is a *homo-factus ad unguem*. Mr. Burke, Bryan,' I proceeded, 'is a gentleman in the—hem—true sense of that word. He is generous, candid, faithful, and honest; and in association wid all his other excellent qualities, he is celebrated, among the select few who know him best, for an extraordinary attachment to—truth.' Now, if that wasn't misrepresentation, Mr. Hycy, I don't know what was. Ha! ha! ha!"

"You're half drunk," replied Hycy, "or I should rather say whole drunk, I think, and scarcely know what you're saying; or rather, I believe you're a bit of a knave, Mr. O'Finigan."

"Thanks, sir; many thanks for the prefix. Proceed."

"I have nothing more to add," replied Hycy, rising up and preparing to go.

"Ay," said Finigan, with another grin, "a bit of a knave, am I? Well, now, isn't it better to be only a bit of a knave than a knave all out—a knave in full proportions, from top to toe, from head to heel—like some accomplished gentlemen that I have the! honor of being acquainted wid. But in the I meantime, now, don't be in a hurry, man alive, nor look as if you were fatted on vinegar. Sit down again; ordher in another libation, and I shall make a disclosure that will be worth your waiting for."

"You shall have the libation, as you call it, at all events," said Hycy, resuming his seat, but feeling, at the same time, by no means satisfied with the lurking grin which occasionally played over Finigan's features.

After much chat and banter, and several attempts on the part of Hycy to insinuate himself into the pedagogue's confidence, he at length rose to go. His companion was now in that state which strongly borders on inebriety, and he calculated that if it were possible to worm anything out of him, he was now in the best condition for it. Every effort, however, was in vain; whenever he pressed the schoolmaster closely, the vague, blank expression of intoxication disappeared for a moment, and was replaced by the broad, humorous ridicule, full of self-possession and consciousness, which always characterized Finigan, whether drunk or sober. The man was naturally cunning, and ranked among a certain class of topers who can be made drunk to a certain extent, and upon some particular subjects, but who, beyond that, and with these limitations, defy the influence of liquor.

Hycy Burke was one of those men who, with smart and showy qualities and great plausibility of manner, was yet altogether without purpose or steadfast principle in the most ordinary affairs of life. He had no fixed notions upon either morals, religion, or politics; and when we say so, we may add, that he was equally without motive—that is, without *adequate* motive, in almost everything he did.

The canvass was now going on with great zeal on the part of Chevydale and Vanston. Sometimes Hycy was disposed to support the one and sometimes the other, but as to feeling a firm attachment to the cause or principles of either, it was not in his nature.

Indeed, the approach of a general election was at all times calculated to fill the heart of a thinking man with a strong sense of shame for his kind, and of sorrow for the unreasoning and brutal tendency to slavery and degradation which it exhibits. Upon this occasion the canvass, in, consequence of the desperate struggle that must ensue, owing to the equality of the opposing forces, was a remarkably early one. Party feeling and religious animosity, as is usual, ran very high, each having been made the mere stalking-horse or catchword of the rival candidates, who cared nothing, or at least very little, about the masses on either side, provided always that they could turn them to some advantage.

It was one morning after the canvass had been going forward with great activity on both sides for about a week, that Hycy, who now felt himself rather peculiarly placed, rode down to Clinton's for the purpose of formally paying his addresses to the gauger's interesting niece, and, if possible, ascertaining his fate from her own lips. His brother Edward had now been brought home in accordance with the expressed determination of his father, with whom he was, unquestionably, a manifest favorite, a circumstance which caused Hycy to detest him, and also deprived him in a great degree of his mother's affection. Hycy had now resolved to pay his devoirs to Kathleen Cavanagh, as a *dernier* resort, in the event of his failing with Miss Clinton; for, as regarding affection, he had no earthly conception what it I meant. With this view he rode down to Clinton's as we said, and met Harry coming out of the stable.

"Harry," said he, after his horse was put I up, "I am about to ask an interview with your sister."

"I don't think she will grant it," replied her brother, "you are by no means a favorite; with her; however, you can try; perhaps she may. You know the old adage, *'varium et imutabile semper.'* Who knows but she may have changed her mind?"

"Is your uncle within?" asked Hycy.

"No," replied his nephew, "he's gone to Fethertonge's upon some election business."

"Could you not contrive," said Hycy, "to leave her and me together, then, and allow me to ascertain what I am to expect?"

"Come in," said Harry—"never say it again. If I can I will."

Hycy, as we have stated before, had vast confidence in his own powers of persuasion; and general influence with women, and on this occasion, his really handsome features were made vulgar by a smirk of self-conceit which he could not conceal, owing to his natural vanity and a presentiment of success that is almost inseparable from persons of his class, who can scarcely look even upon the most positive and decided rejection by a woman as coming seriously from her heart. Even Harry Clinton himself, though but a young man, thought, as he afterwards stated to his sister, that he never saw Hycy have so much the appearance of a puppy as upon that occasion. As had been proposed, he withdrew, however, and the lover being left in the drawing-room with Miss Clinton began, with a simper that was rather coxcombical, to make allusions to the weather, but in such a way as if there was some deep but delightful meaning veiled under his commonplaces. At length he came directly to the 'point.

"But passing from the weather, Miss Clinton, to a much more agreeable topic, permit me to ask if you have ever turned your thoughts upon matrimony?"

The hectic of a moment, as Sterne. says, accompanied by a look that slightly intimated displeasure, or something like it, was the only reply he received for a quarter of a minute, when she said, after the feeling probably had passed away—"No, indeed, Mr. Burke, I have not."

"Come, come, Miss Clinton," said Hycy, with another smirk, "that won't pass. Is it not laid down by the philosophers that you think of little else from the time you are marriageable?"

"By what philosophers?"

"Why, let me see—by the philosophers in general—ha! ha! ha!"

"I was not aware of that," she replied; "but even if they have so ruled it, I see no inference we can draw from that, except their ignorance of the subject."

"It is so ruled, however," said Hycy, "and philosophy is against you."

"I am willing it should, Mr. Burke, provided we have truth with us."

"Very good, indeed, Miss Clinton—that was well said; but, seriously, have you ever thought of marriage?"

"Doesn't philosophy say that we seldom think of anything else?" she replied, smiling. Ask philosophy, then."

"But this really is a subject in which I feel a particular interest—a personal interest; but, as for philosophy, I despise it—that is as it is usually understood. The only philosophy of life is love, and that is my doctrine."

"Is that your only doctrine?"

"Pretty nearly; but it is much the same as that which appears in the world under the different disguises of religion."

"I trust you do not mean to assert that love and religion are the same thing, Mr. Burke?"

"I do; the terms are purely convertible. Love is the universal religion of man, and he is most religious who feels it most; that is your only genuine piety. For instance, I am myself in a most exalted state of that same piety this moment, and have been so for a considerable time past."

Miss Clinton felt a good deal embarrassed by the easy profligacy that was expressed in these sentiments, and she made an effort to change the subject.

"Are you taking part in the canvass which is going on in the country, Mr. Burke?"

"Not much," said he; "I despise politics as much as I cherish the little rosy god; but really, Miss Clinton, I feel anxious to know your opinions on marriage, and you have not stated them. Do you not think the nuptial state the happiest?"

"It's a subject I feel no inclination whatsoever to discuss, Mr. Burke; it is a subject which, personally speaking, has never occupied from me one moment's thought; and, having said so much, I trust you will have the goodness to select some other topic for conversation."

"But I am so circumstanced, just now, Miss Clinton, that I cannot really change it. The truth is, that I have felt very much attached to you for some time past—upon my word and honor I have: it's a fact, I assure you, Miss Clinton; and I now beg to make you a tender of myself and—and—of all I am possessed of. I am a most ardent admirer of yours; and the upmost extent of my ambition is to become an accepted one. Do then, my dear Miss Clinton, allow me the charming privilege—pray, do."

"What will be the consequence if I do not?" she replied, smiling.

"Upon my word and honor, I shall go nearly distracted, and get quite melancholy; my happiness depends upon you, Miss Clinton; you are a very delightful girl, quite a *nonpareil*, and I trust you will treat me with kindness and consideration."

"Mr. Burke," replied the lady, "I am much obliged for the preference you express for me; but whether you are serious or in jest, I can only say that I have no notion of matrimony; that I have never had any notion of it; and that I can safely say, I have never seen the man whom I should wish to call my husband. You will oblige me very much, then, if in future you forbear to introduce this subject. Consider it a forbidden one, so far as I am concerned, for I feel quite unworthy of so gifted and accomplished a gentleman as Mr. Burke."

"You will not discard me surely, Miss Clinton?"

"On that subject, unquestionably."

"No, no, my dear Miss Clinton, you will not say so; do not be so cruel; you will distress me greatly, I assure you. I am very much deficient in firmness, and your cruelty will afflict me and depress my spirits."

"I trust not, Mr. Burke. Your spirits are naturally good, and I have no doubt but you will ultimately overcome this calamity—at least I sincerely hope so."

"Ah, Miss Clinton, you little know the heart I have, nor my capacity for feeling; my feelings, I assure you, are exceedingly tender, and I get quite sunk under disappointment. Come, Miss Clinton, you must not deprive me altogether of hope; it is too cruel. Do not say no forever."

The arch girl shook her head with something of mock solemnity, and replied, "I must indeed, Mr. Burke; the fatal no must be pronounced, and in connection with forever too; and unless you have much virtue to sustain you, I fear you run a great risk of dying a martyr to a negative. I would fain hope, however, that the virtue I allude to, and your well-known sense of religion, will support you under such a trial."

This was uttered in a tone of grave ironical sympathy that not only gave it peculiar severity, but intimated to Hycy that his character was fully understood.

"Well, Miss Clinton," said he, rising with a countenance in which there was a considerable struggle between self-conceit and mortification, a struggle which in fact was exceedingly ludicrous in its effect, "I must only hope that you probably may change your mind."

"Mr. Burke," said she, with a grave and serious dignity that was designed to terminate the interview, "there are subjects upon which a girl of delicacy and principle never can change her mind, and this I feel obliged to say, once for all, is one of them. I am now my uncle's housekeeper," she added, taking up a bunch of keys, "and you must permit me to wish you a good morning," saying which, with a cool but very polite inclination of her head, she dismissed Hycy the accomplished, who cut anything but a dignified figure as he withdrew.

"Well," said her brother, who was reading a newspaper in the parlor, "is the report favorable?"

"No," replied Hycy, "anything but favorable. I fear, Harry, you have not played me fair in this business."

"How is that?" asked the other, rather quickly.

"I fear you've prejudiced your sister against me, and that instead of giving me a clear stage, you gave me the 'no favor' portion of the adage only."

"I am not in the habit of stating a falsehood, Hycy, nor of having any assertion I make questioned; I have already told you, I think, that I would not prejudice my sister against you. I now repeat that I have not done so; but I cannot account for her prejudices against you any more than I shall attempt to contradict or combat them, so far from that I now tell you, that if she were unfortunately disposed to many you, I would endeavor to prevent her."

"And pray why so, Harry, if it is a fair question?"

"Perfectly fair; simply because I should not wish to see my sister married to a man unburthened with any kind of principle. In fact, without the slightest intention whatsoever, Hycy, to offer you offence, I must say that you are not the man to whom I should entrust Maria's peace and happiness; I am her only brother, and have a right to speak as I do. I consider it my duty."

"Certainly," replied Hycy, "if you think so, I cannot blame you; but I see clearly that you misunderstand my character—that is all."

They separated in a few minutes afterwards, and Hycy in a very serious and irritable mood rode homewards. In truth his prospects at this peculiar period were anything but agreeable. Here his love-suit, if it could be called so, had just been rejected by Miss Clinton, in a manner that utterly precluded all future hope in that quarter. With Kathleen Cavanagh he had been equally unsuccessful. His brother Edward was now at home, too, a favorite with, and inseparable from his father, who of late maintained any intercourse that took place between himself and Hycy, with a spirit of cool, easy sarcasm, that was worse than anger itself. His mother, also, in consequence of her unjustifiable attempts to defend her son's irregularities, had lost nearly all influence with her husband, and if the latter should withdraw, as he had threatened to do, the allowance of a hundred a year with which he supplied him, he scarcely saw on what hand he could turn. With Kathleen Cavanagh and Miss Clinton he now felt equally indignant, nor did his friend Harry escape a strong portion of his ill-will. Hycy, not being overburthened with either a love or practice of truth himself, could not for a moment yield credence to the assertion of young Clinton, that he took no stops to prejudice his sister against him. He took it for granted, therefore, that it was to his interference he owed the reception he had just got, and he determined in some way or other to repay him for the ill-services he had rendered him.

The feeling of doubt and uncertainty with which Bryan M'Mahon parted from his landlord and Fethertonge, the agent, after the interview we have already described, lost none of their strength by time. Hycy's memorial had been entrusted to Chevydale, who certainly promised to put his case strongly before the Commissioners of Excise; and Bryan at first had every reason to suppose that he would do so. Whether in consequence of that negligence of his promise, for which he was rather remarkable, or from some sinister influence that may have been exercised over him, it is difficult to say, but the fact was that Bryan had now only ten days between him and absolute ruin. He had taken the trouble to write to the Secretary of Excise to know if his memorial had been laid before them, and supported by Mr. Chevydale, who, he said, knew the circumstances, and received a reply, stating that no such memorial had been sent, and that Mr. Chevydale had taken no steps in the matter whatsoever. We shall not now enter into a detail of all the visits he had made to his landlord, whom he could never see a second time, however, notwithstanding repeated solicitations to that effect. Fethertonge he did see, and always was assured by him that his case was safe and in good hands.

"You are quite mistaken, Bryan," said he, "if you think that either he or I have any intention of neglecting your affair. You know yourself, however, that he has not a moment for anything at the present time but this confounded election. The contest will be a sharp one, but when it is over we will take care of you."

"Yes, but it will then be too late," replied Bryan; "I will be then a ruined man."

"But, my dear Bryan, will you put no confidence in your friends? I tell you you will not be ruined. If they follow up the matter so as to injure you, we shall have the whole affair overhauled, and justice done you; otherwise we shall bring it before Parliament."

"That may be all very well," replied Bryan, "but it is rather odd that he has not taken a single step in it yet."

"The memorial is before the Board," said the other, "for some time, and we expect an answer every day."

"But I know to the contrary," replied Bryan, "for here is a letther from the Secretary stating that no such memorial ever came before them."

"Never mind that," replied Fethertonge, "he may not have seen it. The Secretary! Lord bless you, he never reads a tenth of the memorials that go in. Show me the letter. See there now—he did not write it all; don't you see his signature is in a different, hand? Why will you not put confidence in your friends, Bryan?"

"Because," replied the independent and honest young fellow, "I don't think they're entitled to it—from me. They have neglected my business very shamefully, after having led me to think otherwise. I have no notion of any landlord suffering his tenant to be ruined before his face without lifting a finger to prevent it."

"Oh! fie, Bryan, you are now losing your temper. I shall say no more to you. Still I can make allowances. However, go home, and keep your mind easy, we shall take care of you, notwithstanding your ill humor. Stay—you pass Mr. Clinton's—will you be good! enough to call and tell Harry Clinton I wish to speak to him, and I will feel obliged?"

"Certainly, sir," replied Bryan, "with pleasure. I wish you good morning."

"Could it be possible," he added, "that the hint Hycy Burke threw out about young Clinton has any truth in it—'Harry Clinton will do you an injury;' but more he would not say. I will now watch him well, for I certainly cannot drame why he should be my enemy."

He met Clinton on the way, however, to whom he delivered the message.

"I am much obliged to you," said he, "I was already aware of it; but now that I have met you, M'Mahon, allow me to ask if you have not entrusted a memorial to the care of Mr. Chevydale, in order that it might be sent up strongly supported by him to the Board of Excise?"

"I have," said Bryan, "and it has been sent, if I am to believe Mr. Fethertonge."

"Listen to me, my honest friend—don't believe Fethertonge, nor don't rely on Chevydale, who will do nothing more nor less than the agent allows him. If you depend upon either or both, you are a ruined man, and I am very much afraid you are that already. It has not been sent; but observe that I mention this in confidence, and with an understanding that, for the present, you will not name me in the matter."

"I sartinly will not," replied Bryan, who was forcibly struck with the truth and warmth of interest that were evident in his language and manner; "and here is a letter that I received this very mornin' from the Secretary of Excise, stating that no memorial on my behalf has been sent up to them at all."

"Ay, just so; that is the true state of the matter."

"What, in God's name, am I to do, then?" asked Bryan, in a state of great and evident perplexity.

"I shall tell you; go to an honest man—I don't say, observe, that Chevydale is not honest; but he is weak and negligent, and altogether the slave and dupe of his agent. Go to-morrow morning early, about eight o'clock, fetch another memorial, and wait upon Major Vanston; state your case to him plainly and simply, and, my life for yours, he will not neglect you, at all events. Get a fresh memorial drawn up this very day."

"I can easily do that," said Bryan, "for I have a rough copy of the one I sent; it was Hycy Burke drew it up."

"Hycy Burke," repeated Clinton, starting with surprise, "do you tell me so?"

"Sartinly," replied the other, "why do you ask?"

Clinton shook his head carelessly. "Well," he said, "I am glad of it; it is better late than never. Hycy Burke"—he paused and looked serious a moment,—"yes," he added, "I am glad of it. Go now and follow my advice, and you will have at least a chance of succeeding, and perhaps of defeating your enemies, that is, if you have any."

The pressure of time rendered energy and activity necessary in the case of Bryan; and, accordingly, about eight o'clock next morning, he was seeking permission to speak to the man against whom he and his family had always conscientiously voted—because he had been opposed to the spirit and principles of their religion.

Major Vanston heard his case with patience, inquired more minutely into the circumstances, asked where Ahadarra was, the name of his landlord, and such other circumstance as were calculated to make the case clear.

"Pray, who drew up this memorial?" he asked.

"Mr. Hycy Burke, sir," replied Bryan.

"Ah, indeed," said he, glancing with a singular meaning at M'Mahon.

"You and Burke are intimate then?"

"Why, we are, sir," replied Bryan, "on very good terms."

"And now—Mr.'Burke has obliged you, I suppose, because you have obliged him?"

"Well, I don't know that he has obliged me much," said Bryan, "but I know that I have obliged him a good deal."

Vanston nodded and seemed satisfied.

"Very well," he proceeded; "but, with respect to this memorial. I can't promise you much. Leave it with me, however, and you shall probably hear from me again. I fear we are late in point of time; indeed, I have but faint hopes of it altogether, and I would not recommend you to form any strong expectations from the interference of any one; still, at the same time," he added, looking significantly at him, "I don't desire you to despair altogether."

"He has as much notion," thought Bryan, "of troubling his head about me or my memorial, as I have for standin' candidate for the county. D—n them all! they think of nobody but themselves!"

CHAPTER XVIII.—A Family Dialogue

—Ahadarra not in for it—Bryan's Vote.

Honest Jemmy Burke, we have already said, had brought home his second son, Edward, from school, for the purpose of training him to agricultural pursuits, having now abandoned all notions of devoting him to the Church, as he would have done had Hycy manifested towards him even the ordinary proofs of affection and respect.

"You druv me to it, Rosha," said he to his wife; "but I'll let you both know that I'm able to be masther in my own house still. You have made your pet what he is; but I tell you that if God hasn't said it, you'll curse one another with bitther hearts yet."

"Well, sure you have your own way," replied his wife, "but you wor ever and always self-willed and headstrong. However, it's all the mane blood that's in you; it breaks your heart to see your son a gintleman; but in spite of your strong brogues and felt caubeen, a gentleman he is, and a gentleman he will be, an' that's all I have to say about it. You'll tache your pet to hate his brother, I'll go bail."

"No, indeed, Rosha," he replied, "I know my duty to God and my childre' better than to turn them against one another; but it's only a proof of how little you know about Edward and his warm and lovin' heart, when you spake as you do."

This indeed was true. Edward Burke was but a short time at home when he saw clearly how matters stood in the family. He was in fact a youth of a most affectionate and generous disposition, and instead of attempting to make the breach wider, as Hycy had he been in his place would have done, he did everything in his power to put the parties into a good state of feeling with each other, and to preserve peace and harmony in the family.

One morning, a few days after Hycy's rejection by Miss Clinton, they were all at breakfast, "the accomplished" being in one of his musical and polite moods, his father bland but sarcastic, and Edward in a state of actual pain on witnessing the wilful disrespect or rather contempt that was implied by Hycy towards his parents. "Well,

Ned," said his father, "didn't we spend a pleasant evenin' in Gerald Cavanagh's last night? Isn't Kathleen a darlin'?"

"She is a delightful girl," replied Edward, "it can't be denied; indeed, I don't think I ever saw so beautiful a girl, and as for her figure, it is perfect—perfect."

"Ay," said the father, "and it's she that knows the difference between a decent sensible boy and a—gintleman—a highflyer. She was both kind and civil to you, Ned."

"I don't know as to the kindness," replied Edward; "but she was certainly civil and agreeable, and I don't think it's in her nature to be anything else."

"Except when she ought," said his father; "but listen, Ned—dress yourself up, get a buff waistcoat, a green jockey coat, a riding whip, and a pair o' shinin' top-boots, titivate yourself up like a dandy, then go to her wid lavendher water on your pocket-handkerchy, an' you'll see how she'll settle you. Be my sowl, you'll be the happy boy when you get her; don't you think so, Misther Hycy?"

"Unquestionably, Mr. Burke, when you speak you shame an Oracle; as for Master Ned—why—

> "'I'm owre young,—I'm owre young,
> I'm owre young to marry yet,
> I'm owre young, 'twould be a sin
> To take me from my Daddy yet.'

I think, Master Edward, the Boy-god has already taken occupation; the vituline affection for the fair Katsey has set in; heigho, what a delightful period of life is that soft and lickful one of calf love, when the tongue rolls about the dripping lips, the whites of the eyes are turned towards the divine, the ox-eyed Katsey, and you are ready to stagger over and blare out the otherwise unutterable affection."

"Very well described, Hycy, I see you have not forgotten your Homer yet; but really Kathleen Cavanagh is a perfect Juno, and has the large, liquid, soft ox-eye in perfection."

"Let me look at you," said Hycy, turning round and staring at him with a good deal of surprise; "begad, brother Ned, let me ask where you got your connoisseurship upon women? eh? Oh, in the dictionary, I suppose, where the common people say everything is to be found. Observe me, Mr. Burke, you are taking your worthy son out of his proper vocation, the Church. Send him to 'Maynewth,' he is too good a connoisseur on beauty to be out of the Tribunal."

"Hycy," replied his brother, "these are sentiments that do you no credit, it is easy to sneer at religion or those who administer it,—much easier than to praise the one, it would appear, or imitate the virtues of the other."

"Beautiful rebuke," said Hycy, again staring at him; *"why, Masther Edward, you are a prodigy of wonderful sense and unspotted virtue; love has made you eloquent—"'I gaed a waefu' gate yestreen,*
   A gate, I fear, I'll dearly rue,
   I gat my death frae twa sweet e'en,
   Twa lovely e'en o' bonnie blue, &c, &c.'"

"I am not in love yet, Hycy, but as my father wishes to bring about a marriage between Kathleen and myself, you know," he added, smiling, "it will be my duty to fall in love with her as fast as I can."

"Dutiful youth! what a treasure you will prove to a dignified and gentlemanly parent,—to a fond and doting wife! Shall I however put forth my powers? Shall Hycy the accomplished interpose between Juno and the calf? What sayest thou, my most amiable maternal relative, and why sittest thou so silent and so sad?"

"Indeed, it's no wondher I would, Hycy," replied his mother, whom Edward's return had cast into complete dejection, "when I see your father strivin' to put between his own childre'."

"Me, Rosha!" exclaimed her husband; "God forgive you for that! but when I see that one of my childre' wont spake a word to me with respect or civility—no, not even in his natural voice, it is surely time for ma to try if I can't find affection in his brother."

"Ay," said she, "that's your own way of it; but it's easy seen that your eggin' up Ned agin his brother, bringin' ill will and bad feelin' among a family that was quiet before; ay, an' I suppose you'd be glad to see my heart broke too, and indeed I didn't care it was," and as she spoke the words? were accompanied by sobbings and tears.

"Alas!" said Hyoy, still in the mock heroic—"where is the pride and dignity of woman? Remember, oh maternal relative, that you are the mother of one Gracchus at least! Scorn the hydraulics, I say; abandon the pathetic; cast sorrow to the winds, and—give me another cup of tea."

Edward shook his head at him, as if remonstrating against this most undutiful and contemptuous style of conversation to his mother. "Don't give way to tears, my dear mother," he said; "indeed you do my father injustice; he has neither said nor done anything to turn me against Hycy. Why should he? So far from that, I know that he loves Hycy at heart, all that he wishes is that Hycy would speak to him in his natural voice, and treat him with respect, and the feeling that surely is due to him. And so Hycy will, father; I am sure he respects and loves you in spite of this levity and affectation. All we want is for each to give up a little of his own way—when you become more respectful, Hycy, my father's manner will change too: let us be at least sincere and natural with each other, and there is nothing that I can see to prevent us from living very happily."

"I have some money saved," said Burke, turning to his wife—"a good penny—too, more than the world thinks; and I declare to my God I would give it twice over if I could hear that young man," pointing to Hycy, "speak these words with the same heart and feelings of him that spoke them; but I fear that 'ud be a hopeless wish on my part, an' ever will."

"No, father," said Edward, "it will not—Hycy and you will soon understand one another. Hycy will see what his duty towards you is, and, sooner than be the means of grieving your heart, he will change the foolish and thoughtless habit that offends you."

"Well, Edward, may God grant it," exclaimed his father rising up from breakfast, "and that's all I have to say——God grant it!"

"Why, Sir Oracle, junior," said Hycy, after his father had gone out, "or rather Solomon Secundus, if you are now an unfledged philosopher on our hand, what will you not be when your opinions are grown?"

"My dear brother," replied Edward, I cannot see what on earth you can propose to yourself by adopting this ridiculous style of conversation I cannot really see any object you can have in it. If it be to vex or annoy my father, can you blame him if he feels both vexed and annoyed at it.

"Most sapiently said, Solomon Secundus—

> "'Solomon Lob was a ploughman stout,
> And a ranting cavalier;
> And, when the civil war broke out,
> It quickly did appear
> That Solomon Lob was six feet high,
> And fit for a grenadier.
> So Solomon Lob march'd boldly forth
> To sounds of bugle horns
> And a weary march had Solomon Lob,
> For Solomon Lob had corns.
> Row,—ra—ra—row—de—dow.'

"And so I wish you a good morning, most sapient Solomon. I go on business of importance affecting—the welfare of the nation, or rather of the empire at large—embracing all these regions, antipodial and otherwise, on which the sun never sets. Good morning, therefore; and, maternal relative, wishing the same to thee, with a less copious exhibition of the hydraulics, a-hem!"

"Where is he going, mother, do you know?" asked Edward.

"Indeed I don't know, Edward," she replied; "he seldom or never tells us anything about his motions; but it vexes me to think that his father won't make any allowance for his lightheartedness and fine spirits. Sure now, Edward, you know yourself it's not raisonable to have a young man like him mumpin' and mopin' about, as if there was a wake in the house?"

The only reply Edward made to this weak and foolish speech was, "Yes; but there is reason in everything, my dear mother. I have heard," he added, "that he is working for the Tory candidate, Vanston, and hope it is not true."

"Why," said his mother, "what differ does it make?"

"Why," replied the other, "that Vanston votes to keep us slaves, and Chevydale to give us our political freedom: the one is opposed to our religion and our liberty, and the other votes for both."

"Troth, as to religion," observed the mother, "the poor boy doesn't trouble his head much about it—bat it's not aisy for one that goes into jinteel society to do so—an' that's what makes Hycy ait mate of a Friday as fast as on any other day."

"I am sorry to hear that, mother," replied Edward; "but Hycy is a very young man still, and will mend all these matters yet."

"And that's what I'm tellin' his father," she replied; "and if you'd only see the way he looks at me, and puts a *cuir* (* a grin—mostly of contempt) upon him so bitther that it would a'most take the skin off one."

Edward's observations with respect to Hycy's having taken a part in forwarding the interests of Major Vanston were not without foundation. He and Bryan M'Mahon had of late been upon very good terms; and it so happened that in the course of one of their conversations about Kathleen Cavanagh, Bryan had mentioned to him the fact of Kathleen's having heard that he was pledged to vote with Vanston, and repeated the determination to which she had resolved to come if he should do so. Now, it so happened, that a portion of this was already well known to Hycy himself, who, in fact, was the very individual who had assured Major Vanston, and those who canvassed for him, that he himself had secured Bryan. On hearing now from Bryan that Kathleen had put the issue of their affection upon his political truth and consistency he resolved to avail himself of that circumstance if he could. On hearing, besides, however, that Harry Clinton had actually sent him (M'Mahon) to Vanston, and on being told, in the course of conversation, that that gentleman asked who had drawn up the memorial, he felt that every circumstance was turning in his favor; for he determined now to saddle Clinton with the odium which, in this treacherous transaction, was most likely to fall upon himself.

It is not our intention here to describe the brutal and disgraceful scenes that occur at an election. It is enough to say that, after a long, bitter, and tedious struggle, the last day of it arrived. Bryan

M'Mahon, having fully satisfied himself that his landlord had not taken a single step to promote his interests in the matter of the memorial, resolved from the beginning not to vote in his favor, and, of course, not to vote at all.

On the morning of the last day, with the exception of himself alone, a single voter had not been left unpolled; and the position of the two candidates was very peculiar, both having polled exactly the same number of votes, and both being consequently equal.

Bryan, having left home early, was at breakfast about eleven o'clock, in a little recess off the bar of the head-inn, which was divided from one end of the coffee-room by a thin partition of boards, through which anything spoken in an ordinary tone of voice in that portion of the room could be distinctly heard. Our readers may judge of his surprise on hearing the following short but pithy dialogue of which he himself formed the subject matter. The speakers, with whom were assembled several of his landlord's committee, being no other than that worthy gentleman and his agent.

"What's to be done?" asked Chevydale; "here is what we call a dead heat. Can no one prevail on that obstinate scoundrel, the Ahadarra man—what do ye call, him? M'Master—M'Manus—-M'—eh?"

"M'Mahon," replied Fethertonge, "I fear not; but, at all events, we must try him again. Vote or not, however, we shall soon clear him out of Ahadarra—we shall punish his insolence for daring to withhold his vote; for, as sure as my name is Fethertonge, out he goes. The fine and distillation affair, however, will save us a good deal of trouble, and of course I am very glad you declined to have anything to do with the support of his petition. The fellow is nothing else than shuffler, as I told you. Vote or not, therefore, out of Ahadarra he goes; and, when he does, I have a good tenant to put in his place."

M'Mahon's blood boiled on hearing this language, and he inwardly swore that, let the consequences be what they might, a vote of his should never go to the support of such a man.

Again we return to Hycy Burke, who, when the day of the great struggle arrived, rode after breakfast on that same morning into

Ballymacan, and inquired at the post-office if there were any letters for him.

"No," replied the postmaster; "but, if you see Bryan M'Mahon, tell him I have here one for him, from Major Vanston—it's his frank and his handwriting."

"I'm going directly to him," said Hycy, "and will bring it to him; so you had better hand it here."

The postmaster gave him the letter, and in a few minutes Hycy was on his way home with as much speed as his horse was capable of making.

"Nanny," said he, calling upon Nanny Peety, when he had put his horse in the stable and entered the parlor, "will you fetch me a candle and some warm water?"

"Yes, sir," said Nanny; "but you must wait till I boil some, for there's none hot."

"Be quick, then," said he, "for I'm in a devil of a hurry. Shut the door after you, I say. What is the reason that you never do so, often as I have spoken to you about it?"

"Becaise it's never done," she replied; "nobody ever bids me shut it but yourself, an' that's what makes me forget it."

"Well, I'll thank you," he said, "to pay more attention to what I say to you I have reason to think you both intrusive and ungrateful, Nanny; and, mark, unless you show me somewhat more submission, madam, you shall pitch your camp elsewhere. It was I brought you here."

"Ax your own conscience why, Mr. Hycy."

"Begone now and get me the hot water," he said, with a frown of anger and vexation, heightened probably by the state of agitation into which the possession of Vanston's letter had already put him.

We shall not follow him through all the ingenious and dishonorable manoeuvres by which he got the communication safely open-ed; it is enough to say that, in the course of a few minutes, he was enabled to peruse the contents of Vanston's communication, which were as follows:—

Sir,—I beg to enclose you a letter which I received yesterday from the Secretary to the Board of Excise, and to assure you that I feel much pleasure in congratulating you upon its contents, and the satisfactory result of your memorial.

"I am, sir, very sincerely yours,

"Egbert Vanston.

"To Mr. Bryan M'Mahon,

"Ahadarra."

(The enclosed.)

"Sir,—I have had the honor of reading your communication in favor of Bryan M'Mahon, of Ahadarra, and of submitting that and his own memorial to the Commissioners of Excise, who, after maturely weighing the circumstances, and taking into consideration the excellent character which memorialist has received at your hands, have been pleased to reduce the fine originally imposed upon him to the sum of fifty pounds. The Commissioners are satisfied that memorialist, having been in no way connected with the illicit distillation which was carried on upon his property, is not morally liable to pay the penalty; but, as they have not the power of wholly remitting it they have reduced it as far the law has given them authority.

"I have the honor to be, sir, your faithful and obedient servant,

"Francis Fathom.

"To Major Vanston, &c, &c."

Hycy, having perused these documents, re-sealed them in such a manner as to evade all suspicion of their having been opened.

"Now," thought he, "what is to be done? Upon the strength of this, it is possible I may succeed in working up M'Mahon to vote for Vanston; for I know into what an enthusiasm of gratitude the generous fool will be thrown by them. If he votes for Vanston, I gain several points. First and foremost, the round some of three hundred.

If I can get his vote, I establish my own veracity, which, as matters stand, will secure Vanston the election; I, also, having already secretly assured the Tory gentleman that I could secure him, or rather, I can turn my lie into truth, and make Vanston my friend. Secondly, knowing as I do, that it was by Harry Clinton's advice the clod-hopper went to him, I can shift the odium of his voting for Vanston upon that youth's shoulders, whose body, by the way, does not contain a single bone that I like; and, thirdly, having by his apostacy and treachery, as it will be called, placed an insurmountable barrier between himself and the divine Katsey, I will change my course with Jemmy, the gentleman—my sarcastic dad—return and get reconciled with that whelp of a brother of mine, and by becoming a good Christian, and a better Catholic, I have no doubt but I shall secure the 'Ox-eyed,' as I very happily named her the other morning. This, I think, will be making the most of the cards, and, as the moment is critical, I shall seek the clod-hopper and place this seasonable communication in his hands."

He accordingly rode rapidly into town again, where he had not been many minutes when he met M'Mahon, burning with indignation at the language of his landlord and the agent.

"I cannot have patience, Hycy," he exclaimed, "under such scoundrelly language as this; and while I have breath in my body, he never shall have my vote!"

"What's the matter, Bryan?" he asked; "you seem flushed."

"I do, Hycy, because I am flushed, and not without reason. I tell you that my landlord, Chevydale, is a scoundrel, and Fethertonge a deceitful villain."

"Pooh, man, is that by way of information? I thought you had something in the shape of novelty to tell me. What has happened, however, and why are you in such a white heat of indignation?"

M'Mahon immediately detailed the conversation which he had overheard behind the bar of the inn, and we need scarcely assure our readers that Hycy did not omit the opportunity of throwing oil upon the fire which blazed so strongly.

"Bryan," said he, "I know the agent to be a scoundrel, and what is nearer the case still, I have every reason—but you must not ask me to state them yet,—I have every reason to suspect that it is Fethertonge, countenanced by Chevydale, who is at the bottom of the distillation affair that has ruined you. The fact is, they are anxious to get you out of Ahadarra, and thought that by secretly ruining you, they could most plausibly effect it."

"I have now no earthly doubt of it, Hycy," replied the other.

"You need not," replied Hycy; "and maybe I'm not far astray when I say, that the hook-nosed old Still-hound, Clinton, is not a thousand miles from the plot. I could name others connected with some of them—but I wont, now."

When M'Mahon recollected the conversation which both Clinton and the agent had held with him, with respect to violating the law, the truth of Hycy's remark flashed upon him at once, and of course deepened his indignation almost beyond endurance.

"They are two d—d scoundrels," pursued Hycy, "and I have reasons, besides, for suspecting that it was their wish, if they could have done it successfully, to have directed your suspicions against myself."

M'Mahon was, in fact, already convinced of this, and felt satisfied that he saw through and understood the whole design against him, and was perfectly aware of those who had brought him to ruin.

"By the way," said Hycy, "let me not forget that I have been looking for you this hour or two; here is a letter I got for you in! the post-office this morning. It has Vanston's frank, and I think is in his handwriting."

M'Mahon's face, on perusing the letter, beamed with animation and delight. "Here, Hycy," said he, "read that; I'm safe yet, thank God, and not a ruined man, as the villains thought to make me."

"By my soul and honor, Bryan," exclaimed the other, "that is noble on the part of Vanston, especially towards an individual from whom, as well as from his whole family, he has ever experienced the strongest opposition. However, if I were in your coat, I certainly would not suffer him to outdo me in generosity. Good heavens! only contrast such conduct with that of the other scoundrel, his opponent, and then see the conclusion you must come to."

"Let Vanston be what he may, he's an honest man," replied Bryan, "and in less than ten minutes I'll have him the sittin' member. I would be ungrateful and ungenerous, as you say, Hycy, not to do so. Come along—come along, I bid you. I don't care what they say. The man that saved me—who was his enemy—from ruin, will have my vote."

They accordingly proceeded towards the court house, and on their way Hycy addressed him as follows:—"Now, Bryan, in order to give your conduct an appearance of greater generosity, I will pretend to dissuade you against voting for Vanston, or, rather, I will endeavor, as it were, to get your vote for Chevydale. This will make the act more manly and determined on your part, and consequently one much more high-minded and creditable to your reputation. You will show them, besides, that you are not the cowardly slave of your landlord."

It was accordingly so managed; the enthusiastic gratitude of the young man overcame all considerations; and in a few minutes Major Vanston was declared by the sheriff duly elected, by a majority of one vote only.

It is no part of our intention to describe the fierce sensation which this victory created among the greater portion of the people. The tumult occasioned by their indignation and fury was outrageous and ruffianly as usual; but as the election had now terminated, it soon ceased, and the mobs began to disperse to their respective homes. Bryan for some three hours or so was under the protection of the military, otherwise he would have been literally torn limb from limb. In the mean time we must follow Hycy.

This worthy and straightforward young gentleman, having now accomplished his purpose, and been the means of M'Mahon having exposed himself to popular vengeance, took the first opportunity of withdrawing from him secretly, and seeking Vanston's agent. Having found him, and retired out of hearing, he simply said—

"I will trouble you for three hundred."

"You shall have it," replied that honest gentleman; "you shall have it. We fully acknowledge the value of your services in this matter; it is to them we owe our return."

"There is no doubt in the matter," replied Hycy; "but you know not my difficulty, nor the dexterous card I had to play in accomplishing my point."

"We are sensible of it all," replied the other; "here," said he, pulling out his pocket-book, "are three notes for one hundred each."

"Give me two fifties," said Hycy, "instead of this third note, and you will oblige me. By the way, here is the major." With this the other immediately complied, without the major having been in any way cognizant of the transaction.

On entering the inner room where they stood, Vanston shook hands most cordially with Hycy, and thanked him in very warm language for the part he took, to which he had no hesitation in saying he owed his return.

"Look upon me henceforth as a friend, Mr. Burke," he added, "and a sincere one, who will not forget the value of your influence with the young man whose vote has gained me the election. I have already served him essentially,—in fact saved him from ruin, and I am very glad of it."

"I really feel very much gratified, Major Vanston, that I have had it in my power," replied Hycy, "to render you any service of importance; and if I ever should stand in need of a favor at your hands, I shall not hesitate to ask it."

"Nor I to grant it, Mr. Burke, if it be within the reach of my influence."

"In the mean time," said Hycy, "will you oblige me with a single franc?"

"Certainly, Mr. Burke; with half a dozen of them."

"Thank you, sir, one will be quite sufficient; I require no more."

The major, however, gave him half a dozen of them, and after some further chat, and many expressions of obligation on the part of the new M.P., Hycy withdrew.

CHAPTER XIX.—Bryan Bribed—is Rejected by Kathleen.

In the course of about two or three hours after the transaction already stated, old Peety Dim was proceeding towards the post-office with a letter, partly in his closed hand, and partly up the inside of his sleeve, so as that it might escape observation. The crowds were still tumultuous, but less so than in the early part of the day; for, as we said, they were diminishing in numbers, those who had been so long from home feeling a natural wish to return to their families and the various occupations and duties of life which they had during this protracted contest been forced to neglect. Peety had got as far as the market-house—which was about the centre of the street—on his way, we say, to the post-office, when he met his daughter Nanny, who, after a few words of inquiry, asked him where he was going.

"Faith, an' that's more than I dare tell you," he replied.

"Why," she said, "is there a saicret in it, I'm sure you needn't keep it from me, whatever it is."

This she added in a serious and offended tone, which, however, was not lost on the old man.

"Well," said he, "considherin' the man he is, an' what you know about him, I think I may as well tell you. It's a letther I'm bringin' to slip into the post-office, unknownst."

"Is it from Hycy?" she asked.

"From Hycy, and no other."

"I'll hould a wager," she replied, "that that's the very letther I seen him openin' through the key hole doar this mornin'. Do you know who it's to?" she inquired.

"Oh, the sorra know; he said it was a love-letther, and that he did not wish to be seen puttin' it in himself."

"Wait," said she, "give it to me here for a minute; here's Father M'Gowan comin' up, and I'll ax him who it's directed to."

She accordingly took the letter out of his hand, and approaching the priest, asked him the name of the person to whom it was addressed.

"Plaise your reverence," she said, "what name's on the back of this?—I mane," said she, "who is goin' to?"

The priest looked at it, and at once replied, "It is goin' to Bryan M'Mahon, of Ahadarra, the traitor, and it comes from Major Vanston, the enemy to his liberty and religion, that his infamous vote put into Parliament, to rivet our chains, and continue our degradation. So there, girl, you have now the bigot from whom it comes, and the apostate to whom it goes. Who gave it to you?"

Nanny, who from some motives of her own, felt reluctant to mention Hycy's name in the matter, hastily replied, "A person, plaise your reverence, from Major Vanston."

"Very well, girl, discharge your duty," said the priest; "but I tell you the devil will never sleep well till he has his clutches in the same Major, as well as in the shameless apostate he has corrupted."

Having uttered these words, he passed on, and Nanny in a minute or two afterwards returned the letter to her father, who with his own hands put it into the post-office.

"Now," said she to her father, "the people is scatterin' themselves homewards; and the streets is gettin' clear—but listen—that letter is directed to Bryan M'Mahon; will you keep about the post-office here; Bryan's in town, an' it's likely when the danger's over that he may be passin'. Now you know that if he does, the people in the shop where the post-office is kep' will see him, an' maybe he'll get the letter to-day, or I'll tell you what, watch Hycy; take my word for it, he has some scheme afoot."

"Hycy's no favorite wid you, Nanny."

"Why you know he's not, an' indeed I don't know why he's one wid you."

"Throth an' he is, many a shillin' an' sixpence he throws me,—always does indeed wherever he meets me."

"No matter, maybe the day will soon come when you'll change your opinion of him, that's all I say, except to keep your eye on him; and I'll tell you why I bid you, some day soon."

"Well, achora, maybe I may change my opinion of him; but at present I say he is my favorite, an' will be so, till I know worse about him."

Nanny, having bade him good-bye, and repeated her wish that the old man would watch the post-office for some time, proceeded up the street in the direction of the grocer's, to whom she had been dispatched for groceries.

Two hours more had now elapsed, the crowds were nearly dispersed, and the evening was beginning to set in, when Hycy Burke called at the post-office, and for the second time during the day, asked if there was a letter for him.

The post-master searched again, and replied, "No; but here's another for Bryan M'Mahon."

"What!" he exclaimed, "another for Bryan! Why he must have an extensive correspondence, this Bryan M'Mahon. I wonder who it's from."

"There's no wonder at all about it," replied the post-master, "it's from Major Vanston. Here's his frank and handwriting in the direction and all."

"Allow me to look," said Hycy, glancing at it. "Yes, you are quite right, that is the gallant Major's hand, without any mistake whatsoever. I will not fetch him this letter," he proceeded, "because I know not when I may see him; but if I see him, I shall tell him."

Peety Dim, who had so placed himself in the shop attached to the post-office, on seeing Hycy approach, that he might overhear this conversation without being seen, felt, considerably surprised that Hycy should seem to have been ignorant that there was a letter for M'Mahon, seeing that it was he himself who had sent it there. He consequently began to feel that there was some mystery in the matter; but whatever it might be, he knew that it was beyond his power to develop.

On coming forward from the dark part of the shop, where he had been standing, he asked the post-master if there was a second letter for M'Mahon.

"No," replied the man, "there is only the one. If you see him, tell him there's a letter from Major Vanston in the office for him."

We must still trace Hycy's motions. On leaving the post-office, he went directly to the Head Inn, where he knew Bryan M'Mahon was waiting until the town should become perfectly calm and quiet. Here he found Bryan, whose mind was swayed now to one side and now to another, on considering the principle on which he had voted, and the consequences to which that act might expose him.

"I know I will have much to endure," he thought, while pacing the room by himself in every way, "but I little value anything the world at large may think or say, so that I don't lose the love and good opinion of Kathleen Cavanagh."

"Why, Bryan," said Hycy, as he entered, "I think you must provide a secretary some of these days, your correspondence is increasing so rapidly."

"How is that?" inquired the other.

"Simply that there's another letter in the post-office for you, and if I don't mistake, from the same hand—that of our friend the Major."

"I'm not aware of anything he could have to write to me about now," replied Bryan; "I wonder what can it be?"

"If you wish I shall fetch you the letter," said Hycy, "as you have an objection I suppose to go out until the town is empty."

"Thank you, Hycy, I'll feel obliged to you if you do; and Hycy, by the way, I am sorry that you and I ever mistook or misunderstood one another; but sich things happen to the best of friends, and why should we hope to escape?"

"Speak only for yourself, Bryan," replied Hycy, "the misunderstanding was altogether on your side, not on mine. I always knew your value and esteemed you accordingly. I shall fetch your letter immediately."

On returning he placed the document aforesaid in M'Mahon's hands, and said, in imitation of his friend Teddy Phats—"Come now, read her up." Bryan opened the letter, and in the act of doing so a fifty pound note presented itself, of which, as it had been cut in two, one half fell to the ground.

"Hallo!" exclaimed Hycy, suddenly taking it up, "this looks well—what have we here? A fifty pound note!"

"Yes," replied Bryan; "but why cut in two? here however is something written, too—let me see—

"'Accept this as an earnest of better things for important services. The fine imposed upon you has been reduced to fifty pounds—this will pay it.

"A DEEPLY OBLIGED FRIEND.'"

The two young men looked at each other for some time without speaking. At length M'Mahon's face became crimsoned with indignation!

"Who could have dared to do this?" said he, once more looking at the bank-note and the few lines that accompanied it. "Who durst suppose that a M'Mahon would sell his vote for a bribe? Did Vanston suppose that money would sway me? for this I am sure must be his work."

"Don't be too sure of that," replied Hycy; "don't be too sure that it's not some one that wishes you worse than Vanston does. In my opinion, Bryan, that letter and the note contained in it were sent to you by some one who wishes to have it whispered abroad that you were bribed. It surely could not be Vanston's interest to injure your character or your circumstances in any sense; and I certainly think him too honorable to deal in an anonymous bribe of that kind."

"Some scoundrel has done it, that's clear; but what would you have me to do, Hycy? You are up to life and know the world a great deal better than I do; how ought I to act now?"

"I'll tell you candidly, my dear Bryan, how I think you ought to act, or at least how I would act myself if I were in your place." He then paused for a minute and proceeded:—"You know I may be wrong, Bryan, but I shall advise you at all events honestly, and to the best of my ability. I would keep this letter and this note, and by the way, what else can you do?—I would say nothing whatsoever about it.

The secret, you know, rests with yourself and me, with the exception of the party that sent it. Now, mark me, I say—if the party that sent this be a friend, there will be no more about it—it will drop into the grave; but if it came from an enemy the cry of bribery will be whispered about, and there will be an attack made on your character. In this case you can be at no loss as to the source from whence the communication came—Fethertonge will then most assuredly be the man; or, harkee, who knows but the whole thing is an electioneering trick resorted to for the purpose of impugning your vote, and of getting Vanston out on petition and scrutiny. Faith and honor, Bryan, I think that this last is the true reading."

"I'm inclined to agree with you there," replied Bryan, "that looks like the truth; and even then I agree with you still that Fethertonge is at the bottom of it. Still how am I to act?"

"In either case, Bryan, precisely as I said. Keep the letter and the bank-note; say nothing about it—that is clearly your safest plan; do not let them out of your hands, for the time may come when it will be necessary to your own character to show them."

"Well, then, I will be guided by you, Hycy. As you say no one knows the secret but yourself and me; if it has come from a friend he will say nothing about it, but if it has come from an enemy it will be whispered about; but at all events I have you as proof that it did not come to me by any bargain of mine."

Hycy spoke not a word, but clapped him approvingly on the shoulder, as much as to say—"Exactly so, that is precisely the fact," and thus ended the dialogue.

We all know that the clearer the mirror the slighter will be the breath necessary to stain it; on the breast of an unsullied shirt the most minute speck will be offensively visible. So it is with human character and integrity. Had Bryan M'Mahon belonged to a family of mere ordinary reputation—to a family who had generally participated in all the good and evil of life, as they act upon and shape the great mass of society, his vote might certainly have created much annoyance to his party for a very brief period—just as other votes given from the usual motives—sometimes right and honorable—sometimes wrong and corrupt—usually do. In his case, however, there was something calculated to startle and alarm all those who knew and were capable of appreciating the stainless honor and hereditary integrity of the family. The M'Mahon's, though inoffensive and liberal in their intercourse with the world, even upon matters of a polemical nature, were nevertheless deeply and devotedly attached to their own religion, and to all those who in any way labored or contributed to relieve it of its disabilities, and restore those who professed it to that civil liberty which had been so long denied them. This indeed was very natural on the part of the M'Mahons, who would sooner have thought of taking to the highway, or burning their neighbor's premises, than supporting the interests or strengthening the hands of any public man placed, in a position to use a hostile influence against them. There was only one other family in the barony, who in all that the M'Mahon's felt respecting their religion and civil liberty, Were far in advance of them. These were the Cavanaghs, between whom and the M'Mahons their existed so many strong points of resemblance that they only differed from the others in degree—especially on matters connected with religion and its privileges. In these matters the Cavanaghs were firm, stern, and inflexible—nay, so heroic was the enthusiasm and so immovable the attachment of this whole family to their creed, that we have no hesitation whatever in saying that they would have laid down their lives in its defence, or for its promotion, had such a sacrifice been demanded from them. On such a family, then, it is scarcely necessary to describe the effects of what was termed Bryan M'Mahon's apostacy. The intelligence came upon them in fact like a calamity. On the very evening before, Gerald Cavanagh, now a fierce advocate for Edward Burke, having, in compliance with old Jemmy, altogether abandoned Hycy, had been urging upon Kathleen the prudence and propriety of giving Bryan M'Mahon up, and receiving the address of young Burke, who was to inherit the bulk of his father's wealth and property; and among other arguments against M'Mahon he stated a whisper then gaining ground, that it was his intention to vote for Vanston.

"But I know to the contrary, father," said Kathleen, "for I spoke to him on that very subject, and Bryan M'Mahon is neither treacherous nor cowardly, an' won't of course abandon his religion or betray it into the hands of its enemies. Once for all, then," she added, calmly, and with a smile full of affection and good humor, "I say you may spare both yourself and me a great deal of trouble, my dear father, I grant you that I like and esteem Edward Burke as a friend, an' I think that he really is what his brother Hycy wishes himself to be thought—a true gentleman—but that is all, father, you know; for I would scorn to conceal it, that Bryan M'Mahon has my affections, and until he proves false to his God, his religion, and his country, I will never prove false to him nor withdraw my affections from him."

"For all that," replied her father, "it's strongly suspected that he's goin' over to the tories, an' will vote for Vanston to-morrow."

Kathleen rose with a glowing cheek, and an eye sparkling with an enthusiastic trust in her lover's faith; "No, father," said she, "by the light of heaven above us, he will never vote for Vanston—unless Vanston becomes the friend of our religion. I have only one worthless life, but if I had a thousand, and that every one of them was worth a queen's, I'd stake them all on Bryan M'Mahon's truth. If he ever turns traitor—let me die before I hear it, I pray God this night!"

As she spoke, the tears of pride, trust, and the noble attachment by which she was moved, ran down her cheeks; in fact, the natural dignity and high moral force of her character awed them, and her father completely subdued, simply replied:—

"Very well, Kathleen; I'll say no more, dear; I won't press the matter on you again, and so I'll tell Jemmy Burke."

Kathleen, after wiping away her tears, thanked him, and said with a smile, and in spite of the most boundless confidence in the integrity of her lover, "never, at any rate, father, until Bryan M'Mahon turns a traitor to his religion and his country."

On the evening of the next day, or rather late at night, her father returned from the scene of contest, but very fortunately for Kathleen's peace of mind during that night, he found on inquiry that she and Hanna had been for a considerable time in bed. The following morning Hanna, who always took an active share in the duties of the family, and who would scarcely permit her sister to do anything, had been up a short time before her, and heard from her mother's lips the history of Bryan's treachery, as it was now termed by all. We need scarcely say that she was deeply affected, and wept bitterly. Kathleen, who rose a few minutes afterwards, thought she saw her sister endeavoring to conceal her face, but the idea passed away without leaving anything like a fixed impression upon it. Hanna, who was engaged in various parts of the house, contrived still to keep her face from the observation of her sister, until at length the latter was ultimately struck by the circumstance as well as by Hanna's unusual silence. Just as her father had entered to breakfast, a sob reached her ears, and on going over to inquire if anything were wrong, Hanna, who was now fairly overcome, and could conceal her distress no longer, ran over, and throwing herself on Kathleen's neck, she exclaimed in a violent burst of grief, "Kathleen, my darling sister, what will become of you! It's all true. Bryan has proved false and a traitor; he voted for Vanston yesterday, and that vote has put the bitter enemy of our faith into Parliament."

"Bryan M'Mahon a traitor!" exclaimed Kathleen; "no, Hanna—no, I say—a thousand times no. It could not be—the thing is impossible—impossible!"

"It is as true as God's in heaven, that he voted yesterday for Vanston," said her father; "I both seen him and heard him, an' that vote it was that gained Vanston the election."

Hanna, whose arms were still around her sister's neck, felt her stagger beneath her on hearing those words from her father.

"You say you saw him, father, and h'ard him vote for Vanston. You say you did?"

"I both seen the traitor an' h'ard him," replied the old man.

"Hanna, dear, let me sit down," said Kathleen, and Hanna, encircling her with one hand, drew a chair over with the other, on which, with a cheek pale as death, her sister sat, whilst Hanna still wept with her arms about her. After a long silence, she at last simply said:—

"I must bear it; but in this world my happiness is gone."

"Don't take it so much to heart avourneen," said her mother; "but, any way, hadn't you betther see himself, an' hear what he has to say for himself. Maybe, afther all, it's not so bad as it looks. See him, Kathleen; maybe there's not so much harm in it yet."

"No, mother, see him I will not, in that sense—Bryan M'Mahon a traitor! Am I a dreamer? I am not asleep, and Bryan M'Mahon is false to God and his country! I did think that he would give his life for both, if he was called upon to do so; but not that he would prove false to them as he has done."

"He has, indeed," said her father, "and the very person you hate so much, bad as you think him, did all in his power to prevent him from doin' the black deed. I seen that, too, and h'ard it. Hycy persuaded him as much as he could against it; but he wouldn't listen to him, nor pay him any attention."

"Kathleen," said her sister, "the angels in heaven fell, and surely it isn't wonderful that even a good man should be tempted and fall from the truth as they did?"

Kathleen seemed too much abstracted by her distress to hear this. She looked around at them all, one after another, and said in a low, composed, and solemn voice, "All is over now between that young man and me—and here is one request which I earnestly entreat you—every one of you—to comply with."

"What is it darling?" said her mother.

"It is," she replied, "never in my hearing to mention his name while I live. As for myself, I will never name him!"

"And think, after all," observed her father, "of poor Hycy bein' true to his religion!"

It would seem that her heart was struggling to fling the image of M'Mahon from it, but without effect. It was likely she tried to hate him for his apostacy, but she could not. Still, her spirit was darkened with scorn and indignation at the act of dishonor which she felt her lover had committed, just as the atmosphere is by a tempest. In fact, she detested what she considered the baseness and treachery of the vote; but could not of a sudden change a love so strong, so trusting, and so pure as hers, into the passions of enmity and hatred. No sooner, however, had her father named Hycy Burke with such approval, than the storm within her directed itself against him, and she said, "For God's sake, father, name not that unprincipled wretch to me any more. I hate and detest him more than any man living he has no good quality to redeem him. Ah! Hanna, Hanna, and is it come to this? The dream of my happiness has vanished, and I awake to nothing now but affliction and sorrow. As for happiness, I must think of that no more, father, after breakfast, do you go up to that young man and tell him the resolution I have come to, and that it is over for ever between him and. me."

Soon after this, she once more exacted a promise from them to observe a strict silence on the unhappy event which had occurred, and by no means ever to attempt offering her consolation. These promises they religiously kept, and from this forth neither M'Mahon's name nor his offence were made the topics of any conversation that occurred between them.

CHAPTER XX.—M'Mahon is Denounced from the Altar

—Receives his Sentence from Kathleen, and Resolves to Emigrate.

Whatever difficulty Bryan M'Mahon had among his family in defending the course he had taken at the election, he found that not a soul belonging to his own party would listen to any defense from him. The indignation, obloquy, and spirit of revenge with which he was pursued and harassed, excited in his heart, as they would in that of any generous man conscious of his own integrity, a principle of contempt and defiance, which, however they required independence in him, only made matters far worse than they otherwise would have been. He expressed neither regret nor repentance for having voted as he did; but on the contrary asserted with a good deal of warmth, that if the same course lay open to him he would again pursue it.

"I will never vote for a scoundrel," said he, "and I don't think that there is anything in my religion that makes it a duty on me to do so. If my religion is to be supported by scoundrels, the sooner it is forced to depend on itself the better. Major Vanston is a good landlord, and supports the rights of his tenantry, Catholic as well as Protestant; he saved me from ruin when my own landlord refused to interfere for me, an' Major Vanston, if he's conscientiously opposed to my religion, is an honest man at all events, and an honest man I'll ever support against a rogue, and let their politics go where they generally do, go to the devil."

Party is a blind, selfish, infatuated monster, brutal and vehement, that knows not what is meant by reason, justice, liberty, or truth. M'Mahon, merely because he gave utterance with proper spirit to sentiments of plain common sense, was assailed by every description of abuse, until he knew not where to take refuge from that cowardly and ferocious tyranny which in a hundred shapes proceeded from the public mob. On the Sunday after the election, his parish priest, one of those political fire-brands, who whether under a mitre or a white band, are equally disgraceful and detrimental to religion and the peaceful interests of mankind—this man, we say, openly denounced him from the altar, in language which must have argued but little reverence for the sacred place from which it was uttered, and which came with a very bad grace from one who affected to be an advocate for liberty of conscience and a minister of peace.

"Ay," he proceeded, standing on the altar, "it is well known to our disgrace and shame how the election was lost. Oh, well may I say to our disgrace and shame. Little did I think that any one, bearing the once respectable name of M'Mahon upon him, should turn from the interests of his holy church, spurn all truth, violate all principle, and enter into a league of hell with the devil and the enemies of his church. Yes, you apostate," he proceeded, "you have entered into a league with him, and ever since there is devil within you. You sold yourself to his agent and representative, Vanston, You got him to interfere for you with the Board of Excise, and the fine that was justly imposed on you for your smugglin' and distillin' whiskey—not that I'm runin' down our whiskey, because it's the best drinkin of that kind we have, and drinks beautiful as scalhleen, wid a bit of butther and sugar in it—but it's notorious that you went to Vanston, and offered if he'd get the fine off you, that you'd give him your vote; an' if that's not sellin' yourself to the devil, I don't know what is. Judas did the same thing when he betrayed our Savior—the only difference is—that he got a thirty shilling note—an' God knows it was a beggarly bargain—when his hand was in he ought to have done the thing dacent—and you got the fine taken off you; that's the difference—that's the difference. But there's more to come—more corruption where that was. Along wid the removal of the fine you got a better note than Mr. Judas got. Do you happen to know anything about a fifty pound note cut in two halves? Eh? Am I tickling you? Do you happen to know anything about that, you traicherous apostate? If you don't, I do; and plaise God before many hours the public will know enough of it, too. How dare you, then, polute the house of God, or come in presence of His Holy altar, wid such a crust of crimes upon your soul? Can you deny that you entered into a league of hell wid the devil and Major Vanston, and that you promised him your vote if he'd get the fine removed?"

"I can," replied Bryan; "there's not one word of truth in it."

"Do you hear that, my friends?" exclaimed the priest; "he calls your priest a liar upon the altar of the livin' God."

Here M'Mahon was assailed by such a storm of groans and hisses as, to say the least of it, was considerably at variance with the principles of religion and the worship of God.

"Do you deny," the priest proceeded, "that you received a bribe of fifty pounds on the very day you voted? Answer me that."

"I did receive a fifty-pound note in a—"

Further he could not proceed. It was in vain that he attempted to give a true account of the letter and its enclosure; the enmity was not confined to either groans or hisses. He was seized upon in the very chapel, dragged about in all directions, kicked, punched, and beaten, until the apprehension of having a murder committed in presence of God's altar caused the priest to interfere. M'Mahon, however, was ejected from the chapel; but in such a state that, for some minutes, it could scarcely be ascertained whether he was alive or dead. After he had somewhat recovered, his friends assisted him home, where he lay confined to a sick bed for better than a week.

Such is a tolerably exact description of scenes which have too frequently taken place in the country, to the disgrace of religion and the dishonor of God. We are bound to say, however, that none among the priesthood encourage or take a part in them, unless those low and bigoted firebrands who are alike remarkable for vulgarity and ignorance, and who are perpetually inflamed by that meddling spirit which tempts them from the quiet path of duty into scenes of political strife and enmity, in which they seem to be peculiarly at home. Such scenes are repulsive to the educated priest, and to all who, from superior minds and information, are perfectly aware that no earthly or other good, but, on the contrary, much bitterness, strife, and evil, ever result from them.

Gerald Cavanagh was by no means so deeply affected by M'Mahon's vote as were his two daughters. He looked upon the circumstance as one calculated to promote the views which he entertained for Kathleen's happiness. Ever since the notion of her marriage with Hycy Burke or his brother—it mattered little to him which—he felt exceedingly dissatisfied with her attachment to M'Mahon. Of this weakness, which we may say, was the only one of the family, we have already spoken. He lost little time, however, in going to communicate his daughter's determination to that young man. It so happened, however, that, notwithstanding three several journeys made for the purpose, he could not see him; the fact being that Bryan always happened to be from home when he went. Then came the denouncing scene which we have just described, when his illness put it out of his power, without danger to himself, to undergo anything calculated to discompose or disturb him. The popular feeling, however, was fearfully high and indignant against him. The report went that he had called Father M'Pepper, the senior curate, a liar upon the very altar; and the commencement of his explanation with respect to the fifty-pound note, was, not unnaturally—since they would not permit him to speak—construed into an open admission of his having been bribed.

This was severe and trying enough, but it was not all. Chevydale, whom he unseated by his vote, after having incurred several thousand pounds of expense, was resolved to make him suffer for the loss of his seat, as well as for having dared to vote against him— a purpose in which he was strongly supported, or into which, we should rather say, he was urged by Fethertonge, who, in point of fact, now that the leases had dropped, was negotiating a beneficial bargain with the gauger, apart from Chevydale's knowledge, who was a feeble, weak-minded man, without experience or a proper knowledge of his duties. In fact, he was one of,those persons who, having no fixed character of their own, are either good or evil, according to the principles of those by whom they happen for the time to be managed. If Chevydale had been under the guidance of a sensible and humane agent, he would have been a good landlord; but the fact being otherwise, he was, in Fethertonge's hands, anything but what a landlord ought to be. Be this as it may, the period of M'Mahon's illness passed away, and, on rising from his sick bed, he found the charge of bribery one of universal belief, against which scarcely any person had the courage to raise a voice. Even Hycy suffered himself, as it were, with great regret and reluctance, to become at length persuaded of its truth. Kathleen, on hearing that he himself had been forced to admit it in the chapel, felt that the gloom which had of late wrapped her in its shadow now became so black and impervious that she could see nothing distinctly. The two facts—that is to say, the vote and the bribery—

seemed to her like some frightful hallucination which lay upon her spirits—some formidable illusion that haunted her night and day, and filled her whole being with desolation and sorrow.

With respect to his own feelings, there was but one thought which gave him concern, and this was an apprehension that Kathleen might be carried away by the general prejudice which existed against him.

"I know Kathleen, however," he would say; "I know her truth, her good sense, and her affection; and, whatever the world may say, she won't follow its example and condemn me without a hearing. I will see her tomorrow and explain all to her. Father," he added, "will you ask Dora if she will walk with me to the Long-shot Meadow? I think a stroll round it will do me good. I haven't altogether recovered my strength yet."

"To be sure I will go with you, Bryan," said the bright-eyed and affectionate sister; "to be sure I will; it's on my way to Gerald Cavanagh's; and I'm going down to see how they are, and to know if something I heard about them is thrue. I want to satisfy myself; but they musn't get on their high horse with me, I can tell them."

"You never doubted me, Dora," said Bryan, as they went along—"you never supposed for a moment that I could"—he paused. "I know," he added, "that it doesn't look well; but you never supposed that I acted from treachery, or deceit, or want of affection or respect for my religion? You don't suppose that what all the country is ringin' with—that I took a bribe or made a bargain with Vanston—is true?"

"Why do you ask me such questions?" she replied. "You acted on the spur of the minute; and I say, afther what you heard from the landlord and agent, if you had voted for him you'd be a mane, pitiful hound, unworthy of your name and family. You did well to put him out. If I had been in your place, 'out you go,' I'd say, 'you're not the man for my money.' Don't let what the world says fret you, Bryan; sure, while you have Kathleen and me at your back, you needn't care about them. At any rate, it's well for Father M'Pepper that I'm not a man, or, priest as he is, I'd make a stout horsewhip tiche him to mind his religion, and not intermeddle in politics where he has no business."

"Why, you're a great little soldier, Dora," replied Bryan, smiling on her with affectionate admiration.

"I hate anything tyrannical or overbearing," she replied, "as I do anything that's mane and ungenerous."

"As to Father M'Pepper, we're not to take him as an example of what his brother priests in general are or ought to be. The man may think he is doing only his duty; but, at all events, Dora, he has proved to me, very much at my own cost, I grant, that he has more zeal than discretion! May God forgive him; and that's the worst I wish him. When did you see or hear from Kathleen? I long to give her an explanation of my conduct, because I know she will listen to raison."

"That's more than I know yet, then," replied Dora. "She has awful high notions of our religion, an' thinks we ought to go about huntin' after martyrdom. Yes, faix, she thinks we ought to lay down our lives for our religion or our counthry, if we were to be called on to do so. Isn't that nice doctrine? She's always reading books about them."

"It is, Dora, and thrue doctrine; and so we ought—that is, if our deaths would serve either the one or the other."

"And would you die for them, if it went to that? because if you would, I would; for then I'd know that I ought to do it."

"I don't know, Dora, whether I'd have strength or courage to do so, but I know one who would."

"I know too—Kathleen."

"Kathleen? you have said it. She would, I am certain, lay down her life for either her religion or the welfare of her country, if such a sacrifice could be necessary."

"Bryan, I have heard a thing about her, and I don't know whether I ought to tell it to you or not."

"I lave that to your own discretion, Dora; but you haven't heard, nor can you tell me anything, but what must be to her credit."

"I'll tell you, then; I heard it, but I won't believe it till I satisfy myself—that your family daren't name your name to her at home, and that everything is to be over between you. Now, I'm on my way there to know whether this is true or not; if it is, I'll think less of her than I ever did."

"And I won't Dora; but will think more highly of her still. She thinks I'm as bad as I'm reported to be."

"And that's just what she ought not to think. Why not see you and ask you the raison of it like a—ha! ha!—I was goin' to say like a man? Sure if she was as generous as she ought to be, she'd call upon you to explain yourself; or, at any rate, she'd defend you behind your back, and, when the world's against you, whether you wor right or wrong."

"She'd do nothing at the expense of truth," replied her brother.

"Truth!" exclaimed the lively and generous girl, now catching the warmth from her own enthusiasm, "truth! who'd regard truth—"

"Dora!" exclaimed Bryan, with a seriocomic smile.

"Ha! ha! ha!—truth! what was I sayin'? No, I didn't mean to say anything against truth; oh, no, God forgive me!" she added, immediately softening, whilst her bright and beautiful eyes filled with tears, "oh, no, nor against my darlin' Kathleen either; for, Bryan, I'm tould that she has never smiled since; and that the color that left her cheeks when she heard of your vote has never come back to it; and that, in short, her heart is broken. However, I'll soon see her, and maybe I won't plade your cause; no lawyer could match me. Whisht!" she exclaimed, "isn't that Gerald himself comin' over to us?"

"It is," replied Bryan, "let us meet him;" and, as he spoke, they turned their steps towards him. As they met, Bryan, forgetting everything that had occurred, and influenced solely by the habit of former friendship and good feeling, extended his hand with an intention of clasping that of his old acquaintance, but the latter withdrew, and refused to meet this usual exponent of good will.

"Well, Gerald," said M'Mahon, smiling, "I see you go with the world too; but, since you won't shake hands with me, allow me to ask your business."

"To deliver a message to you from my daughter, and she'd not allow me to deliver it to any one but yourself. I came three times to see you before your sickness, but I didn't find jou at home."

"What's the message, Gerald?"

"The message, Bryan, is—that you are never to spake to her, nor will she ever more name your name. She will never be your wife; for she says that the heart that forgets its duty to God, and the hand that has been soiled by a bribe, can never be anything to her but the cause of shame and sorrow; and she bids me say that her happiness is gone and her heart broken. Now, farewell, and think of the girl you have lost by disgracin' your religion and your name."

Bryan paused for a moment, as if irresolute how to act, and exchanged glances with his high-minded little sister.

"Tell Kathleen, from me," said the latter, "that if she had a little more feeling, and a little less pride or religion, I don't know which, she'd be more of a woman and less of a saint. My brother, tell her, has disgraced neither his religion nor his name, and that he has too much of the pride of an injured man to give back any answer to sich a message. That's my answer, and not his, and you may ask her if it's either religion or common justice that makes her condemn him she loved without a hearing? Goodbye, now, Gerald; give my love to Hanna, and tell her she's worth a ship-load of her stately sister."

Bryan remained silent. In fact, he felt so completely overwhelmed that he was incapable of uttering a syllable. On seeing Cavanagh return, he was about to speak, when he looked upon the glowing cheeks, flashing eyes, and panting bosom of his heroic little sister.

"You are right, my darling Dora. I must be proud on receiving such a message. Kathleen has done me injustice, and I must be proud in my own defence."

The full burthen of this day's care, however, had not been yet laid upon him. On returning home, he heard from one of his laborers that a notice to quit his farm of Ahadarra had been left at his house. This, after the heavy sums of money which he had expended in its improvement and reclamation, was a bitter addition to what he was forced to suffer. On hearing of this last circumstance, and after perusing the notice which the man, who had come on some other message, had brought with him, he looked around him on every side for a considerable time. At length he said, "Dora, is not this a fine country?"

"It is," she replied, looking at him with surprise.

"Would you like," he added, "to lave it?"

"To lave it, Bryan!" she replied. "Oh, no, not to lave it;" and as she spoke, a deadly paleness settled upon her face.

"Poor Dora," he said, after surveying her for a time with an expression of love and compassion, "I know your saicret, and have done so this long time; but don't be cast down. You have been a warm and faithful little friend to me, and it will go hard or I'll befriend you yet."

Dora looked up into his face, and as she did, her eyes filled with tears. "I won't deny what you know, Bryan," she replied; "and unless he— —"

"Well, dear, don't fret; he and I will have a talk about it; but, come what may, Dora, in this neglected and unfortunate country I will not stay. Here, now, is a notice to quit my farm, that I have improved at an expense of seven or eight hundred pounds, an' its now goin' to be taken out of my hands, and every penny I expended on it goes into the pocket of the landlord or agent, or both, and I'm to be driven out of house and home without a single farthing of compensation for the buildings and other improvements that I made on that farm."

"It's a hard and cruel case," said Dora; "an there can be no doubt but that the landlord and Fethertonge are both a pair of great rogues. Can't you challenge them, an' fight them?"

"Why, what a soldier you are, Dora!" replied her brother, smiling; "but you don't know that their situation in life and mine puts that entirely out o' the question. If a landlord was to be called upon to fight every tenant he neglects, or is unjust to, he would have a busy time of it. No, no, Dora dear, my mind's made up. We will lave the country. We will go to America; but, in the mean time, I'll see what I can do for you."

"Bryan, dear," she said in a voice of entreaty, "don't think of it. Oh, stay in your own country. Sure what other country could you like as well?"

"I grant you that, Dora; but the truth is, there seems to be a curse over it; whatever's the raison of it, nothing goes right in it. The landlords in general care little about the state and condition of their tenantry. All they trouble themselves about is their rents. Look at my own case, an' that's but one out of thousands that's happenin' every day in the country. Grantin' that he didn't sarve me with this notice to quit, an' supposin' he let me stay in the farm, he'd rise it on me in sich a way as that I could hardly live in it; an' you know, Dora, that to be merely strugglin' an' toilin' all one's life is anything but a comfortable prospect. Then, in consequence of the people depondin upon nothing but the potato for food, whenever that fails, which, in general, it does every seventh or eighth year, there's a famine, an' then the famine is followed by fever an' all kinds of contagious diseases, in sich a way that the kingdom is turned into one great hospital and grave-yard. It's these things that's sendin' so many thousands out of the country; and if we're to go at all, let us go like the rest, while we're able to go, an' not wait till we become too poor either to go or stay with comfort."

"Well, I suppose," replied his sister, "that what you say is true enough; but for all that I'd rather bear anything in my own dear country than go to a strange one. Do you think I'd not miss the summer sun rising behind the Althadawan hills? an' how could I live without seein' him set behind Mallybeney? An' then to live in a country where I'd not see these ould hills, the green glens, and mountain rivers about us, that have all grown into my heart. Oh, Bryan, dear, don't think of it—don't think of it."

"Dora," replied the other, his fine countenance overshadowed with, deep emotion as he spoke, "you cannot love these ould hills, as you cull them, nor these beautiful glens, nor the mountain rivers better than I do. It will go to my heart to leave them; but leave them I will— ay, and when I go, you know that I will leave behind me one that's dearer ten thousand times than them all. Kathleen's message has left me a heavy and sorrowful heart."

"I pity her now," replied the kind-hearted girl; "but, still, Bryan, she sent you a harsh message. Ay, I pity her, for did you observe how the father looked when he said that she bid him tell you her happiness was gone, and her heart broken; still, she ought to have seen yourself and heard your defence."

"I can neither blame her, nor will; neither can I properly justify my vote, I grant; it was surely very wrong or she wouldn't feel it as she does. Indeed. I think I oughtn't to have voted at all."

"I differ with you there, Bryan," replied Dora, with animation, "I would rather, ten times over, vote wrongly, than not vote from cowardice. It's a mane, skulkin', shabby thing, to be afeard to vote when one has a vote—it's unmanly."

"I know it is; and it was that very thought that made me vote. I felt that it would look both mane and cowardly not to vote, and accordingly I did vote."

"Ay, and you did right," replied his spirited sister, "and I don't care who opposes you, I'll support you for it, through thick and thin."

"And I suppose you may say through right and wrong, too?"

"Ay, would I," she replied; "eh?—what am I sayin?—throth, I'm a little madcap, I think. No, I won't support you through right and wrong—it's only when you're right you may depend on me."

They had now been more than an hour strolling about the fields, when Bryan, who did not feel himself quite so strong as he imagined he was, proposed to return to his father's, where, by the way, he had been conveyed from the chapel on the Sunday when he had been so severely maltreated.

They accordingly did so, for he felt himself weak, and unable to prolong his walk to any greater distance.

CHAPTER XXI.—Thomas M'Mahon is forced to determine on Emigration.

Gerald Cavanaugh felt himself secretly relieved by the discharge of his message to M'Mahon.

"It is good," thought he, "to have that affair settled, an' all expectation of her marriage with him knocked up. I'll be bound a little time will cool the foolish girl, and put Edward Burke in the way of succeeding. As for Hycy, I see clearly that whoever is to succeed, he's not the man—an' the more the pity, for the sorra one of them all so much the gentleman, nor will live in sich style."

The gloom which lay upon the heart of Kathleen Cavanagh was neither moody nor captious, but on the contrary remarkable for a spirit of extreme gentleness and placidity. From the moment she had come to the resolution of discarding M'Mahon, she was observed to become more silent than she had ever been, but at the same time her deportment was characterized by a tenderness towards the other members of the family that was sorrowful and affecting to the last degree. Her sister Hanna's sympathy was deep and full of sorrow. None of them, however, knew her force of character, nor the inroads which, under guise of this placid calm, strong grief was secretly making on her health and spirits. The paleness, for instance, which settled on her cheeks, when the news of her lover's apostasy, as it was called, and as she considered it, reached her, never for one moment left it afterwards, and she resembled some exquisitely chiselled statue moving by machinery, more than anything else to which we can compare her.

She was sitting with Hanna when her father returned, after having delivered her message to M'Mahon. The old man seemed, if one could judge by his features, to feel rather satisfied, as in fact was the case, and after having put up his good hat, and laid aside his best coat, he said, "I have delivered your message, Kathleen, an' dear knows I'm glad there's an end to that business—it never had my warm heart."

"It always had mine, then," replied Hanna, "an' I think we ought not to judge our fellow creatures too severely, knowin' as we do that there's no such thing as perfection in this world. What the sorra could have come over him, or tempted him to vote as he did? What did he say, father, when you brought him the message?"

"Afther I declared it," replied her father, "he was struck dumb, and never once opened his lips; but if he didn't spake, his sister Dora did."

"An' what did she say—generous and spirited little Dora!—what did she say, father?"

He then repeated the message as accurately as he could—for the honest old man was imbued with too conscientious a love for truth to disguise or conceal a single syllable that had been intrusted to him on either side—"Throth," said he, "the same Dora has the use of her tongue when she pleases; 'ax her,' said she, spakin' of Kathleen, here, 'if it's either religion or common justice that makes her condemn my brother without hearin' his defence. Good-bye, now,' says she; 'give my love to Hanna, and tell her 'she's worth a ship-load of her stately sister.'"

"Poor Dora!" exclaimed Hanna, whilst the tears came to her eyes, "who can blame her for defending so good and affectionate a brother? Plague on it for an election! I wish there was no sich thing in the country."

"As for me," said Kathleen, "I wouldn't condemn him without a hearing, if I had any doubt about his conduct, but I have not. He voted for Vanston—that can't be denied; and proved himself to have less honesty and scruple than even that profligate Hycy Burke; and if he made a bargain with Vanston, as is clear he did, an' voted for him because the other got his fine reduced, why that is worse, because then he did it knowingly an' with his eyes open, an' contrary to his conscience—ay, an' to his solemn promise to myself; for I'll tell you now what I never mentioned before, that I put him on his guard against doing so; and he knew that if he did, all would and must be over between him and me."

"Is that true, Kathleen?" said Hanna with surprise; "but why need I ask you such a question—it's enough that you say it—in that case then I give him up at last; but who, oh, who could a' believed it?"

"But that is not all," continued Kathleen, in the same mournful and resigned tone of voice—"there's the bribe—didn't hundreds hear him acknowledge publicly in the chapel that he got it? What more is wanting? How could I ever respect a man that has proved himself to be without either honesty or principle? and why should it happen, that the man who has so openly and so knowingly disgraced his religion and his name fall to my lot? Oh, no—it matters little how I love him, and I grant that in spite of all that has happened I have a lingering affection for him even yet; still I don't think that affection will live long—I can now neither respect or esteem him, an' when that is the case I can't surely continue long to love him. I know," she proceeded, "that it's not possible for him ever to clear himself of this shocking and shameful conduct; but lest there might be any chance of it, I now say before you all, that if something doesn't come about within three months, that may and ought to change my feelings towards him, I'll live afterwards as if I had never known him."

"Mightn't you see him, however, an' hear what he has to say for himself?" asked Hanna.

"No," the other replied; "he heard my message, and was silent. You may rest assured if he had anything to say in his own defence, he would have said it, or asked to see me. Oh, no, no, because I feel that he's defenceless."

In this peculiar state of circumstances our readers need not feel surprised that every possible agency was employed to urge her beyond the declaration she had made, and to induce her to receive the addresses of Edward Burke. Her own parents, old Jemmy Burke, the whole body of her relatives, each in turn, and sometimes several of them together, added to which we may mention the parish priest, who was called in by both families, or at least by old Jemmy Burke and the Cavanaghs—all we say perpetually assailed her on the subject of a union with Edward Burke, and assailed her so pertinaciously, that out of absolute apathy, if not despair, and sick besides of their endless importunities, she at last said—"If Edward Burke can be satisfied with a wife that has no heart to give him, or that cannot love him, I don't care much how I am disposed of; he may as well call me wife as another, and better, for if I cannot love, I can at least respect him."

These circumstances, together with the period allowed to M'Mahon for setting himself, if possible, right with Kathleen, in due time reached his ears. It soon appeared, however, that Kathleen had not all the pride—if pride it could be called—to herself. M'Mahon, on being made acquainted with what had occurred, which he had heard from his sister Dora, simply said—"Since she has not afforded myself any opportunity of tellin' her the truth, I won't attempt to undeceive her. I will be as proud as she is. That is all I say."

"And you are right, Tom," replied Dora, "the name of M'Mahon mustn't be consarned with anything that's mane or discreditable. The pride of our old blood must be kept up, Tom; but still when we think of what she's sufferin' we musn't open our lips against her."

"Oh, no," he replied; "I know that it's neither harshness nor weakness, nor useless pride that makes her act as she's doin', but a great mind and a heart that's full of truth, high thoughts, and such a love for her religion and its prosperity as I never saw in any one. Still, Dora, I'm not the person that will ever sneak back to entreat and plead at her feet like a slave, and by that means make myself look still worse in her eyes; I know very well that if I did so she'd despise me. God bless her, at all events, and make her happy! that's the worst I wish her."

"Amen," replied Dora; "you have said nothing but the truth about her, and indeed. I see, Tom, that you know her well."

Thus ended the generous dialogue of Dora and her affectionate brother, who after all might have been induced by her to remain in his native country and share whatever fate it might allot him, were it not that in a few days afterwards, his father found that the only terms on which he could obtain his farm were such as could scarcely be said to come within the meaning and spirit of the landlord's adage, "live and let live." It is true that for the terms on which his farm was offered him he was indebted to Chevydale himself, who said that as he knew his father had entertained a high respect for old M'Mahon, he would not suffer him to be put out. The father besides voted for him, and always had voted for the family. "Do what you please with the son," he proceeded—"get rid of him as you like, but I shan't suffer the father to be removed. Let him have the farm upon reasonable terms; and, by the way, Fethertonge, don't you think now it was rather an independent act of the young fellow to vote for Vanston, although he knew that I had it in my power to send him about his business?"

"It was about as impudent a piece of gratitude and defiance as ever I witnessed," returned the other. "The wily rascal calculated upon your forbearance and easiness of disposition, and so imagined that he might do what he pleased with impunity. We shall undeceive him, however."

"Well, but you forget that he, had some cause of displeasure against us, in consequence of having neglected his memorial to the Commissioners of Excise."

"Yes; but as I said before, how could we with credit involve ourselves in the illegal villany of a smuggler? It is actually a discredit to have such a fellow upon the estate. He is, in the first place, a bad example, and calculated by his conduct and influence to spread dangerous principles among the tenantry. However, as it is, he is, fortunately for us, rather well known at present. It is now perfectly notorious—and I have it from the best authority—one of the parties who was cognizant of his conduct—that his vote against you was the result of a deliberate compact with our enemy, Vanston, and that he received a bribe of fifty pounds from him. This he has had the audacity to acknowledge himself, being the very amount of the sum to which the penalty against him was mitigated by Vanston's interference. In fact the scoundrel is already infamous in the country."

"What, for receiving a bribe!" exclaimed Chevydale, looking at the agent with a significant smile; "and what, pray, is the distinction between him who gives and him who takes a bribe? Let us look at home a little, my good Fethertonge, and learn a little charity to those who err as we do. A man would think now to hear you attack M'Mahon for bribery, that you never had bribed a man in your life; and yet you know that it is the consciousness of bribery on our own part that prevents us from attempting to unseat Vanston."

"That's all very true, I grant you," replied the other; "but in the mean time we must keep up appearances. The question, so far as regards M'Mahon, is—not so much whether he is corrupt or not, as whether he has unseated you; that is the fatal fact against him; and if we allow that to pass without making him suffer for it, you will find that on the next election he may have many an imitator, and your chances will not be worth much—that's all."

"Very well, Fethertonge," replied the indolent and feeble-minded man, "I leave him to you; manage him or punish him as you like; but I do beg that you will let me hear no more about him. Keep his father, however, on the property; I insist on that; he is an honest man, for he voted for me; keep him on his farm at reasonable terms too, such,—of course, as he can live on."

The reasonable terms proposed by Fethertonge were, however, such as old Tom M'Mahon could not with any prospect of independence encounter. Even this, however, was not to him the most depressing consideration. Faith had been wantonly and deliberately broken with him—the solemn words of a dying man had been disregarded—and, as Fethertonge had made him believe, by that son who had always professed to regard and honor his father's memory.

"I assure you, M'Mahon," replied the agent, in the last interview he ever had with him, "I assure you I have done all in my power to bring matters about; but without avail. It is a painful thing to have to do with an obstinate man, M'Mahon; with a man who, although he seems quiet and easy, will and must have everything his own way."

"Well, sir," replied M'Mahon, "you know what his dying father's words wor to me."

"And more than I know them, I can assure you," he whispered, in a very significant voice, and with a nod of the head that seemed to say, "your landlord knows them as well as I do. I have done my duty, and communicated them to him, as I ought."

M'Mahon shook his head in a melancholy manner, and said,—

"Well, sir, at any rate I know the worst. I couldn't now have any confidence or trust in such a man; I could depend upon neither his word or his promise; I couldn't look upon him as a friend, for he didn't prove himself one to my son when he stood in need of one. It's clear that he doesn't care about the welfare and prosperity of his tenantry; and for that raison—or rather for all these raisons put together—I'll join my son, and go to a country where, by all accounts, there's better prospects for them that's honest and industrious than there is in this unfortunate one of ours,—where the interest of the people is so much neglected—neglected! no, but never thought of at all! Good-bye, sir," he added, taking up his hat, whilst the features of this sterling and honest man were overcast with a solemn and pathetic spirit, "don't consider me any longer your tenant. For many a long year has our names been—but no matther—the time is come at last, and the M'Mahon's of Carriglass and Ahadarra will be known there no more. It wasn't our fault; we wor willin' to live—oh! not merely willin' to live, but anxious to die there; but it can't be. Goodbye, sir." And so they parted.

M'Mahon, on his return home, found Bryan, who now spent most of his time at Carriglass, before him. On entering the house his family, who were all assembled, saw by the expression of his face that his heart had been deeply moved, and was filled with sorrow.

"Bryan," said he, "you are right—as indeed you always are. Childre'," he proceeded, "we must lave the place that we loved so much; where we have lived for hundreds of years. This counthry isn't one now to prosper in, as I said not long since—this very day. We must lave the ould places, an' as I tould Fethertonge, the M'Mahons of Ahadarra and Carriglass will be the M'Mahons of Ahadarra and Carriglass no more; but God's will be done! I must look to the intherest of you all, childre'; but, God help us, that's what I can't do here for the future. Every one of sense and substance is doin' so, an' why shouldn't we take care of ourselves as well as the rest? What we want here is encouragement and fair play; but *fareer gair*, it isn't to be had."

The gloom which they read in his countenance was now explained, but this was not all; it immediately settled upon the other members of the family who were immediately moved,—all by sorrow, and some even to tears. Dora, who, notwithstanding what her brother had said with regard to his intention of emigrating, still maintained a latent hope that he might change his mind, and that a reconciliation besides might yet be brought about between him and Kathleen, now went to her father, and, with tears in her eyes, threw her arms about his neck, exclaiming: "Oh, father dear, don't think of leaving this place, for how could we leave it? What other country could we ever like as well? and my grandfather—here he's creepin' in, sure he's not the same man within the last few months,—oh, how could you think of bringin' him, now that he's partly in his grave, an' he," she added, in a whisper full of compassion, "an' he partly dotin' with feebleness and age."

"Hush!" said her father, "we must say nothing of it to him. That must be kept a secret from him, an' it's likely he won't notice the change."

Kitty then went over, and laying her hand on her father's arm, said: "Father, for the love of God, don't take us from Carriglass and Ahadarra:—whatever the world has for us, whether for good or evil, let us bear it here."

"Father, you won't bring us nor you won't go," added Dora; "sure we never could be very miserable here, where we have all been so happy."

"Poor Dora!" said Bryan, "what a mistake that is! I feel the contrary; for the very happiness that I and all of us enjoyed here, now only adds to what I'm sufferin'."

"Childre'," said the father, "our landlord has broken his own father's dyin' promise—you all remember how full of delight I came home to you from Dublin, and how she that's gone"—he paused;—he covered his face with his open hands, through which the tears were seen to trickle. This allusion to their beloved mother was too much for them. Arthur and Michael sat in silence, not knowing exactly upon what grounds their father had formed a resolution, which, when proposed to him by Bryan, appeared to be one to which his heart could never lend its sanction. No sooner was their mother named, however, than they too became deeply moved, and when Kitty and Dora both rushed with an outcry of sorrow to their father, exclaiming, "Oh, father dear, think of her that's in the clay—for her sake, change your mind and don't take us to where we can never weep a tear over her blessed grave, nor ever kneel over it to offer a prayer within her hearin' for her soul!"

"Childre," he exclaimed, wiping away his tears that had indeed flowed in all the bitterness of grief and undeserved affliction;

"childre'," he replied, "you must be manly now; it's because I love you an' feels anxious to keep you from beggary and sorrow at a future time, and destitution and distress, such as we see among so many about us every day in the week, that I've made up my mind to go. Our landlord wont give us our farm barrin' at a rent that 'tid bring us down day by day, to poverty and distress like too many of our neighbors. We have yet some thrifle o' money left, as much as will, by all accounts, enable us to take—I mane to purchase a farm in America—an' isn't it betther for us to go there, and be independent, no matther what it may cost our hearts to suffer by doin' so, than to stay here until the few hundre' that I've got together is melted away out of my pocket into the picket of a landlord that never wanst throubles himself to know how we're gettin' on, or whether we're doin' well or ill. Then think of his conduct to Bryan, there; how he neglected him, and would let him go to ruin widout ever movin' a finger to save him from it. No, childre', undher sich a man I won't stay. Prepare yourselves, then, to lave this. In biddin' you to do so, I'm actin' for the best towards you all. I'm doin' my duty by you, and I expect for that raison, an' as obedient childre'—which I've ever found you—that you'll do your duty by me, an' give no further opposition to what I'm proposin' for your sakes. I know you're all loath—an' you will be loath—to lave this place; but do you think?—do you?—'that I—I—oh, my God!—do you think, I say, that I'll feel nothing when we go? Oh! little you know of me if you think so! but, as I said, we must do our duty. We see our neighbors fallin' away into poverty, and distress, and destitution day by day, and if we remain in this unfortunate country, we must only folly in their tracks, an' before long be as miserable and helpless as they are."

His family were forced to admit the melancholy truth and strong sense of all he had uttered, and, although the resolution to which he had come was one of bitterness and sorrow to them all, yet from a principle of affection and duty towards him, they felt that any opposition on their part would have been unjustifiable and wrong.

"But, sure," the old man proceeded, "there's more than I've mentioned yet, to send us away. Look at poor Bryan, there, how he was nearly ruined by the villany of some cowardly scoundrel, or scoundrels, who set up a still upon his farm; that's a black business, like many other black business that's a disgrace to the country—an inoffensive young man, that never made or did anything to make an enemy for himself, durin' his whole life! An' another thing, bekaise he voted for the man that saved him from destruction, as he ought to do, an' as I'm proud he did do, listen now to the blackguard outcry that's against him; ay, and by a crew of vagabonds that 'ud sell Christ himself, let alone their country, or their religion, if they were bribed by Protestant goold for it! Throth I'm sick of the counthry and the people; for instead of gettin' betther, it's worse they're gettin' every day. Make up your minds then, childre'; there's a curse on the counthry. Many o' the landlords are bad enough, too bad, and too neglectful, God knows; but sure the people themselves is as bad, an' as senseless on the other hand; aren't they blinded so much by their bad feelin's, and short-sighted passions, that it is often the best landlords they let out their revenge upon. Prepare then, childre'; for out of the counthry, or at any rate from among the people, the poverty and the misery that's in it, wid God's assistance, we'll go while we're able to do so."

CHAPTER XII.—Mystery Among the Hogans

—Finigan Defends the Absent.

The three Hogans, whom we have lost sight of for some time, were, as our readers already know, three most unadulterated ruffians, in every sense of that most respectable term. Yet, singular as it may appear, notwithstanding their savage brutality, they were each and all possessed of a genius for mechanical inventions and manual dexterity that was perfectly astonishing when the low character of their moral, and intellectual standard is considered. Kate Hogan, who, from her position, could not possibly be kept out of their secrets, at least for any length of time, was forced to notice of late that there was a much closer and more cautious intimacy between Hycy Burke and them than she had ever observed before. She remarked, besides, that not only was Teddy Phats excluded from their councils, but she herself was sent out of the way, whenever Hycy paid them a visit, which uniformly occurred at a late hour, in the night.

Another circumstance also occurred about this time which puzzled her not a little: we mean the unusual absence of Philip for about a fortnight from home. Now, there certainly nothing more offensive, especially to a female, than the fact of excluding her from the knowledge of any secret, a participation in which she may consider as a right. In her case she felt that it argued want of confidence, and as she had never yet betrayed any trust or secret reposed in her, she considered their conduct towards her, not merely as an insult, but such as entitled them to nothing at her hands but resentment, and a determination to thwart their plans, whatever they might be, as soon as she should succeed in making herself acquainted with them. What excited her resentment the more bitterly was the arrival of a strange man and woman in company with Philip, as she was able to collect, from the metropolis, to the former of whom they all seemed to look with much deference as to a superior spirit of the secret among them this man and his wife were clearly in possession, as was evident from their whisperings and other conversations, which they held apart, and uniformly out of her hearing. It is true the strangers did not reside with the Hogans, but in a small cabin adjacent to that in which Finigan taught his school. Much of the same way of thinking was honest Teddy Phats, whom they had now also abandoned, or rather completely cast off, and, what was still worse, deprived of the whole apparatus for distillation, which, although purchased by Hycy Burke's money, they very modestly appropriated to themselves. Teddy, however, as well as Kate, knew that they were never cautious without good reason, and as it had pleased them to cut him, as the phrase goes, so did he, as Kate had done, resolve within himself to penetrate their secret, if human ingenuity could effect it.

In this position they were when honest Philip returned, as we have said, after a fortnight's absence, from some place or places unknown. The mystery, however, did not end here. Kate observed that, as before, much of their conversation was held aloof from her, or in such enigmatical phrases and whisperings, as rendered the substance of it perfectly inscrutable to her. She observed, besides, that two of them were frequently absent from the kiln where they lived; but that one always remained at home to make certain that she should not follow or dog them to the haunt they frequented. This precaution on their part was uniform. As it was, however, Kate did not seem to notice it. On the contrary, no one could exhibit a more finished appearance of stupid indifference than she assumed upon these occasions, even although she knew by the removal of the tools, or a portion of them, that her friends were engaged in some business belonging to their craft. In this manner matters proceeded for some weeks subsequent to the period of Philip's return.

Kate also observed, with displeasure, that among all those who joined in the outcry against Bryan M'Mahon, none made his conduct, such as it was conceived to have been, a subject of more brutal and bitter triumph than the Hogans. The only circumstance connected with him which grieved them to the heart, was the fact that the distillation plot had not ruined him as they expected it would have done. His disgrace, however, and unjust ejectment from Ahadarra filled them with that low, ruffianly sense of exultation, than which, coming from such scoundrels, there is scarcely anything more detestable in human nature.

One evening about this time they were sitting about the fire, the three brothers, Kate, and the young unlicked savages of the family, when Philip, after helping himself to a glass of quints, said,—

"At any rate, there'll be no match between Miss Kathleen and that vagabond, Bryan M'Mahon. I think we helped to put a nail in his coffin there, by gob."

"Ay," said Kate, "an' you may boast of it, you unmanly vagabone; an' yet you purtind to have a regard for the poor girl, an' a purty way you tuck to show it—to have her as she is, goin' about wid a pale face an' a broken heart. Don't you see it's her more than him you're punishin', you savage of hell?"

"You had betther keep your tongue off o' me," he replied; "I won't get into grips wid you any more, you barge o' blazes; but, if you provoke me wid bad language, I'll give you a clink wid one o' these sotherin'-irons that'll put a clasp on your tongue."

"Never attempt that," she replied fiercely, "for, as sure as you do, I'll have this knife," showing him a large, sharp-pointed one, which, in accordance with the customs of her class, hung by a black belt of strong leather from her side—"I'll have this customer here greased in your puddins, my buck, and, when the win's out o' you, see what you'll be worth—fit for Captain James's hounds; although I dunno but the very dogs themselves is too clane to ait you."

"Come," said Bat, "we'll have no more o' this; do you, Philip, keep quiet wid your sotherin'-iron, and, as for you, Kate, don't dhraw me upon you; *na ha nan shin*—it isn't Philip you have. I say I'm right well plaised that we helped to knock up the match."

"Don't be too sure," replied Kate, "that it is knocked up; don't now, mind my words; an' take care that, instead of knockin' it up, you haven't knocked yourselves down. Chew your cud upon that now."

"What does she mane?" asked Ned, looking on her with a baleful glance, in which might be read equal ferocity and alarm. "Why, traichery, of coorse," replied Philip, in his deep, glowing voice. "Kate," said her husband, starting into something' like an incipient fit of fury, but suddenly checking himself—"Kate, my honey, what do you mane by them words?"

"What do I mane by them words?" she exclaimed, with an eye which turned on him with cool defiance; "pick that out o' your larnin', Bat, my pet. You can all keep your saicrets; an' I'll let you know that I can keep mine."

"Be the Holy St. Lucifer," said her husband, "if I wanst thought that traichery 'ud enter your head, I'd take good care that it's in hell you'd waken some fine mornin' afore long. So mind yourself, Kate, my honey."

"Are you in nobody else's power but mine?" she replied, "ax yourselves that—an' now do you mind yourself, Bat, my pet, and all o' yez."

"What is the raison," asked her husband, "that I see you an' Nanny Peety colloguin' an' huggermuggerin' so often together of late?"

"Ah," she replied, with a toss of disdain, "what a manly fellow you are to want to get into women's saicrets! you may save your breath though."

"Whatever you collogue about, all I say is, that I don't like a bone in the same Nanny Peety's body. She has an eye in her head that looks as if it knew one's thoughts."

"An' maybe it does. One thing I know, and every one knows it, that it's a very purty eye."

"Tell her, then, to keep out o' this; we want no spies here."

"Divil a word of it; she's my niece, an' the king's highway is as free to her as it is to you or anybody else. She'll be welcome to me any time she comes, an' let me see who'll dare to mislist her. She feels as she ought to do, an' as every woman ought to do, ay, an' every man, too, that is a man, or anything but a brute an' a coward—she feels for that unfortunate, heart-broken girl 'ithout;' an' it'll be a strange thing if them that brought her to what she's sufferin' won't suffer themselves yet; there's a God above still, I hope, glory be to His name! Traichery!" she exclaimed; "ah, you ill-minded villains, it's yourselves you're thinkin' of, an' what you desarve. As for myself, it's neither you nor your villainy that's in my head, but the sorrowful heart that's in that poor girl 'ithout—ay, an' a broken one; for, indeed, broked it is; and it's not long she'll be troub'lin' either friend or foe in this world. The curse o' glory upon you all, you villains, and upon every one that had a hand in bringing her to this!"

Having uttered these words, she put her cloak and bonnet upon her, and left the house, adding as she went out, "if it's any pleasure to you to know it, I'll tell you. I'm goin' to meet Nancy Peety this minute, an' you never seen sich colloguin' an' hugger-muggerin' as we'll have, plaise goodness—ah, you ill-thinkin', skulkin' villains!"

Kate Hogan, though a tigress when provoked, and a hardened, reckless creature, scarcely remarkable for any particular virtue that could be enumerated, and formidable from that savage strength and intrepidity for which she was so well known, was yet not merely touched by the sufferings of Kathleen Cavanagh, but absolutely took an interest in them, at once so deep and full of sympathy, as to affect her temper and disturb her peace of mind. Notwithstanding her character she was still a woman; and, in matters involving the happiness of an innocent and beautiful creature of her own sex, who had been so often personally kind to herself, and whose family were protectors and benefactors to her and her kindred, she felt as a woman. Though coarse-minded upon most many matters, she was yet capable of making the humane distinction which her brutal relatives could not understand or feel;—we mean the fact that, in having lent themselves to the base conspiracy planned and concocted by Hycy Burke, and in having been undoubtedly the cause of M'Mahon's disgrace, as well as of his projected marriage with Kathleen having been broken up, they did not perceive that she was equally a sufferer; or, if they did, they were either too cunning or too hardened to acknowledge it. For this particular circumstance, Kate, inasmuch as it involved deep ingratitude on their part, could not at all forgive them.

At this time, indeed, the melancholy position of Kathleen Cavanagh was one which excited profound and general sorrow; and just in proportion as this was sincere, so was the feeling of indignation against him whose corruption and want of principle were supposed to have involved her in their consequences. Two months or better of the period allotted by Kathleen to the vindication of his character, had now elapsed, and yet nothing had been done to set himself right either with her or the world. She consequently argued and with apparent reason, that everything in the shape of justification was out of his power, and this reflection only deepened her affliction. Yes, it deepened her affliction; but it did not; on that account succeed in enabling her to obliterate his image the more easily from her heart. The fact was, that despite the force and variety of the rumors that were abroad against him—and each succeeding week brought in some fresh instance of his duplicity and profligacy, thanks to the ingenious and fertile malignity of Hycy the accomplished—despite of this, and despite of all, the natural reaction of her heart had set in—their past endearments, their confidence their tenderness, their love, now began, after the first vehement expression of pride and high principle had exhausted the offended mind of its indignation, to gradually resume their influence over her. A review, besides, of her own conduct towards her lover was by no means satisfactory to her. Whilst she could not certainly but condemn him, she felt as if she had judged him upon a principle at once too cold and rigorous. Indeed, now that a portion of time had enabled her mind to cool, she could scarcely understand why it was that she had passed, so harsh a sentence upon him. She was not, however, capable of analyzing her own mind and feelings upon the occasion, or she might have known that her severity towards the man I was the consequence, on her part, of that innate scorn and indignation which pure and lofty minds naturally entertain against everything dishonorable and base, and that it is a very difficult thing to disassociate the crime from the criminal, even in cases where the latter may have had a strong hold upon the affections of such a noble nature. Nay, the very fact of finding that one's affections have been fixed upon a person capable of such dishonor, produces a double portion of indignation at the discovery of their profligacy, because it supposes, in the first place, that something like imposture must have been practised upon us in securing our affections, or what is still more degrading, that we must have been materially devoid of common penetration, or we could not have suffered ourselves to become the dupe of craft and dissimulation.

Our high-minded heroine, however, had no other theory upon the subject of her own feelings, than that she loved her religion and its precepts, and detested every word that was at variance with truth, and every act inconsistent with honesty and that faithful integrity which resists temptation and corruption in whatever plausible shapes they may approach it.

Be this, however, as it may, she now found that, as time advanced, her heart began to fall into its original habits. The tumult occasioned by the shock resulting from her lover's want of integrity, had now nearly passed away, and the affection of the woman began to supersede the severity of the judge. By degrees she was enabled, as we have said, to look back upon her conduct, and to judge, of her lover through the more softened medium of her reviving affection. This feeling gained upon her slowly but surely, until her conscience became, alarmed at the excess of her own severity towards him. Still, however, she would occasionally return, as it were, to a contemplation of his delinquency, and endeavor, from an unconscious principle of self-love, to work herself up into that lofty hatred of dishonor which had prompted his condemnation; but the effort was in vain. Every successive review of his guilt was attended by a consciousness that she had been righteous overmuch, and that the consequences of his treason, even against their common religion, were not only rapidly diminishing in her heart, but yielding to something that very nearly resembled remorse.

Such was the state of her feelings on the day when Kate Hogan and her male relatives indulged in the friendly and affectionate dialogue we have just detailed. Her heart was smitten, in fact, with sorrow for the harsh part she had taken against her lover, and she only waited for an opportunity to pour out a full confession of all she felt into the friendly ear of her sister.

Gerald Cavanagh's family at this period was darkened by a general spirit of depression and gloom. Their brother James, from whatever cause it may have proceeded, seemed to be nearly as much cast down as his sister; and were it not that Cavanagh himself and his wife sustained themselves by a hope that Kathleen might ultimately relax so far as to admit, as she had partly promised to do, the proposals of Edward Burke, it would have been difficult to find so much suffering apart from death under the same roof.

On the day in question, our friend O'Finigan, whose habits of intemperance had by no means diminished, called at Cavanagh's, as he had been in the habit of doing. Poor Kathleen was now suffering, besides, under the consequences of the injunction not to mention M'Mahon's name, which she had imposed upon her own family—an injunction which they had ever since faithfully observed. It was quite evident from the unusually easy fluency of O'Finigan's manner, that he had not confined his beverages, during the day, to mere water. Hanna, on seeing him enter, said to Kathleen, in a whisper,—

"Hadn't you better come out and take a walk, Kathleen? This O'Finigan is almost tipsy, and you know he'll be talking about certain subjects you don't wish to hear."

"Time enough, dear Hanna," she replied, with a sorrowful look at her sister, "my heart is so full of suffering and pain that almost anything will relieve it. You know I was always amused by Finigan's chat." Her sister, who had not as yet been made acquainted with the change which had taken place in her heart, on hearing these words looked at her closely, and smiled sorrowfully, but in such a manner as if she had at that moment experienced a sensation of pleasure, if not of hope. Hitherto, whenever a neighbor or stranger came in, Kathleen, fearing that the forbidden name might become the topic of conversation, always retired, either to another room or left the house altogether, in order to relieve her own family from the painful predicament in which their promise of silence to her had placed them. On this occasion, however, Hanna perceived with equal surprise and pleasure that she kept her ground.

"Sit ye, merry jinteels!" said Finigan, as he entered; "I hope I see you all in good health and spirits; I hope I do; although I am afraid if what fame—an' by the way, Mrs. Cavanagh, my classicality tells me, that the poet Maro blundered like a Hibernian, when he made the same fame a trumpeter, in which, wid the exception of one point, he was completely out of keeping. There's not in all litterature another instance of a female trumpeter; and for sound raisons—if the fair sex were to get possession of the tuba, God help the world, for it would soon be a noisy one. However, let me recollect myself—where was I? Oh! ay—I am afraid that if what fame says—an' by the way, her trumpet must have been a speaking one—be true, that there's a fair individual here whose spirits are not of the most exalted character; and indeed, and as I am the noblest work of God—an honest man—I feel sorry to hear the fact."

The Emigrants of Ahadarra

The first portion of this address, we need scarcely say, was the only part of it which was properly understood, if we except a word or two at the close.

"God save you, Misther Finigan."

"O'Finigan, if you plase, Mrs. Cavanagh."

"Well, well," she replied, "O'Finigan, since it must be so; but in troth I can!t always remember it, Misther Finigan, in regard that you didn't always stand out for it yourself. Is there any news stirrin', you that's abroad?"

"Not exactly news, ma'am; but current reports that are now no novelty. The M'Mahon's—"

"Oh, never mind them," exclaimed Mrs. Cavanagh, glancing at her daughter, "if you have any 'other news let us hear it—pass over the M'Mahons—they're not worth our talk, at least some o' them."

"Pardon me, Mrs. Cavanagh;—if Achilles at the head of his myrmidons was to inform me to that effect, I'd tell him he had mistaken his customer. My principle, ma'am—and 'tis one I glory in—is to defend the absent in gineral, for it is both charitable and ginerous to do so—in gineral, I say; but when I know that they are unjustly aspersed, I contemplate it as' an act of duty on my part to vindicate them."

"Well," replied Mrs. Cavanagh, "that's all very right an' thrue, Mr. Finigan."

"It is, Mr. Finig—O'Finigan," observed James Cavanagh, who was present, "and your words are a credit and an honor to you."

"Thanks, James, for the compliment; for it is but truth. The scandal I say (he proceeded without once regarding the hint thrown out by Mrs. Cavanagh) which has! been so studiously disseminated against Bryan M'Mahon—spare your nods and winks, Mrs. Cavanagh, for if you winked at me with as many eyes as Argus had, and nodded at me wid as many heads as Hydra, or that baste in the Revelaytions, I'd not suppress a syllable of truth;—no, ma'am, the *suppressio veri's* no habit of mine; and I say and assert—ay, and asseverate— that that honest and high-spirited young man, named Bryan or

Bernard M'Mahon, is the victim of villany and falsehood—ay, of devilish hatred and ingenious but cowardly vituperation."

"Kathleen," whispered her sister, "will you come out, darlin'? this talk must be painful to you."

Kathleen gave her a look of much mingled sorrow and entreaty as went to her heart. Hanna, whose head had been lovingly reclining on her sister's bosom, pressed her gently but affectionately to her heart, and made no reply.

"You wor always a friend of his," replied Mrs. Cavanagh, "an' of course you spake as a friend."

"Yes," said Finigan, "I always was a friend of his, because I always knew his honesty, his love of truth, his hatred of a mane action, ay, and his generosity and courage. I knew him from the very egg, I may say—*ab ovo*—Mrs. Cavanagh; it was I instilled his first principles into him. Oh! I know well! I never had a scholar I was so proud out of. Hycy Burke was smart, quick, and cunning; but then he was traicherous—something of a coward when he had his match—strongly addicted to fiction in most of his narratives, and what was still a worse point about him, he had the infamous ingenuity, whenever he had a point to gain—such as belying a boy and taking away his characther—of making truth discharge all the blackguard duties of falsehoood. Oh! I know them both well! But who among all I ever enlightened wid instruction was the boy that always tould the truth, even when it went against himself?—why, Bryan M'Mahon. Who ever defended the absent?—why, Bryan M'Mahon. Who ever and always took the part of the weak and defenceless against the strong and tyrannical?—why, Bryan M'Mahon. Who fought for his religion, too, when the young heretics used to turn it, or try to turn it, into ridicule—ay, and when cowardly and traicherous Hycy used to sit quietly by, and either put the insult in his pocket, or curry favor wid the young sneering vagabonds that abused it? And yet, at the time Hycy was a thousand times a greater little bigot than Bryan. The one, wid a juvenile rabble at his back, three to one, was a tyrant over the young schismatics; whilst Bryan, like a brave youth as he was, ever and always protected them against the disadvantage of numbers, and insisted on showing them fair play. I am warm, Mrs. Cavanagh," he continued, "and heat, you know, generates thirst. I know that a drop o' the right sort used to be somewhere undher this same roof; but I'm afraid if the *fama clamosa* be thrue, that the side of the argument I have taken isn't exactly such as to guarantee me a touch at the native—that is, taking it for granted that there's any in the house."

This request was followed by a short silence. The Cavanagh's all, with the exception of Kathleen, looked at each other, but every eye was marked either by indecision or indifference. At length Hanna looked at her sister, and simply said, "dear Kathleen!"

"He has done," replied the latter, in a low voice, "what I had not the generosity to do—he has defended the absent."

"Darling Kathleen," Hanna whispered, and then pressed her once more to her heart. "You must have it, Mr. O'Finigan," said she—"you must have it, and that immediately;" and as she spoke, she proceeded to a cupboard from which she produced a large black bottle, filled with that peculiar liquid to which our worthy pedagogue was so devotedly addicted.

"Ah," said he, on receiving a bumper from the fair hand of Hanna, "let the M'Mahons alone for the old original—indeed I ought to say—aboriginal hospitality. Thanks, Miss Hanna; in the meantime I will enunciate a toast, and although we shall not draw very strongly upon sentiment for the terms, it shall be plain and pithy; here is 'that the saddle of infamy may be soon placed upon the right horse,' and maybe there's an individual not a thousand miles from us, and who is besides not altogether incognizant of the learned languages, including a tolerably comprehensive circle of mathematics, who will, to a certain extent, contribute to the consummation of that most desirable event; here then, I repate, is the toast—'may the saddle of infamy soon be placed upon the right horse!'"

Having drunk off the glass, he turned the mouth of it down upon his corduroy breeches, as an intimation that he might probably find it necessary to have recourse to it again.

Hanna observed, or rather we should say, felt, that as Finigan proceeded with his reminiscences of M'Mahon's school-boy days and the enumeration of his virtues, her sister's heart and bosom quivered with deep and almost irrepressible emotion. There was a good deal of enthusiasm in the man's manner, because he was in earnest, and it was quite evident that Kathleen's spirit had caught it as he went along, and that her heart recognized the truth of the picture which he was drawing. We say she literally felt the quiverings of her sister's heart against her own, and to do the admirable girl justice, she rejoiced to recognize these manifestations of returning affection.

"It was only yesterday," continued Finigan, resuming the discourse, "that I met Bryan M'Mahon, and by the way, he has sorrow and distress, poor fellow, in his face. 'Bryan,' said I, 'is it true that you and your father's family are preparing to go to that *refugium peccatorum*, America—that overgrown cupping-glass which is drawing the best blood of our country out of it?'

"'The people of Ireland,' he replied, 'have a right to bless God that there is such a country to fly to, and to resave them from a land where they're neglected and overlooked. It is true, Mr. O'Finigan,' he proceeded—!' we have nothing in this country to live for now.'

"'And so you are preparing?' I asked.

"'I ought rather say,' he replied, 'that we are prepared; we go in another month; I only wish we were there already.'

"'I fear, Bryan,' said I, 'that you have not been well trated of late.' He looked at me with something like surprise, but said nothing; and in a quarter, I added, 'that was the last from which you were prepared to expect justice without mercy.'

"'I don't understand you,' he replied sharply; 'what do you mean?'

"'Bryan,' said I, 'I scorn a moral circumbendibus where the direct truth is necessary; I have heard it said, and I fear it is burthened wid too much uncomfortable veracity, that Kathleen Cavanagh has donned the black cap* in doing the judicial upon you, and that she considers her sentence equal to the laws of the Medes and Persians, unchangeable—or, like those of our own blessed church—wid reverence be the analogy made—altogether infallible.' His eye blazed as I spoke; he caught me where by the collar wid a grip that made me quake—'Another word against Kathleen Cavanagh,' he replied, 'and I will shake every joint of your carcass out of its place.' His little sister, Dora, was wid him at the time; 'Give him a shake or two as it is,' she added, egging him on, 'for what he has said already;' throth she's a lively little lady that, an' if it wasn't that she has a pair of dark shining eyes, and sweet features—ay, and as coaxin' a figure of her own—however, sorra may care, somehow, I defy any one to, be angry wid her."

* Alluding to the practice of putting on the black cap when the Judge condemns a felon to death.

"Come, Mr. O'Finigan," said James, approaching him, "you must have another glass."

"Well no, James," he replied, "I think not."

"Faith, but I say you will; if it was only to hear what Dora—hem—what Bryan said.

"Very well," said the master, allowing him to take the glass which he received again brimming, "thanks, James."

"'Well,' said Bryan, lettin' go my collar, 'blame any one you like; blame me, blame Vanston, blame Chevydale, Fethertonge, anybody, everybody, the Priest, the Bishop, the Pope,—but don't dare to blame Kathleen Cavanagh.'

"'Why,' said I, 'has she been right in her condemnation of you?'

"'She has,' he replied, with a warmth of enthusiasm which lit up his whole features; 'she has done nothing but what was right. She just acted as she ought, and all I can say is, that I know I'm not worthy of her, and never was. God bless her!'

"'And don't let me hear,' said Dora, taking up the dialogue, 'that ever you'll mention her name wid disrespect mark that, Mr. O'Finigan, or it'll be worse for you a thrifle.'

"Her brother looked on her wid complacent affection, and patting her on the head, said, 'Come, darling, don't beat him now. You see the risk you run,' he added, as they went away, 'so don't draw down Dora's vengeance on your head. She might forgive you an offence against herself; but she won't forgive you one against Kathleen Cavanagh; and, Mister O'Finigan, neither will I.'"

"Masther," said James Cavanagh, "you'll stop to-night with us?"

"No, James, I have an engagement of more importance than you could ever dhrame of, and about—but I'm not free or at liberty to develop the plot—for plot it is—at any greater length. Many thanks to you in the mane time for your hospitable intentions; but before I go, I have a word to say. Now, what do you think of that young man's ginerosity, who would rather have himself thought guilty than have her thought wrong; for, whisper,—I say he's not guilty, and maybe—but, no ruatther, time will tell, and soon tell, too, plaise God."

So saying he took up his hat, and politely wished them a pleasant evening, but firmly refused to taste another drop of liquor, "lest," he added, "it might denude him of the necessary qualifications for accomplishing the enterprise on which he was bint."

When he was gone, Kathleen brought her sister to their own room, and throwing herself on her bosom, she spoke not, but wept calmly and in silence for about twenty minutes.

"Kathleen," said Hanna, "I am glad to see this, and I often wished for it."

"Whisht, dear Hanna," she replied; "don't speak to me at present. I'm not fit to talk on that unfortunate subject yet. 'Forgive us our trespasses as we—we—forgive them that trespass against us!' Oh! Hanna darling, how have I prayed?" They then rejoined the family.

CHAPTER XXIII.—Harry Clinton's Benevolence Defeated

—His Uncle's Treachery—The Marriage of Kathleen and Edward Burke Determined on

This partial restoration of M'Mahon to the affections of Kathleen Cavanagh might have terminated in a full and perfect reconciliation between them, were it not for circumstances which we are about to detail. From what our readers know of young Clinton, we need not assure them that, although wild and fond of pleasure, he was by no means devoid of either generosity or principle. There were indeed few individuals, perhaps scarcely any, in the neighborhood, who felt a deeper or manlier sympathy for the adverse fate and evil repute which had come so suddenly, and, as he believed in his soul, undeservedly, upon Bryan M'Mahon. He resolved accordingly to make an effort for the purpose of setting the unfortunate young man's character right with the public, or if not with the public, at least in that quarter where such a service might prove most beneficial to him, we mean in Gerald Cavanagh's family. Accordingly, one morning after breakfast as his uncle sat reading the newspaper, he addressed him as follows:—

"By the way, uncle, you must excuse mo for asking you a question or two."

"Certainly, Harry. Did I not often desire you never to hesitate asking me any question you wish? Why should you not?"

"This, however, may be trenching a little upon the secrets of your—your—profession."

"What is it?—what is it?"

"You remember the seizure you made some time ago in the townland of Ahadarra?"

"I do perfectly well."

"Now, uncle, excuse me. Is it fair to ask you if you know the person who furnished you with information on that subject. Mark, I don't wish nor desire to know his name; I only ask if you know it?"

"No, I do not."

"Do you not suspect it? It came to you anonymously, did it not?"

"Why, you are raking me with a fire of cross-examination, Harry; but it did."

"Should you wish to know, uncle?"

"Undoubtedly, I wish to know those to whom we are indebted for that fortunate event."

"Don't say we, uncle; speak only for yourself."

"I should wish to know, though."

"Pray have you the letter?"

"I have: you will find it in one of the upper pigeon holes; I can't say which; towards the left hand. I placed it there yesterday, as it turned up among some other communications of a similar stamp."

In a few moments his nephew returned, with the precious document in his hands.

"Now, uncle," he proceeded, as he seated himself at the table, "you admit that this is the letter?"

"I admit—why, you blockhead, does not the letter itself prove as much?"

"Well, then, I know the scoundrel who sent you this letter."

"I grant you he is a scoundrel, Harry; nobody, I assure you, despises his tools more than I do, as in general every man does who is forced to make use of them. Go on."

"The man who sent you that letter was Hycy Burke."

"Very likely," replied the cool old Still-Hound; "But I did not think he would ever place us—"

"You, sir, if you please."

"Very well, me, sir, if you please, under such an important obligation to him. How do you know, though, that it was he who sent it?"

His nephew then related the circumstance of his meeting with Nanny Peety, and the discovery he had made through her of the letter having been both written and sent by Hycy to the post-office. In order, besides, to satisfy his relative that the getting up of the still was a plan concocted by Hycy to ruin M'Mahon, through the medium of the fine, he detailed as much of Hycy's former proposal to him as he conveniently could, without disclosing the part which he himself had undertaken to perform in this concerted moment.

"Well, Harry," replied the old fellow after a pause, "he's a d—d scoundrel, no doubt; but as his scoundrelism is his own, I don't see why we should hesitate to avail ourselves of it. With respect, however, to M'Mahon, I can assure you, that I was informed of his intention to set up a Still a good while before I made the capture, and not by anonymous information either. Now, what would you say if both I and Fethertonge knew the whole plot long before it was put in practice?"

As he spoke, he screwed his hard keen features into a most knavish expression.

"Yes," he added; "and I can tell you that both the agent and I forwarned M'Mahon against suffering himself to engage in anything illegal—which was our duty as his friends you know—hem!"

"Is that possible?" said his nephew, blushing for this villianous admission.

"Quite possible," replied the other; "however, as I said, I don't see why we should hesitate to avail ourselves of his villany."

"That is precisely what I was about to say, sir," replied his nephew, still musing on what he had heard.

"Right, Harry; the farm is a good thing, or will be so, at least."

"The farm, sir! but I did not speak with reference to the farm."

"Then with reference to what did you speak?"

"I meant, sir, that we should not hesitate to avail ourselves of his villany, in setting M'Mahon right with the public as far as we could."

"With the whole public!—whew! Why, my good young man, I thought the days of giants and windmills had gone by."

"Well, sir," continued the nephew, "at all events there is one thing you must do for me. I wish you to see old Gerald Cavanagh, and as far as you can to restore his confidence in the honesty and integrity of young M'Mahon. State to him that you have reason to know that his son has a bitter enemy in the neighborhood; that great injustice had been done to him in many ways, and that you would be glad that a reconciliation should take place between the families."

"And so I am to set out upon the wild goose chase of reconciling a wench, and a fellow, without knowing why or wherefore."

"No, sir—not at all—-I will make Cavanough call upon you."

"I don't understand this," replied the uncle, rubbing behind his ear; "I don't perceive; but pray what interest have you in the matter?"

"Upon my honor, uncle, none in life, unless an anxiety to serve poor M'Mahon. The world is down upon him about that vote which, considering all the circumstances, was more creditable to him than otherwise. I know, however, that in consequence of the estrangement between him and Miss Cavanagh, he is bent on emigrating. It is that fact which presses upon him most. Now will you oblige me in this, uncle?"

"Let Cavanagh call upon me," he replied, "and if I can say anything to soften the old fellow, perhaps I will."

"Thank you, uncle—thank you—I shall not forget this kindness."

"Well, then," said his uncle, "I am going down to Fethertonge on a certain matter of business, you understand, and—let me see—why, if Cavanagh calls on me tomorrow about eleven, I shall see him at all events."

Young Clinton felt surprised and grieved at what his uncle had just hinted to him; but on the other hand, he felt considerably elated at the prospect of being able to bring about a reconciliation between these two families, and with this excellent motive in view he went to Cavanagh, with whom he had a private conversation. Having been made aware by M'Mahon himself of Cavanagh's prejudice against him, and the predilections of himself and his wife for an alliance into Burke's family, he merely told him that his uncle would be glad to see him the next day about eleven o'clock, upon which the other promised to attend to that gentleman.

Old Clinton, on his way to Fethertonge's, met that worthy individual riding into Ballymacan.

"I was going down to you," said he; "but where are you bound for?"

"Into town," replied the agent; "have you any objection to ride that way?"

"None in the world; it is just the same to me. Well, how are matters proceeding?"

"Not by any means well," replied the other, "I begin to feel something like alarm. I wish we had those M'Mahons out of the country. Vanston has paid that d—d goose Chevydale a visit, and I fear that unless the Ahadarra man and his father, and the whole crew of them, soon leave the country, we shall break down in our object."

"Do you tell me so?" said the gauger, starting; "by Jove, it is well I know this in time."

"I don't understand."

"Why," continued. Clinton, "I was about to take a foolish step tomorrow morning, for the express purpose, I believe, of keeping him, and probably the whole family in the country."

He then detailed the conversation that he had with his nephew, upon which Fethertonge convinced him that there was more in the wind with respect to that step, than either he or his nephew, who he assured him was made a cat's paw of in the business, suspected. "That's a deep move," said the agent, "but we shall defeat them, notwithstanding. Everything, however, depends upon their leaving the country before Chevydale happens to come at the real state of the case; still, it will go hard or we shall baffle both him and them yet."

Whether Clinton was sure that the step urged upon him by his nephew was the result of a generous regard for M'Mahon, or that the former was made a mere tool for ultimate purposes, in the hands of the Ahadarra man, as he called him it is not easy to determine. Be this as it may, when the hour of eleven came the next morning, he was prepared to set his nephew's generosity aside, and act upon Fethertonge's theory of doing everything in his power to get the whole connection out of the country, "Ha," he exclaimed, "I now understand what Harry meant with respect to their emigration—'It is that fact which presses upon him most.' Oh ho! is it so, indeed! Very good, Mr. M'Mahon—we shall act accordingly."

Gerald Cavanaugh had been made acquainted by his wife on the day before with the partial revival of his daughter's affection for Bryan M'Mahon, as well as with the enthusiastic defense of him made by Finigan, two circumstances which gave him much concern and anxiety. On his return, however, from Clinton's, his family observed that there was something of a satisfactory expression mingled up with a good deal of grave thought in his face. The truth is, if the worthy man thought for a moment that the ultimate loss of M'Mahon would have seriously injured her peace of mind, he would have bitterly regretted it, and perhaps encourage a reconciliation. This was a result, however, that he could scarcely comprehend. That she might fret and pine for a few months or so was the worst he could calculate upon, and of course he took it for granted, that the moment her affection for one was effaced, another might step in, without any great risk of disappointment.

"Well, Gerald," said his wife, "what did Ganger Clinton want with you?"

Gerald looked at his two daughters and sighed unconsciously. "It's not good news," he proceeded, "in one sense, but it is in another; it's good news to all my family but that girl sittin' there," pointing to Kathleen.

Unfortunately no evil intelligence could have rendered the unhappy girl's cheek paler than it was; so that, so far as appearances went, it was impossible to say what effect this startling communication had upon her.

"I was down wid Misther Clinton," he proceeded; "he hard a report that there was about to be a makin' up of the differences between Kathleen there and Bryan, and he sent for me to say, that, for the girl's sake—who he said was, as he had heard from all quarthers, a respectable, genteel girl—he couldn't suffer a young man so full of thraichery and desate, as he had good raisons to know Bryan M'Mahon was, to impose himself upon her or her family. He cautioned me," he proceeded, "and all of us against him; and said that if I allowed a marriage to take place between him and my daughter, he'd soon bring disgrace upon her and us, as well as himself. 'You may take my word for it, Mr. Cavanagh,' says he, 'that is not a thrifle 'ud make me send for you in sich a business; but, as I happen to know the stuff he is made of, I couldn't bear to see him take a decent family in so distastefully. To my own knowledge, Cavanagh,' said he, 'he'd desave a saint, much less your innocent and unsuspectin' daughter.'"

"But, father," said Hanna, "you know there's not a word of truth in that report; and mayn't all that has been said, or at least some of what has been said against Bryan, be as much a lie as that? Who on earth: could sich a report come from?"

"I axed Mr. Clinton the same question," said the father, "and it appears that it came from Bryan himself."

"Oh, God forbid!" exclaimed Hanna; "for, if it's a thing that he said that, he'd say anything."

"I don't know," returned the father, "I only spake it as I hard it, and, what is more, I believe it—I believe it after what I hard this day; everybody knows him now—man, woman, an' child, Gheernah! what an escape that innocent girl had of him!"

Kathleen rose up, went over to her father, and, placing her hand upon his shoulder, was about to speak, but she checked herself; and, after looking at them all, as it were by turns, with a look of distraction and calm but concentrated agony, she returned again to her seat, but did not sit down.

"After all," she exclaimed, "there has been no new crime brought against him, not one; but, if I acted wrongly and ungenerously once, I won't do so again. Hanna, see his sister Dora, say I give him the next three weeks to clear himself; and, father, listen! if he doesn't do so within that time, take me, marry me to Edward Burke if you wish—of course Hycy's out of the question—since you must have it so, for the sooner I go to my grave the better. There's his last chance, let him take it; but, in the mean time, listen to me, one and all of you. I cannot bear this long; there's a dry burning pain about my heart, and a weight upon it will soon put me out of the reach of disappointment and sorrow. Oh, Bryan M'Mahon, can you be what is said of you! and, if you can, oh, why did we ever meet, or why did I ever see you!"

Her sister Hanna attempted to console her, but for once she failed. Kathleen would hear no comfort, for she said she stood in need of none.

"My mind is all dark," said she, "or rather it is sick of this miserable work. Why am I fastened upon by such suffering and distraction? Don't attempt at present to console me, Hanna; I won't, because I can't be consoled. I wish I knew this man—whether he is honest or not. If he is the villain they say he is, and that with a false mask upon him, he has imposed himself on me, and gained my affections by hypocrisy and deceit, why, Hanna, my darling sister, I could stab him to the heart. To think that I ever should come to love a villain that could betray his church, his country, me—and take a bribe; yes, he has done it," she proceeded, catching fire from the force of her own detestation of what was wrong. "Here, Hanna, I call back my words—I give him no further warning than he has got: he knows the time, the greater part of it is past, and has he ever made a single attempt to clear himself? No, because he cannot. I despise him; he is unworthy of me, and I fear he ever was. Here, father," she said with vehemence, "listen to me, my dear father; and you, my mother, beloved mother, hear me! At the expiration of three weeks I will marry Edward Burke; he is a modest, and I think an honest young man, who would not betray his religion nor his country, nor—nor— any unhappy girl that might happen to love him; oh, no, he would not—and so, after three weeks—I will marry him. Go now and tell him so—say I said so; and you may rest assured I will not break my word, although—I may break—break my heart—my heart! Now, Hanna, come out and walk, dear—come out, and let us chat of other matters; yes, of other matters; and you can tell me candidly whether you think Bryan M'Mahon such a villain." Struck by her own words she paused almost exhausted, and, bending down, put her face upon her hands, and by a long persevering effort, at length raised her head, and after a little time appeared to have regained a good deal of composure; but not without tears—for she had wept bitterly.

On that night she told her sister that the last resolution she had come to was that by which she was determined to abide.

"You would not have me like a mere girl," she said, "without the power of knowing my own mind—no; let what may come I will send no messages after him—and as sure as I have life I will marry Edward Burke after the expiration of three weeks, if Bryan doesn't—but it's idle to talk of it—if he could he would have done it before now. Good-night, dear Hanna—good-night," and after many a long and heavy sigh she sank to an uneasy and troubled slumber.

The next morning Gerald Cavanagh, who laid great stress upon the distracted language of his daughter on the preceding night paid an early visit to his friend, Jemmy Burke. He found the whole family assembled at breakfast, and after the usual salutations, was asked to join them, which invitation, however, having already breakfasted, he declined. Hycy had of late been very much abroad—that is to say he was out very much at night, and dined very frequently in the head-inn of Ballymacan, when one would suppose he ought to have dined at home. On the present occasion he saluted honest Gerald with a politeness peculiarly ironical.

"Mr. Cavanagh," said he, "I hope I see you in good health, sir. How are all the ladies?—Hannah, the neat, and Kathleen—ah, Kathleen, the divine!"

"Troth, they're all very well, I thank you, Hycy; and how is yourself?"

"Free from care, Mr. Cavanagh—a chartered libertine."

"A libertine!" exclaimed the honest farmer; "troth I've occasionally heard as much; but until I heard it from your own lips divil a word of it I believed."

"He is only jesting, Mr. Cavanagh," said his brother; "he doesn't mean exactly, nor indeed at all, what you suppose he does."

"Does he mean anything at all, Ned?" said his father, dryly, "for of late it's no aisy matther to understand him."

"Well said, Mr. Burke," replied Hycy; "I am like yourself, becoming exceedingly oracular of late—but, Mr. Cavanagh, touching this exquisite union which is contemplated between Adonis and Juno the ox-eyed—does it still hold good, that, provided always she cannot secure the corrupt clod-hopper, she will in that ease condescend upon Adonis?"

"Gerald," said the father, "as there's none here so handy at the nonsense as to understand him, the best way is to let him answer himself."

"Begad, Jemmy," said Cavanagh, "to tell you the truth, I haven't nonsense enough to answer the last question at any rate; unless he takes to speakin' common-sense I won't undhertake to hould any further discourse wid him."

"Why will you continue," said his brother in a low voice, "to render yourself liable to these strong rebuffs from plain people?"

"Well said, most vituline—*Solomon secundus*, well said."

"Hycy," said his mother, "you ought to remember that every one didn't get the edi cation you did—an' that ignorant people like your father and Gerald Kavanagh there can't undhercomestand one-half o' what you say. Sure they know nothing o' book-lamin', and why do you give it them?"

"Simply to move their metaphysics, Mrs. Burke. They are two of the most notorious metaphysicians from this to themselves; but they don't possess your powers of ratiocination, madam?"

"No," replied his father; "nayther are we sich judges of horseflesh, Hycy."

Hycy made him a polite bow, and replied, "One would think that joke is pretty well worn by this time, Mr. Burke. Couldn't you strike out something original now?"

"All I can say is," replied the father, "that the joke has betther bottom than the garran it was made upon."

Edward now arose and left the parlor, evidently annoyed at the empty ribaldry of his brother, and in a few minutes Hycy mounted his horse and rode towards Ballymacan.

It is not our intention here to follow Gerald Cavanagh in the account, unconsciously one sided as it was, of the consent which he assured them Kathleen had given, on the night before, to marry their son Edward. It is sufficient to say, that before they separated, the match was absolutely made by the two worthies, and everything arranged, with, the exception of the day of marriage, which they promised to determine on at their next meeting.

CHAPTER XXIV.—Thoughts on Our Country and Our Countrymen
—Dora and Her Lover.

The state of the country, at this period of our narrative, was full of gloom and depression. Spring had now set in, and the numbers of our independent and most industrious countrymen that flocked towards our great seaports were reckoned by many thousands; and this had been the case for many a season previously. That something was wrong, and that something is wrong in the country must, alas! be evident from the myriad's who, whilst they have the means in their hands, are anxious to get out of it as fast as they can. And yet there is not a country in the world, a population so affectionately attached to the soil—to the place of their birth—as the Irish. In fact, the love of their native fields, their green meadows, the dark mountains, and the glorious torrents that gush from them, is a passion of which they have in foreign lands been often known to die. It is called Home Sickness, and we are aware ourselves of more than one or two cases in which individuals, in a comparatively early stage of life, have pined away in secret after their native hills, until the malady becoming known, unfortunately too late, they sought once more the green fields and valleys among which they had spent their youth, just in time to lay down their pale cheeks and rest in their native clay for ever those hearts which absence and separation from the very soil had broken.

Now, nothing can be a greater proof of the pressure, the neglect, the hopelessness of independence or comfort, which the condition of the people, and the circumstances which occasioned it, have produced, than the fact that the strong and sacred attachment which we have described is utterly incapable of attaching them as residents in a country so indescribably dear to their best affections. People may ask, and do ask, and will ask, why Ireland is in such a peculiarly distressed state—why there is always upon its surface a floating mass of pauperism without parallel in Europe, or perhaps in the world? To this we reply simply because the duties of property have uniformly been neglected. And in what, may it be asked, do the duties of property consist? To this we reply again, in an earnest fixed resolution to promote, in the first place, the best social and domestic interests of the people, to improve their condition, to stock their minds with, useful and appropriate knowledge, to see that they shall be taught what a sense of decent comfort means, that they shall not rest satisfied with a wad of straw for a bed, and a meal of potatoes for food, and that they shall, besides, come to understand the importance of their own position as members of civil society. Had the landlords of Ireland paid attention to these and other matters that directly involve their own welfare and independence, as well as those of their neglected tenantry, they would not be, as they now are, a class of men, some absolutely bankrupt, and more on the very eve of it; and all this, to use a commercial phrase painfully appropriate,—because they neglect their business.

Who, until lately, ever heard of an Irish landlord having made the subject of property, or the principles upon which it ought to be administered, his study? By this we do not mean to say that they did not occasionally bestow a thought upon their own interests; but, in doing so, they were guided by erroneous principles that led them to place these interests in antagonism with those of the people. They forgot that poverty is the most fertile source of population, and that in every neglected and ill-regulated state of society, they invariably reproduce each other; but the landlords kept the people poor, and now they are surprised, forsooth, at their poverty and the existence of a superabundant population.

"We know," said they, "that the people are poor; but we know also that, by subsisting merely upon the potato, and excluding better food and a higher state of comfort, of course the more is left for the landlord." This in general was their principle and its consequences are now upon themselves.

This, however, is a subject on which it is not our intention to expatiate here. What we say is, that, in all the relations of civil life, Her people were shamefully and criminally neglected. They were left without education, permitted to remain ignorant of the arts of life, and of that industrial knowledge on which, or rather on the application of which, all public prosperity is based.

And yet, although the people have great errors, without which no people so long neglected can ever be found, and, although they have been for centuries familiarized with suffering, yet it is absolute dread

The Emigrants of Ahadarra

of poverty that drives them from their native soil; They understand, in fact, the progress of pauperism too well, and are willing to seek fortune in any clime, rather than abide its approach to themselves — an approach which they know is in their case inevitable and certain. For instance, the very class of our countrymen that constitutes the great bulk of our emigrants is to be found among those independent small farmers who appear to understand something like comfort. One of these men holding, say sixteen or eighteen acres, has a family we will suppose of four sons and three daughters. This family grows up, the eldest son marries, and the father, having no other way to provide for him, sets apart three or four acres of his farm, on which he and his wife settle. The second comes also to marry, and hopes his father won't treat him worse than he treated his brother. He accordingly gets four acres more, and settles down as his brother did. In this manner the holding is frittered away and subdivided among them. For the first few years—that is, before their children rise—they may struggle tolerably well; but, at the expiration of twenty or twenty-five years, each brother finds himself with such a family as his little strip of land cannot adequately support, setting aside the claims of the landlord altogether; for rent in these cases is almost out of the question.

What, then, is the consequence? Why, that here is to be found a population of paupers squatted upon patches of land quite incapable of their support; and in seasons of famine and sickness, especially in a country where labor is below its value, and employment inadequate to the demand that is for it, this same population becomes a helpless burthen upon it—a miserable addition to the mass of poverty and destitution under which it groans.

Such is the history of one class of emigrants in this unhappy land, of ours; and what small farmer, with such a destiny as that we have detailed staring him and his in the face, would not strain every nerve that he might fly to any country—rather than remain to encounter the frightful state of suffering which awaits him in this.

Such, then, is an illustration of the motives which prompt one class of emigrants to seek their fortune in other climes, while it is yet in their power to do so. There is still a higher class, however, consisting of strong farmers possessed of some property and wealth, who, on looking around them, find that the mass of destitution which is so rapidly increasing in every direction must necessarily press upon them in time, and ultimately drag them down to its own level. But even if the naked evils which pervade society among us were not capable of driving these independent yeomen to other lands, we can assure our legislators that what these circumstances, appalling as they are, may fail in accomplishing, the recent act for the extra relief of able-bodied paupers will complete—an act which, instead of being termed a Relief Act, ought to be called an act for the ruin of the country, and the confiscation of its property, both of which, if not repealed, it will ultimately accomplish. We need not mention here cases of individual neglect or injustice upon the part of landlords and agents, inasmuch as we have partially founded our narrative upon a fact of this description.

It has been said, we know, and in many instances with truth, that the Irish are a negligent and careless people—without that perseverance and enterprise for which their neighbors on the other side of the channel are so remarkable. We are not, in point of fact, about to dispute the justice of this charge; but, if it be true of the people, it is only so indirectly. It is true of their condition and social circumstances in this country, rather than of any constitutional deficiency in either energy or industry that is inherent in their character. In their own country they have not adequate motive for action—no guarantee that industry shall secure them independence, or that the fruits of their labor may not pass, at the will of; their landlords, into other hands. Many, therefore, of the general imputations that are brought against them in these respects, ought to be transferred rather to the depressing circumstances in which they are placed than to the people themselves. As a proof of; this, we have only to reflect upon their industry, enterprise, and success, when relieved from the pressure of these circumstances in other countries—especially in America, where exertion and industry never, or at least seldom, fail to arrive at comfort and independence. Make, then, the position of the Irishman reasonable—such, for instance, as it is in any other country but his own—and he can stand the test of comparison with any man.

Not only, however, are the Irish flying from the evils that are to come, but they feel a most affectionate anxiety to enable all those who are bound to them by the ties of kindred and domestic affection to imitate their example. There is not probably to be found in records of human attachment such a beautiful history of unforgotten affection, as that presented by the heroic devotion of Irish emigrants to those of their kindred who remain here from inability to accompany them.*

The following extract, from a very sensible pamphlet by Mr. Murray, is so appropriate to this subject, that we cannot deny ourselves the pleasure of quoting it here:—

"You have been accustomed to grapple with and master figures, whether as representing the produce of former tariffs, or in constructing new ones, or in showing the income and expenditure of the greatest nation on the earth. Those now about to be presented to you, as an appendix to this communication, are small, very small, in their separate amounts, and not by any means in the aggregate of the magnitude of the sums you have been accustomed to deal with; but they are large separately, and heaving large in the aggregate, in all that is connected with the higher and nobler parts of our nature—in all that relates to and evinces the feelings of the heart towards those who are of our kindred, no matter by what waters placed asunder or by what distance separated. They are large, powerfully large, in reading lessons of instruction to the statesman and philanthropist, in dealing with a warm-hearted people for their good, and placing them in a position of comparative comfort to that in which they now are. The figures represent the particulars of 7,917 separate Bills of Exchange, varying in amount from £1 to £10 each—a few exceeding the latter sum; so many separate offerings from the natives of Ireland who have heretofore emigrated from its shores, sent to their relations and friends in Ireland, drawn and paid between the 1st of January and the 15th of December, 1846—not quite one year; and amount in all to £41,261 9s. 11d. But this list, long though it be, does not measure the number and amount of such interesting offerings. It contains only about one-third part of the whole number and value of such remittances that have crossed the Atlantic to Ireland during the 349 days of 1846. The data from which this list is complied enable the writer to estimate with confidence the number and amount drawn otherwise; and he calculates that the entire number, for not quite one year, of such Bills, is £24,000, and

the amount £125,000, or, on an average, £5 4s. 3d. each. *They are sent from husband to wife, from father to child, from child to father, mother, and grand-parents, from sister to brother, and the reverse; and from and to those united by all the ties of blood and friendship that bind us together on earth.*

In the list, you will observe that these offerings of affection are classed according to the parts of Ireland they are drawn upon, and you will find that they are not confined to one spot of it, but are general as regards the whole country." —Ireland. its Present Condition and Future Prospects, In n letter addressed to the Right Honorable Sir Robert Peel, Baronet, by Robert Murray. Esq. Dublin, James M'Olashan, 21 D'Olier Street, 1847.

Let it not be said, then, that the Irishman is deficient in any of the moral elements or natural qualities which go to the formation of such a character as might be made honorable to himself and beneficial to the country. By the success of his exertions in a foreign land, it is clear that he is not without industry, enterprise, and perseverance; and we have no hesitation in saying that, if he were supplied at home with due encouragement and adequate motive, his good qualities could be developed with as much zeal, energy, and success as ever characterized them in a foreign country.

We trust the reader may understand what the condition of the country, at the period of our narrative to which we refer, must have been, when such multitudes as we have described rushed to our great seaports in order to emigrate; the worst feature in this annual movement being that, whilst the decent, the industrious, and the moral, all influenced by creditable motives, went to seek independence in a distant land, the idle, the ignorant, and the destitute necessarily remain at home—all as a burthen, and too many of them as a disgrace to the country.

Our friends the M'Mahons, urged by motives at once so strong and painful, were not capable of resisting the contagion of emigration which, under the circumstances we have detailed, was so rife among the people. It was, however, on their part a distressing and mournful resolve. From the, moment it was made, a gloom settled upon the whole family. Nothing a few months before had been farther from their thoughts; but now there existed such a combination of arguments for their departure, as influenced Bryan and his father, in spite of their hereditary attachment to Ahadarra and Carriglass.

Between them and the Cavanaghs, ever since Gerald had delivered Kathleen's message to Bryan, there was scarcely any intercourse. Hanna, 'tis true, and Dora had an opportunity of exchanging a few words occasionally, but although the former felt much anxiety for a somewhat lengthened and if possible confidential conversation with her sparkling little friend, yet the latter kept proudly if not haughtily silent on one particular subject, feeling as she did, that anything like a concession on her part was humiliating, and might be misconstrued into a disposition to compromise the independence of her brother and family. But even poor Dora, notwithstanding her affectionate heart and high spirit, had her own sorrows to contend with, sorrows known only to her brother Bryan, who felt disposed to befriend her in them as far as he could. So indeed would every one of the family, had they known them, for we need scarcely say that the warm and generous girl was the centre in which all their affections met. And this indeed was only justice to her, inasmuch as she was willing on any occasion to sacrifice her interests, her wishes, or anything connected with her own welfare, to their individual or general happiness. We have said, however, that she had her own sorrows, and this was true. From the moment she felt assured that their emigration to America was certain, she manifested a depression so profound and melancholy, that the heart of her brother Bryan, who alone knew its cause, bled for her. This by the rest of the family was imputed to the natural regret she felt, in common with themselves, at leaving the old places for ever, with this difference to be sure—they imagined that she felt the separation more acutely than they did. Still, as the period for their departure approached, there was not one of the family, notwithstanding what she felt herself, who labored so incessantly to soothe and sustain the spirits of her father, who was fast sinking under the prospect of being "forever removed," as he said, "from the places his heart had grown into." She was in fact the general consoler of the family, and yet her eye scarcely ever met that of her brother that a tear did not tremble in it, and she felt disposed to burst out into an agony of unrestrained grief.

It was one evening in the week previous to their departure, that she was on her return from Ballymacan, when on passing a bend of the road between Carriglass and Fenton's farm, she met the cause of the sorrow which oppressed her, in the handsome person of James Cavanaugh, to whom she had been for more than a year and a half deeply and devotedly attached, but without the knowledge of any individual living, save her lover himself and her brother Bryan.

On seeing him she naturally started, but it was a start of pleasure, and she felt her cheek flush and again get pale, and her heart palpitated, then was still a moment, and again resumed its tumultuous pulsations.

"Blessed be God, my darlin' Dora, that I've met you at last," said James; "in heaven's name how did it happen that we haven't met for such a length of time?"

"I'm sure that's more than I can tell," replied Dora, "or rather it's what both, you and I know the cause of too well."

"Ah, poor Dora," he exclaimed, "for your sake I don't wish to spake about it at all; it left me many a sore heart when I thought of you."

Dora's natural pale cheek mantled, and her eyes deepened with a beautiful severity, as she hastily turned them on him and said, "what do you mane, James?"

"About poor Bryan's conduct at the election," he replied, "and that fifty-pound note; and may hell consume it and him that tempted him with it!"

"Do you forget," she said, "that you're spaking to his sister that knows the falsehood of it all; an' how dare you in my presence attempt to say or think that Bryan M'Mahon would or could do a mane or dishonest act? I'm afeard, James, there's a kind of low suspicion in your family that's not right, and I have my reasons for thinking so. I fear there's a want of true generosity among you; and if I could be sure of it, I tell you now, that whatever it might cost me, I'd never—but what am I sayin'? that's past."

"Past! oh, why do you spake that way, Dora dear?"

"It's no matter what I may suffer myself," she replied; "no matter at all about that; but wanst and for all, I tell you that let what may happen, I'm not the girl to go into a family that have treated my dear brother as yours has done. Your sister's conduct has been very harsh and cruel to the man she was to be married to."

"My sister, Dora, never did anything but what was right."

"Well, then, let her go and marry the Pope, with reverence be it spoken, for I don't know any other husband that's fit for her. I'd like to see the girl that never did anything wrong; it's a sight I never saw yet, I know."

"Dora, dear," replied her lover, "I don't blame you for being angry. I know that such a load of disgrace upon any family is enough to put one past their temper. I don't care about that, however," he proceeded; "if he had betrayed his church and his country ten times over, an' got five hundred pounds instead of fifty, it wouldn't prevent me from makin' you my wife."

Her eyes almost emitted fire at this unconsciously offensive language of Cavanagh. She calmed herself, however, and assumed a manner that was cool and cuttingly ironical.

"Wouldn't you, indeed?" she replied; "dear me! I have a right to be proud of that; and so you'd be mane enough to marry into a family blackened by disgrace. I thought you had some decent pride, James."

"But you have done nothing wrong, Dora," he replied; "'you're free from any blame of that kind."

"I have done nothing wrong, haven't I?" she returned. "Ay, a thousand things—for, thank God, I'm not infallible like your sister. Haven't I supported my brother in every thing he did? and I tell you that if I had been in his place I'd just 'a' done what he did. What do you think o' me now?"

"Why, that every word you say, and every lively look—ay, or angry if you like—that you give—makes me love you more and more. An' plase God, my dear Dora, I hope soon to see you my own darlin' wife."

"That's by no means a certain affair, James; an' don't rely upon it. Before ever I become your wife Kathleen must change her conduct to my brother."

"'Deed and I'm afraid that shell never do, Dora."

"Then the sorra ring ever I'll put on you while there's, breath in my body."

"Why, didn't she give him three months to clear himself?"

"Did she, indeed? And do you think that any young man of spirit would pay attention to such a stilted pride as that? It was her business to send for him face to face, and to say—'Bryan M'Mahon, I never knew you or one of your family to tell a lie or do a dishonest or disgraceful act'—and here as she spoke the tears of that ancient integrity and hereditary pride which are more precious relics in a family than the costliest jewels that ever sparkled in the sun, sprang from her eyes—'and now, Bryan M'Mahon, I ax no man's word but your own—I ax no other evidence but your own—I put it to your conscience—to that honor that has never yet been tarnished by any of your family, I say I put it to yourself, here face to face with the girl that loves you—and answer me as you are in the presence of God—did you do what they charge you with? Did you do wrong knowingly and deliberately, and against your own conscience?"

The animated sparkle of her face was so delightful and fascinating that her lover attempted to press her to his bosom; but she would not suffer it.

"Behave now," she said firmly; "sorra bit—no," she proceeded; "and whilst all the world was against him, runnin' him down and blackenin' him—was she ever the girl to stand up behind his back and defend him like a—hem—defend him, I say, as a girl that loved him ought, and a generous-girl would?"

"But how could she when she believed, him to be wrong?"

"Why did she believe him to be wrong upon mere hearsay? and granting that he was wrong! do you think now if you had done what they say he did (and they lie that say it), an' that I heard the world down on you for your first slip, do you think, I say, that I'd not defend you out of clane contrariness,—and to vex them—ay, would I."

"I know, darlin', that you'd do everything that's generous an' right; but settin' that affair aside, my dear Dora, what are you and I to do?"

"I don't know what we're to do," she replied; "it's useless for you to ax me from my father now; for he wouldn't give me to you,—sorra bit."

"But you'll give me yourself, Dora, darling."

"Not without his consent, no nor with it,—as the families stand this moment; for I tell you again that the sorra ring ever I'll put on you till your sister sends for my brother, axes his pardon, and makes up with him, as she ought to do. Oh why, James dear, should she be so harsh upon him," she said, softening at once; "she that is so good an' so faultless afther all? but I suppose that's the raison of it—she doesn't know what it is to do anything that's not right."

"Dora," said her lover, "don't be harsh on Kathleen; you don't know what she's sufferin'. Dora, her heart's broke—broke."

The tears were already upon Dora's cheeks, and her lover, too, was silent for a moment.

"She has," resumed the warm-hearted girl, "neither brother nor sister that loves her, or can love her, better than I do, afther all."

"But in our case, darling, what's to be done?" he asked, drawing her gently towards him.

"I'll tell you then what I'd recommend you to do," she replied; "spake to my brother Bryan, and be guided by him. I must go now, it's quite dusk."

There was a moment's pause, then a gentle remonstrance on the part of Dora, followed, however, by that soft sound which proceeds from the pressure of youthful lips—after which she bade her lover a hasty good-night and hurried home.

CHAPTER XXV.—The Old Places—Death of a Patriarch.

As the day appointed for the auction of the M'Mahon's stock, furniture, etc., etc., at Carriglass drew near, a spirit of deep and unceasing distress settled upon the whole family. It had not been their purpose to apprise the old man of any intention on their part to emigrate at all, and neither indeed had they done so. The fact, however, reached him from the neighbors, several of whom, ignorant that it was the wish of his family to conceal the circumstance from him—at least as long as they could—entered into conversation with him upon it, and by this means he became acquainted with their determination. Age, within the last few months—for he was now past ninety—had made sad work with both his frame and intellect. Indeed, for some time past, he might be said to hover between reason and dotage. Decrepitude had set in with such ravages on his constitution that it could almost be marked by daily stages. Sometimes he talked with singular good sense and feeling; but on other occasions he either babbled quite heedlessly, or his intellect would wander back to scenes and incidents of earlier life, many of which he detailed with a pathos that was created and made touching by the unconsciousness of his own state while relating them. They also observed that of late he began to manifest a child-like cunning in many things connected with himself and family, which, though amusing from its very simplicity, afforded at the same time a certain indication that the good old grandfather whom they all loved so well, and whose benignant character had been only mellowed by age into a more plastic affection for them all, was soon to be removed from before their eyes, never again to diffuse among them that charm of domestic truth and love, and the holy influences of all those fine old virtues which ancestral integrity sheds over the heart, and transmits pure and untarnished from generation to generation.

On the day he made the discovery of their intention, he had been sitting on a bench in the garden, a favorite seat of his for many a long year previously; "And so," said he to the neighbor with whom he had been speaking, "you tell me that all our family is goin' to America?"

"Why, dear me," replied his acquaintance, "is it possible you didn't know it?"

"Ha!" he exclaimed, "I undherstand now why they used to be whisperin' together so often, and lookin' at me; but indeed they might spake loud enough now, for I'm so deaf that I can hardly hear anything. Howaniver, Ned, listen—they all intend to go, you say; now listen, I say—I know one that won't go; now, do you hear that? You needn't say anything about it, but this I tell you—listen to me, what's your name? Barney, is it?"

"Why, is it possible, you don't know Ned Gormley?"

"Ay, Ned Gormley—och, so it is. Well listen, Ned—there's one they won't bring; I can tell you that—the sorra foot I'll go to—to—where's this you say they're goin' to, Jemmy?"

Gormley shook his head. "Poor Bryan," said he, "it's nearly all over wid you, at any rate. To America, Bryan," he repeated, in a loud voice.

"Ay, to America. Well, the sorra foot ever I'll go to America—that one thing I can tell them. I'm goin' in. Oh! never mind," he exclaimed, on Gormley offering him assistance, "I'm stout enough still; stout an' active still; as soople as a two-year ould, thank God. Don't I bear up wonderfully?"

"Well, indeed you do, Bryan; it is wonderful, sure enough."

In a few minutes they arrived at the door; and the old man, recovering as it were a portion of his former intellect, said, "lavin' this place—these houses—an' goin' away—far, far away—to a strange country—to strange people! an' to bring me, the ould white haired grandfather, away from all! that would be cruel; but my son Tom will never do it."

"Well, at any rate, Bryan," said his neighbor, "whether you go or stay, God be wid you. It's a pity, God knows, that the like of you and your family should leave the country; and sure if the landlord, as they say, is angry about it, why doesn't he do what he ought to do? an' why does he allow that smooth-tongued rap to lead him by the nose as he does? Howandiver, as I said, whether you go or stay, Bryan, God be wid you!"

During all that morning Thomas M'Mahon had been evidently suffering very deeply from a contemplation of the change that was about to take place by the departure of himself and his family from Carriglass. He had been silent the greater part of the morning, and not unfrequently forced to give away to tears, in which he was joined by his daughters, with the exception of Dora, who, having assumed the office of comforter, felt herself bound to maintain the appearance of a firmness which she did not feel. In this mood he was when "grandfather," as they called him, entered the house, after having been made acquainted with their secret. "Tom," said he, approaching his son, "sure you wouldn't go to bring an ould man away?"

"Where to, father?" asked the other, a good deal alarmed.

"Why, to America, where you're all goin' to. Oh! surely you wouldn't bring the old man away from the green fields of Carriglass? Would you lay my white head in a strange land, an' among a strange people? Would you take poor ould grandfather away from them that expects him down, at Carndhu where they sleep? Carndhu's a holy churchyard. Sure there never was a Protestant buried in it but one, an' the next mornin' there was a boortree bush growin' out o' the grave, an' it's there yet to prove the maricle. Oh! ay, Carndhu's holy ground, an' that's where I must sleep."

These words were uttered with a tone of such earnest and childlike entreaty as rendered them affecting in a most extraordinary degree, and doubly so to those who heard him. Thomas's eyes, despite of every effort to the contrary, filled with tears. "Ah!" he exclaimed, "he has found it out at last; but how can I give him consolation, an' I stands in need of it so much myself?"

"Father," said he, rising and placing the old man in the arm-chair, which for the last half century had been his accustomed seat, "father, we will go together—we will all be wid you. You'll not be among strangers—you'll have your own about you still."

"But what's takin' you all away?"

"Neglect and injustice, an' the evil tongues of them that ought to know us betther. The landlord didn't turn out to be what he ought to be. May God forgive him! But at any rate I'm sure he has been misled."

"Ould Chevydale," said his father, "never was a bad landlord, an' he'd not become a bad one now. That's not it."

"But the ould man's dead, father, an' its his son we're spakin' of."

"And the son of ould Chevydale must have something good about him. The heart was always right wid his father, and every one knows there's a great deal in true blood. Sooner or later it'll tell for itself—but what is this? There was something troublin' me this minute. Oh! ay, you're goin' away, then, to America; but, mark my words:—I won't go. You may, but I'll stay here. I won't lave the green fields of Carriglass for any one. It's not much I'll be among them now, an' it isn't worth your while to take me from them. Here's where I was born—here's where the limbs that's now stiff an' feeble was wanst young and active—here's where the hair that's white as snow was fair an' curlin' like goold—here's where I was young—here's where I grew ould—among these dark hills and green fields—here you all know is where I was born; and, in spite o' you all, here's where I'll die."

The old man was much moved by all these recollections; for, as he proceeded, the tears fell fast from his aged eyes, and his voice became tremulous and full of 'sorrow.

"Wasn't it here, too," he proceeded, "that Peggy Slevin, she that was famed far an' near for her beauty, and that the sweet song was made upon—'Peggy Na Laveen'—-ay—ay, you may think yourselves fine an' handsome; but, where was there sich a couple as grandfather and Peggy Na Laveen was then?"

As he uttered these words, his features that had been impressed by grief, were lit up by a smile of that simple and harmless vanity which often attends us to the very grave; after which he proceeded:—

"There, on the side of that hill is the roofless house where she was born; an' there's not a field or hill about the place that her feet didn't make holy to me. I remember her well. I see her, an' I think I hear her voice on the top of Lisbane, ringin' sweetly across the valley of the

Mountain Wather, as I often did. An' is it to take me away now from all this? Oh! no, childre', the white-haired grandfather couldn't go. He couldn't lave the ould places—the ould places. If he did, he'd die—he'd die. Oh, don't, for God's sake, Tom, as you love me!"

There was a spirit of helpless entreaty in these last words that touched his son, and indeed all who heard him, to the quick.

"Grandfather dear, be quiet," he replied; "God will direct all things for the best. Don't cry," he added, for the old man was crying like an infant; "don't cry, but be quiet, and everything will be well in time. It's a great trial, I know; but any change is better than to remain here till we come, like so many others, to beggary. God will support us, father."

The old man wiped his eyes, and seemed as if he had taken comfort from the words of his son; whereas, the fact was, that his mind had altogether passed from the subject; but not without that unconscious feeling of pain which frequently remains after the recollection of that which has occasioned it has passed away.

It was evident, from the manner of the old man, that the knowledge of their intended emigration had alarmed into action all the dormant instincts of his nature; but this was clearly more than they were competent to sustain for any length of time. Neither the tottering frame, nor the feeble mind was strong enough to meet the shock which came so unexpectedly upon them. The consequence may be easily anticipated. On the following day he was able to be up only for an hour; yet he was not sick, nor did he complain of any particular pain. His only malady appeared to consist in that last and general prostration of bodily and intellectual strength, by which persons of extreme old age, who have enjoyed uninterrupted health, are affected at, or immediately preceding their dissolution. His mind, however, though wandering and unsteady, was vigorous in such manifestations as it made. For instance, it seemed to be impressed by a twofold influence,—the memory of his early life,—mingled with a vague perception of present anxiety, the cause of which he occasionally was able to remember, but as often tried to recollect in vain.

On the second day after his discovery he was unable to rise at all; but, as before, he complained of nothing, neither were his spirits depressed. On the contrary they were rather agitated—sometimes into cheerfulness, but more frequently into an expression of sorrow and lamentation, which were, however, blended with old by-gone memories that were peculiarly reflecting to those who heard them. In this way he went on, sinking gradually until the day previous to the auction. On that morning, to their surprise, he appeared to have absolutely regained new strength, and to have been gifted with something like renovated power of speech.

"I want to get up," said he, "and it's only Tom an' Dora that I'll allow to help me. You're all good, an' wor always good to grandfather, but Tom was my best son, and signs on it—everything thruv wid him, an' God will prosper an' bless him. Where's Dora?"

"Here, grandfather."

"Ay, that's the voice above all o' them that went like music to my heart; but well I know, and always did, who you have that voice from; ay, an' I know whose eyes—an' it's them that's the lovely eyes—Dora has. Isn't the day fine, Dora?"

"It is, grandfather, a beautiful day."

"Ay, thank God. Well then I want to go out till I look—take one look at the ould places; for somehow I think my heart was never so much in them as now."

It is impossible to say how or why the feeling prevailed, but the fact was, that the whole family were impressed with a conviction that this partial and sudden restoration of his powers was merely what is termed the lightening before death, and the consequence was, that every word he spoke occasioned their grief, for the loss of the venerable and virtuous patriarch, to break out with greater force. When he was dressed he called Dora to aid her father in bringing him out, which she did with streaming eyes and sobbings that she could scarcely restrain. After having reached a little green eminence that commanded a glorious view of the rich country beneath and around them, he called for his chair; "an', Bryan," said he, "the manly and honest-hearted, do you bring it to me. A blessin' will follow you, Bryan—a blessin' will follow my manly grandson, that I often had a proud heart out of. An'; Bryan," he proceeded, when the latter had returned with the chair and placed him in it, "listen, Bryan—when you and Kathleen Cavanagh's married—but I needn't say it—where was there one of your name to do an unmanly thing in that respect?—but when you and Kathleen's married, be to her as your own father was to her that's gone—ever and always kind and lovin', an' what your grandfather that's now spaking to you, maybe for the last time, was to her that's long, long an angel in heaven—my own Peggy Slevin—but it's the Irish sound of it I like—Peggy Na Laveen. Bring them all out here—but what is this?—why are you all cryin'? Sure; there's nothing wrong—an' why do you cry?"

The other members of the family then assembled with tearful faces, and the good old man proceeded:—

"Thomas M'Mahon, stand before me." The latter, with uncovered head, did so; and his father resumed:—"Thomas M'Mahon, you're the only livin' son I have, an' I'm now makin' my Will. I lave this farm of Carriglass to you, while you live, wid all that's on it and in it;—that is, that I have any right to lave you—I lave it to you wid my blessin', and may God grant you long life and health to enjoy it. Ahadarra isn't mine to give, but, Bryan, it's your's; an' as I said to your father, God grant you health and long life to enjoy it, as he will to both o' you."

"Oh! little you know, grandfather dear," replied Shibby, "that we've done wid both of them for ever."

"Shibby, God bless you, achora," he returned; "but the ould man's lips can spake nothing now but the truth; an' my blessin' an' my wish, comin' from the Almighty as they do, won't pass away like common words." He then paused for a few minutes, but appeared to take a comprehensive view of the surrounding country.

"But, grandfather," proceeded simple-hearted Shibby, "sure the match between Bryan and Kathleen Cavanagh is broken up, an' they're not to be married at all."

"Don't I say, darlin', that they will be married, an' be happy—ay, an' may God make them happy! as He will, blessed be His holy name! God, acushla, can bring about everything in His own good way."

After another pause of some minutes he murmured to himself—"Peggy Na Laveen—Peggy Na Laveen—how far that name has gone! Turn me round a little. What brought us here, childre'? Oh! ay—I wanted to see the ould places—there's Claghleim, where the walls of the house she was born in, and the green garden, is both to the fore; yet I hope they won't be disturbed, if it was only for the sake of them that's gone; an' there's the rock on the top of Lisbane, where, in the summer evening, long, long ago, I used to sit an' listen to Peggy Na Laveen singin' over our holy songs—the darlin' ould songs of the counthry. Oh! clear an' sweet they used to ring across the glen of the Mountain Wather. An' there's the hills an' the fields where she an' I so often sported when we wor both young; there they are, an' many a happy day we had on them; but sure God was good to us, blessed be His name, as He ever will be to them that's obadient to His holy will!"

As he uttered the last words he clasped his two hands together, and, having closed his eyes, he muttered something internally which they could not understand. "Now," said he, "bring me in again; I have got my last look at them all—the ould places, the brave ould places! oh, who would lave them for any other country? But at any rate, Tom, achora, don't take me away from them; sure you wouldn't part me from the green fields of Carriglass? Sure you'd not take me from the blessed graveyard of Carndhu, where we all sleep. I couldn't rest in a sthrange grave, nor among strange people; I couldn't rest, barrin' I'm wid her, Peggy Na Laveen." These words he uttered after his return into the house.

"Grandfather," said Bryan, "make your mind aisy; we won't take you from the brave ould places, and you will sleep in Carndhu with Peggy Na Laveen; make your heart and mind easy, then, for you won't be parted."

He turned his eyes upon the speaker, and a gleam of exultation and delight settled upon his worn but venerable features; nor did it wholly pass away, for, although his chin sank upon his breast, yet the placid expression remained. On raising his head they perceived that this fine and patriarchal representative of the truthful integrity and simple manners of a bygone class had passed into a life where neither age nor care can oppress the spirit, and from whose enjoyment no fear of separation can ever disturb it.

It is unnecessary to describe the sorrow which they felt. It must be sufficient to say that seldom has grief for one so far advanced in years been so sincere and deep. Age, joined to the knowledge of his affectionate heart and many virtues, had encircled him with a halo of love and pious veneration which caused his disappearance from among them to be felt, as if a lamb of simple piety and unsullied truth had been removed from their path for ever.

That, indeed, was a busy and a melancholy day with the M'Mahons; for, in addition to the death of the old grandfather, they were obliged to receive farewell visits to no end from their relations, neighbors, and acquaintances. Indeed it would be difficult to find a family in a state of greater distress and sorrow. The auction, of course, was postponed for a week—that is, until after the old man's funeral—and the consequence was that circumstances, affecting the fate of our *dramatis personae* had time to be developed, which would otherwise have occurred too late to be available for the purposes of our narrative. This renders it necessary that we should return to a period in it somewhat anterior to that at which we have now arrived.

CHAPTEE XXVI.—Containing a Variety of Matters.

Our readers cannot have forgotten the angry dialogue which Kate Hogan and her male relations indulged in upon the misunderstanding that had occurred between the Cavanaghs and M'Mahons, and its imputed cause. We stated at the time that Hycy Burke and the Hogans, together with a strange man and woman, were embarked in some mysterious proceedings from which both Kate Hogan and Teddy Phats had been excluded. For some time, both before and after that night, there had been, on the other hand, a good, deal of mysterious communication between several of our other characters. For instance Kate Hogan and Nanny Peety had had frequent interviews, to which, in the course of time, old Peety, Teddy Phats, and, after him, our friend the schoolmaster had been admitted. Nanny Peety had also called on Father Magowan, and, after him, upon young Clinton; and it was evident, from the result of her disclosures to the two latter, that they also took a warm interest, and were admitted to a participation in, the councils we mention. To these proceedings Clinton had not been long privy when he began to communicate with Vanston, who, on his part, extended the mystery to Chevydale, between whom and himself several confidential interviews had already taken place. Having thrown out these hints to our readers, we beg them to accompany us once more to the parlor of Clinton the gauger and his nephew.

"So, uncle, now that you have been promoted to the Supervisorship, you abandon the farm; you abandon Ahadarra?"

"Why, won't I be out of the district, you blockhead? and you persist in refusing it besides."

"Most positively; but I always suspected that Fethertonge was a scoundrel, as his conduct in that very business with you was a proo—hem, ahem."

"Go on," said the uncle, coolly, "don't be ashamed, Harry; I was nearly as great a scoundrel in that business as he was. I told you before that I look upon the world as one great pigeon, which every man who can, without exposing, himself, is obliged to pluck. Now, in the matter of the farm, I only was about to pluck out a feather or two to put in my own nest—or yours, if you had stood it."

"At any rate, uncle, I must admit that you are exceedingly candid."

"No such thing, you fool; there is scarcely an atom of candor in my whole composition—I mean to the world, whatever I may be to you. Candor, Harry, my boy, is a virtue which very few in this life, as it goes, can afford to practice—at least I never could."

"Well but, uncle, is it not a pity to see that honest family ruined and driven out of the country by the villany of Burke on the one hand, and the deliberate fraud and corruption of Fethertonge, on the other. However, now that you are resolved to unmask Fethertonge, I am satisfied. It's a proof that you don't wish to see an honest family oppressed and turned, without reasonable compensation, out of their property."

"It's a proof of no such thing, I tell you. I don't care the devil had the M'Mahons; but I am bound to this ninnyhammer of a landlord, who has got me promoted, and who promises, besides, to get an appointment for you. I cannot see him, I say, fleeced and plucked by this knavish agent, who winds him about his finger like a thread; and, as to those poor honest devils of M'Mahons, stop just a moment and I will show you a document that may be of some value to them. You see, Fethertonge, in order to enhance the value of his generosity to myself, or, to come nearer the truth, the value of Ahadarra, was the means of placing a document, which I will immediately show you, in my hands."

He went to his office or study, and, after some search, returned and handed the other a written promise of the leases of Ahadarra and Carriglass, respectively, to Thomas M'Mahon and his son Bryan, at a certain reasonable rent offered by each for their separate holdings.

"Now," he proceeded, "there's a document which proves Fethertonge, notwithstanding his knavery, to be an ass; otherwise he would have reduced it to ashes long ago; and, perhaps, after having turned it to his account, he would have done so, were it not that I secured it. Old Chevydale, it appears, not satisfied with giving his bare word, strove, the day before he died, to reduce his promise

The Emigrants of Ahadarra

about the lease to writing, which he did, and entrusted it to the agent for the M'Mahons, to whom, of course, it was never given."

"But what claim had you to it, uncle?"

"Simply, if he and I should ever come to a misunderstanding, that I might let him know he was in my power, by exposing his straightforward methods of business; that's all. However, about the web that this fellow Burke has thrown around these unfortunate devils the M'Mahons, and those other mighty matters that you told of, let me hear exactly what it is all about and how they stand. You say there is likely to be hanging or transportation among them."

"Why, the circumstances, sir, are these, as nearly as I am in possession of them:—There is or was, at least a day or two ago, a very pretty girl—"

"Ay, ay—no fear but there must be that in it; go along."

"A very pretty girl, named Nanny Peety, a servant in old Jemmy Burke's, Hycy's father. It appears that his virtuous son Hycy tried all the various stratagems of which he is master to debauch the morals of this girl, but without success. Her virtue was incorruptible."

"Ahem! get along, will you, and pass that over."

"Well, I know that's another of your crotchets, uncle; but no matter, I should be sorry, from respect to my mother's memory, to agree with you there: however to proceed; this Nanny Peety at length—that is about a week ago—was obliged to disclose to her father the endless persecution which she had to endure at the hands of Hycy Burke; and in addition to that disclosure, came another, to the effect that she had been for a considerable period aware of a robbery which took place in old Burke's—you may remember the stir it made—and which robbery was perpetrated by Bat Hogan, one of these infamous tinkers that live in Gerald Cavanagh's kiln, and under the protection of his family. The girl's father—who, by the way, is no other than the little black visaged mendicant who goes about the country—"

"I know him—proceed."

"Her father, I say, on hearing these circumstances, naturally indignant at Hycy Burke for his attempts to corrupt the principles of his daughter, brought the latter with him to Father Magowan, in whose presence she stated all she knew; adding, that she had secured Bat Hogan's hat and shoes, which, in his hurry, he had forgotten on the night of the robbery. She also requested the priest to call upon me, 'as she felt certain,' she said, 'in consequence of a letter of Burke's which I happened to see as she carried it to the post-office, that I could throw some light upon his villany. He did so.' It was on that affair the priest called here the other day, and I very candidly disclosed to him the history of that letter, and its effect in causing the seizure of the distillery apparatus—the fact being that everything was got up by Hycy himself—I mean at his cost, with a view to ruin M'Mahon. And this I did the more readily, as the scoundrel has gone far to involve me in the conduct imputed to M'Mahon, as his secret abbettor and enemy."

"Well," observed his uncle, "all that's a very pretty affair as it stands; but what are you to do next?"

"There is worse behind, I can assure you," continued his nephew. "Hycy Burke, who is proverbially extravagant, having at last, in an indirect way, ruined young M'Mahon, from the double motive of ill-will and a wish to raise money by running illicit spirits—"

"The d—d scoundrel!" exclaimed the gauger, seized with a virtuous fit of (professional) indignation, "that fellow would scruple at nothing—proceed."

"By the way," observed the other, rather maliciously, "he made a complete tool of you in M'Mahon's affair."

"He did, the scoundrel," replied his uncle, wincing a good deal; "but, as the matter was likely to turn up, he was only working out my purposes."

"He is in a bad mess now, however," continued his nephew.

"Why, is there worse to come?"

"This same Nanny Peety, you must know, is a relative, it seems, to Bat Hogan's wife. For some time past there has come a strange man named Vincent, and his wife, to reside in the neighborhood, and this fellow in conjunction with the Hogans, was managing some secret proceedings which no one can penetrate. Now, it appears that

Hogan's wife, who has been kept out of this secret, got Nanny Peety to set her father to work in order to discover it. Peety, by the advice of Hogan's wife, called in Teddy Phat's—"

"What's that? Teddy Phats? Now, by the way, Harry, don't abuse poor Teddy. You will be surprised, Hal, when I tell you that he and I have played into each other's hands for years. Yes, my boy, and I can assure you that, owing to him, both Fethertonge and I were aware of Hycy's Burke's plot against M'Mahon long before he set it a-going. The fellow, however, will certainly be hanged yet."

"Faith, sir," replied Harry, "instead of being hanged himself, he's likely to hang others. In consequence of an accidental conversation which Teddy Phats, and Finigan the tippling schoolmaster had, concerning Vincent, the stranger I spoke of, who, it appears, lives next to Finigan's school-house, Teddy discovered, through the pedagogue, who, by the way, is abroad at all hours, that the aforesaid Vincent was in the habit of going up every night to the most solitary part of the mountains, but for what purpose, except upon another distillation affair, he could not say."

The old gauger or supervisor, as he now considered himself, became here so comically excited—or, we should rather say, so seriously excited—that it was with difficulty the nephew could restrain his laughter. He moved as if his veins had been filled with quicksilver, his eyes brightened, and his naturally keen and knavish-looking features were sharpened, as it were, into an expression so acutely sinister, that he resembled a staunch old hound who comes unexpectedly upon the fresh slot of a hare.

"Well," said he, rubbing his hands—"well, go on—what happened? Do you hear, Harry? What happened? Of course they're at the distillation again. Don't you hear me, I say? What was the upshot?"

"Why, the upshot was," replied the other, "that nothing of sufficient importance has been discovered yet; but we have reason to suppose that they're engaged in the process of forgery or coining, as they were in that of illicit distillation under the patronage of the virtuous Hycy Burke, or Hycy the accomplished, as he calls himself."

"Tut, tut!" exclaimed Clinton, disappointed—"so after all, there has been nothing done?"

"Oh, yes, there has been something done; for instance, all these matters have been laid before Mr. Vanston, and he has had two or three interviews with Chevydale, in whose estimation he has exonerated young M'Mahon from the charge of bribery and ingratitude. Fethertonge holds such a position now with his employer that an infant's breath would almost blow him out of his good opinion."

"I'll tell you what, Harry, I think you have it in your power among you to punish these rogues; and I think, too, it's a pity that Fethertonge should escape. A breath will dislodge him, you say; but for fear it should not, we will give him a breeze."

"I am to meet Vanston at Chevydale's by-and-by, uncle. There's to be an investigation there; and by the way, allow me to bring Hycy's anonymous letter with me—it may serve an honest man and help to punish a rogue. What if you would come down with me, and give him the breeze?"

"Well," replied the uncle, "for the novelty of the thing I don't care if I do. I like, after all, to see a rogue punished, especially when he is not prepared for it."

After a little delay they repaired to Chevydale's house, armed with Hycy's anonymous letter to Clinton, as well as with the document which the old squire, as he was called, had left for Thomas M'Mahon and his son. They found the two gentlemen on much better terms than one would have expected; but, in reality, the state of the country was such as forced them to open their eyes not merely to the folly of harboring mere political resentments or senseless party prejudices against each other, but to the absolute necessity that existed for looking closely into the state of their property, and the deplorable condition to which, if they did not take judicious and decisive steps, it must eventually be reduced. They now began to discover a fact which they ought, long since, to have known—viz.:—that the condition of the people and that of their property was one and the same—perfectly identical in all things; and that a poor tenantry never yet existed upon a thriving or independent estate, or one that was beneficial to the landlord.

Vanston had been with his late opponent for some time before the arrival of Clinton and his nephew; and, as their conversation may not, perhaps, be without some interest to our readers, we shall detail a portion of it.

"So," says Vanston, "you are beginning to feel that there is something wrong on your property, and that your agent is not doing you justice?"

"I have reason to suspect," replied Chevydale, "that he is neither more nor less than feathering his own nest at the expense of myself and my tenantry. I cannot understand why he is so anxious to get the M'Mahons off the estate; a family unquestionably of great honesty, truth, and integrity, and who, I believe, have been on the property before it came into our possession at all. I feel—excuse me, Vanston, for the admission, but upon my honor it is truth—I feel, I say, that, in the matter of the election—that is, so far as M'Mahon was concerned, he—my agent—made a cat's paw of me. He prevented me from supporting young M'Mahon's memorial; he—he—prejudiced me against the family in several ways, and now, that I am acquainted with the circumstances of strong and just indignation against me under which M'Mahon voted, I can't at all blame him. I would have done the same thing myself."

"There is d——d villany somewhere at work," replied Vanston. "They talk of a fifty-pound note that I am said to have sent to him by post. Now, I pledge my honor as an honest man and a gentleman, that I have sifted and examined all my agents, and am satisfied that he never received a penny from me. Young Burke did certainly promise to secure me his vote; but I have discovered Burke to be a most unprincipled profligate, corrupt and dishonest. For, you may think it strange that, although he engaged to procure me M'Mahon's vote, M'Mahon himself, whom I believe, assured me that he never even asked him for it, until after he had overheard, in the head inn, a conversation concerning himself that filled him with bitter resentment against you and your agent."

"I remember it," replied Chevydale, "and; yet my agents told me that Burke did everything in his power to prevent M'Mahon from voting for you."

"That," replied the other, "was to preserve his own character from the charge of inconsistency; for, I again assure you that he had promised us M'Mahon's vote, and that he urged him privately to vote against you. But d—n the scoundrel, he is not worth the conversation we had about him. Father Magowan, in consequence of whose note to me I wrote to ask you here, states in the communication I had from him, that the parties will be here about twelve o'clock—Burke himself, he thinks, and M'Mahon along with the rest. The priest wishes to have these Hogans driven out of the parish—a wish in which I most cordially join him. I hope we shall soon rid the country of him and his villanous associates. Talking of the country, what is to be done?"

"Simply," replied Chevydale, "that we, the landed proprietors of Ireland, should awake out of our slumbers, and forgetting those vile causes of division and subdivision that have hitherto not only disunited us, but set us together by the ears, we should take counsel among ourselves, and after due and serious deliberation, come to the determination that it is our duty to prevent Irish interests from being made subservient to English interests, and from being legislated for upon English principles."

"I hope, Chevydale, you are not about to become a Repealer."

"No, sir; I am, and ever have been sickened by that great imposture. Another half century would scarcely make us fit for home legislation. When we look at the conduct of our Irish members in the British Parliament—I allude now, with few exceptions, to the Repeal members—what hope can we entertain of honesty and love of country from such men? When we look, too, at many of our Corporations and strike an average of their honesty and intellect, have we not a right to thank God that the interests of our country are not confided to the management of such an arrogant, corrupt, and vulgar crew as in general compose them. The truth is, Vanston, we must become national in our own defense, and whilst we repudiate, with a firm conviction of the folly on the one hand, and the dishonesty on the other, of those who talk about Repeal, we shall find it our best policy to forget the interests of any particular class, and suffer ourselves to melt down into one great principle of national love and good-will toward each other. Let us only become unanimous, and England will respect us as she did when we were unanimous upon other occasions."

"I feel, and am perfectly sensible of the truth of what you say," replied Vanston, "and I am certain that, in mere self-defence, we must identify ourselves with the people whose interests most unquestionably are ours."

"As to myself," continued Chevydale, "I fear I have much to repair in my conduct as an Irish landlord. I have been too confiding and easy—in fact, I have not thought for myself; but been merely good or evil, according to the caprice of the man who managed me, and whom, up until now, I did not suspect."

"The man, my good friend, is probably not worse in general than others," replied Vanston; "but the truth is, that there has been such a laxity of management in Irish property—such indifference and neglect upon our part, and such gross ignorance of our duties, that agents were, and in most cases are, at liberty to act as they please in our names, and under show of our authority; you can scarcely suppose this man, consequently, much worse than others who are placed in similar circumstances."

The dialogue was here interrupted by the entrance of old Clinton and his nephew; but, as our readers are already in possession of the proofs they brought against Hycy Burke and Fethertonge, it is not necessary that we should detail there conversation at full length.

"I must confess," said Clinton, "that I would have some reason to feel ashamed of my part in the transactions with respect to Ahadarra, were it not, in the first place, that I have never been much afflicted with the commodity; and, in the next, that these transactions are too common to excite any feeling one way or the other."

"But you must have known, Clinton," said Chevydale, "that it was a most iniquitous thing in you to enter into a corrupt bargain with a dishonest agent for the property which you knew to belong to another man."

"What other man, Mr. Chevydale? Had not M'Mahon's lease expired?"

"But had you not in your own possession my father's written promise—written, too, on his death-bed—to these honest men, that they should have their leases renewed?"

"Yes, but that was your agent's affair, and his dishonesty, too, not mine."

"As much yours as his; and, by the way, I don't see upon what principle you, who are equally involved with him in the profligacy of the transaction, should come to bear testimony against him now. They say there is honor among thieves, but I see very little of it here."

"Faith, to tell you the truth," replied Clinton, "as I said to Harry here, because *I like to see a rogue punished, especially when he is not prepared for it.*"

"Well," said Chevydale, with a very solemn ironical smile, "I am myself very much of your way of thinking; and, as a proof of it, I beg to say that, as your appointment to the office of Supervisor has not yet been made out, I shall write to my brother, the Commissioner, to take care that it never shall. To procure the promotion of a man who can deliberately avow his participation in such shameless profligacy would be to identify myself with it. You have been doubly treacherous, Mr. Clinton; first to me, whom you know to be your friend, and, in the next place, to the unfortunate partner in your villany, and at my expense; for d——d if I can call it less. What noise is that?"

Clinton the elder here withdrew, and had scarcely disappeared when two voices were heard in the hall, in a kind of clamorous remonstrance with each other, which voices were those of Father Magowan and our friend O'Finigan, as we must now call him, inasmuch as he is, although early in the day, expanded with that hereditary sense of dignity which will not allow the great O to be suppressed.

"Behave, and keep quiet, now," said his Reverence, "you unfortunate pedagogue you; I tell you that you are inebriated."

"Pardon me, your Reverence," replied O'Finigan; "*non ebrius sed vino gravatus,* devil a thing more."

"Get out, you profligate," replied the priest, "don't you know that either, at this time o' day, is too bad?"

"*Nego, dominie—nego, Dominie revendre*—denial is my principle, I say. Do you assert that there's no difference between *ebrius* and *gravatus vino*?"

"In your case, you reprobate, I do. Where would you get the vino? However," he proceeded, "as you are seldom sober, and as I know it is possible you may have something of importance to say on a particular subject, I suppose you may as well say it now as any other time, and it's likely we may get more truth out of you."

"Ay," said the schoolmaster, "upon the principle that *in vino veritas*; but you know that *gravatus vino* and *ebrius* are two different things—*gravatus vino*, the juice o' the grape—och, och, as every one knows, could and stupid; but *ebrius* from blessed poteen, that warms and gives ecstatic nutrition to the heart."

The altercation proceeded for a little, but, after a short remonstrance and bustle, the priest, followed by O'Finigan, entered the room.

"Gentlemen," said the priest, "I trust you will excuse me for the society in which I happen to appear before you; but the truth is that this Finigan—"

"Pardon me, your Reverence, O'Finigan if you plaise; we have been shorn of—"

"Well, then, since he will have it so, this O'Finigan is really inebriated, and I cannot exactly say why, in this state, his presence can be of any advantage to us."

"He says," replied the master, "that I am *ebrius*, whereas I replied that I was only *vino gravatus*, by which I only meant *quasi vino gravatus*; but the truth is, gentlemen, that I'm never properly sober until I'm half seas over—for it is then that I have all my wits properly about me."

"In fact, gentleman," proceeded the priest, "in consequence of certain disclosures that have reached me with reference to these Hogans, I deemed it my duty to bring Nanny Peety before Mr. Chevydale here. She is accompanied by Kate Hogan, the wife of one

The Emigrants of Ahadarra

of these ruffians, who refuses to be separated from her—and insists, consequently, on coming along with her. I don't exactly know what her motive may be in this; but I am certain she has a motive. It is a gratification to me, however, to find, gentlemen, that you both happen to be present upon this occasion. I sent word to Hycy Burke and to Bryan M'Mahon; for I thought it only fair that Hycy should be present, in order to clear himself in case any charge may be brought against him. I expect M'Mahon, too."

"Let us remove, then, to my office," said, Chevydale—"it is now a few minutes past twelve, and I dare say they will soon be here."

They accordingly did so; and, as he had said, the parties almost immediately made their appearance.

"Now, gentlemen," said Father Magowan, "I am of opinion that the best way is for this girl to state what she knows concerning these Hogans; but I think I can now persave the raison why Kate Hogan has made it a point to come with her. It is quite evident from her manner that she wishes to intimidate this girl, and to prevent her from stating fully and truly what she knows."

"No," replied Kate, "it is no such thing—she must either state the whole truth or nothing; that's what I want, an' what she must do—put the saddle on the right horse, Nanny—since you will spake."

"It is a good proverbial illustration," observed Finigan, "but I will improve it—put the saddle of infamy, I say, upon the right horse, Nanny. You see, gintlemen," he added, turning to the magistrates, "my improvement elevates the metaphor—proceed, girsha."

"Gentlemen," said Hycy, "I received a note from Father Magowan informing me that it was probable certain charges might be brought against me—or at least some complaints made," he added, softening the expression—"and I should be glad to know what they are all about, before this girl commences formally to state them; I say so in order that I may not be taken by surprise."

"You know," replied the priest, "that you cannot be taken by surprise; because I myself told you the substance of the strong suspicions that are against you."

Bryan M'Mahon now entered, and was cordially greeted by Vanston—and we may add rather kindly, in manner at least, by Chevydale.

"By the way," asked the former of these gentlemen, "does this investigation bear in any way upon your interests, M'Mahon?"

"Not, sir, so far as I am aware of—I come here because Father Magowan wished me to come. I have no interests connected with this country now," he added in a tone of deep melancholy, "there's an end to that for ever."

"Now, my good girl," said Chevydale, "you will state all you know connected with these Hogans fully and truly—that is, neither more nor less than the truth."

"All the truth, Nanny," said Kate Hogan, in a voice of strongly condensed power; "Hycy Burke," she proceeded, "you ruined Bryan M'Mahon here—and, by ruinin' him, you broke Miss Kathleen Cavanagh's heart—she's gone—no docthor could save her now; and for this you'll soon know what Kate Hogan can do. Go on, Nanny."

"Well, gintlemon," Nanny began, "in the first place it was Mr. Hycy here that got the Still up in Ahadarra, in ordher to beggar Bryan M'Mahon by the fine."

Hycy laughed. "Excellent!" said he; "Why, really, Mr. Chevydale, I did not imagine that you could suffer such a farce as this is likely to turn out to be enacted exactly in your office."

"Enacted! well, that's, appropriate at any rate," said the schoolmaster; "but in the mane time, Mr. Hycy, take care that the farce won't become a tragedy on your hands, and you yourself the hero of it. Proceed, girsha."

"How do you know," asked Chevydale, "that this charge is true?"

"If I don't know it," she replied, "my aunt here does,—and I think so does Mr. Harry Clinton an' others."

"Pray, my woman, what do you know about this matter?" asked Chevydale, addressing Kate.

"Why that it was Mr. Hycy Burke that gave the Hogans the money to make the Still, set it up—and to Teddy Phats to buy barley; and although he didn't tell them it was to ruin Bryan M'Mahon he did it, sure they all knew it was—'spishly when he made them change from Glendearg above, where they were far safer, down to Ahadarra."

"I assure you, gentlemen," said Hycy, "that the respectability of the witnesses you have fished up is highly creditable to your judgments and sense of justice;—a common vagabond and notorious thief on the one hand, and a beggarman's brat on the other. However, proceed—I perceive that I shall be obliged to sink under the force of such testimony—ha! ha! ha!"

At this moment old Jemmy Burke, having accidentally heard that morning that such an investigation was to take place, and likely to bear upon the conduct of his eldest son, resolved to be present at it, and he accordingly presented himself as Hycy had concluded his observations.

The high integrity of his character was at once recognized—he was addressed in terms exceedingly respectful, if not deferential, by the two magistrates—Chevydale having at once ordered the servant in attendance to hand him a chair. He thanked him, however, but declined it gratefully, and stood like the rest.

In the meantime the investigation proceeded. "Mr. Burke," said Chevydale, addressing himself to the old man, whose features, by the way, were full of sorrow and distress—"it may be as well to state to you that we are not sitting now formally in our magisterial capacity, to investigate any charges that may be brought against your son, but simply making some preliminary inquiries with respect to other charges, which we have been given to understand are about to be brought against the notorious Hogans."

"Don't lay the blame upon the Hogans," replied Kate, fiercely—"the Hogans, bad as people say they are, only acted under Hycy Burke. It was Hycy Burke."

"But," said Chevydale, probably out of compassion for the old man, "you must know we are not now investigating Mr. Burke's conduct."

"Proceed, gintlemen," said his father, firmly but sorrowfully; "I have heard it said too often that he was at the bottom of the plot that ruined Bryan M'Mahon, or that wint near to ruin him; I wish to have that well sifted, gintlemen, and to know the truth."

"I can swear," continued Kate, "that it was him got up the whole plan, and gave them the money for it. I seen him in our house—or, to come nearer the truth, in Gerald Cavanagh's kiln, where we live—givin' them the money."

"As you are upon that subject, gentlemen," observed Harry Clinton, "I think it due to the character of Bryan M'Mahon to state that I am in a capacity to prove that Hycy Burke was unquestionably at the bottom—or, in point of fact, the originator—of his calamities with reference to the act of illicit distillation, and the fine which he would have been called on to pay, were it not that the Commissioners of Excise remitted it."

"Thank you, Mr. Clinton," replied Hycy; "I find I am not mistaken in you—I think you are worthy of your accomplices"—and he pointed to Kate and Nanny as he spoke—"proceed."

"We are passing," observed Vanston, "from one to another rather irregularly, I fear; don't you think we had better hear this girl fully in the first place; but, my good girl," he added, "you are to understand that we are not here to investigate any charges against Mr. Hycy Burke, but against the Hogans. You will please then to confine your charges to them."

"But," replied Nanny, "that's what I can't do, plase your honor, widout bringin' in Hycy Burke too, bekaise himself an' the Hogans was joined in everything."

"I think, gintlemen," said the priest, "the best plan is to let her tell her story in her own way."

"Perhaps so," said Chevydale; "proceed, young woman, and state fully and truly whatever you have got to say."

"Well, then," she proceeded, "there's one thing I know—I know who robbed Mr. Burke here;" and she pointed to the old man, who started.

The magistrates also looked surprised. "How," said Vanston, turning his eyes keenly upon her, "you know of the robbery; and pray, how long have you known it?"

"Ever since the night it was committed, plaise your honor."

"What a probable story!" exclaimed Hycy; "and you kept it to yourself, like an honest girl as you are, until now!"

"Why, Mr. Burke," said Vanston, quickly and rather sharply, "surely you can have no motive in impugning her evidence upon that subject?"

Hycy bit his lip, for he instantly felt that he had overshot himself by almost anticipating the charge, as if it were about to be made against himself;—"What I think improbable in it," said Hycy, "is that she should, if in possession of the facts, keep them concealed so long."

"Oh, never fear, Mr. Hycy, I'll soon make that plain enough," she replied.

"But in the mean time," said Chevydale, "will you state the names of those who did commit the robbery?"

"I will," she replied.

"The whole truth, Nanny," exclaimed Kate.

"It was Bat Hogan, then, that robbed Mr. Burke," she replied; "and—and—"

"Out wid it," said Kate.

"And who besides, my good girl?" inquired Vanston.

The young woman looked round with compassion upon Jemmy Burke, and the tears started to her eyes. "I pity him!" she exclaimed, "I pity him—that good old man;" and, as she uttered the words, she wept aloud.

"This, I fear, is getting rather a serious affair," said Vanston, in a low voice to Chevydale—"I see how the tide is likely to turn."

Chevydale merely nodded, as if he also comprehended it. "You were about to add some other name?" said he; "in the mean time compose yourself and proceed."

The Emigrants of Ahadarra

Hycy Burke's face at this moment had become white as a sheet; in fact, to any one of common penetration, guilt and a dread of the coming disclosure were legible in every lineament of it.

"Who was the other person you were about to mention?" asked Vanston.

"His own son, sir, Mr. Hycy Burke, there."

"Ha!" exclaimed Chevydale; "Mr. Hycy Burke, do you say? Mr. Burke," he added, addressing that gentleman, "how is this? Here is a grave and serious charge against you. What have you to say to it?"

"That it would be both grave and serious," replied Hycy, "if it possessed but one simple element, without which all evidence is valueless—I mean truth. All I can say is, that she might just as well name either of yourselves, gentlemen, as me."

"How do you know that Hogan committed the robbery?" asked Hycy.

"Simply bekaise I seen him. He broke open the big chest above stairs."

"How did you see him?" asked Vanston.

"Through a hole in the partition," she replied, "where a knot of the deal boards had come out. I slep', plaise your honor, in a little closet off o' the room the money was in."

"Is it true that she slept there, Mr. Burke?" asked Vanston of the old man.

"It is thrue, sir, God help me; that at all events is thrue."

"Well, proceed," said Chevydale.

"I then throw my gown about my shoulders; but in risin' from my bed it creaked a little, an' Bat Hogan, who had jest let down the lid of the chest aisily when he hard the noise, blew out the bit of candle that he had in his hand, and picked his way down stairs as aisily as he could. I folloyed him on my tippy-toes, an' when he came opposite the door of the room where the masther and misthress sleep, the door opened, an' the mistress wid a candle in her hand met him full—but in the teeth. I was above upon the stairs at the time, but from the way an' the place she stood in, the light didn't rache me, so that I could see them widout bein' seen myself. Well, when the mistress met him she was goin' to bawl out wid terror, an' would, too, only that Masther Hycy flew to her, put his hand on her mouth, an' whispered something in her ear. He then went over to Bat, and got a large shafe of bank-notes from him, an' motioned him to be off wid himself, an' that he'd see him to-morrow. Bat went down in the dark, an' Hycy an' his mother had some conversation in a low voice on the lobby. She seemed angry, an' he was speakin' soft an' strivin' to put her into good humor again. I then dipt back to bed, but the never a wink could I get till mornin'; an' when I went down, the first thing I saw was Bat Hogan's shoes. It was hardly light at the time; but at any rate I hid them where they couldn't be got, an' it was well I did, for the first thing I saw was Bat himself peering about the street and yard, like a man that was looking for something that he had lost."

"But how did you know that the shoes were Hogan's?" asked Vanston.

"Why, your honor, any one that ever seen the man might know that. One of his heels is a trifle shorter than the other, which makes him halt a little, an' he has a bunion as big as an egg on the other foot."

"Ay, Nanny," said Kate, "that's the truth; but I can tell you more, gentlemen. On the evenin' before, when Mr. Hycy came home, he made up the plan to rob his father wid Phil Hogan; but Phil got drunk that night an' Bat had to go in his place. Mr. Hycy promised to see the Hogans that mornin' at his father's, about ten o'clock; but when they went he had gone off to Ballymacan; an' as they expected him every minute, they stayed about the place in spite o' the family, an' mended everything they could lay their hands on. Bat an' Mr. Hycy met that night in Teddy Phat's still-house, in Glendearg, an' went home together across the mountains afterward."

"Well, Mr. Burke, what have you to say to this?" asked Chevydale.

"Why," replied Hycy, "that it's a very respectable conspiracy as it stands, supported by the thief and vagabond, and the beggar's brat."

"Was there any investigation at the time of its occurrence?" asked Vanston.

"There was, your honor," replied Nanny; "it was proved, clearly enough that Phil and Ned Hogan were both dead drunk that night an' couldn't commit a robbery; an' Masther Hycy himself said that he knew how Bat spent the night, an' that of course he couldn't do it; an' you know, your honors, there was no gettin' over that. I have, or rather my father has, Bat Hogan's shoes still."

"This, I repeat, seems a very serious charge, Mr. Burke," said Chevydale again.

"Which, as I said before, contains not one particle of truth," replied Hycy. "If I had resolved to break open my father's chest to get cash out of it, it is not likely that I would call in the aid of such a man as Bat Hogan. As a proof that I had nothing to do with the robbery in question, I can satisfy you that my mother, not many days after the occurrence of it, was obliged to get her car and drive some three or four miles' distance to borrow a hundred pounds for me from a friend of hers, upon her own responsibility, which, had I committed the outrage in question, I would not have required at all."

Old Burke's face would, at this period of the proceedings, have extorted compassion from any heart. Sorrow, distress, agony of spirit, and shame, were all so legible in his pale features—that those who were present kept their eyes averted, from respect to the man, and from sympathy with his sufferings.

At length he himself came forward, and, after wiping away a few bitter tears from his cheeks, he said—"Gentlemen, I care little about the money I lost, nor about who took it—let it go—as for me, I won't miss it; but there is one thing that cuts me to the heart—I'm spakin' about the misfortune that was brought, or near bein' brought, upon this honest an' generous-hearted young man, Bryan M'Mahon, through manes of a black plot that was got up against him—I'm spakin' of the Still that was found on his farm of Ahadarra. That, if my son had act or part in it, is a thousand times worse than the other; as for the takin' of the money, I don't care about it, as I said—nor I won't prosecute any one for it; but I must have my mind satisfied about the other affair."

It is not our intention to dwell at any length upon the clear proofs of his treachery and deceit, which were established against him by

Harry Clinton, who produced the anonymous letter to his uncle—brought home to him as it was by his own evidence and that of Nanny Peety.

"There is, however," said Vanston, "another circumstance affecting the reputation and honesty of Mr. Bryan M'Mahon, which in your presence, Mr. M'Gowan, I am anxious to set at rest. I have already contradicted it with indignation wherever I have heard it, and I am the more anxious to do so, now, whilst M'Mahon and Burke are present, and because I have been given to understand that you denounced him—M'Mahon—with such hostility from the altar, as almost occasioned him to be put to death in the house of God."

"You are undher a mistake there, Major Vanston, with great respect," replied the priest. "It wasn't I but my senior curate, Father M'Pepper; and he has already been reprimanded by his Bishop."

"Well," replied the other, "I am glad to hear it. However, I, now solemnly declare, as an honest man and an Irish, gentleman, that neither I, nor any one for me, with my knowledge, ever gave or sent any money to Bryan M'Mahon; but perhaps we may ascertain who did. M'Mahon, have you got the letter about you?"

"I have, sir," replied Bryan, "and the bank-note, too."

"You will find the frank and address both in your own handwriting," said Hycy. "It was I brought him the letter from the post-office."

"Show me the letter, if you plaise," said Nanny, who, after looking first at it and then at Hycy, added, "and it was I gave it this little tear near the corner, and dhrew three scrapes of a pin across the paper, an' there they are yet; an' now I can take my oath that it was Mr. Hycy that sent that letther to Bryan M'Mahon—an' your Reverence is the very man I showed it to, and that tould me who it was goin' to, in the street of Ballymacan."'

On a close inspection of the letter it was clearly obvious that, although there appeared at a cursory glance a strong resemblance between the frank and the address, yet the difference was too plain to be mistaken.

"If there is further evidence necessary," said Vanston, looking at Hycy significantly, "my agent can produce it—and he is now in the house."

"I think you would not venture on that," replied Hycy.

"Don't be too sure of that," said the other, determinedly.

"Sir," replied Father Magowan, "there is nothing further on that point necessary—the proof is plain and clear; and now, Bryan M'Mahon, give me your hand, for it is that of an honest man—I am proud to see that you stand pure and unsullied again; and it shall be my duty to see that justice shall be rendered! you, and ample compensation made for all that you have suffered."

"Thank you, sir," replied Bryan, with an air of deep dejection, "but I am sorry to say it is now too late—I am done with the country, and with those that misrepresented me, for ever."

Chevydale looked at him with deep attention for a moment, then whispered something to Vanston, who smiled, and nodded his head approvingly.

Jemmy Burke now prepared to go. "Good mornin', gintlemen," he said, "I am glad to see the honest name cleared and set right, as it ought to be; but as for myself, I lave you wid a heavy—wid a breakin' heart."

As he disappeared at the door, Hycy rushed after him, exclaiming, "Father, listen to me—don't go yet till you hear my defence. I will go and fetch him back," he exclaimed—"he must hear what I have to say for myself."

He overtook his father at the bottom of the hall steps. "Give me a hundred pounds," said he, "and you will never see my face again."

"There is two hundre'," said his father; "I expected this. Your mother confessed all to me this mornin', bekaise she knew it would come out here, I suppose. Go now, for undher my roof you'll never come again. If you can—reform your life—an' live at all events, as if there was a God above you. Before you go answer me;—what made you bring in Bat Hogan to rob me?"

"Simply," replied his son, "because I wished to make him and them feel that I had them in my power—and now you have it."

Hycy received the money, set spurs to his horse, and was out of sight in a moment—"Ah!" exclaimed the old man, with bitterness of soul, "what mightn't he be if his weak and foolish mother hadn't taken it into her head to make a gentleman of him! But now she reaps as she sowed. She's punished—an' that's enough."—And thus does Hycy the accomplished make his exit from our humble stage.

"Gintlemen," said Finigan, "now that the accomplished Mr. Hycy is disposed of, I beg to state, that it will be productive of much public good to the country to expatriate these three virtuous worthies, *qui nomine gaudent* Hogan—and the more so as it can be done on clear legal grounds. They are a principal means of driving this respectable young man, Bryan M'Mahon, and his father's family, out of the land of their birth; and there will be something extremely appropriate—and indicative besides of condign and retributive punishment—in sending them on their travels at his Majesty's expense. I am here, in connection with others, to furnish you with the necessary proof against them; and I am of opinion that the sooner they are sent upon a voyage of discovery it will be so much the better for the rejoicing neighborhood they will leave behind them."

The hint was immediately taken with respect to them and Vincent, all of whom had been engaged in coming under Hycy's auspices—they were apprehended and imprisoned, the chief evidence against them being Teddy Phats, Peety Dhu, and Finigan, who for once became a stag, as he called it. They were indicted for a capital felony; but the prosecution having been postponed for want of sufficient evidence, they were kept in durance until next assizes;—having found it impossible to procure bail. In the meantime new charges of uttering base coin came thick and strong against them; and as the Crown lawyers found that they could not succeed on the capital indictment—nor indeed did they wish to do so—they tried them on the lighter one, and succeeded in getting sentence of transportation passed against every one of them, with the exception of Kate Hogan alone.—So that, as Finigan afterwards said, "instead of Bryan M'Mahon, it was they themselves that became 'the Emigrants of Ahadarra,' at the king's expense—and Mr. Hycy at his own."

CHAPTER XXVII.—Conclusion.

How Kathleen Cavanagh spent the time that elapsed between the period at which she last appeared to our readers and the present may be easily gathered from what we are about to write. We have said already that her father, upon the strength of some expressions uttered in a spirit of distraction and agony, assured Jemmy Burke that she had consented to marry his son Edward, after a given period. Honest Jemmy, however, never for a moment suspected the nature of the basis upon which his worthy neighbor had erected the superstructure of his narrative; but at the same time he felt sadly puzzled by the melancholy and declining appearance of her whom he looked upon as his future daughter-in-law. The truth was that scarcely any of her acquaintances could recognize her as the same majestic, tall, and beautiful girl whom they had known before this heavy disappointment had come on her. Her exquisite figure had lost most of its roundness, her eye no longer flashed—with its dark mellow lustre, and her cheek—her damask cheek—distress and despair had fed upon it, until little remained there but the hue of death itself. Her health in fact was evidently beginning to go. Her appetite had abandoned her; she slept little, and that little was restless and unrefreshing. All her family, with the exception of her father and mother, who sustained themselves with the silly ambition of their daughter being able to keep her jaunting-car—for her father had made that point a *sine qua non*—all, we say, with the above exceptions, became seriously alarmed at the state of her mind and health.

"Kathleen, dear," said her affectionate sister, "I think you have carried your feelings against Bryan far enough."

"My feelings against Bryan!" she exclamed.

"Yes," proceeded her sister, "I think you ought to forgive him."

"Ah, Hanna darling, how little you know of your sister's heart. I have long since forgiven him, Hanna."

"Then what's to prevent you from making up with him?"

"I have long since forgiven him, Hanna; but, my dear sister, I never can nor will think for a moment of marrying any man that has failed, when brought to the trial, in honest and steadfast principal—the man that would call me wife should be upright, pure, and free from every stain of corruption—he must have no disgrace or dishonor upon his name, and he must feel the love of his religion and his country as the great ruling principles of his life. I have long since forgiven Bryan, but it is because he is not what I hoped he was, and what I wished him to be, that I am as you see me."

"Then you do intend to marry?" asked Hanna, with a smile.

"Why do you ask that, Hanna?"

"Why, because you've given me sich a fine description of the kind o' man your husband is to be."

"Hanna," she replied, solemnly, "look at my cheek, look at my eye, look at my whole figure, and then ask me that question again if you can. Don't you see, darling, that death is upon me? I feel it."

Her loving and beloved sister threw her arms around her neck, and burst into an irrepressible fit of bitter grief.

"Oh, you are changed, most woefully, Kathleen, darlin'," she exclaimed, kissing her tenderly; "but if you could only bear up now, time would set everything right, and bring you about right, as it will still, I hope."

Her sister mused for some time, and then added—"I think I could bear up yet if he was to stay in the country; but when I recollect that he's going to another land—forever—I feel that my heart is broken: as it is, his disgrace and that thought are both killin' me. To morrow the auction comes on, and then he goes—after that I will never see him. I'm afraid, Hanna, that I'll have to go to bed, I feel that I'm hardly able to sit up."

Hanna once more pressed her to her heart and wept.

"Don't cry, Hanna dear—don't cry for me; the bitterest part of my fate will be partin' from you."

Hanna here pressed her again and wept aloud, whilst her spotless and great-minded sister consoled her as well as she could. "Oh, what would become of me!" exclaimed Hanna, sobbing; "if anything was to happen you, or take you away from me, it would break my heart, too, and I'd die."

"Hanna," said her sister, not encouraging her to proceed any further on that distressing subject; "on to-morrow, the time I allowed for Bryan to clear himself, if he could, will be up, and I have only to beg that you'll do all you can to prevent my father and mother from distressing me about Edward Burke; I will never marry him, but I expect to see him your husband yet, and I think he's worthy of you — that's saying a great deal, I know. You love him, Hanna — I know it, and he loves you, Hanna, for he told me so the last day but one he was here; — you remember they all went out, and left us together, and then he told me all."

Hanna's face and neck became crimson, and she was about to reply, when a rather loud but good-humored voice was heard in the kitchen, for this dialogue took place in the parlor — exclaiming, "God save all here! How do you do, Mrs. Cavanagh? How is Gerald and the youngsters?"

"Indeed all middlin' well, thank your reverence, barrin' our eldest girl that's a little low spirited for some time past."

"Ay, ay, I know the cause of that — it's no secret — where is she now? If she's in the house let me see her."

The two sisters having composed their dress a little and their features, immediately made their appearance.

"God be good to us!" he exclaimed, "here's a change! Why, may I never sin, if I'd know her no more than the mother that bore her. Lord guard us! look at this! Do you give her nothing, Mrs. Cavanagh?"

"Nothing on airth," she replied; "her complaint's upon the spirits, an' we didn't think that physic stuff would be of any use to her."

"Well, perhaps I will find a cure for her. Listen to me, darling. Your sweetheart's name and fame are cleared, and Bryan M'Mahon is what he ever was — an honest an' upright young man."

Kathleen started, looked around her, as if with amazement, and without seeming to know exactly what she did, went towards the door, and was about to walk out, when Hanna, detaining her, asked with alarm—"Kathleen, what ails you, dear? Where are you going?"

"Going," she replied; "I was going to—where?—why?—what—what has happened?"

"The news came upon her too much by surprise," said Hanna, looking towards the priest.

"Kathleen, darlin'," exclaimed her mother, "try and compose yourself. Lord guard us, what can ail her?"

"Let her come with me into the parlor, mother, an' do you an' Father Magowan stay where you are."

They accordingly went in, and after about the space of ten minutes she recovered herself so far as to make Hanna repeat the intelligence which the simple-hearted priest had, with so little preparation, communicated. Having listened to it earnestly, she laid her head upon Hanna's bosom and indulged in a long fit of quiet and joyful grief. When she had recovered a little, Father Magowan entered at more length into the circumstances connected with the changes that had affected her lover's character so deeply, after which he wound up by giving expression to the following determination—a determination, by the way, which we earnestly recommend to all politicians of his profession.

"As for my part," said he, "it has opened my eyes to one thing that I won't forget:—a single word of politics I shall never suffer to be preached from the altar while I live; neither shall I allow denouncements for political offences. The altar, as the bishop told me—and a hard rap he gave Mr. M'Pepper across the knuckles for Bryan's affair—'the altar,' said he, 'isn't the place for politics, but for religion; an' I hope I may never hear of its being desecrated with politics again,' said his lordship, an' neither I will, I assure you."

The intelligence of the unexpected change that had taken place in favor of the M'Mahon's, did not reach them on that day, which was the same, as we have stated, on which their grandfather departed this life. The relief felt by Thomas M'Mahon and his family at this old man's death, took nothing from the sorrow which weighed them down so heavily in consequence of their separation from the abode of their forefathers and the place of their birth. They knew, or at least they took it for granted that their grandfather would never have borne the long voyage across the Atlantic, a circumstance which distressed them very much. His death, however, exhibiting, as it did, the undying attachment to home which nothing else could extinguish, only kindled the same affection more strongly and tenderly in their hearts. The account of it had gone abroad through the neighborhood, and with it the intelligence that the auction would be postponed until that day week. And now that he was gone, all their hearts turned with sorrow and sympathy to the deep and almost agonizing' struggles which their coming departure caused their father to contend with. Bryan whose calm but manly firmness sustained them all, absolutely feared that his courage would fail him, or that his very health would break down. He also felt for his heroic little sister, Dora, who, although too resolute to complain or urge her own sufferings, did not endure the less on that account.

"My dear Dora," said he, after their grandfather had been laid out, "I know what you are suffering, but what can I do? This split between the Cavanaghs and us has put it out of my power to serve you as I had intended. It was my wish to see you and James Cavanagh married; but God knows I pity you from my heart; for, my dear Dora, there's no use in denyin' it, I understand too well what you feel."

"Don't fret for me, Bryan," she replied; "I'm willin' to bear my share of the affliction that has come upon the family, rather than do anything mane or unworthy. I know it goes hard with me to give up James and lave him for ever; but then I see that it must be done, and that I must submit to it. May God strengthen and enable me! and that's my earnest prayer. I also often prayed that you an' Kathleen might be reconciled; but I wasn't heard, it seems. I sometimes think that you ought to go to her; but then on second thoughts I can hardly advise you to do so."

"No, Dora, I never will, dear; she ought to have heard me as you said face to face; instead o' that she condemned me without a hearin'. An' yet, Dora," he added, "little she knows—little she drames, what I'm sufferin on her account, and how I love her—more now than ever, I think; she's so changed, they say, that you could scarcely know her." As he spoke, a single tear fell upon Dora's hand which he held in his.

"Come. Bryan," she said, assuming a cheerfulness which she did not feel, "don't have it to say that little Dora, who ought and does look up to you for support, must begin to support you herself; tomorrow's the last day—who knows but she may relent yet?" Bryan smiled faintly, then patted her head, and said, "darling little Dora, the wealth of nations couldn't purchase you."

"Not to do any thing mane or wrong, at any rate," she replied; after which she went in to attend to the affairs of the family, for this conversation took place in the garden.

As evening approached, a deep gloom, the consequence of strong inward suffering, overspread the features and bearing of Thomas M'Mahon. For some time past, he had almost given himself over to the influence of what he experienced—a fact that was observable in many ways, all more or less tending to revive the affection which he felt for his departed wife. For instance, ever since their minds had been made up to emigrate, he had watched, and tended, and fed Bracky, her favorite cow, with his own hands; nor would he suffer any one else in the family to go near her, with the exception of Dora, by whom she had been milked ever since her mother's death, and to whom the poor animal had now transferred her affection. He also cleaned and oiled her spinning-wheel, examined her clothes, and kept himself perpetually engaged in looking at every object that was calculated to bring her once more before his imagination.

About a couple of hours before sunset, without saying where he was going, he sauntered down to the graveyard of Gamdhu where she lay, and having first uncovered his head and offered up a prayer for the repose of her soul, he wept bitterly.

"Bridget," said he, in that strong figurative language so frequently used by the Irish, when under the influence of deep, emotion; "Bridget, wife of my heart, you are removed from the thrials and throubles of this world—from the thrials and throubles that have come upon us. I'm come, now—your own husband—him that loved you beyant everything on this earth, to tell you why the last wish o' my heart, which was to sleep where I ought to sleep, by your side, can't be granted to me, and to explain to you why it is, in case you'd miss me from my place beside you. This unfortunate counthry, Bridget, has changed, an' is changin' fast for the worse. The landlord hasn't proved himself to be towards us what he ought to be, and what we expected he would; an' so, rather than remain at the terms he axes from us, it's better for us to thry our fortune in America; bekaise, if we stay here, we must only come to poverty an' destitution, an' sorrow; an' you know how it 'ud break my heart to see our childre' brought to that, in the very place where they wor always respected. They're all good to me, as they ever wor to' us both, acushla machree; but poor Bryan, that you loved so much—your favorite and your pride—has had much to suffer, darlin', since you left us; but blessed be God, he bears it manfully and patiently, although I can see by the sorrow on my boy's brow that the heart widin him is breakin'. He's not, afther all, to be married, as you hoped and wished he would, to Kathleen Cavanagh. Her mind has been poisoned against him; but little she knows him, or she'd not turn from him as she did. An' now, Bridget, asthore machree, is it come to this wid me? I must lave you for ever. I must lave—as my father said, that went this day to heaven as you know, now—I must lave, as he said, the ould places. I must go to a strange country, and sleep among a strange people; but it's for the sake of our childre' I do so, lavin' you alone there where you're sleepin'? I wouldn't lave you if I could help it; but we'll meet yet in heaven, my blessed wife, where there won't be distress, or injustice, or sorrow to part us. Achora machree, I'm come, then, to take my last farewell of you. Farewell, then, my darlin' wife, till we meet for evermore in heaven!"

He departed from the grave slowly, and returned in deep sorrow to his own house.

About twelve o'clock the next morning, the family and those neighbors who were assembled as usual at the wake-house, from respect to the dead, were a good deal surprised by the appearance of Mr. Vanston and their landlord, both of whom entered the house.

"Gentlemen, you're welcome," said old M'Mahon; "but I'm sorry to say that it's to a house of grief and throuble I must welcome you—

death's here, gentlemen, and more than death; but God's will be done, we must be obaidient."

"M'Mahon," said Chevydale, "give me your hand. I am sorry that either you or your son have suffered anything on my account. I am come now to render you an act of justice—to compensate both you and him, as far as I can, for the anxiety you have endured. Consider yourselves both, therefore, as restored to your farms at the terms you proposed originally. I shall have leases prepared—give up the notion of emigration—the country cannot spare such men as you and your admirable son. I shall have leases I say prepared, and you will be under no necessity of leaving either Carriglass or Ahadarra."

Need we describe the effect which such a communication had upon this sterling-hearted family? Need we assure our readers that the weight was removed from all their hearts, and the cloud from every brow? Is it necessary to add that Bryan M'Mahon and his high-minded Kathleen were married? that Dora and James followed their example, and that Edward Burke, in due time, bestowed his hand upon sweet and affectionate Hanna Cavanagh?

We have little now to add. Young Clinton, in the course of a few months, became agent to Chevydale, whose property soon gave proofs that kindness, good judgment, and upright principle were best calculated not only to improve it, but to place a landlord and his tenantry on that footing of mutual good-will and reciprocal interest upon which they should ever stand towards each other.

We need scarcely say that the sympathy felt for honest Jemmy Burke, in consequence of the disgraceful conduct of his son, was deep and general. He himself did not recover it for a long period, and it was observed that, in future, not one of his friends ever uttered Hycy's name in his presence.

With respect to that young gentleman's fate and that of Teddy Phats, we have to record a rather remarkable coincidence. In about three years after his escape, his father received an account of his death from Montreal, where it appears he expired under circumstances of great wretchedness and destitution, after having led, during his residence there, a most profligate and disgraceful life. Early the same day on which the intelligence of his death reached his family, they also received an account through the M'Mahons to the effect that Teddy Phats had, on the preceding night, fallen from one of the cliffs of Althadawan and broken his neck; a fate which occasioned neither surprise nor sorrow.

We have only to add that Bryan M'Mahon and his wife took Nanny Peety into their service; and that Kate Hogan and Mr. O'Finigan had always a comfortable seat at their hospitable hearth; and the latter a warm glass of punch occasionally, for the purpose, as he said himself, of keeping him properly sober. him properly sober.

Copyright © 2023 Esprios Digital Publishing. All Rights Reserved.

Milton Keynes UK
Ingram Content Group UK Ltd.
UKHW050447280324
440101UK00016B/1257